Praise for
Cyndere's Midnight

"Delving deeper into the vividly imagined world of the Expanse, with characters both diverse and sympathetic, and a story filled with heartbreak, hope, and wonder, *Cyndere's Midnight* is a worthy follow-up to Jeffrey's fantasy debut and another enchanting entry in the Auralia Thread."
—ROBERT THOMPSON, FantasyBookCritic.blogspot.com

"Astonishing, arresting, rich, and profound. Jeffrey Overstreet's beauty of prose reveals the vileness of human nature and then, just as deftly, awakens hope."
—DONITA K. PAUL, author of *DragonLight* and *DragonSpell*

"With *Cyndere's Midnight*, Jeffrey Overstreet fulfills the promise of *Auralia's Colors:* he has created a fully realized imaginative world, at once utterly distinctive and hauntingly familiar. I can't wait for the next volume."
—JOHN WILSON, editor, *Books & Culture*

"It's entering a beautiful dream you don't want to leave, with exhilarating tension that takes you beyond story and into deep truths."
—SIGMUND BROUWER, author of *Broken Angel*

"When the Inklings (C. S. Lewis and J. R. R. Tolkien) met at the 'Bird and Baby' pub each week, they would read excerpts from their work, then critique and improve it. With *Cyndere's Midnight*, the inventive and imaginative Jeffrey Overstreet delivers another well-crafted, artful work of fantasy, rewarding thoughtful readers and reminding us that the spirit of the Inklings is alive and well and at least one living writer could have held his own at their table!"
—DICK STAUB, broadcaster (The Kindlings Muse) and author of
The Culturally Savvy Christian and *Christian Wisdom of the Jedi Masters*

Praise for
Jeffrey Overstreet and *Auralia's Colors*

"Overstreet's writing is precise and beautiful, and the story is masterfully told."

—*Publishers Weekly*

"Overstreet paints vividly imagined scenes and develops his characters and story with thought-provoking insights into human motivations."

—*CBA Retailers+Resources*

"Overstreet writes gorgeous and gritty fantasy that leaves us wanting more."

—*YouthWorker Journal*

"If you're a fan of fantasy such as *Lord of the Rings* and J. R. R. Tolkien, then you'll love *Auralia's Colors*, an awesome tale for young and old alike."

—*Midwest Book Review*

CYNDERE'S
MIDNIGHT

A NOVEL

ALSO BY JEFFREY OVERSTREET

Fiction:
Auralia's Colors

Nonfiction:
Through a Screen Darkly:
Looking Closer at Beauty, Truth and Evil at the Movies

CYNDERE'S
MIDNIGHT

A NOVEL

JEFFREY
OVERSTREET

WATERBROOK
PRESS

CYNDERE'S MIDNIGHT
PUBLISHED BY WATERBROOK PRESS
12265 Oracle Boulevard, Suite 200
Colorado Springs, Colorado 80921
A division of Random House Inc.

The characters and events in this book are fictional, and any resemblance to actual persons or events is coincidental.

ISBN: 978-1-4000-7253-8

Published in association with the literary agency of Alive Communications Inc., 7680 Goddard Street, Suite 200, Colorado Springs, CO 80920, www.alivecommunications.com.

Published in the United States by WaterBrook Multnomah, an imprint of The Doubleday Publishing Group, a division of Random House Inc., New York.

WATERBROOK and its deer colophon are registered trademarks of Random House Inc.

Library of Congress Cataloging-in-Publication Data
Overstreet, Jeffrey.
   Cyndere's midnight : a novel / Jeffrey Overstreet ; author of Auralia's colors. —
1st ed.
       p. cm.
   ISBN 978-1-4000-7253-8
   I. Title.
   PS3615.V474C96 2008
   813'.6—dc22

                                        2008025015

Printed in the United States of America
2008—First Edition

10 9 8 7 6 5 4 3 2 1

For Anne,

Once upon a time, there was a beauty and there was a beast.

*Thank you for being a patient, perceptive, inspiring beauty,
while we wrestled this beast to the ground.*

CONTENTS

THE EXPANSE

AS CONCERNS THE STORY OF
CYNDERE AND JORDAM

1 Deep Lake
2 Ruins of House Abascar
3 Blackstone Caves
4 Baldridge Hill
5 Auralia's Caves
6 Cragavar Forest
7 Cent Regus Ruins
8 The Four Brothers' Den
9 Standing Stones
10 Tilianpurth
11 House Bel Amica
12 The River Throanscall

PROLOGUE

A magnificent viscorcat paws at the trunk of the coil tree, yearning for a summer sun spot up in the branches, his black fur glossed from grooming. The cat's rider, a girl no more than thirteen, slides from his back.

Impatient, the cat claws neat lines down through the bark. "Go ahead, Dukas," says the girl, running her hand from his neck to his tail, tracing sturdy links of spine through the fur. The cat leaps into the tree and stretches out on a sun-warmed branch.

The girl is tempted to follow. She has wandered far from her lakeside caves, feeling confident as a queen. Her realm has provided everything she might need—nourishment, shelter, color, and materials for her art. But she has yet to offer something in response.

She descends through fern fronds into a quiet glen and finds a place to rest, sitting against a young cloudgrasper tree. Rummaging through her ribbon-weave bag, she considers an array of unfinished crafts. Blue curtains—she's making them for Krawg, the old man who rescued her from the wilderness when she was a baby. The floppy, fur-spun hats are for the Gatherers. There are lake-fishing lures of dragonfly wings and throwing dice fashioned from acorns. But none of these seems the right subject for this afternoon's play. She shoves them back inside and listens to the trees' ideas.

A murmur of water deep underground draws her into a stroll around a flowered mound of stones, a weathered well. Something about that distant song is familiar. *How curious,* she thinks. *Why would anyone need a well here?*

She climbs up on the wellstones. Ivy has stitched the well's mouth shut, shielding it from summer's slow, golden dust. She tears the ivy loose and shoves her head in, then withdraws, brushing cobwebs and tiny white spiders from her silverbrown hair. Her eyes are wide. The sad, familiar music of the rushing water far below inspires her to imagine its source—a place of fierce purity, high above the world, in skies alive with color and light.

Inside the well a rope is bound to an iron ring. She seizes it and feels resistance. Persisting, she pulls until a sturdy bucket appears. Swirling water mirrors the layered ceiling of dark boughs, delicate leaves, the shining sky. She splashes it across her face. It is surprisingly warm.

She pours the water over the wellstones, washing away dust, webs, fragments of leaves, old spider-egg sacs. Beetles scramble, looking for new homes.

Arranging small glass jars of dye beside her, she takes tiny brushes of vawn-tail hair and sets about painting.

She daubs one wellstone, pauses, considers what should come next. Proceeding like a worryworm, she feels around for a sure step, then teases the air before her in search of the next certainty. She examines the cloudgrasper, its bark green as olives. She scoops up handfuls of leaves, lays them over each other, holds them up to the light. Mixing the paints and spreading them thick and bright across another boulder, she considers how the colors fit. She wishes for more stones, a larger well, something mountain sized.

When she is finished, Dukas has dropped down from the tree, disgruntled by the fading sunlight. He sniffs at the well, blinks, and sneezes in disgust.

The girl scowls. "Thanks for nothing."

Dukas slinks off to search for a madweed patch where he can roll and dream, leaving her to grumble. "But I suppose you're right," she sighs. "I mean, what's the use?" She shrugs and tosses the paintbrush aside. "Who's ever gonna see it? Just a pile of painted stones. In a few harsh winters, it'll all be gone."

The cat snarls, dragging his claws down the trunk of a maple this time.

"Hunting and eating. That's all you think about. You know you'll be fed by sundown. I'm hungry too. I just can't say for what."

A cloud passes over, hastening the night.

"We should go."

While she gathers up her brushes and jars, buds open on the frail stems, blessing the glen with their tiny, cerulean stars. "Why bother?" she snaps at the flowers. "Nobody notices."

But as she sits back down before their constellations, she relaxes, seduced by the light. "Dukas, have you seen the beastman who comes to my caves? He comes to see the colors. And he's got a strange liking for blue. He should see this."

She shivers. The tree shadows have shifted, darkening every color they find.

"He doesn't hurt me. Never has. But I wonder what he's like when he's out on his own." She sighs. "No. I don't wonder. I think I know."

She plucks a cluster of the blooms, careful to draw the shallow, fragile roots along with them. She'll replant them where she lives. They're a color with possibilities. "A little something I'm working on," she mumbles. "Another splash of nothing."

When she's gone, the starflowers go on glowing, testifying to the water beneath their roots, raising their own version of its song in perfume and light. Travelers might pass without pausing to observe. No matter. They shine as if for joy.

1

THE HEIRESS AND
THE OCEANDRAGON

Cyndere walked down to the water to make her daily decision—turn
and go back into House Bel Amica, or climb Stairway Rock and
throw herself into the sea.

It had become a habit. Leaving her chamber early, while the mirror-
lined corridors were empty of all but servants, she would traverse many
bridges, stairs, and passages and emerge on the shores of the Rushtide Inlet,
escaping the gravity of distraction. Today in the autumn bluster, she wore her
husband's woolen stormcloak at the water's edge. She brought her anger. She
brought her dead.

While the fog erased the wild seascape, waves exploded against the
ocean's scattered stone teeth, washed wide swaths of pebbles, and sighed into
the sand. They carried her father's whispers from many years past, mornings
when he had walked with her along the tide's edge and dreamt aloud. His
bristling grey beard smelled of salt, prickling when he rested his chin on her
head. He would place one hand on her shoulder and with the other hold a
seashell to her ear. "Hear that?" he'd say. "That's your very own far-off country. You will walk on ground no one has ever seen. And I'm going to find it
for you when I venture out to map the Mystery Sea."

He had done just that. While Cyndere's mother, Queen Thesera, stayed
home to govern her people within House Bel Amica's massive swell of stone,
King Helpryn discovered islands, sites for future Bel Amican settlements.

A shipwreck took the king when he tried to cross a stormy span between
those islands. Within hours of the report, Bel Amica's cloud-bound city
turned volcanic with theories and superstitions. From one sphere of their

society to another, all the way down to the shipyards of the inlet, the people competed to interpret their ambitious king's demise, their rumors full of words like *iceberg, pirates,* and *oceandragon.* The Seers, quarrelsome as gulls, debated whether this might be a portent of judgment by the moon-spirits or whether Helpryn's celestial guardian had reached down from the sky and carried him away to live in his own peaceful paradise.

Meanwhile, Cyndere mourned the loss of her father's smiling eyes, his confidence in her, his vision for her future. "You will walk on ground no one has ever seen." From the day he vanished, the young heiress never grew taller, and the sun was burnt out of her sky.

She did not weep. Given no chance to mourn in private, she concerned herself with the comfort of her mother and her older brother, Partayn.

Partayn slept with his head on the windowsill as though he listened for the king's counsel in the ocean's roar. Did those crashing lullabies awaken his father's wanderlust within him? She wondered. King Helpryn had answered the call of the horizon, but the boy would set sail on a different sea, striving to master all manner of music.

Partayn's quest was tragically brief. When an armored escort carried him southward to study the music of House Jenta, an ambush of Cent Regus beastmen silenced his songs.

The people, having only just regained their footing, were cast into despair. Even Queen Thesera believed someone had cursed House Bel Amica.

The pressure of an impending inheritance fell hard on Cyndere. She was expected now to stand beside her mother and prepare to take her place someday. More urgently, she should find a husband, bring a new generation of royalty to Bel Amica, and ensure that the line of Tammos Raak, father of the four houses, would continue.

But Cyndere had already determined that she would not become her mother. She still dreamt of breaking ground all her own. She was capable. She had the respect of her people, and in Bel Amica's courtrooms she was famous for her temper and tenacity. Her helplessness to save her father and her brother only stoked her passions to help others and prevent further calamity.

Such ambitions made her lonely. As her people groped for distractions to numb their fears, the Seers provided potions for reckless indulgences. Those meddling conjurers caught even her mother with their hooks. The thought of inheriting such counselors made Cyndere want to sail for that far-off country of her own, wherever it might be. The sea's call was more seductive every morning. Her days became rituals of counting the few, feeble cords that bound her to Bel Amica. Hope to become what her father had envisioned quickly dimmed.

If it were not for Deuneroi, a young man who often fought with Cyndere in the court, she might have let the ocean carry her to her father. Even in the midst of their famous courtroom collisions, Deuneroi discerned Cyndere's sadness. He saw her right through and wove subtle threads of sympathy into his eloquence. Sensing this, she conspired that their feud should spread into private debate, and soon their minds and hearts were inseparably entangled, furious in love.

Before long, Cyndere realized that while two cords had broken, a new cord had been strung. Deuneroi became her consort, her refuge, strong enough to keep her from the sea.

Today she missed hearing the footfalls of Deuneroi's casual stride. He was off, led by courage she both admired and resented, to search for survivors buried in the rubble of the fallen House Abascar. She had tried to stop him. Tempers flared in their hottest debate. But in the end, she had surrendered, moved by his compassion and by his promise.

"Deuneroi, look what you've done. This cat was wild once. Now he's a lazy pile of fur."

On their last evening before her husband's departure, Cyndere sulked through their argument's aftermath. Gazing into their bedchamber fireplace, she stroked a black viscorcat whose head filled her lap while his furry, muscled body sprawled limp across the braided rug. The viscorcat hummed, kneading the air with his claws.

"I don't think he was ever very wild at all," said Deuneroi, rolling a woolen tunic and pressing it into his pack. "Once I lured him into my camp with some fish, he warmed up quickly, as if he had known someone who treated him kindly before."

When fireglow lulled the cat into sleep, Cyndere bit her lip and gingerly untangled the snare around the animal's tail. A prankster had tied a ring of keys there with a thread, then set him loose to run, terrified, with the keys clanging along the corridor behind him.

As the knot slipped free, the cat raised his head and growled. "It's all right now," Cyndere whispered. "You're free." His purr slowly returned, resonating. She pondered the keys, wondered what they fit, and set them on the floor next to her.

She touched the scar on the cat's hind leg where Deuneroi had drawn out an arrow's poisoned head. "I'm glad you found him. That wound might have killed him."

"I'm surprised he trusted me."

"I'm not. You're a born healer, Deun."

"And so are you." Deuneroi sat on the edge of the bed, smiling at her.

"Then I should be going with you. If there are survivors in Abascar's ruins, they'll need special care."

"Your mother will never let you venture into such danger."

"What good is royalty if we just sit in our palace when people are in trouble?"

"Your mother's lost too much already. She won't risk losing you."

"She's not the only one who's grieving, Deun. I'm grieving too. And I can't bear the risk of this. Don't go. Don't put so much distance between us."

"You urged your mother to send rescuers. Remember?"

"Months ago…and she refused to send help while it mattered. Now she's just doing this to separate us, to interrupt our work. You won't find anything in the ruins of Abascar except scavenging beastmen."

"Then I'll bring back some beastmen. We'll have real subjects for our study." He was trying to make her laugh, but she would have none of it. He shifted to a softer approach. "Won't you sleep better knowing that there's nobody clinging to hope in Abascar's ruins? We've both had nightmares, imagining someone trapped there, praying to the moon-spirits for a rescuer."

"The people of Abascar don't pray to moon-spirits. Didn't."

"This isn't the daughter of brave King Helpryn talking. Where is the bold heiress who dares to dream even of curing the beastmen of their curse?"

Cyndere pressed her lips together. She was angry with her mother, the Seers, and the court. She needed to strike at something, and Deuneroi was the easiest target. But she knew that he was right. She reached for a poker and began to jab recklessly at the smoldering firewood. "Life was so much easier before Mother got word of our plans for the beastmen."

"It was in the glen near Tilianpurth, wasn't it? That's where we first dreamt of taming them."

"No more talk about the Cent Regus, Deun. Not if you insist on running off into their territory. You're not ready for this road. You're a court scholar. Will you stab at the beastmen with a scroll?"

He sat down beside her. "I'm afraid too. But I lost faith in my fears a long time ago, Cyn. People used to tell me, 'Deuneroi, you're a weakling. When the soldiers eat what they catch on a hunt, you're stuck with broth. While others run along the wall, you can't climb a flight of stairs without losing your breath. You're not fit for an heiress.' But then an heiress proved them wrong."

"This is different, Deun. You're not a soldier. You're not a ranger or even a merchant."

"And I have no skill with horses or vawns. I couldn't hunt a stag if you turned one loose in this very chamber." He turned and looked her in the eye. "But I must do this. If we run into the Cent Regus, so be it. What good is this dream of helping beastmen if we're too afraid to face them?"

Cyndere picked up a scrap of burnt firewood and began to sketch the outline of the viscorcat on one of the stone tiles. "You know what they did to my brother."

"Your brother headed south with inexperienced guards. Your mother's sending Ryllion with us. He can shoot the eye out of a rabbit running. He can chase down a fox in his bare feet. He can hear a flea on a fangbear. He'll protect me. And don't forget." Deuneroi's warm palm slid across Cyndere's belly. "Your mother has a compelling reason to keep me safe."

"She only wants a grandchild to extend the line of Tammos Raak."

"But *I* want a child, Cyn, because you and I perform wonders whenever we work together." He took the brittle charcoal from her hand and entangled his fingers in hers. "Don't despair."

She pulled her hands away, reached to massage the nape of the viscorcat's neck. A ripple of white moved under her fingers as she stroked the black-tipped fur. The cat stiffened at her touch, murmured in delight, and then eased back into sleep.

Deuneroi stood. "Remember the tigerfly?"

She laughed, although she tried to avoid it. Deuneroi had rescued the bright orange insect during a walk in the woods around the faraway bastion of Tilianpurth. It had been trapped inside a curled leaf floating in the bucket beside the old well. "It sat in your hand for an hour."

"And then it flew. When I go to Abascar, I'll bring something out of those ruins. Something worth saving. I promise."

"Right." She dabbed at her eyes. "You promise."

"I promise. And then we'll go to the well at Tilianpurth. And celebrate."

"Will we?"

He knelt behind her, ran his fingers through her strawgold hair, and tipped her head back so he could look into her eyes. "Yes. Or you could just close your eyes and dream a little, and we could be there right now."

When she reached up to pull his dark hair down around her face, the cat grumbled, unhappy to have been forgotten.

"Be brave, little bird," Deuneroi whispered between their kisses. "Be brave."

Without her husband beside her, Cyndere felt exposed.

The only remaining child of Queen Thesera, she lived with constant surveillance. Cyndere was the last link in the chain—and it felt so much like a chain—leading back to Tammos Raak. She would never be allowed to walk unguarded. She would never walk on ground that had not been secured.

The fog unveiled the long, winding stair down the rugged cliffs to the sandy strand. The chorus of waves grew louder. The cold grew mean.

Cyndere would have her meditation, nevertheless. She would wear out those forerunners who scanned the path ahead and tax the strength of those who crept behind. The cold did not dissuade her. She was always cold.

Buffeted by wind, she clasped Deuneroi's black stormcloak at her throat. When she reached the beach at last, she left her silver slippers on the final stair. Her feet were numb with cold by the time she reached the line where the surf slid frothy beneath the fog.

A tree trunk nudged the shore, rolling and waving its sprawl of roots. Above her, two great lights gleamed like eyes—the rising sun, a coin of gold, and the setting moon, a pool of shifting shapes believed by the Seers to be powerful spirits. Every so often the fog strained at its seams and tore, and Cyndere peered through to the ocean. Once she saw a dark, departing ship, sails pregnant with wind, carrying dreamers her father had inspired.

She scooped up wet sand and cast it into the rippling shallows, tempted again. *Come out into the water,* the waves seemed to say. *Come out to me, my daughter. You have suffered so much loss. You can escape here in the deep, where I am waiting for you. You'll never again have to worry about losing what you love.*

As the rippling tide washed over her feet, a commotion ahead of her broke the silence. Screams. And curses too dark for the morning.

She stepped into the water and hid behind the tree stump as it rocked in the surf.

Her forerunners ran, wailing, back toward Bel Amica. "Wyrm! Ocean-dragon!"

She braced herself as the freezing currents swirled about her ankles and her feet turned to ice. Water tugged at Deuneroi's cloak. She felt a faint spark, the flare of her father's courage. "Row," he would have said. "Row against the current."

"Cyndere!" they were calling into the mist. "Heiress! Where is she?"

The sound of their panic blew past.

Cyndere splashed out of the tide.

There it was. A jagged line of darkness ahead, like a mountain range. As it took on detail, she heard its hollow groaning.

The oceandragon's gargantuan form loomed, its snout resting on the sand, head large enough to swallow a herd of wild tidehorses. The fog withdrew, and she could see the spiked tip of its tail curling about and resting on the sand beside her, ten times the size of the harpoons her father had hurled at seawraiths and horned whales.

She stood still, waited for the dragon to writhe and twist and thrash down upon her. "Is this what took you down into the sea?" she whispered to her father. "Is this what you saw as the ship came apart?"

The fog thinned.

The oceandragon's eyes were hollow, the head but a skull. Its sides did not heave; they were no more than rows of towering ribs. Its tail, a chain with links of bone. Perhaps it had been dead an age. The sea had carried it into the inlet by night and cast it onto the shore, having taken every scrap of its flesh, offering up its unbreakable skeleton.

That reverberating moan—it was only the wind moving through the skull's cavities.

"Beautiful," she said.

She stepped through the gap of a missing tooth. The lower jaw was gone, probably resting at the bottom of the sea. Within the hollow thrumming of its head, she stood tall enough to see out through the gaping windows of its eyes. She reached out, touched the edge of a socket.

What was it like to be an oceandragon? What was its purpose? Had it enjoyed the open sea, redirecting currents with the twitch of a tail or the fling of a fin? Did oceandragons sing, as some drunken sailors insisted? Or did the creatures think only of eating?

She found a small, exquisitely detailed stone on the edge of the opposite eye. She set it on her palm, amazed, for it was an exact replica of the oceandragon's white skull, sculpted as only a stonemaster could shape it. She held it up to the light and looked through its vacant eyes. And then she laughed. "Scharr ben Fray."

She put it to her lips and blew softly. The whistle's tone struck a haunting counterpoint to the low hum of the dragon's skull. He had been here. That eccentric old mage, so famously exiled from House Abascar when Cyndere was a child, had walked among these bones. Scharr ben Fray was known across the Expanse as a man obsessed with mysteries. And he had studied these bones already. His sculptures were his signatures, and this whistle in Cyndere's hand was unmistakable.

She would have given the whistle to Partayn for his collection, were he still alive. Scharr ben Fray had shown both her and her brother a grandfatherly affection during his occasional visits to House Bel Amica. King Helpryn had coveted the old man's advice and respected his knowledge of the Expanse. Partayn had pestered him for verses from songs he heard in his travels. The queen had only tolerated him, jealous of his stonemastery and his gift of speaking with animals. But Scharr ben Fray was a solitary wanderer, appearing when least expected, slipping away whenever they tried to hold him.

Cyndere stepped through the skull's oceanward ear. The tide's tentative shallows moved around her feet again, alive with wavering seaweed and scuttling crabs.

She traced her fingers along the edge of the ribs, then stepped into their vast cage. These bones were gashed as if by claws or teeth. Either the dragon had died violently, or vigorous scavengers had carved up the carcass.

When she pulled her hand away, her skin was smudged with black from the decomposing dragon bone. Not stopping to wonder why, she followed an impulse and traced the ashes around her eyes and across her forehead, thinking of her father.

Another rush of water. The tide was turning in earnest now. Cyndere tucked the whistle into her pocket. "You'll regret missing this, Deun." She felt a strong tug of the tether, longing to share all wonders with Deuneroi. That desire would bring her home again.

Something moved. She turned, half expecting the mage. But this figure was taller and robed in something colorless. Light passed through it, and it cast no shadow.

Her father's courage flickered again. She stepped from between the oceandragon's ribs to get a better look. But swift currents of fog moved in, erasing the phantom. She thought to call out, but distant voices approaching from Bel Amica distracted her.

Walking back, clutching the whistle in her pocketed fist, Cyndere guessed that her guardians meant to rescue her. She hastened toward them, smug with her discovery. How Deuneroi would laugh.

But then she slowed. Figures emerged from the mist. Their silhouettes became robes, wringing hands, fretful faces. Some were Seers, stalking forward like white mantises. Some, her attendants—sisterlies—in their heavy brown stormcloaks, with her lifelong friend Emeriene limping along ahead of them, one leg bound in a cast.

"Cyndere." Emeriene opened her arms and stumbled forward in her haste as a mother lunges to save her child from a fall.

"Em." Cyndere's voice seized in her throat. Her body knew, somehow, before any tidings reached her ears. "No. Not Deuneroi..."

Cyndere's tether broke. Like a kite cut loose in a storm, she surrendered, turning and splashing out into the tide. Half in ocean, half in fog, she felt wet sand give way beneath her feet. Water closed over her head.

When Emeriene's hands seized Cyndere's robes, the heiress of House Bel Amica fought to break free and dive into her father's embrace.

2

PREDATORS IN THE RUINS

T he back of Deuneroi's neck prickled, a premonition of pursuit. He looked over his shoulder across the dark glass of Deep Lake. Autumn mist swirled over the surface as if it had been disturbed. He thought he caught traces of the vee cut by a swimmer.

But the waters smoothed, fields of floating stars reappeared, and the mist settled like a suspended breath. The only creatures that Cyndere's royal consort could discern were zigzagging lakebats snapping their way through clouds of water bugs.

Meanwhile, his companions were contemplating a different sort of danger—the devastation of House Abascar, which lay ahead beyond the forest.

"I've seen terrible things in my seventy years." Slagh was a windbag, a timeworn merchant full of half-imagined stories. But Deuneroi believed the old man's claim that he had been bargaining in Abascar on the day of the great calamity. So Deuneroi had paid the talkative fellow to lead the rain-burdened party from House Bel Amica to the edge of Abascar's wreckage. And even though the travelers exchanged weary glances whenever the merchant opened his mouth, Deuneroi listened.

"I've seen summer's forest fires blacken miles of earth," Slagh continued. "I've choked on the foul fog that the beastmen breathe in the wasteland of House Cent Regus. I've watched a mountainside turn to porridge and collapse during a quake. I stood in the Rushtide Inlet during the Red Moon Flood, and my father carried me on his shoulders while the water rose to his chin. I've lived through all those nightmares. But I've *never* seen anything like the day House Abascar fell. I've never seen the earth open up its fiery throat and swallow a whole kingdom. I've never seen that. You ever seen that?"

Deuneroi looped a strap of his heavy pack around a broken tree branch, then called up into the tree. "Ryllion, what do you see?"

Ryllion's answer fell with the rain. "Looks like somebody kicked apart an anthill. Abascar's been smashed into the earth. It's buried treasure. Our merchant must be worried that we'll take the spoils. He's trying to scare us home."

Deuneroi smiled to his companions, who scowled while waterfalls poured off their hoods. "Imagine what Ryllion will be like when he's grown up. He'll see through the morning fog and tell us who's misbehaving on the islands. It's frightening, how far our boy can see."

"I heard that," Ryllion growled. "And I'll have you know I'm—"

"Twenty-two years old!" chorused Ryllion's thirteen companions. Raucous laughter broke the tension, a welcome moment of levity along their soggy, treacherous course.

There were only four. But four would be enough to finish these Bel Amicans.

Picking at his fangs with a polished claw, Jordam huffed impatiently. He and his brothers were famous along the roads of the Expanse. He liked to think that the travelers would see him tonight in their dreams underneath these agitated trees.

Tomorrow my brothers and I will teach them that nightmares are real.

He lay on the high branch of a long-beard tree, listening through rainpatter to the Bel Amicans as they muttered in their shadowy camp. Syllables. Phrases. Whispers. Hiding out of the lantern's glow, he sifted their chatter, but he caught only a few puzzling scraps in the damaged nets of his memory and mind. *Fires. Fog. Mountain. Throat.*

Like his brothers, Jordam had learned some of these words. Fragments of Common still endured in the brusque tongue of the Cent Regus, but he rarely managed to understand what one of the weakerfolk's words had to do with the other. It was clear, however, that these nervous travelers had decided to wait until morning to proceed into Abascar's ruin.

To Jordam's surprise his older brother, Mordafey, had insisted that they wait until morning as well. Tomorrow, Mordafey had explained, when the Bel Amicans' attention faltered—that would be the time to strike.

Rain seeped into Jordam's mane and dripped from his browbone, the blunt horn that jutted from his forehead.

Two of his brothers were already asleep. The youngest, Jorn—the hairless one with dark stripes on his grey hide—mumbled curses, his tongue twitching behind jutting tusks. Jordam's twin, Goreth, lay on his back like a big brown ape, smiling and thumping the ground with his long, hairy tail, the only distinctive feature that Jordam did not share. *Dreaming of honey and rockbeetles,* Jordam guessed.

Below Jordam's perch Mordafey sat against the base of the long-beard tree picking fleas out of his brindled fur. His black ears were cupped forward, and his leonine nose twitched in irritation. Mordafey did not like the language of weakerfolk. Everything about such people enraged him. "Deuneroi," he muttered softly, gnawing rough edges from his claws. "Deuneroi. Deuneroi."

Jordam felt his eyelids grow heavy. But then something unusual brought him back to full attention.

Mordafey sprang to his feet and broke one of the rules he had set for the brothers. He prowled off into the night. Alone.

As much as he wanted to follow, Jordam knew better than to test his older brother's temper. Mordafey was larger and stronger than all of them. But he would not forget this. Mordafey was up to something.

As Deuneroi beheld the ruinous crater, the Underkeep into which House Abascar had crumbled, he began to wonder if he had won the wrong argument with Cyndere. Perhaps she had been right to favor fear.

For hours the company descended into the maze, all sense of direction lost, prodding dead ends with their spear tips in search of concealed paths and stairs. Stone and clay corridors had collapsed in tangles. Some wove crookedly; some led to walls or chasms. Most were crowded with rockslides and boulders, rivers of sand, fragments of walls. Massive columns—what Ryllion called "the ribs"—lay long and pale beneath slanted, smoke-blackened ceilings.

The air, caliginous with ash, moved in currents through the glow of their sparking torches. The Bel Amicans breathed through thick scarves and moved gingerly, as though wary of some hibernating giant.

At one turn in the tunnel, the searchers glimpsed the rattling tail of a rockwyrm before it vanished into a burrow. That unsettled what little remained secure within them. Oblivion lapped at the edges of the rooms, and a sound like slippery tendrils rose from the abyss. Every shudder in the walls whispered, *Wise men do not walk here. This is death's den.* Even Ryllion cursed when he found that the jutting obstacles in his path were not stones at all, but bones.

"*Crolca.*" Deuneroi draped another layer of his scarf across his nose to muffle the stench. "Abascar's a corpse too big for burying." He stared at a skeletal hand that still clutched a broken spear. Teeth marks lined the bones of the forearm. Rumors claimed that beastmen had slaughtered survivors or dragged them off as prisoners. His spirits sank further when he observed his companions' relief, for they assumed that he was defeated and ready to go home.

But Ryllion's yellow-bearded jaw was set, his eyes wild. Deuneroi had seen this look before—a drive for satisfaction. Ryllion's heart was set on treasure.

Devoted to the study of moon-spirits, Ryllion believed the Seers when they said that each person was guarded by a personal spirit. This moon-dwelling spirit would bestow desire—"sacred destinies," a mysterious cargo carried on moonlight—within a subject's heart by night and then punish him if he did not pursue that call by day. But if he strove with passion, he would be blessed. Ryllion's zeal had become famous throughout Bel Amica. No one could deny his desire to become a captain, to attain the stature of a legendary defender. It was only a matter of time for a man of such uncanny talents. Ryllion would not return from Abascar without some trophy.

"Hold," said Ryllion. "Master, look."

The soldiers' silence spoke their objection as Deuneroi joined Ryllion, surveying the wall's three open mouths. The royal consort used his sword as a crutch. His feet had blistered on the journey; he was more accustomed to riding in royal processions. He waved his torch at the three tunnels and watched shadows shift.

"I smell possibilities." Ryllion cocked his head like an attentive bird. "And I suspect, from the look of this third passage, that it leads down to the dungeons. We might find survivors there."

Deuneroi could not bear to surrender their mission while anyone still had the spirit to search. "We'll take one look further, and then we'll. . ." He leaned against the entrance, clenched his eyes and teeth.

"Master?" Ryllion grabbed his arm. "You're pale as a ghost."

"Don't the Seers teach that ghosts don't exist?" He forced a smile. "I just need my breath. I suppose this adventure is a quick game of hide-and-bother for you. But me, I feel like I've just climbed over the Forbidding Wall."

"I can revive you. I've brought some of the Seers' cures."

"Potions? When have I ever trusted their elixirs?" Deuneroi stepped away from the wall, turning to the company. "Break up; three groups. Sound an alarm at any sign of trouble."

"If you won't take the potions, then you're coming with me, master. Just in case I need to carry you back out." Ryllion directed some of the group into the largest tunnel and others down the broken stair.

"How will we know when to return here?" squeaked Slagh. It seemed that dark memories had seized him by the throat. "We have no sands or sunlight for marking the hour."

"Recite the 'Song of Tammos Raak's Escape.' It's a long and tedious song, but it will give us a good measure on when to rendezvous." Deuneroi paused, then added, "Whisper it."

With shared glances that spoke of fears darker than any morbid ballad, they parted ways.

"I doubt that anyone trapped here is better than bones by now." Deuneroi fingered the golden eagle emblem that clasped the collar of his cape.

"Wouldn't Cyndere have searched deeper?" Ryllion's laugh was edged with worry, echoing ahead in the narrow passage. "There's no one bolder or sharper in Bel Amica. If you hadn't married her, I might have pursued her myself."

Deuneroi grinned. "You think the boldest and sharpest would have accepted you?"

"Choosing *you* was a flourish of genius?"

"A rare lapse in judgment." Laughing, he clapped Ryllion's shoulder, glad for anyone who could find levity in such a tomb. Startled, the soldier grabbed his sword hilt.

"Forgive me!" said Deuneroi. "Did I scare you?"

Ryllion scowled. "It's my training."

It was an answer, but not enough to set Deuneroi at ease. "Should we turn back? What's troubling you?"

Ryllion wiped his dripping brow, and without answering he pressed on.

As the Bel Amicans' torchflares faded into the tunnels, Jordam and his brothers moved with the darkness, creeping like insects along the sloped, boulder-strewn walls. Together they dropped to the floor and walked, leaning slightly forward with the weight of the heavy browbones that jutted from their foreheads like sawed-off horns.

Mordafey hissed instructions to his younger brothers. "Quiet. We follow. Bel Amicans may lead us to treasure."

While Jordam wanted nothing more than to hurl himself, claws extended, at the Bel Amicans' backs, he held the reins of his appetite hard. Restraint wasn't easy for the Cent Regus, but the brothers had learned that cooperation often brought greater spoils. This advantage and their capacity for strategy made them famously successful hunters among their kind.

Mordafey proceeded alone, low to the ground, muscled legs tensed for a jump. Jordam watched his brother vanish into the narrow crevasse where Deuneroi and his guardsman had gone.

"Claims the best prize for himself," Goreth whispered.

Jordam gestured for silence. Corridors like these could carry echoes of the slightest disturbance. The Bel Amicans would be on their guard. But he was nervous for other reasons as well. By Mordafey's instructions, this would not be a typical ambush. The brothers would be divided, attacking soldiers from behind.

Jordam moved to the passage of the cold stair. He paused and watched Goreth push their younger brother, Jorn, into the second passageway, like a master releasing a hound for a hunt. As they disappeared, Jordam felt a fever rise, an eagerness for blood. He crouched, flexed his jaws, sniffed the air, and then padded softly downward.

Inhaling, he detected simple elements—sweat, the clean metal of drawn swords, dried scraps of fish. The Bel Amicans moved quickly, chanting in rhythm.

On a platform where the crooked stair took a sudden turn, he ducked behind two stacked barrels. Excited whispers echoed in some large space around a corner. Jordam's red-furred ear flicked free of his black mane.

"Do you believe this?" a woman gasped.

"These footprints must be ten hands wide," a man replied. "No creature so large could make it through passageways so small. Look, seven toes."

"I don't need more convincing. This is the sign that says 'Go home.'"

"What kind of animal would Abascar keep down here? Deuneroi will want to see this."

"Deuneroi must not hear about this. His curiosity will ruin us. Do you want to be here when this…this *thing* comes back?"

"Haven't we all just completed the 'Song of Tammos Raak's Escape'?"

Footprints. Creature. Animal. Abascar. The words were familiar musical notes. But Jordam could not discern the song. As much as he hated the weakerfolk and their language, he knew that Cent Regus who could understand them demonstrated an unusual capacity for patience, concentration, and memory, giving them advantages over their brutish kin. Jordam suspected Mordafey understood more than he let on. Mordafey kept secrets.

These Bel Amicans in the chamber below—they had changed their minds. They were moving quickly back up the stairs. Their torchlight would carve his image from the darkness long before he could return to the crossroads.

Jordam tapped the top barrel. It made a hollow *fffumm*. He clambered up, swung his legs over the opening, landed in ankle-deep ash, and crouched inside. The barrel fit as if crafted to hold him, an ideal place to hide.

But the barrel beneath him, also empty, its wooden slats charred from Abascar's fire, could not sustain the new weight. It buckled and splintered, then crumbled to soot. The top barrel, tipping, fell into the stairwell.

Jordam rolled down the first few steps, then began picking up speed. Before he could escape, the barrel was hurtling downward. He heard a shout. His barrel struck the ascending soldiers as they rounded the corner. A clamor of armor. Dropped weapons clattering. The barrel continued down the last stretch of stairs. And then a hard impact, a rapid roll, and a spin across the floor. He choked on clouds of ash. And he felt the ground open into another abysm.

When the barrel crashed at last into a chamber far below, it began to break apart, rolling crookedly. Light flickered through the cracks. It slowed, spun, and stopped against a wall.

Jordam's crooked browbone, half of which had been smashed off in a fall long ago, vibrated from the jolt. Pain daggered his head. He lay exhausted, listening. No sounds of pursuit. No hints of investigation.

But the scent—it cut through the haze of cold ash and caught him like a snare. A whiff of clear water. Something familiar.

On the ceiling colors glimmered in a wavering array. At first Jordam thought he imagined them. When they did not dissipate, he pulled himself out of the wreckage and crawled through ash, rocks, and bones to stare. Threads of memory gathered, braiding themselves together into a cord that stretched back through time. He knew these colors.

A washbasin teetered on broken floorboards. Like a bowl of burning candles, the vessel revealed a lustrous aura, casting a beacon to the ceiling. Jordam approached it warily, sensing that his discovery would carry consequences. But he could not resist.

Inside the basin a cloth turned and twisted like a living thing. It slipped free of the murky water easily as if glad to be discovered. Rivers of oily brine streamed away without leaving a stain. He was enveloped in the glow.

The light rushed in, illuminating dark corners of his past, details he had forgotten in the seasons since the colors' disappearance. He had touched this weave before. A deep ache dissolved in his long and weary sigh. Something missing from his mind was restored.

The colors sang in harmonic tones—just as they had in the caves on the edge of Deep Lake where he had watched a lonely misfit weaving them. The colors had seeped into his skull and somehow lulled a throbbing ache to sleep. Not long ago when the girl and this, her most extravagant creation, vanished, the pain had returned like a patch of weeds spreading behind his eyes, staining every sunrise, burdening every step.

"O-raya...here?"

He hadn't told his brothers about discovering those caves. He hadn't told them about the girl who enchanted him with her otherworldly craft. Mordafey would not have understood.

Examining more basins and an overturned washtub on the far side of the room, he pressed the cloth to his chest. He would take this prize. He would steal away with it and conceal it. And then he would return to the ruins and search for the girl.

He had only a moment's warning—a rain of debris—before two figures dropped into the chamber. By the time they landed, he had cast the glowing fabric back into its cauldron and lunged to hide behind the overturned tub. Peering over its rounded metal edge, Jordam stifled a snarl.

Cent Regus creatures slunk and spat across the floor. Not killers, but rodentlike scavengers who followed more powerful hunters in hopes of steal-ing. One noticed the colors and, in a gurgling gasp, jerked out the magnifi-cent fabric. "Shiny," she hissed.

The other laughed, guttural and greedy. "Chieftain wants shiny things. Abascar prizes. To taunt his favorite Abascar prisoner. The queen. Big reward for me."

"I had it first."

Tugging at the corners, they kicked at each other with long-toed feet, naked tails lashing.

Wrath boiled in Jordam's throat. If he saw so much as a strand of color severed, he would strike. While he had rested in those lakeside caves with his discovery, he had imagined what he would do to anyone who dared disrupt the designs of O-raya's nimble fingers. But when she vanished, he had found no one to punish, his anger remaining unsatisfied until it dwindled into embers.

So when the rodentlike beastmen scuttled up the walls of this Under-keep chamber and through the tear in the ceiling, yanking the cloak of colors between them, Jordam pursued like an angry swarm.

When he reached the crossing, he found himself in the midst of a skirmish. The smell of slaughter clouded his concentration, demanded his attention. Swords clashed. Arrows sang past and thudded into the walls.

Enthused by his twin's arrival, Goreth laughed. Jordam marched past him, growling as his instincts sought to distract him from his goal. He stumbled into hot Bel Amican blood and stopped, looking back.

A merchant, the one Deuneroi had called "Slagh," came up behind Goreth and raised a bloodied Bel Amican sword. Cursing, Jordam abandoned his pursuit of the thieves. He could not bear to see Goreth scarred by such a feeble fool. He snatched a short blade from its sheath just below his knee and flung it. The merchant fell against the wall, grasping at the hilt that protruded from his chest. As the blade came out, a sigh spluttered from the wound. The merchant collapsed.

"Rockbeetles!" Goreth exclaimed, as he did when anything pleased him.

The killing frenzy seized Jordam, burning all the hotter for his anger at losing O-raya's colors. He turned to roar at the remaining Bel Amicans, who stood back to back as they steadied their swords. In their desperate shouts, he heard Deuneroi's name. Then he, Goreth, and Jorn finished them.

When Mordafey emerged from the third passage, his boastful grin was like a rack of knives. He threw something into a puddle of blood. "Deuneroi," he snarled in the darkness, trembling with satisfaction. "Deuneroi."

The severed hand lay open like a question while the last Bel Amican torches gasped and went out.

3

RESCUE ON
BALDRIDGE HILL

I t's getting darker." The boy peered from beneath the broad leaves of a
shield fern. "Are you watching this, 'Ralia?"

He always listened, just in case she might answer him.

It was a chilly evening in the Cragavar's southernmost fringe, and halfway up an overgrown incline the ale boy watched a predator with yellow eyes
and a crocodile grin dip arrows into poison and laugh quietly to herself.

The boy had been searching for the Keeper's tracks, just as Auralia had
instructed him before her sudden farewell many months ago. The trail of that
elusive creature had led him back into House Abascar's fiery collapse and all
about the surrounding region. He had never caught up with the Keeper, but
he had pulled hundreds from the ruins, found many more wandering distraught. He led them southward to join the assembly of displaced people
hiding at the Cliffs of Barnashum, leaving them in the care of Abascar's new
king, Cal-raven.

The once-thriving Underkeep was a haunted graveyard now. Abascar's
embers were cold and signs of survivors scarce. Even the marks of beastmen,
scavengers, and plunderers had vanished, first beneath blankets of red and
gold, then a season of heavy snows. Spring made a timid approach, but winter rose up and drove it back, leaving the ale boy to wonder if Abascar's fall
was only one stage in some greater collapse. Perhaps the Keeper had gone
away for good, leaving the Expanse to its troubles.

Still, he could not shake off that compulsion to bring rescue wherever
it was needed. He traveled in a frenzied state, returning again and again to
those places where wondrous and terrible things had transpired. Once, he

came upon the remains of some Bel Amicans deep within the Underkeep and wondered if they might have been a rescue party arriving too late to do any good. But that was months ago now, and he was too busy to search for answers. He braced himself for horrors over every hill, around every corner, and clung to his sense of purpose.

When he discovered the prints of small, clawed toes and the mark of a heavy tail sliding along behind, he followed. A familiar despair set in when the predator's tracks turned sharply onto a twig-littered path, following the fresh ruts of wagon wheels. Merchants, most likely, had passed through today.

"Last time I saw one of them monsters up close, you stepped outta the trees. You protected me, 'Ralia." He pulled up the hood of the concealing cloak Auralia had draped across him on the day they first met. He touched a tight band of braided colors that kept the chill from his brow. "Abascar soldiers appeared. Remember? They shot the monster down. Right smack in the forehead." He wiped sweat from the cracked skin of his scalp, his tousled hair but a memory after the fires of Abascar. "I could use your help right now. Folks are in trouble."

The beastwoman returned the short arrows to a quiver strapped to her leg and laughed as if she knew he was there, as if she knew how useless his efforts had been when compared to the number of lives lost. He could not fathom the appetites that drove her. *Better to die*, he thought, *than to be twisted into something that laughs in anticipation of bloodshed.*

"If I'd taken a different path, maybe I'd have made some difference," he muttered. "But what good are two hands, two feet, when there's so many monsters like that running loose? I told you I'd do what I could, 'Ralia. But what we need is somebody who can wipe these creatures out of the Expanse forever."

Behind him something cracked and splintered in the trees. The beast-woman turned, cast her bow aside, and then her jaw sagged open. Her eyes crossed, staring at the arrow newly buried in her forehead.

"Again?" The ale boy stood up, almost believing his pleas had been heard. He turned, hoping to see King Cal-raven riding in triumphant on a vawn. But he quickly ducked.

Four beastmen, like a pack of wild dogs, charged up from the deep forest below, their woodscloaks flapping like dark wings behind them. Huge and ferocious, they passed him. In a moment, they had finished the beast-woman. The smallest, a hairless creature with a hound's muzzle, nosed the wagon's trail, his skin drawing in the surrounding colors like a disguise. The brindled giant with the golden mane, standing upright, barked instructions. Two more, almost identical—red-brown fur, coal black manes—consulted in muffled growls. And then all four moved on hungrily in the merchants' direction.

The silence that settled around the ale boy was somehow worse than violence. He turned and trudged down the hill, wiping his sleeve across his eyes. When he found his vawn leashed to a tree in the shadowed lee of a jutting stone, he leaned against her scaly hide, clung to her reins, and fought to catch his breath. "You're...you're safe."

She trilled, relieved by his return.

"You're not gonna like this," he said, climbing into her saddle. "But we're going after them."

"Heartless, wicked beasts." From his precarious perch on a rickety branch ladder, Krawg gestured in sign language that any predator could understand, even the precipice birds glowering down at him from the cliff edge above. "Do you know who I am? Begone with you."

Black wings spread, bellies cherry red, the precipice birds only clucked amongst themselves, kicking frosty debris down on Krawg so that he had to look away. He bared his teeth at them, knowing the power of his crooked snarl to repulse. "We're House Abascar," he coughed, spittle black with grit. "These cliffs don't belong to you anymore. We're not carnage nor carrion. Since you don't lay any eggs good for eatin', I'd like to skewer you and leave you for the howlers."

Unruffled, the birds embraced the sunset as if they could gather heat from its wintry beams before their evening flight north and west to their nests in the Cragavar forest.

Clinging to the sheer face of the wall, Krawg turned his gaze to look across that vast descending stairway of stone, the tiers of the Cliffs of Barnashum, where Abascar survivors collected leaves, seeds, and berries. Harvest packs on their shoulders, they moved about like sipperbugs searching for moisture after a desert rain. Far, far below some picked through the dead scrubweed and huskerbrambles that blanketed the plains from the base of the cliffs to the southern edge of the forest.

Krawg had become a defender of this place. Here on the edge of the known world, the remnant of Abascar had dug in to survive the long winter. Even hungry birds could ignite his temper and cause him to claim this rise of rock for Abascar's young king.

On the fourteenth step of his flimsy ladder, only three from the top, Krawg groped toward a hollow high in the cliff wall. He had built this ladder of crooked birch branches, binding them with reedrope, so he could investigate possibilities like this—the bristled edge of a nest. Probably a canyonhawk's.

"Ballyworms!" came a shrill voice from the narrow ledge below. "Lookit that, Krawg!"

Krawg sighed. "If you interrupt me again, Warney, you'll pay for it. I'm gonna take a bad step and crush you when I fall. We're s'posed to be workin'. Not gazin' at sunsets."

"No. It's not the sun I'm seein', Krawg. I'm lookin' at that bare hill in the woods. Abascar's got visitors comin'. Haulin' a couple of wagons. Merchants, likely."

Krawg lifted his right foot, scraped the tip of his leather slipper along the wall to toe a rough edge and test his weight. Holding fast to the ladder with his left hand, he spidered the fingers of his right hand along the rockface until he gripped an edge. He glanced up at the sky beyond the precipice birds, worried that the mother hawk would return and find him splayed there like a wasp.

"Lookit, Krawg. By the bottomless belly of Wenjee, those merchants have climbed right up into plain view. Why would they do that? Don't they know that beastmen might be prowlin' about? Smart as a pair of boots, they are."

"Baldridge Hill?" Krawg snorted. "Merchants are strange folk. Slept in a patch of madweed, prob'ly, and lost all sense. Now, hush and let me work. I'm reachin' for the day's best catch."

"If you don't look now, you'll miss it, Krawg. Sun's goin' down."

Indeed, the shadowtide had engulfed the cliff's lower tiers, rising to Krawg's knees. He lifted his left foot from the ladder and dug his toe into a rocky notch. As he let the ladder go, it wobbled, spun on one of its crooked wooden feet, and clattered to the ground. Krawg laughed, clinging to the rockface.

He laughed because a year ago he would not have been able to climb a ladder, much less make his way along a cliff. He had been feeble, worn out by the hard life of exile among House Abascar's Gatherers.

After Abascar's collapse, autumn had seen the assembling of survivors in the Blackstone Caves within the Barnashum Cliffs. As winter's first waves dealt harshly with the traumatized gathering, Krawg had grown confident and strong. Abascar's new king had given him responsibility because of his experience in finding food. He worked with others every day to harvest stores that would feed them through the worsening freeze. Without the Gatherers the remnant of Abascar might not survive. While those accustomed to comfort and warmth nursed their wounds in the labyrinth of caves, Gatherers flourished, already toughened by hardships.

The people needed him. It was a joy Krawg did not deserve, and it filled him with a resolve to please them.

He heard Warney scratch at the wall-winding vines on the cliff face. Thick-skinned wintergrapes tumbled onto blankets spread along the ridge. But Warney was easily distracted. "I see the merchants, Krawg. One's tendin' to his vawns, and another's wavin' at...at two children He's chasin' them back into the wagon."

"Warney, we're losin' light. Rake some more grapes."

"He's chasin' them into the wagon."

"And don't talk to me about children."

"Mercy, Krawg! That merchant's wavin' some kind of flag. Maybe we should wave back."

Krawg pressed his forehead against the stone. "Here's a plan for you, Warney. You wave back, and I'll throw you off this ledge! Has the cold frozen your potato?"

"They must be awful hungry for trade. Or they wouldn't bring wagons this far south."

"And what'll we feed them, Warney? We fill our own bowls with stews made outta weeds. And besides, King Cal-raven will never bargain with merchants so close to the hideaways. Nobody can know where we go in and out. We're long-ears hunkered in a warren, and someday the foxes will snoop us out."

"So you're just gonna ignore them?"

"Cal-raven has watchers in the trees, remember? They'll look out for the merchants." But now Krawg was curious. He glanced over his shoulder. Dusk engulfed Baldridge Hill, and he couldn't see the merchants' wagons.

But he could see the low sun—a bright eye staring through the purple miasma that polluted the western sky over the Cent Regus wasteland. He felt exposed, as if the sun were judging him for plotting to take an egg from this nest. "This ain't thieving," he muttered. "Those days are over. I've got my pardon." Darkness rose to his shoulders. He would grab that nest with what light he had left.

"Oh, Krawg. It's just gone worse."

"It'll go even worser, Warney, when I break these eggs on your empty head!" Krawg leaned, reached, clasped the prickly nest. "Got it!" He walked his fingers up over the edge, felt for the shells.

Something sharp pinched his thumb. He drew back, then reached in again and closed his hand around a bundle of feathers. "A baby," he said as if in a game of Blindfold. "A baby bird in winter!"

"Fire!" Warney whispered. "The merchant wagon! Krawg, it's on fire!"

Krawg chanced another glance back and almost lost his grip. In the pooling dark over Baldridge Hill, flames flowered.

"Burrow in!" It was a sharp order from Brevolo, the swordswoman appointed to scan the land for witnesses. "Burrow in! Now!"

"What's happening?" asked Warney.

"Beastmen," Brevolo shouted back. "Attacking merchants on Baldridge Hill. Too close."

Krawg's hand cradled the trembling bird. He bewildered himself with his decision—taking a baby canyonhawk from its mother. But he was compelled by the chick's vulnerability. He wanted to protect something.

He pulled the bird to his chest as it fluttered in a frantic fit. "It's gonna be fine. Trust me. I've been taken from my home too. But by my crackin' knees, know this—I'll make you safe." He held the chick above night's rising tide into the light. It thrust out its puff of a head. It blinked its eyes as if for the first time. He could see that it was not a canyonhawk at all, but an owl.

"Oh, no, Krawg. The merchants, they're—"

"Didn't you hear the woman? Burrow in, you rangy crook!"

"You're gonna ignore what's happening?" Warney was shrieking hysterically.

"What makes you think you'd fare better than merchants against those beastmen?"

"What if it was 'Ralia in that burning wagon?"

"Then Auralia would be dead, Warney. Auralia *is* dead."

Brevolo gave the final order for all harvesters to retreat into the Blackstone Caves. What happened next—a flurry of noise as Abascar's survivors scrambled into concealed tunnels, and then silence—left Krawg choking on a hard fact. With this little feathered life in one hand, and the other clinging to a tenuous edge on the cliff wall, he was stuck. The ladder lay flat on the ledge below.

"Warney? Put the ladder up."

There was no reply.

"Warney? Brevolo?"

Krawg's appeal was answered by a breath of wind, the first pulse of the night's hard freeze. His bones began to ache in dread. He might not survive a night in the open. And his weakening fingers could not hold him up much longer.

"Don't you worry," he told the bird.

He thought of another risk he had taken, gathering a life into his hands without any sense of the future. For almost sixteen years he had counted that his finest decision. And then House Abascar had swallowed her.

Somewhere above, he heard the screech of the mother owl signaling her approach.

"Well, just saw me in two with a tree branch," he muttered.

As the ale boy climbed the brambled slope, smoke erupted from the top of Baldridge Hill. Gorrels fled past, seeking refuge in the forest. The boy pressed on, faster, braver.

Emerging from the bushes, he heard the beastmen gnarring at one another. He could see their hunched, hulking shapes leaping in and out of the smokestorm, probably trying to salvage treasure. They did not see him. A tree of darkness grew above the flames, and when the smoke caught in the crisscrossing winds, that tree sprouted billowing branches.

Hurrying toward the burning wagons, he felt a pulse in his forehead. The scar. The mark he had worn since that night when Northchildren cast a strange, protective covering over him in his burning crib. He felt a prickling in his skin. Emboldened, he strode to a curtain of flame and parted it with his hands. He climbed into one of the wagons.

Under the burning canvas canopy, among stacks of sparking and blackening crates, a small boy sat hunched with arms wrapped protectively around an even smaller girl, who lay limp in his arms. The boy did not look up. He stared through the surrounding fires, wild-eyed, listening to the predators' voices, which sounded like saws grinding deep into old wood.

The ale boy did not want to see the beastmen. Nor did he want to see the parents of these children fighting for their lives. And he certainly could not let the children stay here while all the cargo they had gathered through so many seasons in the cold and the wet exploded into flame and ash.

He reached forward and tapped the boy on the shoulder. The boy looked up at him, incredulous. "Follow me," he said. "I'm not a beastman." The flames lashed at his back but did not catch his cloak or his cap.

Everything wavered, illusory, as the wagon's canvas cover was transformed into curtains of flame. The ale boy knew he must be a fearsome sight. "What's your name?" he asked.

"Wynn."

"Wynn, follow me. Or they'll eat the girl for dessert."

The firestorm swallowed the wagon, howling, and the wheels splintered with loud cracks. But the ale boy did not look back, diving into the night's deep tide with the girl slung over his shoulder and her brother running behind them.

"Mummy," he heard the boy whisper. "Pa. Mummy. Pa."

Down in the maze of dead huskerbrambles, they burrowed into a patch of frosted boughs. In the center they found the ancient trunk of a fallen tree overrun with weeds. The ale boy laid the girl alongside it and wiped soot from her brow. "She'll live." He pulled back his hood. "You hurt?"

Wynn looked at him with such wild bewilderment that the ale boy wished for a mirror. He was something from an oven. His clothes glittered with sparks. And while his voice was still as quiet as it had ever been, his skin had changed, red as sunburn, tough and cracked like a roasted potato. Wynn's eyes flickered, reflecting a tongue of flame. The ale boy pulled off his cap and found a flame like a candle's flare wavering on the crown.

"How come you don't burn?"

The ale boy puffed out the light, and brushed sparks from his clothes until it was dark. "What's your sister's name?"

"Cortie. My sister. She…she worked so hard. We both worked so hard. And now it's all burning. And Mummy and Pa—"

"Listen closely, Wynn. We'll cry for them in a little while. All of us. They're gone. I wanted to save them. But I…I'm not big enough to fight beastmen." The ale boy felt that familiar bitterness rising in his throat, the resentment of insufficiency. "Your parents, they're not hurting. Not anymore. Northchildren are gentle. They'll be kind. I've seen them."

"Northchildren?" Wynn scowled. "Northchildren aren't actual, are they? Pa says they're just spooks from stories."

"They gave me this gift. And they've helped others too. I've seen them."

"Are you the one they call Rescue?" Wynn shuddered. "They say the Keeper walks beside you. They say you saved all kinds of folks from the Abascar fires."

"Rescue?" The ale boy looked up. "I'm the ale boy. That's what folks call me. And if the Keeper is walking beside me, well, tell me when you see it."

Wynn's eyes filled with further questions. But there was a sound in the bushes nearby, and the ale boy held out his hands with a clear message—
Be quiet. Be still. Then he crawled back through the thorns.

One of the beastmen came stalking through the huskerbrambles. The ale boy heard him huffing and puffing. The creature did not need to bring a torch. He could see in the dark. Peering through the branches, the ale boy studied him, darker than dusk, a giant draped in a woodscloak, spiked club in hand. The ale boy crawled further on, winding his way between the bursts of dead branches, avoiding the monster's gaze. But when he looked back again, the beastman was just a few paces from the children's patch.

The ale boy sprang up and feigned a startled cry. The beastman turned, advancing without hesitation. He brandished the club and showed his teeth. The boy backed into a hedge of thorns. "Northchildren," he whispered. "I'm ready."

The beastman did not strike. Instead, the creature sniffed the air as if sensing something invisible between them. He set down the club, reached forward with massive hands and grasped the ale boy's shoulders. Lifting him up, the beastman drew him up close to his leathery, pockmarked visage. He did not meet the boy's gaze, but stared at something just above it. Panting like a rabbit in the eagle's talons, the boy squirmed.

"O-raya?" The beastman's question caught the boy by surprise. Holding him firmly with his left hand, the beastman reached up, pushed off the ale boy's hood, and hooked the colored headband with a shiny black claw to draw it off his head. He held it up to the fading light as if it were a treasure and announced, "rrO-raya!"

"Auralia?" The boy nodded. "Yes. *Auralia*. She made that. I found it. You like it? You can have it! There's much more where that came from."

He stared into the beastman's face, discerning only the faintest details in the frame of the shaggy mane.

"O-raya!" the beastman declared, and his breath was so foul that the ale boy sneezed in his face. The beastman dropped him and growled.

From the top of the hill came a sonorous bellow. The ale boy's captor turned. Clearly disgruntled, he folded Auralia's colored band into his massive hand, snatched the club, and with a grumble that sounded like regret, bounded away, back up through the huskerbrambles, toward the smoke at the hill's crest.

Wynn crawled to the edge of the thicket. "Why didn't he kill you?"

Stunned, the ale boy touched his exposed forehead and crawled back into the bramble. "Let's get Cortie and make a run for the trees. Now. Before he changes his mind."

He gathered the girl into his arms. She coughed, said "Papa," but did not wake. He laid her head on his shoulder and rose.

By the time they stood in the forest, anger was darkening Wynn's voice. "Where will we go, Rescue? What do we do now?"

"I'll take you to Abascar. Quickly. Before that beastman changes his mind."

"Abascar? But there's nothing there. Abascar's collapsed!"

"House Abascar's not a place," said the ale boy. "House Abascar's just people. They're hiding not far from here."

"I don't understand. Why didn't that beastman tear you to pieces?"

"Auralia saved me. Again." A blurred memory stirred—the silhouette of a broad-shouldered monster lumbering up the long corridor into the chambers where Auralia worked. Mystified by the creature's attraction to her colors, the girl had let him bask in their illumination.

"Did you know Auralia?" Wynn blinked. "We knew her too. Where is she?"

"I used to ask as many questions as you," the ale boy sighed. "Learning the answers didn't make things much better."

Something shifted in the trees.

"Beastman!"

"No, Wynn. Hush. It's not a beastman."

Wynn gasped. "The Keeper?"

"Didn't you hear me?" The ale boy almost shouted. "The Keeper is gone. That's just my vawn, Rumpa. She wouldn't come out of the trees when she smelled the smoke. It reminds her too much of the Abascar fires. But she'll carry us to King Cal-raven. He'll help you."

Wynn quieted, following as the ale boy approached the timid vawn. The farther they moved into the trees, the more it felt as if a blanket had been cast over them, and all sounds of the dangerous world beyond were erased.

The large, cautious lizard walked out of hiding on her sturdy, clawed hind feet and lowered her gooselike head to the ale boy, muttering and swishing her scaly tail.

"Will you stay with us?" whispered Wynn as the ale boy lifted Cortie to sit at the base of the vawn's neck. "When we get to Abascar's gate?"

The ale boy did not answer.

"I'm tired," said Wynn, his voice fading.

The ale boy whispered into Rumpa's ear and stroked her yellow neck.

"Are you one of those people who can speak the animals' language?" Wynn asked.

"I'm not a wildspeaker. But I know a man who is. He visited me at the caves by Deep Lake. I told him all about Auralia, and he was so glad about what I told him that he gave me this vawn, Rumpa, and commanded her to obey me." He climbed up behind Wynn and took the vawn's reins. "Go," he shouted.

Rumpa sighed, abruptly dropped to her knees, and began to snuffle about in the dirt for rockbeetles.

"Are you sure she obeys you?" Wynn was unimpressed.

"She gets a little confused, that's all. Rumpa, *go!*" The ale boy dug in his heels, and the vawn lurched to her feet. "You should have seen what happened last time I told her to put me down."

Rumpa strode away in a steady rhythm, and her trembling subsided.

"They almost sold us once, Mummy and Pa." Wynn confessed this quietly, perhaps to Cortie, perhaps to the ale boy. Perhaps to himself. "They were gonna trade us to Bel Amican Seers. But then they didn't. They packed up their things, real fastlike. We rode away. We were hungry. But we were together." He embraced Cortie tight.

The ale boy felt his resistance failing. Emotion swelled in his throat, even though he could not fathom what the boy was feeling.

"Can I cry now?" Wynn whispered.

The ale boy patted him on the shoulder. "Of course," he said, choking. "I'll cry with you."

Krawg cringed as the angry mother owl shrieked nearby. The furious bird had retreated after she'd swiped deep scratches into the back of his bald head. He clung to the wall, his grip failing bit by bit. Below him, silence. The laborers had retreated into the caves long ago.

He was left to weigh his options. To jump, hear his feeble knees snap, and lose the baby owl. Or to keep holding and hoping.

He thought back over his life and how this ridiculous end seemed inevitable. "Stealing," he muttered bitterly. "A thief to the end." He held the owl to his chest. "I should have learned by now. I meant to change, you know. But I'm weak. Now I'm out of second chances."

Krawg heard footsteps. Footsteps along the ledge below him.

Beastmen.

Before Krawg could let go of his remaining hopes, he heard the Late Evening verse of House Abascar being sung. He began to sing along.

The singer stopped, apparently surprised. Krawg felt a ripple of heat move through the stone under his hand. And then the stone shifted. Beneath his toes, the thin lip expanded until he could stand flatfooted. He released his grip as tremors shook the wall. The change continued. In the faint moonlight he saw rugged steps emerging from the cliff wall, an easy path for him to follow down to where a hooded figure waited.

"You owe me," said the shadow. Cal-raven, king of Abascar, stonemaster, removed his hands from the wall.

"Thank you, master!" Krawg fell to his knees, more of a baffled collapse than a gesture of servitude. "I'll do anything you ask."

"Oh, I wasn't serious." The king walked a few paces but turned back as Krawg got to his feet. "Then again, there is something you can do."

"Anything, my king."

"Be our storyteller tonight. Remind the people of how you found Auralia and what she grew to become. They need her now."

"I'll tell the story in such detail it'll be as if she's standin' in the middle of our circle. But, well, not in the bonfire, of course."

"Just tell the story. It'll do its work." The king smiled, and Krawg, forgetting he had already done so, dropped again to his knees.

"Let's burrow in and get something to eat," he whispered to the owl. "We're in the care of the king now."

4

JORDAM'S SECRET

Someone would be punished. Jordam was sure of it. Mordafey's tantrums always ended with a thrashing.

He listened intently while his brother ranted beside the fire. He listened for the moment when the anger would find a focus, when the gold-maned brute would choose a weapon and a target. He hoped it wouldn't be him.

But there were other reasons to listen. Mordafey had a plan, an ambition that he kept to himself. Occasionally, in his anger, he let details slip.

Jordam suspected that his brother meant to overthrow the Cent Regus chieftain. And it could happen. Mordafey was stronger and smarter than any Cent Regus in the wild. But even Mordafey would need loyal, familiar, ferocious accomplices to help him overcome the chieftain. So Jordam obeyed. He wanted to live. He wanted to remain Mordafey's trusted helper—indeed, to become indispensable—for the privileges he might win when his brindled brother claimed the throne.

Tonight, infuriated by mistakes made on Baldridge Hill, Mordafey fumed about how he could not trust his brothers, how they were not yet ready to make any dangerous moves. The merchants' cargo, which would have won them greater reward from the Cent Regus chieftain, had gone up in flames. That was Jorn's fault. Young and a glutton for chaos, the striped savage had torched the wagons too early.

Worse, the merchants' children, whom Mordafey had hoped to sell to the chieftain as slaves, had escaped. Jordam knew that was his mistake. He was reasonably certain Mordafey had no idea how they had slipped away, and that he would not be punished for failing to apprehend them. But his scars from past failures prompted him to worry.

Mordafey was distracted, glancing about at the dark forest beyond the reach of the fireglow. Their noisy meal had an audience, observers with jealous eyes that reflected the emberlight. Slitted eyes of viscorcats, shining like gold coins. Glittering black orbs of a low-bellied, eight-legged scissorjaw. Bloodshot simian eyes of a hairless, tree-climbing rawblood. Most wildlife seemed to be slipping away from the Cragavar forest in a mysterious exodus, but these predators, perverted by the poisons of the Cent Regus lands, remained to make meals of each other or whatever they could find.

Jorn, too, was distracted by these ravenous observers. Any one of them might become a tasty second course. He seemed especially interested in the restless rawblood that swung from branch to branch above, its pink face fading in and out of the light's reach. He leapt from the gory bones to the loot that the brothers had pulled from the wagon fire and snatched up a sharp Bel Amican spear, laughing, *"Hel hel hel. . ."*

"Forget the rawblood, Young Brother." Goreth struggled with a faulty memory. Jordam was the only brother whose name he could sometimes recall. "Get burnstuff. For the fire."

Jorn, glowering, tossed the spear aside and rummaged some more. He drew out a broad span of canvas and dragged it to the smoky, glowing coals.

Noticing the cloth's bright colors, Jordam cast aside the vawn bone he had cleaned and lurched to his feet. "rrNo!" Spitting a chunk of gristle, he stepped between Jorn and the embers, firmly seizing an edge of the fabric.

Thrusting out his tusk-pronged jaw, Jorn nodded toward Jordam's twin. "Goreth told Jorn—*get burnstuff.*"

"Burn *branches.* Not this." Jordam yanked the fabric free of his brother's clutches and spread it, examining its decoration. It was the sort of drape travelers would stretch across a makeshift frame for shelter. Firelight glowed dimly through it, illuminating spirals of blue, green, and purple.

As Jorn took the spear and walked bowlegged to find firewood, Jordam studied the designs as though they formed a map.

"We'll get good payment," said Goreth to his twin. "We've got enough now to go and see *him,* yes? Him with the Essence? *Garr,* what do we call him?"

"rrChieftain," Jordam mumbled absently.

"Chieftain," Goreth laughed. "Yes. Give him a spear, canvas, rope, saddles. Then give him stuff we took from Bel Amicans at Abascar. So many prizes. Chieftain will thank us." He licked his nose and stood up, staring off into the trees. "Rockbeetles! Do I smell honey?"

"So many prizes," Mordafey grumbled. "Brothers could have taken much more. But Mordafey is thirsty for Essence. Brothers must go to Skell Wra. Soon."

Mordafey refused to ascribe the title of "chieftain" to Skell Wra. That dominant manipulator had survived for generations, sustained by perpetual absorption of the Essence, gaining power over the wills of the scattered Cent Regus people. Mordafey coveted the chieftain's power and longevity and insisted on calling him by his name.

The oldest brother also referred to himself by name, stamping it in the minds of others like a threat. "All part of Mordafey's plan," he insisted, pacing on the flat surface of a massive boulder that jutted into the clearing from the crowded trees. "Four brothers take *all* of the Bel Amican prizes to Skell Wra. Canvas, weapons, everything. Get bigger payment in Essence. Get stronger. Better for the plan."

Jordam could almost smell the boiling broth that would renew his strength, enhance his senses, make him even more dangerous. He licked his teeth. The more days that passed between helpings of that murky soup, the more anxious the brothers became, and the pain waves in Jordam's head worsened.

And yet Jordam knew that Essence would only interrupt his misery. After another drink and a season of strength, he would weaken, succumbing again to pain as his intoxication subsided.

Jagged bolts of light flashed behind his eyes. Essence would numb this pain, replacing it with power. But O-raya's colors had eased the pain too, diverting his attention by opening his eyes to new things, new pleasures. This Bel Amican canvas was not O-raya's work, but it would serve. For now.

Jordam first encountered O-raya on the night he fell and broke his browbone.
Three years before House Abascar's fall, Jordam had bounded through

the woods under a moon-bright springtime sky, pursuing a horse and rider.

In the forest south of Deep Lake, the four brothers had ambushed a caravan of traveling entertainers. A horse escaped during the attack. From the rhythm of the run, Jordam discerned that the horse had a rider.

He got the jump on his brothers, off on all fours like a viscorcat. He liked nothing more than a chase. To run—alone—after the scent of hot blood.

The mare was fast, but this was unfamiliar wilderness. When she turned to check her pursuer's progress, Jordam saw her terror. He howled to unsettle her. A cry like a wolf's.

The rider, a small boy, tainted the air with salty tears. Then he suddenly let go of the horse's mane, grasping at his side where Jordam's throwing knife had lodged. The mare's sudden turn threw the boy sideways, and his head thudded against a low tree branch.

Jordam pulled off the boy's silver bracelet, slipped it on his thumb as a ring, and tore open the boy's shoulder bag. Glowstones—the sort mined deep within Abascar's Underkeep—spilled into his leathery palm.

The boy wheezed a name, staring skyward.

"rrOnly one name matters to you now," Jordam laughed in the crude Cent Regus speech. "Skell Wra. Cent Regus chieftain. He'll make you work."

The hoofbeats grew faint. Jordam wanted the mare. But another scent teased his nostrils. Another of the weakerfolk. A girl, with berries on her breath, nearby.

He looked about for strands with which to tie the boy to the tree. But the boy was coughing blood. He would not be going anywhere. "rrSister?" Jordam asked the boy, a word in the weakerfolk speech. But his interrogation stopped there; the boy was no longer breathing.

Pulling his woodscloak around him, Jordam slipped a curved blade from his belt and crept up a steep bramble incline. He emerged on the stone shoulders of a ridge high above Deep Lake. The full moon's face shone red on the waters that rippled up to the base of the cliff. He flattened against the ground.

Twenty paces away a young girl swung her legs over the cliff and sang,

"Guard me from danger, guard me from lies, guard me from claws and from hearts that despise. Guard me from nightmares, threats to my health. Keeper, come rescue me, yes, from myself."

That brilliant blue cloak of hers—it would make a fine prize to show his brothers.

The girl sighed, said, "Save me from House Abascar," and stared at the moon's reflection. Slowly she laid her head down on a folded cloth and settled into sleep.

Jordam felt her feeble breath on his whiskers when he leaned over her. He drew an imaginary line along her throat for the cut, but then he thought better of it. He would gain a greater reward if he took her as a hostage.

A sound like a wind uprooting trees turned him around in time to see a massive shadow clambering up the slope. Vast, leathery wings spread wide to blot out the sky. Eyes flared, big as bonfires. A chasm of a mouth yawned open.

Jordam whimpered in surprise and threw himself backward off the cliff.

Through cold space Jordam fell. He shattered the moon's wavering reflection, and the shards of light found each other again above him. He sank in deep, murky water. His lungs convulsed. Slippery lakeweed tendrils grasped at his arms and legs.

When his head struck a boulder at the bottom, his browbone split down the middle. A jagged piece broke away, disappearing in the slithering bed of green. He went limp, limbs splayed, collapsing into the clutches of the weeds.

A surge pulled him free, a disturbance caused by the creature as it plunged into the lake. The current carried him far and fast. He broke the surface, pumped water from his lungs, and blinked into the cruel light of the sky's red eye.

In the lake before him, the winged behemoth tilted its head. Fire lined the rows of teeth on that long, terrible face. And then it made a strange sound. An announcement. A verdict. The creature's tentacle tail coiled about Jordam's body, pulling him mightily downward. It released him into a powerful undertow, and he was carried away.

When he surfaced again, Jordam struggled to determine which way he should swim. But then his feet found purchase, and he scrambled shoreward.

He fled into a cave that stretched deep beneath the cliffs, moving upward and inward. Staggering into darkness, he turned a corner and stumbled into a chamber shimmering with light.

Colors emanated from a cloth draped across a stone table in the center of the room. They burnt his eyes just as the water had burnt his lungs. He fell forward onto his hands, cowering before the strange illumination—hues of spring, summer, autumn, winter, and seasons he did not recognize.

In the glow, Jordam's body felt heavier. His strength left him. He slumped into a corner. His hands explored the new shape of his broken browbone, and he found, as his breathing slowed and his panic lessened, that with the breakage his vision was clearer.

He lay gazing at the radiant, simmering pools on the ceiling. Fear subsided. Hunger vanished. The ache began to fade. He felt suspended in the light.

Later, while he hovered in a half sleep, Jordam heard faint footsteps pause in the chamber and then retreat. He knew, somehow, that they belonged to the girl. And as he drifted into a strange, contented dream, he discerned that the child, the colors, and the behemoth were connected, pieces in some great mystery. Inexplicably, he felt safe.

Jordam woke to hear ducks laughing and splashing on the lake. He fingered the break in his browbone. The injury had split his mind in two. Eyes open, Jordam saw that the colors remained. Eyes closed, he could see Mordafey ranting back in the brothers' den.

Despite his desire to stay there in the glory, Jordam moved to the cave entrance. Lakewaters lapped quietly on the shore. There was no sign of the girl.

Jordam hesitated. He could take the colorful weaving with him. But he would have to explain this discovery to his brothers. That would aggravate Mordafey, who would take it straight to the chieftain in trade for Essence. He chose to leave it in the cave, where it seemed to be safe.

Besides, Jordam had no way to be sure that the lake creature was not watching him, lying in wait.

He bounded all the way back to his brothers' den, surprised and exhilarated to find that he could run faster, see farther, now that the burdensome browbone was broken. He ran without stopping, taking a path south and west through the Cragavar forest, across open, hilly ground. Half a day later, climbing through a stony canyon to the four brothers' hideaway, he was home.

Mordafey met him with anger, suspicion, and questions. Jordam's lies were enough to help him escape permanent scars, at least for a while.

That was the beginning of Jordam's visits to the girl's mysterious caves. He would frequently creep in and watch her, hypnotized.

She extracted colors from leaves, roots, even stones. She blended dyes and painted them across bark, skins, and webbing. Her nimble hands wove a gallery of wonders. *O-raya*, she would call herself, scolding her own mistakes. After vowing to bring a work to completion, whatever she touched became a more vivid and dazzling version of itself. Then she would bundle the pieces she had made and venture into the woods to deliver them.

Mordafey's suspicions increased. He soon forbade Jordam, Goreth, and Jorn to make solitary excursions. But Jordam was not going to give up his discovery. He found ways to visit her, again and again, season after season. "O-raya," he would say to himself in her absence, running his hands over the most extravagant work of all—the cloth laid upon the broad stone table. The more he basked in the light of that particular weave, the more he felt like a different version of himself.

One day the colors were missing, and O-raya with them. The many months since then had dragged Jordam into a long, slow decline, a return to his reckless, ravenous state.

At the campfire, Jordam opened his hand, looked at the crumpled band he had torn from the boy's head on the slope of Baldridge Hill. Hope surged within him. Perhaps O-raya was still out there. Perhaps he might find her colors again.

It unsettled him, the return of his willingness to risk punishment for a mysterious and colorful comfort. But the colors gave him something that Essence could not. The intoxication of the Cent Regus elixir could briefly satiate his appetites and slow the anxious pulse within his head. But in the luminous spectacle of O-raya's colors, that cold, cruel grasp of appetite let go. He did not want the Essence when he took refuge there, for he found strength of another kind. He would do whatever he could to find that relief again.

Waiting for the pounding to subside, Jordam lay against the crux of a tree with two trunks—one seemed to strain against the earth's pull with branches that clawed for a hold on the sky, the other surrendering to vines and weeds, winding serpentine along the ground.

Goreth was breaking vawn limbs at their hinges, fitting scraps of meat to the tips of cleaned branches, and roasting them over the flames. Jorn crouched on all fours and shoved his canine snout impatiently into the carcass.

"Why does Jordam eat vawn meat tonight?" Mordafey, sulking, threw debris from his rocky perch into the embers. *Rushhh*—ashes rose like a cloud of fireflies. In that flash, Jordam glimpsed contempt in Mordafey's gold eyes. "Jordam didn't kill anything today. What did he do, down there in the bushes?" Mordafey flung a dripping strand of vawn tail into Jordam's face.

"You were killing vawns, Mordafey," Jordam replied. "rrRunaways. I went after runaways."

"But Jordam didn't catch runaways." Mordafey leapt off the stone and stalked around the firelight's circle, passing behind Jordam. "Jordam came back with nothing. He *let* them go. Why? Did runaways beg? Did Jordam make some secret bargain?"

"I don't talk with weakerfolk. I don't like their jabber."

"Jordam doesn't talk *with* them. But he does talk *like* them. Doesn't he, Goreth?" Jordam felt Mordafey's fiery stare on the back of his head. "He barks the weakerfolk way. In his sleep. Three brothers have heard him."

Jordam pricked his palms with his claws. How could he escape trouble if he betrayed himself in his sleep? "rrWeakerfolk in my dreams," he argued. "I trick weakerfolk into traps. Call them with weakerfolk words. Just dreams, Mordafey."

"Then why does Jordam cry about an Abascar girl? Why talk about secret caves? Jordam has a slave somewhere, and won't tell Mordafey?" Mordafey leaned in, his voice like a rush of jagged stones. "Who's O-raya?"

The question jolted Jordam to his feet. He immediately regretted this.

Goreth cursed while Jorn cackled in glee, happy to watch Mordafey torment someone else.

"Found an Abascar girl called O-raya. Once. By the lake. Swam to catch her, to bring her back to brothers. rrNot fast enough. A gator got her. Gator ate the girl." He snickered, pleased with his own embellishment. "I ate the gator."

Jorn smacked his hands together. Murder stories amused him, the bloodier the better, so long as the blood belonged to someone else. Jordam's tale shook his laughter loose.

Mordafey did not share Jorn's amusement. "Cross Mordafey, Jordam, and you will meet him in a dark place." He sealed this vow by knocking his knuckles against his broad browbone. "And you will not recognize him. He'll be like...like..." He scowled, failing to find any appropriate comparison.

The rawblood in the trees behind them shrieked, anxious for the leftover vawn bones. Mordafey's ears swiveled toward the sound. Circling Jordam, he grabbed the Bel Amican spear and launched it into the darkness. Something heavy fell into the bushes. A viscorcat yowled, and there was a scuffling in the dark.

"Mordafey killed the rawblood," Mordafey hissed. "Mordafey *eats* the rawblood." He hurried into the shadows to claim his prize. Jorn, thrilled, crawled after him to watch.

Goreth and Jordam exchanged a silent glance, a familiar expression of weariness. "Older Brother hates secrets," said Goreth to his twin. "Older Brother wants everything. Takes everything." The jagged blue scar across Goreth's cheek wriggled wormlike. "Older Brother gets everything good." He kicked a merchant skull with his foot.

"He doesn't get everything good," said Jordam.

In the shadows the viscorcat uttered a guttural threat. Mordafey replied. The viscorcat bounded away, whimpering, and left the fallen rawblood for Mordafey.

Apparently forgetting he had already made this discovery, Goreth stood up and announced, "I smell honey!" He strolled around the perimeter of the clearing in search of a hive.

From the pocket of his woodscloak, Jordam drew sharp shards of stone and glass, souvenirs from the ambush, and cast them across the canvas. He distracted himself by moving them with a long stick, aligning them with the spirals of blue in the fabric. It lacked the luminosity of the blue in O-raya's colors, but the memory calmed him.

Mordafey emerged from the shadows, dragging his prey. Jorn scampered around him, barking, "Vawn tracks! *Hel hel hel*…Mordafey found vawn tracks!"

"They go north," said Mordafey. Jordam did not like his triumphant, bloodied grin. "Jordam will prove that he did not let our prey escape. Jordam will lead the hunt. After Mordafey eats"—he cast the rawblood carcass onto the fire—"four brothers catch runaways."

Jorn's laughter turned to howls as Mordafey turned the lash against him, cursing him for burning the wagons too early. Jordam stared fixedly at the Bel Amican cloth. And then he smiled too. If he could find the boy, perhaps he could find O-raya…and relief.

5

HUNTING AND HUNTED

Tensing like a spider that feels a tremor on the web, Jordam flexed his claws. Goreth, standing at the top of a ridge, kept his hand in the air to halt the brothers' pursuit.

If the boy from O-raya's caves was just over this ridge, he was as good as dead. Jordam had given him a chance, but he could do nothing to stop the hunt now.

As Jordam relayed Goreth's silent caution, Jorn collapsed, glad for an excuse to catch his breath. Obeying Mordafey's orders, he had hauled the pile of salvage on a makeshift sled of interwoven reedweed shoots. With straps from the sled bound around his lash-whipped hide, Jorn felt punishment in every step—punishment for the cargo he had cost them on Baldridge Hill.

Mordafey shrugged his woodscloak back over his shoulders, freeing his arms. He held a short spear newly tipped with a rawblood tooth.

"Steps." Goreth's whisper was a gust of rustling leaves. "Not far." He spread his arms to indicate something enormous. Mordafey's eyes widened, and he knelt to press his ear to the ground.

Deep quakes pulsed beneath Jordam's feet. A premonition scrambled up his spine. *The Keeper.* He remembered his fall from the cliff into Deep Lake, and the presence that had prompted it, as if it had only just occurred. Alone, he would have fled. But Mordafey was smiling.

The rider had kept the brothers moving north and west from Baldridge Hill through the Cragavar all night. Mordafey was too stubborn to call off a hunt he had begun, and Jordam refused to give his brothers the pleasure of seeing him surrender, even though their dens were close by, stocked with dried meat, eggs kept cold in deep cavewater, and bowls of crunchy beetles. Pride had pushed them forward. Now, newly inspired, Mordafey would press on to know what manner of creature shook the earth. Nothing frightened Mordafey.

"Wood dragon?" Jorn, afraid, began to fade into moss and ferns, his skin greening to disguise him.

"Cent Regus killed every wood dragon." Mordafey pointed to the top of the rise. "This...something new."

A wave of sound—branches shattering, roots ripping from soil, trees crashing down—broke over the ridge. Jorn jumped into a tree, and the jolt on his tethers caused the heavy salvage sled to dump some of its cargo.

Mordafey rushed past Goreth, weapons ready, and stared down the other side of the forested ridge.

Interlocking branches in the thickly wooded forest had forbidden the brothers' passage in the past, but as Jordam reached the top of the rise he saw that something had tumbled through the trees beyond, blazing a new path. He could smell the shock of sap where boughs had snapped. And something more. Jordam's nostrils flared. Smoke. Hadn't that creature at the lake breathed fire like a dragon?

"Other Cent Regus will fear us if we catch it," said Mordafey. "We will be like...like..."

"rrWe should go back." Jordam groped for words that would convince them to retreat. *I've seen a terrible creature. Same one that roars in bad dreams.* No, Mordafey needed something more substantial. "If we chase it, we leave prizes behind for other Cent Regus. We need prizes. For Essence."

"Mordafey stays with prizes." Mordafey grinned. "Jordam, hunt."

Jordam was about to protest when a firm grip fastened to his arm. He turned to see Goreth scowling. "Older Brother, send me too. For Jordam, too dangerous."

Jordam disliked thinking about a charge before it began. Thinking kindled fear, and fear could slow and distract him. Closing his eyes, baring his teeth, he launched into what he knew very well could be his final run. And Goreth's as well.

The twins bounded over the seven-toed prints as if trying to fly. The world about them melted into a blur. The path led them down, north and west.

"Strange," Goreth barked, trying to keep pace. "Smells of water."

"rrLakewater."

"No. Deeper." He fell behind as the ground rose sharply.

Jordam circled back to find his brother sharpening his claws on a rock. "Don't tell Older Brother," Goreth growled. "I smelled that smell before. In a dream. We were cubs. Big animal, smelled like deep water. I told the Old Dog about it in the morning. He thumped me."

Jordam was amazed and strangely comforted. Goreth had confided in him, confessing something he had withheld from Mordafey. This was new. This changed things.

Jordam and Goreth had always resembled each other, with their black manes and fur the deep red of rust. Their appetites advanced together, and their sufferings for want of Essence slowed and tormented them. But their differences were stark as well. Jordam's browbone was broken, but his mind was quick, while Goreth's memories slipped away as easily as wrigglers through a fishing net. Jordam was obstinate, willing to growl at Mordafey and pay the price; Goreth cowered in conflict. Goreth's expressive whip of a tail betrayed fear, agitation, and delight, while Jordam buried emotions deep.

With this confession, Goreth opened a conversation between them. This, Jordam realized, could be useful should Mordafey ever become too dangerous. If he could teach Goreth to conspire with him, perhaps they could gain an advantage.

"Same Brother dreams of the creature too." Goreth shoved him. "I hear you. In your sleep."

Jordam fought the urge to respond with his own revelation—an account of his fall from the cliff. He could feel the words in his mouth. But Goreth's mind, moods, and memory were unreliable as weather, and Mordafey's suspicions were flammable. "Must hurry now," he said. "rrTracks are deep, but the animal is fast."

Together they climbed through the next run of trampled trees, crested another ridge, and looked out across a valley of long whitegrass. A dark swath parted the field. The creature had crawled into the foggy stand of trees that covered the valley floor like dark brine in the bottom of a white bowl.

"Going back to its den?" Goreth drew in a deep breath. "Could be a hard hunt. Older Brother will scar us if we're gone for long."

Jordam glanced back over his shoulder. "He'll scar us deeper if we come back without a catch."

"Older Brother scars us whatever we do." Goreth seemed relieved to hear Jordam's aggravation. "I want some honey."

Clouds crowded the sky like cattle moping in a pasture. Frost glittered across the low woods in waves. Goreth pointed to a monolith there, the tower of a long-neglected Bel Amican bastion, and Jordam found the source of the smoke on the air—a wisp rising from the tower, spiriting away to the south-east. Perhaps the boy rested there.

Goreth began to rhythmically puncture the soil with his spear. "Weaker-folk."

"Bel Amicans," Jordam mused. "rrWe tell Mordafey, brothers need a new plan."

"Big animal guards Bel Amicans?" Goreth whispered.

"No. Not this animal." *But it guarded a girl.* Jordam realized that he had no choice. If the Keeper was here, and the boy as well, O-raya might have returned. "rrGo back," he said with resolve. "Tell Mordafey, I run on ahead."

"Alone?" Goreth shuddered.

"Mordafey say w'three go catch it!" It was Jorn, released from his burden, arriving on the scene as sudden as lightning. "Mordafey's angry." He rubbed the raw lines where pallet straps had burnt him. "Must catch something for him, he say."

Jordam and Goreth glanced back down the slope. It was not like Mordafey to keep himself out of a hunt.

"rrOrders? *Crolca!*" Jordam pointed to the tower. "Weakerfolk, arrows and swords, not far away. Go back, both of you." He reached down to scratch at a sharp sting in his ankle. "I hunt the animal." His hand closed around the shaft of an arrow. He blinked at it for a moment.

"*Urg!*" snorted Jorn. "*Urg!*" He fell, two arrows protruding from his thigh.

"They're behind us!" Jordam snapped. "In the trees!"

Jorn, his skin flushing white as the grass, shuddered and clutched at the arrows. Goreth dove into the field for cover. Jordam remained where he stood, staring into the shadowed trees behind him. When the next arrow came, a fleeting glint in the faint light, he blocked it with his club, and the arrow embedded there. Jordam sniffed the feathered shaft.

Poison.

As he dropped to the ground, he guessed that the attackers were Bel Amicans securing a perimeter around their newly enlivened fort. Jordam, Goreth, and Jorn had broken that border.

The whitegrass he disturbed would betray his position, but Jordam had no choice. He crawled low, frantic for a place to hide. If the brothers scattered, they might divide their pursuers, but they would lose their combined strength. If he took one of the hunters hostage, he could bring back a trophy for Mordafey's praise.

"There!" rang a cry in the Common tongue. A spear pierced the ground beside him.

Like oil catching fire, bloodlust blazed within him. His toes dug into the earth for the spring. His thoughts blurred as the weakening traces of Essence in his blood quickened. The killing fever, so familiar and invigorating, took hold.

But then a man shouted, "Hunt!" Jordam heard the yelps of unleashed hounds tearing through the grass toward him.

The killing fever faded, replaced by a chilling fear of paralysis. Jordam got up to make a run for the swath of trees that darkened the low valley ground, but his left leg was going numb, and he fell. The arrow had only nicked him, but Jorn...Jorn would already be captured. Or dead.

Jordam ran like a three-legged animal, lurching down the hill. The dogs were close. The numbing sensation spread as if carried by small, crawling things into his hip, up his spine, down into his other leg. It gave him little comfort to think that when the dogs caught him and tore him apart, he would not feel a thing.

At last among trees, he forced himself to his feet and staggered in zigzag. His senses wavered. He smelled rain-wet trees; hot, streaming blood from his wound; smoke from damp wood burning; wet dogs. He heard the hounds rejoicing at his clear trail, and he stumbled to his knees.

A coil tree loomed in his path. He grasped at its bark, reached a low branch, and pulled himself up, legs hanging useless behind him. He swung up through the serpentine sprawl of black, slippery boughs.

And then as he reached for the crook of trunk and branch, his arm plunged directly into a hollow of the tree. A sharp pain pierced his wrist.

Teeth.

He yelped. Instinct charging ahead of thought, his hands closed around a fat, squirming, hairy creature deep inside the coil tree. It shrieked. He yanked it out of its den—a gorrel. With hardly a moment to act, Jordam brought the squealing animal down to his bleeding leg and smeared its head, belly, back, and tail with his own blood.

The scattered dogs converged on the coil tree.

He dropped the gorrel as feeling faded from his arm. The bloodied animal fell into the bushes. With no time to celebrate its survival, it scrambled, dripping Jordam's blood across the frost, and led the howling dogs away.

Jordam crawled into a twist of branches like a dying bird into its nest. He wrapped his arms around a limb. His brothers, the journey, the tracks, the hunt, the arrows—all slipped from his mind's grasp, leaving him to fight the poison. He was conscious of nothing else, until the poison took his consciousness as well.

When Jordam opened his eyes again, daylight fell in soft white flakes all around him. Was it a dream, the blur of motion high in the window of the Bel Amicans' stone tower? The sight brought him swiftly from his daze. He could not see the structure clearly; it was just a straight-edged shadow with one glimmering eye near the top.

A woman of the weakerfolk stood there in an extravagant headdress and gown, a candle glinting starlike in her hands. She watched the woods awhile, then looked up at the blurred smudge of moonlight.

Jordam heard his own voice then, a faint rasp dry as bone. "O-raya." His lungs were open again. He could breathe. But he could not move. Nor could he escape the claws of sleep that closed around him once more.

In his sleep there remained a sensation of falling—not of tumbling down to darkness, but skyward, into light.

6

TROUBLE IN TILIANPURTH

A s the snow dusted the valley, Ryllion spurred his horse down through
the whitegrass field, into the dense wood, and at last across the drawbridge to the ancient Bel Amican bastion of Tilianpurth.

Forty-five days earlier he had staggered across this same bridge. The only
survivor of Deuneroi's company after the slaughter in Abascar's ruins, he was
welcomed by Bauris, the bastion's veteran officer. Bauris questioned him carefully before accepting that this bedraggled stranger was, indeed, the famous
soldier whom House Bel Amica had already mourned.

Ryllion had begged for an escort back to Bel Amica. But when word of
his return reached Queen Thesera, she sent instructions that he should
remain at Tilianpurth until he recovered. This was a blessing and a curse. He
was treated with honor, but he was not invited home or celebrated with any
fanfare, for he had failed to protect the royal consort.

Ryllion wanted to get back to the Seers. He wanted to serve the moon-
spirits and follow their sacred call. So he sought to earn back Queen Thesera's favor by shaping this cold lump of clay into something so essential that
all Bel Amica would clamor for his return.

During the beastman wars, Tilianpurth served as a crucial garrison. That
conflict ended generations ago when beastmen devolved into creatures that
could not organize or cooperate. King Helpryn had considered expanding
the old bastion into a permanent settlement, where inhabitants would work
to draw resources from the woods for shipbuilding. But the plans had moved
slowly, then stopped when the king died. The outpost languished from
neglect, watched over by only a few aging soldiers.

Today, as he had for many days, Ryllion returned from a Cragavar patrol and surveyed Tilianpurth—its yards, towerhouse, and tower—as if it were a prison. "Guide me out of here," he prayed in bursts of clouding breath. "How can I serve you if I'm bound to this pest-infested relic? They had a burial ceremony for me, Spirit. And when they learned I was alive, they decided to bury me again, right here."

He cast the reins of his panting vawn to the wide-eyed stablehand. The boy fumbled with the reins and squeaked, "You're welcome to Tilianpurth, sir."

"First tour, eh? What are you, ten?"

"Twelve, sir."

"Any news?"

"Did you hear, sir? Guards caught a beastman in the whitegrass this morning. They put him in the prison pit."

Ryllion dismounted. "I know. I've been hunting two more that escaped." He felt like a seasoned, middle-aged warrior, his mood as rank and heavy as the fog. It draped over his shoulders. It clung to his yellow beard. It lingered in his wake with a stench that came from sleeping in rain-soaked camps. "What's your name, boy? And what brings you to serve at this chunk of Bel Amican history?"

"I'm Pyroi, sir. My father wants me to be a soldier. He says it pays to start early, and—"

"Your father wants that, eh? What do *you* want to be, Pyroi?"

The boy blinked. "A soldier. Like you!"

"Your father isn't listening, son." Ryllion squeezed the boy's bony shoulder until Pyroi sucked air through his teeth. "What do *you* want? When you want something powerfully, *that's* the voice of your moon-spirit. I wanted to be a soldier. I'm only ten years older than you, but look at what my moon-spirit has given me. I listened for that call, and I answered it. The spirits carry moon-dust down at night, and we breathe it in. Desires take root. And in the morning, we feel them. Urges. Impulses. You're responsible to answer that call, kid. The Seers taught me that."

As the drawbridge lifted and sealed the Tilianpurth gate behind him, Ryllion held Pyroi's shoulder fast. The boy looked down at blotches of drying blood on Ryllion's boots and then at the spear he leaned on as if it were a crutch. The soldier straightened, releasing the boy and flexing hands that had recently been released from bandages. He lifted the spear and propped it against his shoulder. "Listen for your call, boy. Then pursue it, risking everything. I have, and so my moon-spirit had mercy on me and spared my life at Abascar."

The boy bowed his head, and his crumpled expression said everything that he was too afraid to admit to the gruff soldier.

"Trust your feelings. They're the best help the spirits have given you." Ryllion patted the boy's head and glanced up at the towerhouse. "Has the heiress arrived?"

"Not yet, sir." As the boy tried to steer the vawn around the looming shadow of the towerhouse to the low-roofed stable, the weary reptile bellowed her complaint through three flaring nostrils and thumped her clubbed tail against the ground.

Ryllion hoped that the company approaching from Bel Amica would bring his horse. Vawns, fast and sturdy, were necessary in these deep woods. But he preferred to be known as a horseman. He deserved that much, at least. Horses were nobler animals and not nearly so punishing in a long night's ride.

How he wanted to regain a sense of confidence. His convalescence at Tilianpurth had been humiliating. A fever clung for days, and his wounds healed slowly. Nightmares shook him from his bed. He woke fighting his blankets on the floor, shouting at beastmen, calling for Deuneroi. But he rejected his caretakers' instructions and clawed his way back to health, determined to defy rumors that his days as a soldier were over. He proved industrious. He set the bastion's staff to work, shoring up Tilianpurth from the kitchen to the perimeter. He sharpened the small company of guards Thesera had given him into a battle-ready troop, led them on successful hunts, and directed several raids on beastmen that helped appease his conscience. He sent those Cent Regus skulls back to Bel Amica as trophies to placate the masses distraught over Deuneroi's death.

His ploy failed to open Bel Amica's gates. Reportedly impressed with stories of his success, Queen Thesera thanked him by "asking" him to stay at Tilianpurth. She sent additional staff to make the place more livable and provided soldiers for training. Deuneroi's death had cast Thesera's daughter,

Cyndere, into despair, and the queen wanted to hear daily news of beastmen being trapped, punished, and killed.

"How many skulls will it take, Your Loftiness?" he snapped. "Or would you be happier if I packaged my own head as a prize? Would that assuage your sorrow at last?"

Ryllion marched up the pebbled path across the east yard toward Tilian-purth's central fortification and tower. The old grey structure sulked like a cantankerous ancestor, waiting to wheeze and snarl stories about hard winters and glory days when it was a furnace full of soldiers, waiting to cough and complain about the ache in its stony joints, the cracks in its mortar, and the chill in its bones.

The south yard showed progress; servants with shears snipped their way through shoulder-high brambles that had grown thick beneath three long rows of fruit trees.

In the north yard, swordmasters led exercises; blindfolded, soldiers shouted and stamped their boots, bared broken teeth, and struck at imaginary Cent Regus combatants. Ryllion had promised them they would learn to depend on senses other than sight, enhancing their reaction time based on smell and sound. The exercise leader saluted him. Ryllion pressed his fist against his chest, against his forehead, and then opened his hand to the sky— a sign of allegiance to his moon-spirit.

He ran up the twelve stone stairs and passed between the two statues. The eagle, a fish in its talons, represented Bel Amican sovereignty over the Mystery Sea. At Ryllion's instruction, the staff had set the bird free from moss and ivy. On the right the smaller shape of a howling wolf had been sculpted from marrowwood, a crescent-cut mirror strung around its neck. Ryllion had ordered that the wolf be carved to represent disciples of the moon-spirits. Tilianpurth's old-timers resisted at first. But when Ryllion suggested an appeal to the queen, they quieted. They knew what her answer would be.

He stopped before the heavy burdenwood doors, one of which stood open. Laughing in disbelief, he stepped into the stale air of the towerhouse.

"Where are you, Caroon?" The guard's empty suit of armor lay in pieces beside an abandoned chair. "Wilus Caroon?" He thudded the butt of his spear against the floor. The guard's name echoed down the long, candlelit passage with its many mirrors, past the ascending stairway, past the gold-framed lift on its suspension chains.

He closed the doors. The entryway darkened. He regarded his faint reflection in the mirror on the wall beside the door. Mirrors were an art in House Bel Amica. Even in Tilianpurth, they gleamed in elaborate frames at every turn. This mirror flattered him, erasing lines on his face, accentuating his height and the breadth of his shoulders with such artful subtlety that he could almost ignore the distortion. He tugged at tangles of his yellow hair, which had not been cut since his departure from Bel Amica. He let it fall down and frame his wiry beard that made a weak chin seem bold.

He touched the cut under his eye—a fresh scratch from a beastman claw—and smiled. "You'll pay for that tonight, beastman."

In the reflection he watched the door to the antechamber open. He heard the rustle of cloth and bare feet on stone. Squaring his shoulders, he planted his feet a bit farther apart and formed an expression that could paralyze an opponent.

Broom in hand, one of the heiress's blue-robed attendants limped into view, one leg wrapped in a brace of toughweed. Ryllion gasped. "Emeriene! When did you arrive?"

"I hear you've been out chasing beastmen," she yawned, as if no subject could be less interesting. "Forgive us for interrupting the fun."

Waves of heat from a stove filled the entryway. But it was more than the stove that put the pulse in Ryllion's veins. "I'm just surprised. Surprised that you'd arrive before the heiress. There's no need for you to come early. I've overseen the tower's preparation."

"Cyndere seeks a place to grieve. She needs solitude. This place smells like soldiers. It sounds like soldiers. And what do I see? Why, the place is crawling with soldiers!"

"The woods around Tilianpurth are teeming with the very creatures that widowed the heiress. This isn't the cozy towerhouse you remember from childhood, Emeriene. You need these soldiers."

"Don't take that tone with me, child." She shoved him with the broom brush. "I'm older than you."

"Four years older by the numbers. But if you're measuring experience, well, call me Uncle Ryllion."

"Is that what your nurse calls you? She was just telling me how she tucks you in at night so you don't fall out of bed."

"I only fall out of bed because it's crowded when she climbs in with me." Ryllion loved to offend Emeriene. It was the only way to command her full attention, and this was a rare opportunity—she was away from her husband, away from the gossips who would spend secrets like coins.

"We'll keep Cyndere safe," he said, smiling. "And we'll drive the beastmen across the Expanse back into their holes." He propped the spear in the corner beside the guard's chair, pulled off his gloves, and winced as he opened and closed his hands. He sat down and began to remove his heavy, shielded boots.

"You do your work. I'll do mine," said Emeriene. "Cyndere will sleep here tonight, and I'll watch over her. But there's still much to do. Keep your fellow officers clear of the corridors. And stay out of sight. If she sees you, well, that's not going to ease her burden."

Ryllion scowled. "Clear the corridors? You'd better keep clear of my temper, Sisterly. You think your work is hard? Thanks to the heiress's mother, I live here now. And my instructions from Her Loftiness are to sift these woods for Cent Regus mutants. I've appealed for reinforcements, for horses, and for a wagonload of those new beastman traps."

"Yes, of course," she said, uninterested. "Fill the woods with traps that can't discern between beastmen and rabbits. Cyndere will be delighted."

"Good to see you haven't changed, Em," he murmured. Even her worst jabs could not annoy him. She was graceful as a dancer and, to his eyes, more attractive than the heiress. Her soot-dark hair fell to her shoulders, framing precise, fierce features that somehow smiled and snarled simultaneously. He dreamt of unbinding the splint from her left leg, which had been wounded in the blast that destroyed her father's laboratory. Her skin, smooth as an eggshell, suggested a fragile temperament, but he knew better. Emeriene was a tempest. She had to be. It was her job to counsel the argumentative heiress and defend her against advisors, suitors, and enemies.

"But *you've* changed." Emeriene reached up and yanked on a strand of his hair so roughly that he barked. "Haven't you, child? After all that you've..." She trailed off, her playfulness engulfed by the subject that neither could bear to discuss. She touched him lightly, almost affectionately, on the arm. "Bel Amica is grateful—"

"You mean *you're* grateful."

"Bel Amica," she insisted, "is grateful that you're alive. That you came back from that—"

"It all went wrong," Ryllion whispered, looking back into the mirror. "So terribly wrong. We're going to make the Cent Regus regret what they've done. My riders charted the best places to conceal snares. We'll catch any beastman that comes close. We'll learn which forms of persuasion will wring answers from them. If they can speak at all, we'll find out where Deuneroi's killers are hiding. And then we'll hunt them down."

Emeriene propped the broom against the wall and seized the spear. "Someday we'll stop their cruelty." The rage boiling beneath her quiet words surprised him.

"I should bring you along on a patrol," he laughed. "I need someone with that kind of passion. It would be safer than letting you stay here. You've only just arrived, and you've already removed the guard from his post." He gestured to the empty suit of armor. "Is that your idea of preparing this place for the heiress?"

"Old Caroon was coughing like a clogged chimney. We wheeled him to the sickroom. Winter plagues persist. The last thing the heiress needs is to catch a fever."

"Caroon hasn't caught a winter plague," Ryllion scoffed. "He was coughing because he smoked madweed all night."

"His lungs are bad. His legs are bad. He wraps himself in a bedbag and shivers at the door. Caroon couldn't fight off a moth, much less a beastman. Find a proper guard, will you?"

"Caroon has served Bel Amica for fifty years. Old men should go out honorably, not in disgrace. My father worked fifty-four years down at the shipyards where he suddenly dropped dead, with never a day—"

"The whole house has heard your lament, child. 'Never a day of reward for my papa's lifetime of work.' Don't worry, I'm not suggesting we dump Caroon in the sea. I'm only asking that we give the heiress a proper welcome." Emeriene pushed the front door open again as if hoping to glimpse

Cyndere's approach. "She's my responsibility, and I tell you, Ryllion, I can manage. Keep to your work, and let her be."

"I can comfort her, Em. I can tell her tales of Deuneroi's determination and courage."

"Cyndere's well aware of Deuneroi's courage. And stop calling me 'Em.' I'm a sisterly."

Ryllion stood beside her in the doorway, sharing the view of the east yard and the path to the front gate. He softened his tone. "How is she?"

"She's been under a close watch. But she's finding her way back to her feet. Her mother asked what would comfort her. 'Tilianpurth,' she said."

"This dungheap? Why?"

"King Helpryn loved to stay here during the summers when Cyndere and I were young. He would spend all day in the tower studying his ancestors' wartime journals. He meant to make this a settlement. And while he made his plans, Officer Bauris watched Cyndere and me out playing in the woods. This was a wild paradise for us. It was just a few years ago that Cyndere brought Deuneroi here and asked him to be her husband. So who knows? She might be right. It may do her good to be here."

"Or it might make things more painful. If Cyndere's hoping to visit all her favorite haunts, she'll be disappointed. She won't set foot outside the walls, not while I'm here. We snared a beastman at the edge of the trees this morning. Caged him and locked him up. There were others—they escaped."

"How is Cyndere going to feel about having a beastman caged here while she's looking for a peaceful place to mourn?"

"I have plans for that creature," Ryllion growled. "Plans that will help bring an end to the heiress's pain. The Feast of the Sacrifice is coming."

"Ryllion, you know how she and Deuneroi felt about..." Emeriene choked and turned away.

He did not dare touch her. Not in the open. Not with his honor still in question, his future so uncertain. Not while her husband, Cesylle, an advisor to Queen Thesera, was still a favorite disciple of the Seers.

Surprised by the rising turmoil inside him, he turned abruptly and stepped back inside. "You'll have to excuse me, but I'm exhausted. And hungry."

He walked into the antechamber, unclasping the brooch that held his burgundy cape about his neck. He cast the cape over a hook beside the stove that ticked quietly in the corner and snatched a slice of bread and a bottle of fresh brook water from an array on the serving table, then slouched into a deep-cushioned chair beside the stove. After wolfing down the bread, he removed shields from his arms, legs, and chest, let them clatter to the floor, and brushed dust from his black tunic and leggings.

Emeriene followed him in. She took flowers lying on the serving table and tucked them into a vase. Fumbling, she upset the vase, then bowed her head. When she spoke again, she whispered. "They say you were beside him when he died. Did he suffer much?"

Ryllion looked down at his hands. Four broken fingers were still healing, and the deep gash across his right palm was still scabbed. His hands quivered. "It was quick. I almost saved him. But you should have seen the beastmen. They were…" He closed his hands into fists, rose, and strode through a heavily curtained door into the dimly lit dining room.

The sisterlies had already prepared the room for the heiress's arrival. Candles flickered down the length of the table, and the place settings glittered as if sprinkled with sparks. Stools along the walls waited for soldiers, a symbolic ring of protection. And at the head of the table, the sisterlies had set two grandly sculpted chairs—just the way they had when Cyndere and Deuneroi dined here together.

"Cyndere won't be dining with us," said Emeriene, following him. "She wants to be alone. But the sisterlies will proceed, working as if she is always with us. It keeps us focused."

Ryllion could not stop staring at Deuneroi's empty chair. He could almost feel the royal consort's gaze. He leaned against the end of the table and turned his eyes to the tapestries that ran down both sides of the room. The dyed canvas depicted musclebound men and women with drawn bows and swords in each hand. Cent Regus beastmen, dead and dying, sprawled on the ground with tongues aloll and carcasses bloodied as if they were but prey from a sporting hunt.

Emeriene wandered beside the wall, trailing her fingertips along a tapestry fringe. "This isn't how it is to fight beastmen, is it?"

"Not at all."

The sharp reminder of his failure had soured his appetite for playful debate. He needed cheering up.

He walked the length of the table, past Deuneroi's chair, and out through the far door into the corridor, where he was engulfed by a cloud that promised a savory feast. Bread. Dragonfish steak. Carrots. Gemberry sauce. Honeywine. He even caught a sweet hint of Clyve's Delight, a Bel Amican specialty. He drained the bottle of water, wishing it was ale.

Kitchen workers had unloaded the heavy supply cart behind the tower-house, and now they wheeled smaller carts of supplies—covered canisters, wrapped cabbages, nets of fresh vegetables—down the passage. Blue-robed sisterlies carried linens, candles, and brooms from an adjoining corridor back to the entryway, where they ascended the winding stair to the watch-tower. Chambers at the top, originally designed for commanders, waited for the heiress.

"I have already overseen the preparation for Cyndere's chamber." The servants refused to acknowledge him, casting displeased expressions at each other on their way up. "Be sure the heiress knows this. Before I rode out yesterday, I cleared out a bird's nest." He waited, but no one thanked him. "I hung curtains to keep out the wind. I arranged spirit bowls on the windowsills. Tapestries reminding her of the proud history of Tilianpurth—"

"I've replaced those tapestries with woven images of the Bel Amican eagle," said Emeriene, catching up with him. "The heiress will not give any thought to wars or to beastmen. As for the spirit bowls, our lady's doubts about the moon-spirits have increased, especially after so many painful losses. You prepared the room for some woman who lives in your head, not Cyndere. Space—that's what she needs. Privacy. Quiet."

Ryllion walked to the iron rail at the bottom of the stairs as a line of sisterlies ascended. He muttered, "I skipped the soldiers' supper last night to prepare that chamber!"

"The last thing Cyndere needs is a bunch of soldiers bungling tasks that her sisterlies are trained to perform." A sense of the game returned to Emeriene's voice. "Clear your tantrums and your troops from the corridors, the kitchens, and the tower, and make sure they keep to their bunkrooms. Do that, and I'll make sure that the sacrifices you've made for Cyndere's pleasure are reported to Queen Thesera herself." Awkwardly, she began to climb the stairs, gripping the iron rail and lifting her unbending leg along behind her, following the sisterlies.

"You'd like that wouldn't you? To be left alone here with Cyndere." Ryllion stepped into the gilded frame of the carpeted lift and pulled the cord slightly. The lift rose alongside the stairs. He ascended next to her, and reached through the bars to hold her elbow. He knew his tenderness would distract her. "Oh, I know you better than you think, Sisterly Emeriene. Now that Deuneroi's a piece of Bel Amican history, you're Cyndere's closest friend again. You've missed those childhood days, haven't you?"

Emeriene wrenched her arm free. "You think I could find pleasure in her suffering?"

"There's no shame in wanting time with your lifelong friend." Honeying his voice, he leaned against the cage frame. "You've been lonely, Em. When Cyndere and Deuneroi married, you lost her companionship. Your husband, he's always preoccupied with... What is it that makes Cesylle a stranger in your home? Does the court have that much business? You won't let anyone else close to you." He leaned forward. She backed against the wall. "I know," he said. "I've tried."

"Don't call me *Em*." He could almost feel the heat from her reddening complexion. She planted her foot on the next step, turned away, and growled, "How dare you?"

"I hear your desires better than you." He pulled the cord, keeping himself beside her. "Enjoy your time with the heiress. If I'm wrong, if you really have no desire for my company, I wonder if Cyndere will." This was a dangerous argument, and he knew it. He had never before tried to make Emeriene jealous for his attention. "You and I both know that it won't be long before the heiress will need another consort."

"Am I to find solace in selfish quarreling?" came a voice from below.

Ryllion's head jerked as if he'd been slapped across the face. He released the cord and grasped the lift's frame to steady himself.

The entryway below him was full of guards wearing hooded green capes. Their heads were bowed, their hands dutifully fixed on the hilts of their broadswords. In their midst a woman in a brown stormcloak and an elaborate blue headdress, a veil concealing all but her eyes, stared up at him. Guards parted to let her through. Her dark makeup could not hide the fury in her gaze, which pinned his words to the back of his throat.

Ryllion's mind reeled. What had he said?

He saw a silent understanding pass between Cyndere and Emeriene. How he hated that. The heiress's eyes smiled suddenly as if she had reached a clever decision. He knew she was laughing at him. "You missed a remarkable ceremony, Ryllion. They spoke of your integrity and your devotion to your moon-spirit. Not many people get a second chance at life after friends and family have said their last good-byes." The heiress grasped one of the two cords that controlled the lift. "We all thought you were buried underground. Maybe it would do you some good to spend a little time there." She gave the cords a strong pull.

Gear wheels clanked and groaned, grinding Ryllion's pride. The ropes sang, dissonant and shrill. With a jolt, the lift descended into a shaft in the floor. Down beneath the towerhouse Ryllion plunged, his view of the heiress and Emeriene vanishing.

The prospect of sharing Tilianpurth with Emeriene and Cyndere had, for a few moments, excited him. He should have known better.

Arriving at the lowest platform, Ryllion stormed into the cellar and grabbed a bottle from an open crate.

"Sir?" Dashing in after him, Pyroi the stablehand presented a small scroll sealed with a distinctive, elaborate stamp. "I almost forgot to give you—"

Ryllion snatched it away and sniffed the wax seal. "It's from one of the Seers." This had been sealed recently, maybe only two days earlier. He opened it, scanned the scrawled message. "The Honorable Pretor Xa is on his way. Good. Excellent."

Dismissing the boy, he pulled the cork from the bottle and emptied it in several gulps. When he looked up, he saw a moon-mirror strung with a wire from the ceiling, slowly turning and casting fragments of torchlight.

"Thank you, Spirit," he whispered. "He's all the help I need. Bring him safely. And bring him soon."

7

THE BLUE GLEN

T hat was not the welcome I had imagined." Cyndere shrugged her heavy stormcloak into the hands of the guard behind her. "Where is the quiet, orderly Tilianpurth?"

She bowed to her guards, and they filed in perfect formation into the antechamber. Two of the towerhouse staff boys followed to gather up their damp woolen capes.

Cyndere turned just in time to catch Emeriene hobbling down the stairs to embrace her, and she laughed at the sisterly's rush of apologies. "You have nothing to be sorry for, Em. It reminds me of chasing off your admirers when we were younger. Remember how my mother complained that you were inspiring more suitors than me?"

Emeriene bowed her head to hide her face.

"Are you still crying?" Cyndere grasped Emeriene's shoulders and leaned in so their foreheads met.

"Someone has to."

"I did not come here to cry." She looked over Emeriene's shoulder. "I came here to begin again." The corridor was empty. They were alone, but she spoke softly anyway. "Officer Bauris met us at the gate. Can you believe how much has changed? He has to keep watch while the cooks gather herbs from the woods. Is it so dangerous here?"

As Emeriene dabbed at her cheeks and shared the report of Ryllion's new prisoner, Cyndere felt willfulness stir like an animal within her. "Then it's good that Bauris has agreed to help us. We'll need him. If anybody discovers our plan, we'll have more trouble than ever. They must believe I'm here for solitude."

Two soldiers led four leashed hunting hounds through the front door. Cyndere knelt to scratch the dogs' backs. "I should have brought my dogs, Em. Some quiet company for my chamber. Mother wouldn't let me bring the viscorcat. He's too wild."

"I thought you'd bring Shakey."

"Shakey? He'd bolt after the first gorrel he saw. We'd never see him again. Willow's tending to two new pups. Drunkard and Trumpet. Mother calls them 'Bad Dog' and 'Worse Dog.'"

One of the hounds shoved a wet nose into Cyndere's cheek. "They know, don't they?" said Emeriene. "They know just what will help—a warm, comforting presence. When the chillplague took your mother, that greenbird of hers would not leave her shoulder for days. He kept calling, 'Hot rags! Hot rags!'"

"Mother could learn a thing or two from that bird. She's never shown a care for people in trouble. I'm going to name the next puppy *Cal-raven*, just to poke at her conscience."

"Cyndere!" Emeriene's glare scolded the heiress. "You said you're here to start over. Time to roll that scroll and put it away."

Cyndere pressed on as if Emeriene had not even spoken. Clapping her hands, she knelt down before an invisible dog. "Here, Cal-raven! Here, boy!"

Emeriene pressed her lips together but too late. The tremors began. Soon they were both shaking with laughter as they had once upon a time. Emeriene shouted down the corridor, "Bad dog, Ryllion! Stay away from me! Where are your manners?"

When the heiress's guards, free of their capes and armor, lumbered back into the corridor in long black tunics and leggings, they were surprised to see the women doubled over and holding their sides. They shared puzzled looks with each other, then bowed in embarrassment.

As the guards thundered up the stairs to their quarters, baths, and drinks, Emeriene steered Cyndere into the antechamber, and her amusement was soured by what she found there. "No, no, no!" She rushed to the empty tray, shaking her head at the scattered crumbs. "They've eaten what I set out for you!"

Cyndere pushed past Emeriene to the table, where she grasped the vase of wildflowers. "How I've missed this forest." She pulled her veil aside and buried her face in the bouquet, breathing deep.

"Officer Bauris remembered how much you love the woods." Emeriene pressed her palms against her forehead. "He doesn't like our plan. He doesn't see why he should risk opening the secret passage. And he is especially upset that you would dare send me into the forest at night. But he's right, Cyndere. The woods are too dangerous now. If anybody discovers our deception, Bauris will be in trouble too."

"I don't care." Cyndere covered her ears. "I came here to say good-bye to Deuneroi in my own way." Pulling the blue headdress from her head, she grabbed fistfuls of her strawgold hair, which was quickly growing back after she had cut it all away. "Must Ryllion play the watchdog?"

Emeriene reminded her that they would be free of Ryllion during the day. Cyndere sighed. "What about at night? After seeing the way he treated you, I'd suggest you bar the door to your chamber. His brush with death in Abascar has only emboldened him." She gazed at the portraits of her elders and at the tapestry. "I hate the way they look at me. I'm going up to my chamber."

They returned to summon the lift, and it carried them up through four levels of the towerhouse. Soldiers on the first two floors bowed and smiled. Emeriene raised her hands as if this adulation was meant for her. She never tired of the joke. On the third level, servants moved between closets and bunkrooms, and sisterlies bowed to them on the fourth. Then it was on up through cooling air into the tower's narrow span. Arriving at the highest platform, they stepped off into the sisterlies' welcome. Cyndere thanked the attendants and dismissed them. While they slipped barefoot down the stairs, Cyndere walked into her bedchamber.

"There it is," said Emeriene. "All you need in the world. A bed, a window, a fire, and hot water in the washtub." She pointed to the cord hanging inside the door, which would summon the sisterlies at any hour, day or night. "And me, if you need any company."

"You've scrubbed the stones on the wall. I have clean canvasses for sketching."

"Who knows you better than I do?" Emeriene embraced her friend once more. "But you've had enough of everyone. Those voices clamoring in your head, they're so loud that I can hear them too." She placed her hands on Cyndere's head. "I'm gathering them up, see? I'm taking those voices with me. All of them." She pulled her hands away and cupped them together as if capturing a struggling creature. "I'm dragging them downstairs to lock them in the prison pit for the duration of your stay."

"You know what to do at midnight, yes?"

"Bauris and I will be ready."

Cyndere clasped her friend's hands in gratitude. "Don't fret, Emeriene."

"Forgive me, but it's my job."

Cyndere's smile was feeble. "Do you remember what we said when we were girls, when we were going to be apart?"

"Distance is an illusion," they said together.

Emeriene departed, and the curtain fell behind her. Cyndere kicked aside the stone that held open the heavy door and then closed it urgently, slamming the iron bar into place as if locking out invaders.

The quiet of the room embraced her as if it had waited for years. She was surprised at how the soldiers' commotion in the yard below sounded miles away. She stood at the sill, gazed out beyond the walls, and scanned the woods. Her memories stirred the way cobwebs waver when windows are opened. The forest. Fallen trees. Aromatic wildflowers. Her father, slashing a trail through dense thorn bushes. The smell of old wood, new leaves, silver tendrils of sap. An ancient well, besieged by ivy. Blue flowers. A bucket of warm water from deep underground. Deuneroi laughing with a crown of feathers on his head.

Cyndere reached out as if the scene were a map and imagined she could touch the frosted crowns of the treetops. "It's a lie, Emeriene," she whispered. "Distance is real and cruel."

"Well, sound the biggest horn." Bauris paused, set down the heavy pack, and stared up through the trees toward the starry sky. "There's the old marrow-wood tree house."

For twenty years he had monitored the slow decline of Tilianpurth, but he had forgotten about this overgrown path, this ancient tree with its suspended shelter. He slapped his glove against its sturdy bark just the way he'd pat an old friend on the back. "We're still standing, aren't we?" he muttered. "Still stuck in the same woods."

To the shivering woman in the hooded woolen cape, he added, "It really hasn't been so long since you and Cyndere played here." Kicking the husk of a lightning-smashed tree stump, he continued, "Back then I just watched over you to keep you out of trouble. But here, tonight, we have to step more carefully. Look at this, Sisterly." He kicked a burnt tree stump. "The old ropeswing tree's been blasted down."

"You don't have to call me 'sisterly.' I'm still the same Emeriene you used to carry on your shoulders." The woman set down her woven basket. "That's the tree house, all right. This is where the heiress told me we should turn and move uphill."

"How can Cyndere's memory be so sharp?" Bauris broke off a shard of burnt tree stump and sniffed it, as if he might discern some hint of smoke. All he smelled was rot. "I've watched over Tilianpurth since both of you were small and full of mischief. And yet I suspect Cyndere could map this patch of woods better than me. I guess that's why she's the heiress and I'm just a soldier."

"She's the heiress because she's the daughter of Thesera and a descendant of Tammos Raak."

"Oh, I'm just throwing elbows around. Don't mind me." He lifted the pack and moved on, watching as she took the basket and limped through the trees. "You know, when you were young and rowdy, you'd both keep secrets from me. I didn't mind. But the secrets you keep now that you're grown...they worry me. Like the reason we're out here. What's so important to Cyndere that she would send you out in the dark?"

No answer. Only a steady step, *thump*, step, *thump* as his companion's cast complicated her steps.

"Nobody tells me much of anything anymore." *And yet*, he argued with himself, *this is more interesting than any task I've had in years.* He felt young and ambitious again. Cyndere trusted him to guard Emeriene, stealing away from the vigilant guards. They had slipped through a secret kitchen door into an ancient escape tunnel known only to the royalty and the highest-ranking guard. Opening that passage for the first time in many years, Bauris had cut a trail through cobwebs. What Emeriene was to gather or achieve out here in these woods, he could not imagine. Her pack was full of heavy objects, but he was not allowed to look inside or ask questions about it.

A cold thrill of danger charged the air. Ryllion's patrols had caught a beastman here yesterday. Any of the fidgeting shadows might come to life and threaten this young woman. She had pulled her hood up over her face as if afraid to survey their wild surroundings, and it pained him to see such a beauty struggle with that broken stride.

"I'll tell you why Cyndere remembers the path so clearly."

"Go on." Bauris drew his sword, tested its edge.

"She spent her happiest days here. You remember?"

"Of course. I still remember Partayn learning to play harmonies on a perys. He'd wear ten bone rings and tap out melodies on the strings. Just ahead, there's the glen where Cyndere asked Deuneroi to marry her." Bauris cleared his throat. Why the heiress would want to mourn at Tilianpurth, closer to memories that would salt her wounds, bewildered him. "Don't take us much farther," he whispered. "The perimeter guards can't hear us out here. These trees silence everything."

They took a path through a patch of gnarled bushes. He watched her touch the silvery veins of a glitter tree. "It's still here," she whispered. "Why does it shimmer?"

"Glitter trees grow deep roots," he answered. "If they find something in the ground that they like, they glow. I remember this tree. She's a happy old sprout and probably one of the strongest in the region for rooting herself so deeply."

"Cyndere said you must wait for me here. I'm going into a glen just ahead. Make sure nobody's followed us."

"You sure this is a good idea? Why risk it?"

"Call it the cost of friendship. Call it trust. The heiress's will is my own. She's not her mother. She'll do things her own way. And you know better than to bother me about this."

She sounded nervous. "No offense, Emeriene," he murmured, but he thought, *I do know better. About this whole endeavor.*

"You gave me the tetherwings." She lifted the basket. "They're asleep. I poured a drop of slumberseed oil on the sponge, just as you taught me. But I'll set them free while I do what Cyndere has sent me to do. They'll watch over me."

Bauris explained again that tetherwings could not protect her if a beastman came. The creatures were as fragile as the eggs that hatched them, and they would only do as they had been trained.

"If I'm wrong," she said, "and if we really are in danger, you might finally get to fight a beastman, Bauris. Isn't that what you've always wanted?" With that, she took the pack from him, hoisted it onto her back, and hobbled off through the trees.

As her footsteps faded, Bauris's old ambition returned. He listened to the spaces between the trees, almost hoping to find a Cent Regus monster lurking there.

Jordam reached for the span of blue fabric that O-raya had spread across the stone table. "I found it in the forest," she said. "It's a quiet color, isn't it? Like the coldest corner of an ice cave. Or like a song that you whisper, a sad song."

"Sad song," Jordam answered, trying to shape the Common words he was learning from the girl with the silverbrown hair. He watched her, entranced, then began to blink sleepily. Details dissolved until only a shimmering blue cloud remained.

Jordam tried to reach for that luminous array. But his body was imprisoned in some invisible shell.

A clump of snow splashed across his nose, startling him.

Moments of memory and dream melted away. He was not in O-raya's cave. He lay limp on the coil tree's bough in the dark, feeling nothing except a burn of thirst in his throat and the ache of an empty stomach. And yet, that mysterious blue light still glowed before him, faintly sketching the outline of his surroundings.

The coil tree stood on the edge of a foggy bowl. He could see down into a dark, grassy glen, where an ancient wall drew a curved barrier around half the open space. Someone had sought to enclose this place, a project never completed. The crumbling wall caught and amplified the rush of a stream, but he could not trace the sound to its source. In the middle of the glen, he saw a mound of colorful stones cloaked in steam that seemed to spill from the top. He moaned, unable to quench the flare of longing that responded to those colors. They were familiar. O-raya had been here.

Scratchwings chirped happily in the grass. Flap-hoppers croaked in the trees. *Better than barking dogs,* he thought. He breathed in deeply, smelling the snow suspended in the trees above him and fragrant, night-blooming flowers. It was strange, the scent of spring in winter.

Something the size of a knuckle-nut bolted across the clearing as a shadow descended into the glen, draped in a brown woodscloak.

Jordam held his breath. If it was a Bel Amican soldier, there was nothing he could do to escape. If it was Mordafey, he would be rescued and promptly thrashed with sharp objects.

The shadow paused at the clearing's edge, as if suspicious of the light. Then it moved in a slow circle about the glow. He clenched his teeth, hoping his woodscloak would conceal him among the branches.

But when the shadow stopped and pushed back its hood, he almost laughed. It was neither hunter nor animal. It was a woman, her black hair gleaming with a blue sheen in the light. She wore a crown of grey feathers and carried a heavy pack on her shoulder. One hand rested on the hilt of her knife, the other held a woven basket. Her left leg was bound with stiff reeds.

It was not O-raya. It was someone else, a woman from Bel Amica, but a mystery all the same. As she limped about the open space, she touched each of the trees as if offering greetings to old friends. A maple of tiny, star-shaped leaves. A slender apple tree, high branched, its shallow roots widespread. Then she returned to the mound in the center. Through the streams of undulating mist, Jordam glimpsed wildflowers rooted between the stones. Their petals glowed—the source of the mysterious blue light.

Leaning back against the stone mound, the woman set the basket down and unbound the brace of reeds from her leg. She reached to touch the small blooms that sprouted from the tips of spiraling green stems, and he heard her voice at last—a question, a note of confusion. "Who's been here? Who's painted the stones?"

Then she opened the basket and withdrew a small vial of golden glass, placing it on the stones. A flurry of small, grey-feathered birds rose soundless from the basket. He recognized them at once. Tetherwings. Wealthy travelers released them at campsites, for the birds' instincts made them subtle sentries. They would stay close together in the trees, watchful, calling out only if they sensed a predator nearby.

Like hummingbirds, the tetherwings hovered about their keeper's head. One by one they dove in to peck at her crown of grey feathers as if in some ritual greeting. She did not wave them off. The birds seemed assured that she was, indeed, the one they must protect. Then they ascended in a widening spiral to higher ground and settled in the trees that surrounded the glen. One perched on the edge of a branch below Jordam, its back to the woman, eyes turned outward from the clearing.

He stared at his hand. He tried to move his fingers. If he were to be discovered here, he would be killed. By a vulnerable woman. With a simple knife.

The woman bowed her head, dark hair falling across her face. She plucked petals from the blue flowers and placed them on her tongue. Her face twisted, souring, and she choked. But instead of spitting them out, she forced more into her mouth until, with some effort, she chewed and swallowed them.

A long, low growl rumbled in Jordam's empty belly. The woman turned abruptly in his direction. He held his breath.

For a moment he could see her face clearly, and he was surprised to see that her brow was beaded with dark droplets that ran in stark lines down her cheeks.

She stood and reached for the mound of stones. There was the sound of an indrawn breath. Something gave way. She staggered, lifting a heavy wooden cover and dropping it to the grass. Steam filled the clearing. The perfume of warm spring water intensified. And the sound was the rush of an underground river.

A well, Jordam realized. *A well that opens to a stream.* He dragged his stone-dry tongue across his lips.

The woman reached into the well. She began to draw out a length of rope with great effort. Hand over hand, she drew the rope. Something solid bumped against the well's stone throat. Then she withdrew a heavy wooden bucket.

She set it on the ground, dropped to one knee, removed black gloves, and laid them on the edge of the well. Cupping her hands, she splashed water from the bucket across her face. Her shaking subsided. She cupped her hands again and drank, eyes closed. Then she stood and let the bucket back down into the well. A cloud of moths fluttered from the well into the air like scraps of ash. Jordam watched them rise toward the night sky, then noticed a light in the tower window far away. A figure in a gown and a headdress stepped into the frame.

After pulling more flowers free from the wellstones and placing them in the basket, the woman rose and walked to the cloudgrasper tree. She laid the pack on the ground and withdrew a sequined tunic. With trembling hands, she draped the tunic over one of the tree's low, slender boughs. "It's time," she whispered to the tree. "You're beautiful. I'll give you all of these treasures. And you can give them back to the king. To Partayn. And to Deuneroi."

Jordam gasped, then clamped his mouth shut.

One of the small grey birds spoke a quiet word of alarm. Jordam braced for the worst. But then he heard a rumor in the brush below.

A winter fox padded around the edge of the clearing. Ears pricked forward, pink tongue wagging, he stared at the woman. He looked as if his skin were wrapped too tight. She watched him. He snorted, changed direction, curiosity fighting with fear. Then he crouched low and inched toward her, sniffing the air. Jordam waited for her to reach for her dagger. But instead she held out her hand, offering a bright blue flower.

"I will not hurt you," came the woman's gentle voice. "I don't think you want to hurt me. Let me help you."

The fox's ears swiveled and cupped, catching her words. His lean white body tensed.

Jordam ran those words through his mind. *Let. Me. Help. You.* He felt a sudden pang, and there was nothing he could do to stop his belly from rumbling again.

The fox's ears flicked back. His tail twitched. He turned and bolted into the woods.

Every fiber in the beastman's body quivered with the instinct to pursue. But he could not move.

The bird on the bough below him suddenly began to hoot. First cautiously, then with some insistence.

The woman looked up toward Jordam, then pulled the tunic from the tree branch and stuffed it into the pack. "I'm sorry," she said. "Tomorrow. I'll come back tomorrow."

She carried the pack quickly from the base of the cloudgrasper to the well and let it down inside. He did not hear a splash. She hefted the lid back over the well, then took the golden glass vial and opened it. She drizzled a clear line of something like honey into the open bird basket and whistled sharply twice. Together the birds lifted from their perches, gathered again in a moving circle, and descended to settle in the basket. After pulling her gloves back on, the woman bound the cast of reeds around her leg. With one parting glance at the silhouette in the tower window, she limped up the path and out of sight.

While the sound of murmuring water teased Jordam's thirst, the delicate blue that glimmered between the wellstones, and the vibrant colors on the stones themselves, filled a void he had learned to ignore. He drank in the sight, and his fears and anxieties melted away like snow in spring.

Startled out of his memories, Bauris sprang to his feet. "Sisterly Emeriene! I was just about to come looking for you! What kept you?"

"One of the tetherwings was slow in returning." The cloaked woman limped back up the slope to the soldier.

Bauris observed that she was not carrying her pack. He had decided to trust her, though, and did not mention it. He followed her back through the bushes. "I trained those birds myself," he said in disbelief. "Give me the basket. I'll test them tomorrow. Perhaps they're out of practice."

"No, no, that won't be necessary." She paused beneath the glitter tree. "I'd like to keep them with me in case the heiress needs my help again."

"Again? Why would she send you again? You won't come back out here without me."

She did not answer. He glanced back over his shoulder, determining that someday he would return to the glen to try to understand what sort of business required such risk, darkness, and secrecy.

8

TWO PRISONERS

The next morning Cyndere slipped out of bed with a wedge of warm salt-bread in her hand, leaving her breakfast unfinished on the plate. She tiptoed halfway across the chamber and set the bread on the floor, then stepped back and waited. Nothing emerged from the small crack at the base of the wall.

The morning chill drove her to the closet, and she drew out a heavy drape of fangbear fur. She hesitated, then returned it to its hook and chose instead her father's long leather sailing jacket. She pushed back the sleeves so her fingers were free to fasten its silver buttons, and then she let them slide down past her hands. She tiptoed to the rug in the middle of her chamber, shivering, and sat down, stretching out to nudge the scrap of bread further toward the breakage.

"What if you trusted me?" Steam rose from her leg, red from the morning bath, and she drew it back under the jacket. "What if you let me give you something?"

"Heiress." The voice came not from the wall, but from beyond the heavy door. Cyndere rose and unbarred it.

Candle flames bowed low as Emeriene stepped inside. Speaking softly as if avoiding spies, the heiress said, "You stayed up all night to help me. Shouldn't you be sleeping now?"

"Ryllion's been storming about the place. Didn't I vow to look after you?"

"Ryllion's not dangerous."

"No, but he's a bother. And, I'm happy to announce, he's finally asleep."

"Soundly?"

"More soundly than a stone. Beneath seaweed. At the bottom of the ocean. On a dark night." Emeriene knelt before the fireplace, snapped a small firestick so that it sparked, and tossed it into the moss and kindling. The timid flame hesitated, then flared to life.

"It's not like him to sleep while Emeriene the Beautiful is within reach. Let me guess. You drugged him."

"I intend to stay out of reach, thank you very much. The man's nocturnal. I suspect he's part bat."

Cyndere glanced toward the hole in the wall. "And speaking of bats..."

Emeriene continued. "Look, I'm your humble servant, but I will not tolerate anyone's suggestion that I feel anything but disgust for Ryllion's advances." The sisterly stood and stamped out a stray spark on the rug. From a pocket in her rumpled skirts, she drew a fold of cloth. "Still, you must admit, some of his attempts to persuade me have been rather impressive." She held up the length of fabric in the firelight. It unfolded and danced in the air as if inspired by the flames.

"Wicked man." Cyndere reached out and caught the cloth, letting it drape across her palm. "Where does a soldier like him find something as exquisite as this?" She fingered its frayed edge. "Had he really loved you, Emmy, he'd have given you something a little more...complete."

"He says he found it," Emeriene answered, a little too quickly. "It must have been torn already."

Cyndere pointed toward the fireplace mantel. "When the sisterlies brought me breakfast, they delivered *that*. From Ryllion."

Emeriene's smile faded. A matching strand of the scarf was draped around a candle. She picked it up and held its frayed edge against the piece she had brought with her. "For all the piles in the stable, I can't believe..." And then her anger evaporated. "I must be sniffing the wrong potions, getting jealous for the attention of such a calculating fool." She folded the pieces together, then threw them at Cyndere.

"He's either setting traps for beastmen, or he's setting traps for us." Cyndere laughed.

Using a pillow from the bed for a cushion, Emeriene sat down across from the heiress, and Cyndere arranged the two halves on the rug between them. She smoothed them together as if hoping they would merge into a whole.

"It is sad, really." Emeriene continued to massage the span of cloth, smoothing its creases. "Who could tear something like this? And where *did* he find it?"

The heiress watched a charred lump of smoking wood tumble onto the hearth. "He's after me for want of power. And he's after you because he knows beauty when he sees it."

"Oh, droppings!"

"Don't deny it, Emmy. Should you dress in greasy dishrags, you'd still break a soldier's concentration as you pass. And Ryllion believes...really believes...that if he has a desire, it's as good as a promise from the moon-spirit who fancies him. He won't stop until he gets what he wants."

"And thus my marriage is merely a problem he means to solve."

"The honor of fidelity seems like nonsense to those who worship moon-spirits. The Seers want us to follow our impulses."

"Enough about moon-spirits, Cyndere. You came here to leave the Seers and their meddling behind, and yet here we are fussing about them. This is Tilianpurth. We're back, you and me."

"Don't you dare say that it's just like it used to be." Cyndere stood and went to the window. As she reached the view, a pillow sailed past her head and out the window. She turned, shocked.

Emeriene, wide-eyed and laughing, rolled onto her back and stuck her reed-bound leg into the air.

Cyndere stifled a smile, unwilling to give up the argument. "It isn't funny."

"It will be when it lands on some poor soldier in the yard," Emeriene laughed. "I'm not going to let you spoil our first day here, Cyn. Last night's secret endeavor was successful. You should be resting. And that means your head as well as your feet. Do you know how long I've wished we could come back here together, away from all the madness at home?"

Cyndere opened her mouth to speak but stopped when Emeriene shrieked and jumped to her feet.

A grey bat had crawled from the hole. Wings draped over its body like a cape, it glanced about as if it could see. Its enormous ears were at full attention, and its snout twitched as it neared the bread. But the sisterly's dismay frightened it, and it withdrew into the wall.

"I've named him Night-scrap. Poor thing. His wings don't work. I found him this morning trying to jump for the window."

"You've had every other kind of pet. But do you have to tame one so ugly?"

"If I can teach a small monster to trust me..." Cyndere immediately wished she could suck the words back in. But Emeriene's eyes flared.

"Cyndere, you told me you were giving that up! What happened to Deuneroi... Hasn't it convinced you that—"

"I'm going to visit this imprisoned beastman, Emmy. What if that's the real reason I came? What if Deuneroi was drawing me out here just to see this monster? If we could learn how to persuade the Cent Regus, if we could tame one of them—"

"Tame a beastman?" Emeriene rose as if to bar Cyndere's path to the door, but when she remembered the bat, she climbed back up on the cushion. "The prison pit is no place for you. You came here for peace."

Cyndere fixed her with a solemn stare. "I asked you to tell me when Ryllion was asleep. I need to do this."

"I brought you here to help you find healing, Cyndere."

"My mother isn't watching, Em. There aren't any Seers in Tilianpurth. This is my purpose. This is a chance to do what Deuneroi and I always meant to do. How perfect that I should accomplish it here, where he and I first dreamt of it."

Emeriene's expression quivered between amazement and outrage.

"You should understand this, Em. Your grandfather devoted his life to the science of healing. He shared this dream. He wanted to help the beastmen."

"Yes, and what my father learned from him led to that explosion. I'm done meddling with that kind of danger." Emeriene reached down to knock on the toughweed shoots that bound up her bad leg. "I've learned, you see."

"From what?" Cyndere narrowed her eyes. "Others' mistakes? Is that what you were going to say?"

Emeriene closed her eyes. "No, no, I'm sorry. I didn't mean—"

"Well, it's not a mistake to try to pull somebody out of trouble, whether they're from House Abascar or House Cent Regus." Cyndere lifted the straw basket from the windowsill. "Now I can try what Deuneroi and I discussed. You know what these blue flowers from the glen can do. They healed Deuneroi's snakebite. They've cooled my fevers. They purge poisons. What if they could calm the Cent Regus fury?"

"You're going to feed those flowers to that...that thing in the dungeon? Cyndere, this might be the very animal that killed your husband, or that..." Emeriene sank back down. Partayn's death had robbed the sisterly of the future she'd desired, and the man who had taken his place had only deepened that wound.

"If all we can do is cut the Cent Regus down, Em, they'll keep springing back like weeds. And more Bel Amicans will live to mourn like we do for Deuneroi and Partayn. But if the curse of the beastmen can be reversed..." She looked back out to the trees. "Deuneroi understood."

Clouds darkened the horizon as if night were trying to win back the sky. "More snow." Cyndere had hoped to see spring rising at Tilianpurth.

She leaned against the sill and watched the bat sink its tiny fangs into the wedge of bread. The animal then began to flap its wings clumsily against the floor and crawl backward, dragging the bread toward the hole. But the bread was too big, and the bat pulled and pulled, unable to wrestle the food back into its hiding place.

"I'm going now. To see the beastman. Before Ryllion wakes up and gets in the way."

Flags.

That was what the ale boy dreamt, folding himself into a ball and denying the cold, hard floor of the dungeon cell.

He would make flags. He would finish his work. He would turn his hand to gathering the remnants of Auralia's scarves, blankets, ribbons, wreathwork, leggings and stockings, banners and braids, and set them flying from the tops of the trees she had climbed, from those sections of Abascar's walls still standing, from the crooked and sinking towers.

He would row his wine raft across Deep Lake during the day, sleep in her caves at night, and never worry about the rest of the world. He would greet each morning from the cliffs where she had gazed out at sky, water, woods, and mountains. He would close each day at the edge of the rippling waters. He would sing the verses of House Abascar to mark the passage of time. He would wait for the Keeper to return.

But then the ale boy's dream took a turn, coming alive with memories of how he had ended up here, in this prison cell at Tilianpurth.

A merchant had wanted to buy from him a bundle of Auralia's unfinished work. But the boy had insisted there was nothing to compare with Auralia's colors in all of the Expanse. How could he possibly trade them for lesser riches?

The answer displeased the merchant so much that a knife sprang into their exchange.

Fearing for his life, the ale boy spurred Rumpa through the forest, taking the rough ground that no wagon could traverse. Auralia had taught him this. "Pack light and roads become unnecessary."

He had learned so much from her. On that night of cataclysm and fire, when Auralia was swept up in a storm of light and cloud and carried away from House Abascar by the Keeper, the ale boy's vision had changed. No, *he* had changed. Glimpsing something outside the borders of what he'd thought possible, he now saw differently, thought more carefully, behaved more boldly.

He had seen the Northchildren. They were real, with their vague, blurred features, their curious and childlike manner. He had seen the Keeper, that creature of myth and forbidden stories, with legs great as tree trunks, a tail like a lightning storm, wings full as sails, and a long face with eyes as rich and deep as oceans. And he had seen Auralia crumpled at his feet and yet speaking to him from one of the Northchildren's shrouds, somehow dead and yet living.

Now he too was a mystery. A fool. And yet, many inquired about the secrets of the extraordinary colors that he carried, longing to know their source. He could not explain more than to speak of Auralia and to let them gaze some more and touch the elaborate weave.

His flight from the furious merchant had led him into a valley of whitegrass. Thick woods waited at the bottom of the valley. Plunging into those shadows, he heard men shouting, dogs howling.

He jumped off the vawn. Rumpa could lead off the pursuers while he sought hiding. "Go," he commanded Rumpa, who fussed and whimpered at the order. "Go and don't come back until it's safe."

Rumpa vanished, and the ale boy pawed at the weeds that had overrun the exposed roots of a leaning tree. He found an empty gorrel hollow and stuffed in the bundle of Auralia's relics. He had just pushed soil in front of the opening when the dogs surrounded him, spittle flying from their snarls.

Then came the yellow-bearded man who did not ask questions. He saw the boy, and he saw the scarf, the one piece of Auralia's work he had dropped. He jumped from his vawn and reached for the scarf, grabbing one end just as the boy took the other. When it tore, the boy released it, crying out as if his own arm had been broken.

"Bring him in," the soldier said. "I'll question him in time. We need to find out what he's seen."

"Question him? He's just a scrap of a boy," another soldier replied. "What threat could he possibly pose?"

"He could be a spy. When I squeeze him, we'll learn plenty."

The ale boy woke suddenly, pressing himself into a corner of the prison pen. In the cell beside his, a slavering, doglike beastman with striped skin and boarlike tusks lay scratching at the dirt, almost entirely paralyzed.

The pimple-faced guard who paced outside the cages had all but forgotten the ale boy, so preoccupied was he with taunting the beastman.

"Just you wait till Officer Ryllion gets some sleep." The guard slouched against the wall, snacking on rocknuts he drew from a bowl and spitting vile remarks about the various ways Ryllion might dispose of the monster.

When the door at the end of the corridor opened, the guard sprang up, kicking the bowl so that nuts tumbled in all directions. After groping for his spear, he stood at attention.

A figure in a long sailor's coat, a woman with golden hair as short as a young boy's, approached. The ale boy discerned immediately from her stride and stature, and from the guard's rigid attention, that she was of some importance. Hoarsely the guard said, "Honorable Heiress, it is an unexpected pleasure to—"

"Hush." The lady stood still, staring fixedly at the beastman, whose red eyes scanned the cell methodically. "Blessed towers of Inius Throan!" she gasped.

"The heiress wishes to address the Cent Regus creature," said another woman. He recognized this one. She had brought him bread and fruit.

"Garbal, who is this?" The heiress gave the ale boy a quick glance, then returned her wary gaze to the beastman.

"Found him prowling outside the walls. He behaved suspiciously when we caught him."

"He's a harmless child."

"He might have seen things, my lady."

"Like what? One of our soldiers smoking madweed or watering a tree?"

"Ryllion has...concerns. We think he may be a thief. He was carrying things that—"

"I'll have words with Ryllion. But first, I wish to speak with the other prisoner." Turning to the guard, the heiress added, "Alone."

"Honorable Heiress, Ryllion commanded me to hold this post and ensure that the creature does not harm anyone. I must obey you above anyone, of course. But Ryllion—"

"Very well, then, you can stay. But do not interfere." The heiress shuddered as if shaking off a bad dream. Without turning her gaze from the creature, she lifted a plain cloth, unfolded it, and presented it to the beastman. The ale boy sat up, squinting. The heiress had brought the creature a fish. He saw her tuck something blue behind the fish's gills. She stepped toward the bars, holding out the cloth with trembling hands.

"Beastman," she said quietly. "No, I won't call you that. I'll call you a man of House Cent Regus. You will find this hard to believe, but I want to help you."

The creature's nose twitched. He grunted, licked his lips, but did not rise.

"Dumb as a tree trunk, my lady," said the guard. "Shot with a poisoned arrow. He won't move for days. Maybe never again."

She hesitated, then edged toward the bars. The beastman began to growl like a guard dog, and his skin faded to match the brittle soil of the floor. She shoved the cloth through the bars in front of his snout. "Are you hungry?" She smoothed out the edges of the cloth. His lips drew back to show his teeth. The heiress stepped away, out of breath.

The guard gaped as if he had just seen the queen's daughter propose marriage to a gorrel.

This, the ale boy marveled, *is Cyndere of Bel Amica.* She was even more courageous than he'd heard.

Cyndere knelt. "I came to help you. But I can only do that if you listen. Do you understand?" Her words sounded forced, rehearsed.

The ale boy watched the sisterly tremble and clutch at her robe.

The beastman inched forward, caught the edge of the cloth between his lips, and in a moment the fish was gone, bones and all, and the cloth lay shredded by sharp teeth.

No one moved. The beastman's eyes blinked sleepily. The heiress did not move, staring as if her gaze alone could change the creature. And the beastman was, in fact, changing. A resentful growl festered in the back of his throat, as if he were beginning to suspect that he had been tricked. His breathing slowed to long, deep inhalations. His claws began to gouge deeper ruts in the dirt, and with some effort he lifted his chin from the floor.

"Quiet," said the woman soothingly. "Quiet now. Listen to my voice. Can you understand me?"

The beastman whimpered.

"I am Cyndere. I want to help you. Deuneroi and I vowed to help you."

The ale boy thought of the Cent Regus monster who had come to Auralia's caves. He recognized Auralia's courage in the Bel Amican heiress. But this beastman was different.

A sneer revealed the monster's teeth. "Doon-roy." The beastman's long pink tongue emerged and lashed across his tusks as if he were remembering a favorite meal. "*Hel hel hel.* Doon-roy."

Cyndere recoiled as if struck. The guard stepped forward, ready to impale the creature if the heiress gave the word. But Cyndere was moving back down the corridor, shaken and silent, taken into her servant's embrace.

The beastman pushed himself tremblingly to his feet, as if prying himself from an invisible cocoon. Cackling, he lurched to the bars, rubbing his belly. "Doon-roy!" he howled. "Doon-roy!"

"The poison," the guard gasped. "Something's counteracting the poison!"

"This is not what you need, Cyndere," said her helper. "What you need is a new start. New dreams."

After the echoes had died and Garbal returned to spewing insults, the ale boy began to wonder if he would ever walk free again. He could not sleep.

The tedium was interrupted by Ryllion, who appeared when one guard relieved the last.

The soldier ignored the boy, stepping to the beastman's bars with such confidence that the creature crawled to the back of the cage.

"Don't fret now, little beastman." Ryllion drew his sword slowly, and the blade hummed in the air. He rattled it between bars of the beastman's cell. The ale boy covered his ears, but it only muffled the soldier's voice. "You think you'll be punished for frightening the heiress? You're meant for something better. I'm not going to harm a single whisker. Not yet. I'm preparing something special. Soon you will give the heiress...you will give *all* of us a certain consolation. And then nothing more will be expected of you. Nothing at all."

Hours later the ale boy's hands still covered his ears, as much for warmth as to shut out the spiteful taunts of the new guard. Behind closed eyes, he tried to retrace his steps through the forest to the tangle of tree roots where he had concealed Auralia's unfinished work. Memory blurred into dream. The forest was a labyrinth. The Keeper's tracks were everywhere and nowhere, crisscrossing and making no sense. He sensed a turbulent darkness on the edge of his vision, like an advancing tide surging up from the ground. It smelled of beastmen. He turned to flee, but for all his effort, he was stuck, unable to take even a step. The tide advanced. And the only choice available set him to shaking like a baby bird abandoned in the nest.

9

MIDNIGHT ENCOUNTER

Questions chirped by curious birds punctuated Jordam's delirium. He heard their hungry speculation as to which parts of his paralyzed shape would taste best. A bold raven's talons pricked his forearm while her beak tore out tufts of hair for a nest. He mustered enough will to hate the bird, then sank back into unconsciousness.

Once he thought he heard Bel Amican soldiers beneath the coil tree. He pried his eyes open to find his brothers pointing up at him, laughing, and gloating that they had gone to drink the Essence without him. *They are not here. This is the poison,* he told himself. *Goreth would not laugh at me.* But he knew that this second day apart from his brothers would try Mordafey's patience.

As the daylight dimmed, the night flowers bloomed again. He could see cool blue light through closed eyelids, which brought O-raya back into his dreams. "It's the color of the lake right before dark." Calmed by the soft blue colors she was stirring in a bowl, he could concentrate on every word she said, stepping from one to the other as if walking up a steep, rocky path toward a view. "What does this blue look like?" she asked.

As he searched for an answer, she offered him a paintbrush. "You know what to do," she said. "You've been watching me. Make something."

He stared at the brush, alarmed, as if she were threatening him.

"Go ahead. I want to see what's inside you, Hairy. Give it a shape."

He tried to take the brush, but that invisible shell of Bel Amican poison held him fast. As he strained against its merciless grip, O-raya's image faded, and he awoke in a world of white.

Snow had dusted the coil-tree boughs and the glen's grassy floor.

Soldiers' bootprints crisscrossed the clearing. He marveled that they had walked beneath his tree. Faint traces of their passage remained in the air—leather, metal, weedsmoke. But they were already far away.

The sky was pregnant with purple storms. O-raya's questions came back to him. "What does this look like?" He wondered how he would answer. *Like. . .like. . .*

His gaze drifted down to the apple tree in the glen. *Plums,* he thought. *Storms look like piles of plums under plum trees.* He thought some more. *Coals. Coals gone cold.*

Such thinking felt unfamiliar, as if he were chewing on something with an awkward shape. But O-raya had talked like this. And there was nothing wrong with her, save for her smallness and weakness. He searched the glen, distracting himself from the maddening paralysis with the play of *this* like *that* and *this* like *that.*

He thought of his brothers. Goreth, like a dog, vicious but faithful. Jorn, like a weasel or a wild pig. Mordafey, a bear or a prongbull. Mordafey, a thunderstorm. Jorn, a miserable blast of sleet. Goreth, maybe a tumble-weed.

Staring at his hands, he thought of how much his claws glinted like daggers. Listening to the wind moan, he thought of Goreth snoring in the brothers' hideaway. Watching bright, precise snowflakes flurry against the dusk, he thought of glowflies. The well, a strange campfire. His aching belly, an empty cave.

He caught a few snowflakes on his pink tongue, imperceptible and flavorless. *Like ash,* he thought. They were worse than nothing. They reminded him of a better, but unattainable source—the well, right there in the glen.

A rustling in the bushes and then a gorrel—no, *the* gorrel—timidly emerged. Having survived its terrifying ordeal with the dogs and washed Jordam's blood from its fur, the animal crawled homeward, gaze fixed upon the tree's high hollow. Its nose wiggled, its tail twitched. He could hear its faltering heartbeat, smell the blood that coursed beneath its furry hide.

As the gorrel arrived at the base of the tree, Jordam focused on moving his feet. Pushing with all his might, he inched to the edge of the branch, desperate to catch some food.

The gorrel stood on the tree's tangled black roots and squinted up into the boughs. It leapt, clung to the trunk with its claws, then slowly lost its hold and scrabbled at the bark until it fell. Shaking itself off, the animal bunched up for another spring, and this time could not even manage a grip.

Jordam felt the pulse of his hunger falter. The gorrel circled the tree. Its furry sides pumped as it fought for breath. Clearly it was injured or exhausted.

Like me, he thought. *Like me, hurt and tired in O-raya's caves.*

Jordam's lips quivered. He would never get out of here if he entertained such useless thoughts. His brothers would drink the Essence without him. They would get stronger while he wasted away in a tree.

He kicked against the tree trunk, shoved himself free of the branch, and began to fall, limbs spread. His growing shadow startled the gorrel. It dodged, escaping by a whisker, and ran screaming back into the forest.

Facedown on the cold knobs of the roots, Jordam was sure that he lay in pieces. *Like the barrel at the bottom of the Abascar stair,* he thought. *Broken. Ruined.*

But as evening deepened, he felt a dull throbbing in his thumbs. The feeling spread to his fingers. He clutched at the tree's tangled tendrils. He dug his toes into the frost and forced his groaning carcass forward about the measure of a maple leaf. The scent of water lured him, and the shining blue flowers pulsed a persistent invitation. Claws digging into the earth, he pulled himself forward.

By the time he grasped the well's low boulders, night had conquered the sky. Snow fell steadily on the forest, but the well was almost warm. Snowflakes melted when they touched the stones. Steam seeped out around the edges of the lid. He dragged the wreckage of his body up against them and rested there awhile.

In the blue glow he could study the weathered paint of the wellstones. It made him feel close to O-raya.

When he could muster the strength, he dragged the cover from the well. The sound of an underground river roared. On his knees he looked through thick vapor into the well's throat and found the bucket's rope bound to an iron ring. Hanging on the ring next to the rope was the woman's pack. He pulled the pack out and set it beside the well. He was curious to know its contents, but thirst compelled him more. He pulled at the rope.

Seizing the bucket, he gulped until it was empty. The warm water stung his cracked tongue, scorched his parched throat, burnt all the way down his gullet, shocking his limbs back to life. He lay back, surprised by the feeling of strength that spread from his belly to his fingertips and toes.

He found a fallen apple, chewed twice, and swallowed. It was flavorless, a withered remnant of summer. But it was food.

Cautious, curious, he took a single, velvet petal from one of the blue flowers, just as the Bel Amican woman had done. He held it to his nose, sniffed it, found nothing of interest. It seemed ordinary. It left a bitter taste that wrinkled the span of his snout.

Then he drew the bucket again, drank some more, and poured the rest across his ankle where the arrow had struck. The wound burnt, but it did not bleed.

He looked up through the snowfall to the tower's silhouette and saw the figure in the window again. He crawled out of the well's glow and lay in the lee of the crumbling wall, spent from his ordeal.

When he woke again, he felt a peace that had eluded him since his visits to O-raya's caves. *She might be close*, he thought. *I should stay here awhile. Hide in the trees. Drink from the well.*

He wiped at his nose and discovered a dark, oily secretion on his face, like the drops he had seen on the Bel Amican woman's brow. *The flowers*, he thought.

Whatever was happening to him, he liked it. He felt lighter, stronger, and his senses were sharper. The glen all around him seemed a concert of life—the rush of the underground river, the *scritch-scratch* of barkbugs, the raucous clamor of clumpfrogs, and the jabber of dreaming gorrels. He heard the Bel Amican flags whipped by the wind atop the tower.

And then he heard another rustle of cloth.

He looked up through the straying fog to see a brown woodscloak hanging in the maple tree. It had not been there before.

His hands clutched the stones of the crumbling wall. His heartbeat broke into a run. And then he heard the first note of a tetherwing's alarm.

The breeze grabbed the fog as if it were a curtain and pulled it aside, laying everything bare.

She stood in the grass beside the open tetherwing basket. She was a slight figure in an ordinary shift of grey. She did not see him, for she stood facing the cloudgrasper tree, drawing out the contents of her pack and hanging them on the green boughs. Already she had arranged a colorful gallery— a hat with a long golden feather, an ornate shield, a toy boat with a sweeping white sail, and an arm-length, serpentine pipe that gave off the spiced scent of old smoke.

Jordam was more concerned about the dagger lying at her feet. He tensed to make a dash for higher ground but worried that he might not even manage to walk.

A tetherwing let loose another cry. The woman paused. Perhaps she was waiting for a third call, a confirmation that a predator was close at hand. Perhaps she was too afraid to move.

She busied herself again, anxious and hurried, drawing out more offerings for the tree. A silver-webbed fishing net. A silver chain bearing an emblem of an eagle with outstretched wings and a fish in its talons.

She pushed heaps of dry twigs against the base of the tree. At last she dropped to her knees and struck a firestick against a stone. It flared up bright and orange, and she held it high. "In the name of Tammos Raak," she murmured, her voice trembling, "I summon King Helpryn, master of the sea. I summon Partayn ker Helpryn, master of music. I summon Deuneroi ker Bekenyr, master of the court."

Jordam blinked, cupping his ears toward her.

"Come and visit me here," she said, raising her voice with increasing confidence. "House Bel Amica has fallen from wisdom. They're abandoning the old ways. The Seers deceive them. I come in secret to offer this sign of gratitude for all you have done and to bid you a proper farewell. Come and take these, your belongings. I speak for many who dare not join me here."

Ornaments in the tree swung on the wind-troubled boughs. The woman cupped a hand around the flaming firestick. "Are you there?" she asked. "Are you listening?"

She touched the firestick to a scrap of kindling. The flame caught and spread along an arching line of bramble, flaring up and dancing. "Take these treasures as a show of our love and remembrance." She stared into the line of flame. "And then...if you would..." She took up the dagger. "Honor my longing, and consider my loneliness. I have no purpose here. I'm a prisoner. I've nothing left to give."

Jordam felt a tremor in the ground. Then another. He recognized the quakes, and he turned his gaze to the trees above the glen, terrified. But no shadow emerged, no great wings were spread against the sky. Still, the wind that roared into the glen felt familiar, as if the Keeper might be answering a summons.

The cloudgrasper swayed. The musical instrument fell from the branch, and when its wooden bowl struck the ground, the strings rang out in a dissonant chord. Buffeted and ripped, the flames flickered and went out. The wind diminished, calming as quickly as it had arrived.

The woman's shoulders sank. She bowed her head, whether in frustration, grief, or exhaustion, Jordam could not tell. He could not see her face.

Tetherwings began to hoot, sounding alarms urgent and sad, as though they knew it was too late for their song. Their tiny, beady eyes glared down at him from their perches.

The woman turned and shuddered when she saw him.

Her gaze made him uneasy, for she was such a different creature. In this light she was like O-raya, small but strong. Older, though, and cloaked in a different kind of costume. Painted by the light of the opening flowers, she was right as green leaves, right as a river. Her skin, red with the cold. Her black hair, bound up in a cloth and pinned with sharp black rods, crowned with the grey tetherwing feathers. Her chin was small as a child's, her lips seemed drawn by the merest tip of a brush. Like the girl at the lake, she was graceful in a way that frightened him.

His fear kindled another feeling—shame. In their hunts he and his brothers reveled in destroying what they did not understand. They enjoyed distorting anything untouched by the influence of the Cent Regus Essence. Jordam hated his victims because they were weak. But here he knew that he hated the weakerfolk because the Essence had taken something away from *him*, something he could not get back.

She did not scream. She did not attack. Instead, she smiled in resignation. Her tense body relaxed, a burdensome question answered. The dagger fell, leaving a cut where she had pressed it through her shift.

She placed the feathered crown in the basket. She took the golden vial and tipped it over the basket, letting one glistening drop fall. A pungent, smoky perfume spread, and Jordam's nostrils tingled. Slumberseed oil. Then she corked the vial, set it aside, and whistled as she had the night before. Tetherwings gathered in a reluctant, mournful spiral, descending one by one into the open basket. "Be still," she whispered. "Be still." The tetherwings quieted as she closed the lid.

He waited for her to run, but she stayed. Black, shiny drops beaded across her brow. She reached up and clasped the eagle emblem on the silver chain the way she might reach for someone's hand. He recognized the emblem.

"*rrDoon-roy,*" he said softly, as surprised to hear his own voice as she was.

Her eyes widened. "Was it you? Were you there?" She seemed to flicker like a dying light. *Like O-raya*, he thought. *Like O-raya before she left.*

"Do to me what you did to him," she continued. "I can't do it. It's like...like he's watching me." She gestured to the tower. "They won't understand. Finish me. Let me join the others you've taken."

In a strange dizziness—whether from the water or from the bitter flowers, from the poison or from the exhaustion, he did not know—Jordam clung to her words. *Do to me what you did to him.* He understood. *Can't do it. Finish me.* The words knotted together into a net, caught meaning.

He lurched to his feet. She seemed so small, trembling there. She bowed and waited, fingers curling into fists.

"*rrNo.*" Speaking to her in Common words was like sorting through loot, trying to discern the use of unfamiliar tools. "No hurt. No finish."

He remembered how she had reached out to the fox. He found words there. "Won't hurt you," he said. Her fear, it covered her. *Like a blanket.* He growled at the nagging sense that inclined him to find comparisons.

She had offered the fox a flower. He stepped to the well and grasped the rope, pulling the bucket up the shaft. "*rr*Good water. Drink." And then another word presented itself. "Help," he said, just as he had heard so many victims cry out. "Help." He was not sure if he was speaking it as an offer or a plea.

She bared her teeth the way a gorrel does when it does not know whether to flee or fight. "Help? I've told you how you can help."

"Help." His voice weakened in his uncertainty.

"Don't you understand?" She reached for the knife, touched its hilt, and then tossed it across the grass to him. She pointed at the tower. "I can't go back. There's nothing for me there now."

He opened his hands and then spewed a gushing roar of language in the Cent Regus' twisted tongue, raging about Mordafey, the pain in his head, the loss of O-raya and her colors. "Can't go back," he echoed to her, but he gestured to the darkness, not the tower.

She fell forward onto her elbows and covered her head with her hands, frozen in place. *Like a cornered animal.*

He knelt across from her. "Help," he said. He unsheathed the knife strapped to his leg and cast it into the grass beside her. She stared at his weapon and its bloodstained hilt. She shook as if naked in cold water.

He backed away toward the edge of the clearing and stood on the root-rumpled ground beneath the boughs of a young apple tree. He waited. "Won't hurt you," he said again.

She stood, lifted the tetherwing basket, and moved toward the crumbling wall. "I don't care if we were right," she snapped. "It's too late. Why couldn't you have come before?"

Panic seized him. He did not understand what he wanted, but he did not want to be alone. He stepped forward. "No... Stop..."

His next step sounded a sudden crack. Rings of gleaming razor wire sprang up from the leaves with the *ping* of plucked strings. Pain seared his legs, arms, and neck, and a tremendous force drew him back hard against the apple tree. Six wire nooses tightened. The commotion ended as quickly as it had begun.

Arms bound to his sides, he pushed against the wires but learned at once that the flesh-splitting lines responded to resistance by tightening further. He roared.

Blinking, choking, he fought back against the pain. Blood beaded and spilled from the lacerations. The wires binding Jordam were held taut by a mechanism in a small metal flywheel that was pinned to the ground out of reach. He could bend his arms, but his hands could only clutch air. He could lift his feet by bending his knees. This gained him nothing. If he touched any of the main lines, the snare tightened, wire cutting closer to bone. *Stuck. Again.*

He groped for clear thought. *The soldiers. They were here.*

He met the woman's gaze. He groped for a word that he could cast out to her as her image blurred.

"Help."

10

WIREBOUND

As Cyndere watched, her fear of the beastman diminished, overcome by revulsion at how the wires constricted and cut. Arms pinned to his sides, hands grasping at nothing, the creature snarled as if trying to frighten the snare. Then his voice faltered to a whimper. Steam curled over the blood that pooled darkly at his feet.

Deuneroi had described these contraptions to Cyndere many months ago. They were easier for soldiers to carry and conceal than the bulky metal spring-jaws. Best of all, they were likely to bind and injure but not kill their catch. The traps could help them round up beastmen for study and observation. But a demonstration of the device quickly changed Deuneroi's mind; in the court he began to argue against their use. Their advantages were obvious, but he hated their cruelty, hated how the wires could not discern between beastmen and more innocent creatures.

Cyndere stared at the struggling beastman. He had not harmed her. Instead, he had raised a question in her mind.

She did not want the question. It prevented her from completing what she had come to do.

The plan had been so simple. She would convince her mother that she could mourn and find peace at Tilianpurth. Disguised as Emeriene, she would get Bauris to lead her through the ancient escape tunnel and into the woods so she could find the glen again.

The glen—where flirtation had given way to confessions and bold vows. Deuneroi had touched each freckle on her back, naming them after constellations, his fingertips soft and cool as these snowflakes. They had imagined a better world and arrived at a common question: Could they purge corruption from the Cent Regus and restore the people of a fallen house? They had practiced conversations with invisible Cent Regus here, dreaming ways to lure the creatures back to conscience and civility.

She wanted to bid a proper farewell to her father, Partayn, and Deuneroi. Seers had convinced the Bel Amicans that the old beliefs were superstitions and that ghosts were fantasy. They insisted that only the moon-spirits' worshipers found life beyond the grave, led away into paradises of their own design, never to return. Cyndere could not accept such a vision. She needed a way to say good-bye. She would decorate a Memory Tree, burn those treasured belongings, and cling to what she had believed as a child—that witnesses surrounded her in clouds, listening to her appeals and laments.

Her first venture to the well had not gone as planned.

Then her visit to the prison pit shattered what remained of her confidence. Emeriene was right. She could not face such hatred alone, and no one would stand beside her to offer help. Deuneroi and his dream were gone, and she felt abandoned, purposeless. She would ask the ghosts to take her away, to set her free from this ruined life.

But now, *this.*

Confronted with this helpless monster, her plan was spoiled again. The opportunity she and Deuneroi had sought was before her, as if someone had brought the beastman here, right at this moment, to knock the knife from her hand. Now she too was caught in a tightening snare of indecision. She could not bring herself to rekindle the fire, nor could she bend and take up that cold, blue-lit blade. Something restrained her.

"I can't," she said to the darkness.

When the beastman's legs weakened and he slumped forward, the wires dug in tighter, shocking him awake. He kicked at the slippery ground and leaned back against the tree, yelping like a wounded dog.

She studied the beastman's face, which was layered with conflicting natures, as if he had ripped away the faces of beasts and pasted patches over his own, merging and melding them into a mask until it was impossible to tell where one ended and the other began.

"You're not like the one we've locked away," she said.

The beastman released a trembling breath. A memory rose, as if from another lifetime before she knew death and despair.

"Cyndere," King Helpryn whispered. With his irrepressible zeal for discovery, he had crawled with her through a stand of tall grass, soil darkening his elbows, arrows in his left hand, a bow in his right.

She had thought it a game. Only seven years old, she had led her father through a maze of passages she carved through the windblown grassfields of the bluffs high above the edge of the Mystery Sea. She would show him the animals that had become her playmates. The coastland creatures were far better friends for an heiress than those children who treated her with fear or false affection.

The king had nodded patiently while she pointed out silverflies and fuzz-worms, bluebeaks, jackrabbits, and fire-coughing candlefrogs. And as they came to the edge of the bluff and looked down to the swirling inlet, she pointed out the sprawling, oil-black bodies of grawlafurrs and the leaping, dancing seals called inysh.

But it was the rapid yipping of lurkdashers that caught the king's attention. She scrambled to keep up as he hurried ahead on all fours, crawling into the tunnels and emerging at the far edge of the field. Together they looked down a long, grassy slope to a patch of thick brush.

A batch of lurkdasher cubs were at play, hopping and wrestling and tumbling together, their long, white-tipped ears flattened against their backs, their red tails bristling and lashing about. They would engage in a furious fracas, then separate and trot on tiptoes in nervous circles, canine smiles betraying rowdy intent, only to jump on each other again and roll, limbs entwined.

The lurkdashers' father suddenly appeared from behind a shrub. His coat seemed made of several shaggy skins, shredded from day after day of crawling through tangles of barbed branches. His towering ears erect, he sniffed at the wind and gave a quick, short bark, then padded on white paws into the open, whiskers straight and bright.

Cyndere's father had thanked his lucky tattoo—eagle wings spread open across his forehead. She did not perceive his intent. Those arrows in his hand, they seemed as much a part of him as his rings and the emblems of royalty.

But then he had drawn an arrow into the bow, set the catch so it would not fire, grasped the curve and fingered the release switch. With his other hand, he quickly sealed Cyndere's open mouth, stopped her sudden cry. He touched the switch. The bowstring sang. The lurkdasher lay on the ground, legs in spasms at his side.

Cyndere ran, her jaw aching from the way she had wrenched free of her father's grasp. He called after her, warned her that the creature was dangerous. But she did not look back. She stumbled and pitched forward, and a thorn pierced the palm of her hand. She ignored it, biting her lip, and continued her run until she reached the creature's side and saw the feathered end of the arrow in its chest. Cyndere looked down the hill in dismay, only to find that there was no sign of the cubs.

The fallen dasher quivered. She reached to touch his shoulder. He snarled, drawing his trembling lips back to show a line of perfect white teeth, pink gums with black spots, a black tongue.

She wept, gripping the arrowshaft, too frightened to pull it free, while blood dripped from the thorn in her hand.

Her father arrived at her side, scolding her for approaching a wounded animal.

She began to feel faint, and her eyes met the lurkdasher's. She saw a kind of understanding in them. With a final, shaky exhalation, light faded from his eyes.

Cyndere turned away. "No, please," she whispered. "I can't bear it."

"Help." The beastman swallowed hard, his body shuddering.

She felt foolish and useless. "I can't do this."

"O-raya," he sighed, and his eyes closed.

"No!" She snatched up the tetherwing basket and drew her cloak from the tree, then stumbled away.

She climbed out of the glen and looked toward the tower. Emeriene stood framed in the window, striking the same regal pose as before, faithful and surely angry that Cyndere had crept away without warning.

"Forgive me, Em," Cyndere whispered. "But I can't come back."

Cyndere seized the wig of black horsehair. It had fooled Bauris into accepting her as Emeriene on the first night and helped her slip past sisterlies into the tunnel tonight. She would not need it anymore. She pulled it from her head.

She pulled up the hood of her cloak to hide her short, golden hair. Then she turned and staggered away in no particular direction. She walked without purpose, without answers, as lost as she had been when she tried to give herself up to the ocean.

As she moved beyond the reach of the blue light, the leaves around her feet rustled. She felt a hot sting across her ankle, and she fell, shocked with pain, her legs wound about with wire. And then she felt nothing, not even the snow that began to settle on her face.

The woods were quiet. The basket lay on its side, the lid open. Sleepy tetherwings trundled about in the snow and then climbed back inside.

At the hint of another's blood on the breeze, Jordam's predatory instincts awoke. He wheezed a desperate breath, shocked to his senses.

The boughs above him cast snow down into the glen. Fog swirled around the glimmering well. He wanted to drift out of this bleeding body and lose himself in that light. Baring his teeth, he fought to keep from falling forward into the wires' tension.

He focused his attention on the snare's mechanism. He could see that it was pinned into the earth. He looked about, hoping to find a low-hanging branch he could use to prod the device loose from the ground.

The lowest of the wires was wrapped about his thighs.

An idea began to take shape.

He pressed his feet between the ridges of the apple tree's shallow roots. He began to dig at the soil around them with his toes. The more he loosened the roots, the more excited he became. Soon he could curl his toes around two roots that ran out from the tree toward the mechanism. Slowly, forcefully, he tugged at them. The more he strained, the farther from the tree the roots broke from their shallow burial.

And then the roots ripped up from the ground on either side of the trap. They caught the flywheel's edges and lifted it, pulling the pin half free. Jordam clenched his teeth, strained against the ground's hold. The roots broke loose. The pin sprang up, free. The trap tilted and fell.

In another mighty pull, Jordam tore the roots free from the soil. He drew the knobby tendrils toward him, and the overturned trap rode along. As the trap came closer, the wire tension slackened.

Jordam pulled the embedded cords from his flesh. When he finally climbed free, he fell against the ground as if to embrace it. Darkness seized him, sought to overcome him, but he wrestled it, cursing.

Behind him, the tree shuddered, leaning into the place where it had lost its grip on the ground. As it did, the rest of the roots tore free. He rolled to the side, and the tree fell toward the well, branches snapping and waving. A few stubborn apples tumbled free.

He caught another trace of the woman's blood on the air. "O-raya," he croaked. "rrWait." He forced himself to his feet and lurched up the slope toward the trees, following the faint sound of her shallow, quivering breath. He climbed through an overhanging patch of ferns, stalked through the brush, and found her. In his delirium he thought she was O-raya, bound up in this wicked Bel Amican wire. Her eyes were closed.

She is trapped. Hurting. Like me.

He reached for her, then paused. "rrNot…O-raya." It was the Bel Amican woman. He remembered now. But as he leaned over her, he remembered O-raya lying on the cliff's edge on the night that the Keeper took him down into the lake. "Not O-raya. *rrLike* O-raya."

Jordam seized the anchor of her trap and pulled the pin free of the ground as easily as plucking out a thorn. Then he took the wires around her legs and slackened them, tenderly and carefully. They had not cut deeply, for she had fallen without any struggle, and the toughweed brace caught most of the snare. She would live.

He knelt there, cradling her cold, bleeding form in his arms as if she were a child. Then he lurched to his feet, carrying her. She was light, not like the bodies of men he had slain. And yet no burden had ever proved so difficult to carry, for every step he took required fierce concentration. The world spun and blurred around him. He moved toward the blue glow, then laid the woman down beside the well. Her hair, which had been long and dark, was now short and golden. He did not understand.

She woke, her eyes widening. She looked at him, looked at the fallen tree, and then looked beyond it, up toward the coil tree, where a figure stepped out of the darkness. "Do you see?" she asked, gesturing to the apparition in the shimmering veil. It held no weapons and made no move to interfere. It seemed to stare at Jordam and the woman intently.

"rrYes," said Jordam.

The diaphanous figure raised a hand as if in greeting.

Jordam slumped against the ground and felt the cold engulf him. He wrapped his arms tightly around himself and was seized with violent shaking.

Water rushed through his mane and down through the lacerations on his arms, chest, and legs. He blinked and saw the woman kneeling and pouring the well water over him. She let the bucket fall and began to draw it out again. She was talking to herself, too quickly for him to understand. "If it's you, Deuneroi," she said. "One more time. One more try."

She poured the next bucket over her own legs, seething as the water cleansed the clotting blood and sealed the wire's stripes. As she did this, she watched the shadows.

Snowflakes drifted down like comforting whispers.

After a while she shook her head as if waking. "I must go back," she said. She stood, wavering weakly. "Hide in the trees," she told him. "Hide well. Tomorrow night I want you to come back. Come back here. To the well. Tomorrow night."

"rrMorrow," he repeated.

She grabbed a broken branch of the apple tree and began to prod about at the ground, testing it for more traps. She walked to the edge of the clearing and onto the path that led to the Bel Amican bastion. She did not look back, but he heard a deep breath, and she said, "What do I call you?"

"rrJordam," he said. "What call?"

She did not answer.

The light from the well glinted on something made of golden glass. She had forgotten her vial of slumberseed oil. "Be still," he said to himself, remembering her stern command. He glanced up at the tower suddenly uneasy. He wondered what had happened to his brothers.

Jordam lay beside the well, caught between desire and fear, half-awake in the light of O-raya's blue.

Standing in her tower chamber as the sun rose, Cyndere stood naked before the mirror, the shreds of her grey shift and the broken toughweed cast scattered about her feet. Daylight coursed through an azure curtain to illuminate her skin pale blue. Her right leg appeared to have been slashed into pieces and then sewn back together, bold red stripes crisscrossing her thigh and calf. The bleeding had stopped, and the wounds had scabbed over. Already. And it was early morning, a few hours after her ordeal.

"The water," she murmured. "Where does it come from?"

Emeriene stirred in her seat at the window, but she did not wake.

Cyndere determined to keep her ordeal a secret. She drew her winter nightgown over her head, and it draped down enough to conceal her wounds. She moved to her bed, where a pitcher of milk waited on a tray beside a plate piled with slices of fresh nectarbread.

On the night of the heiress's first excursion out through the tunnels beneath Tilianpurth, Emeriene had begged her to change her mind. She had even volunteered to go down into the glen herself. But Cyndere would not deviate from her plan. "I must let it go, Em. I must set it all alight and speak to their ghosts." On this second venture, she had gone alone without warning. Bauris slept, oblivious, and Emeriene had found this chamber empty.

Watching the sisterly sleep, Cyndere ached with gratitude. Things were different now. Something unexplainable had happened in the glen, something she would keep to herself. But it gave her a thread of hope, a reason to stay another day.

Emerging from the tunnel in Tilianpurth's kitchen, Cyndere had been surprised to find only young Pyroi the stablehand awake, sneaking biscuits before sunup. He had dropped his plate when the cupboard separated from the wall and the heiress stepped out of the darkness, shaking with cold and smeared with dark blood. He had agreed to keep her secret, and when she promised to recommend him for a promotion, he burst into tears. Sniffing and fighting to regain his composure, he had helped her return to her chamber without being seen.

She took a small bite of nectarbread, then shoved whole slices into her mouth, one after the other, closing her eyes and finding comfort in the food. After she washed down the crumbs with a cup of milk, she rose and carried the pitcher to the foot of the bed. She poured a shallow layer of milk into the empty bowl on the floor, then left the pitcher and crawled beneath the pillowy bed blankets to wait.

Behind closed eyes she could see nothing but Jordam's large, sad face. His ragged, wild mane. His fangs. "Deuneroi, I found him. I found our beastman. Tomorrow, I'll sketch him for you."

As she sank back into the pillows, Emeriene awoke.

"Oh!" Emeriene paused as if questioning her own senses. Then she ran at the bed, seized the heiress by the shoulders, and shook her. "You! You gave me such..." She buried her face in the blankets, and Cyndere embraced her. Her voice muffled in cloth, Emeriene shouted, "I thought you'd gone out again!" Pulling away, she stormed about, a tangle of relief and anger—step, *thump*, step, *thump*. "I've been searching. I wore the headdress and stood at the window. I thought..." And then she rushed to arrange kindling for a new fire.

"I did go out, Em. I saw you in the window." Cyndere's hands clenched fistfuls of the blanket.

Emeriene's mouth opened and closed several times.

"You look like a fish. Listen, Em. I couldn't do it. I couldn't burn the Memory Tree. Instead, I...I had a vision. You must keep this to yourself. No one else can know about this. Not even Bauris."

"You're worse than my sons! Has your mind turned to gravy?" Emeriene wiped tears on her sleeve. "How dare you go outside the wall without telling me? Why? Do you think you'll find a ghost?" Emeriene snapped a dry branch, then held the pieces and stared into the cold fireplace. "I say the most terrible things when I'm angry. Forgive me."

Cyndere smiled feebly. "You've every right to be angry. But I need you to trust me. I'll say more, but first, I'm just..."

"Hungry?" Emeriene struck a firestick. "I'll get us some breakfast."

"Sleepy." Cyndere sank back into the pillows. "I think I'll really sleep. I've almost forgotten what it's like."

"I'll have to teach you how to sleep at night and move about in daylight." Emeriene rose as the fire sprang to life, and she returned to kneel at the bedside. As she took Cyndere's hand, the sisterly's expression took on a frightful intensity. "We've lost so many things," said Emeriene. "But we can start over. Together. Two girls at Tilianpurth. We'll tell each other everything." She stood up and cleared her throat. "First things first."

As Emeriene all but skipped out the door, Cyndere gazed into the flames. She let a forced smile go, felt a furrow in her brow. "No," she said. "No, I can't tell you everything."

It would be complicated, slipping away again to find the beastman. And to look for a ghost.

Abascar's people had told stories of phantoms called Northchildren. But Cyndere didn't believe such things. She was certain that this apparition had known her, greeted her. She was afraid to let herself imagine who it might have been.

A delicate sound interrupted the memories. Drab as one of her father's old sealskin slippers, the bat with the broken wing crawled around inside the milk bowl, his rough tongue scraping the bottom dry. He stretched his weak wings, shook them out as if letting the strength brought by the meal work its way to the edges. He blinked and sniffed at the air. Clenching his eyes, he bared his little teeth and yawned.

Cyndere did not move.

The bat crawled awkwardly until his snout met the cold crystal of the milk pitcher. He licked it. He pawed at it with the tips of his wings, as if knocking to be let in. Soon he had hooked his wingtips over the pitcher's edge and pulled himself up. All the time his nostrils twitched. His small gray body teetered on the lip as he craned his neck to try to reach the milk.

"You're going to fall in," she said.

He fell.

While he splashed and choked and climbed back out again, dripping rivers of milk behind him, Cyndere laughed through her tears until she fell asleep.

11

BROTHERS DIVIDED

Mordafey smelled honey even before he heard Goreth emerge, lips smacking, from the trees. He had tracked Goreth by following the obvious path pressed through the forest by the salvage pallet. He found the pallet alongside an abandoned ranger shack, unguarded, exposed.

Goreth returned hours later, seemingly oblivious to his failure. "Look," he grunted. "See? Ranger house. No rangers."

Hiding just inside, Mordafey dug his claws into the floorboards. In the two days since Jordam and Jorn were captured, his thirst for Essence had worsened. And his fury.

After the Bel Amicans had scattered the brothers, Mordafey waited as long as he could for their return. Goreth found him quickly, but only Goreth. So Mordafey decided to steal away without attempting any kind of rescue for Jordam and Jorn. Unbeknownst to his brothers, Mordafey's Cent Regus conspirators were waiting nearby. He did not dare disappoint them. They were crucial in his plan to seize the Cent Regus throne.

But now, as appetite gnawed at his head and gullet, he hated Jordam and Jorn for complicating his plot. And he hated Goreth for failing to follow simple instructions: *Take the prizes back to the dens.* His brothers were careless, failing to grasp the importance of obedience and sticking together.

"Honeybee," Goreth muttered, closer. "Honeybee stuck in my teeth."

The brothers' fear of Mordafey had slackened. He would remind them to be afraid. And, if necessary, he would leave them behind, take the loot, steal away to the Cent Regus lair, and claim the rewards for himself. The pieces of his strategy were almost in place. He could not afford delays, distractions, or dangerous rescues. He would have that deep drink. He would take another step toward seizure of Skell Wra's throne.

When the first stairstep outside the shack groaned under Goreth's weight, Mordafey froze, still as a stone.

The next step creaked. "Where's Same Brother, Turtle? Always I talk to Same Brother. But he's gone so long. Maybe Bel Amicans killed him." A whimper gusted through Goreth's nostrils, and Mordafey heard him pounding at his head to wake his failing memory. "Was it yesterday, Turtle? We hunted something big. Then Bel Amicans. And Older Brother sent me away with the prizes. Did I show you prizes, Turtle? And then I smelled honey."

Rising suddenly to fill the small doorframe, Mordafey relished Goreth's slack-jawed astonishment. "Found a new home, Goreth?"

Honey still dripping from his beard, Goreth dropped the tree turtle. His eyes rolled in their sockets like thrown marbles. The turtle bounced down the stairs and tumbled to rest in the ferns, retracting its head and long-fingered limbs.

"Mordafey told you, take prizes, go back to the brothers' den." Mordafey stalked down the steps. Goreth's eyes slowed their spin and rested askew. Mordafey recognized this derangement; it happened when the brothers had gone too long without Essence. Unable to recognize his brother or see anything clearly, Goreth brandished the battle-scarred sword he had carried since the ambush on the Bel Amicans at Abascar.

Mordafey seized Goreth's wrist in a crushing grip. He took the sword and swung the flat of the blade against his brother's face. Then he plunged it into the snow-dusted soil and cuffed Goreth again, dropping him to the ground. "You leave Mordafey's prizes out in the open? What if others find them?"

"What others?"

Mordafey clenched his teeth. If his brothers discovered he was conspiring with other Cent Regus, they would worry about their share of the eventual reward. He was determined to prepare his army in secret until the brothers had no choice but to cooperate.

Goreth clutched his head. "Good brother," he squeaked. "Strongest brother. Smartest brother." He gestured into the trees and offered to take Mordafey to the hives and the honey.

Mordafey grabbed the pallet's strongshoot poles and dragged it over to drop them at Goreth's feet. "In the Core, the Sopper Crone will feed you Essence. That will fix your thinking."

"Head hurts." Goreth got to his feet, riding his own private earthquake. Lumbering, he reclaimed and sheathed the sword. Then he found the tree turtle lying on its back, lifted it, and tucked it snugly into his thick, black mane between his ears. "When my head hurts, Same Brother hurts too. Where is Same Brother?"

Mordafey clutched at the air, wishing he could shake Goreth's memory until it righted itself. He recounted for Goreth exactly what had happened the day before, and how the brothers had been separated.

"Where's Turtle?" Goreth reached up to scratch his head and scratched the turtle's shell. Then he laughed and leapt to seize the pallet poles and to haul the brothers' treasure forward. Mordafey ground his knuckles into his eyes and cursed the Old Dog for fathering such a fractured creature, and they walked into the trees.

They advanced through a night of drifting snowfall, moving steadily south and westward.

Goreth endured his searing headache by talking quietly to his new hard-shell pet. The pallet slid along behind, pressing down brush and paving a trail for any Cent Regus followers. Mordafey moved haltingly, listening for signs of an ambush.

"Older Brother wants his brascle," said Goreth to the turtle. "Bird could watch for followers. Bird could warn him."

As cold sunlight revealed the third day since the brothers' separation, the ground grew harder, intolerant of anything green and growing. Midmorning they emerged from the Cragavar onto chalky terrain skiffed with new snow. They kept to high ground across rolling plains of shallow-rooted scrubweed bushes, for the valleys and ravines were choked with impassable brambles.

Mordafey's claws probed burrows trying to snag prey by a hind leg. Most warrens of scramdogs, rabbits, lurkdashers, gorrels, and thick-headed dodgers had mysteriously emptied since summer. Only scavengers, insects, parasites, and slithering things remained.

"Older Brother," Goreth called. "Brothers should bring the Old Dog hunting. Strong and fast, the Old Dog."

"*Crolca!*" Mordafey swore. "You forget everything. The Old Dog's dead many years now. Left Mordafey to tell brothers what to do."

Goreth hung his head. "I forget," he whispered. "But not everything." He could recall days when he would follow the Old Dog, father of the four brothers. He learned to hunt by watching the bearlike giant. "The Old Dog's dead," he remembered. "His head. Big tent spike pounded right through."

"Yes," said Mordafey, a note of contempt in his voice. "Remember who caught the Old Dog's killer? Remember who killed him and ate him? Mordafey. Mordafey made things right. Then Mordafey taught brothers how to fight together, hunt together, and get strong."

"She." Goreth picked at the rough edge of the bone protruding from his brow. "What about She?"

"She?" Mordafey rattled a small wooden box of bones tied with a leather strap to his belt. "The Old Dog killed She. Wanted Mordafey to hunt only for him. Goreth and Jordam came from a different She. And Jorn, another."

The story set Goreth to flinching. His memory tossed like a sea, and at times memories surfaced that had been sunken for many years. "Goreth's She? Did the Old Dog kill her too?"

Mordafey grinned, a glittering in the shadows beneath the hood of his woodscloak. "The Old Dog killed her too."

"Don't say more." Goreth held up his hands.

"Remember the Old Dog's last She? Whipped her cubs, even Jorn. But Jorn…he bit back. First kill." Staring intently at Goreth, Mordafey licked his lips. Goreth felt a nervous chill until he realized that his brother was looking at the turtle. He pulled up his own woodscloak hood then, covering his passenger.

Waves of dead weeds thinned as the brothers entered a labyrinth of stony ridges. Ridges grew larger, and crevasses between them narrowed and deepened. Mordafey led them in zigzag until they were deep within a canyon.

Turning up a slope of layered clay, Goreth recognized stony pillars, and he began to recite what he could remember of the brothers' secret stash.

At last they arrived on a great stone shelf. Near the perilous edge, above a seemingly bottomless chasm, a rugged blister of stone swelled, and on the side that faced the chasm it yawned open, a jagged maw.

"Secret way to brothers' dens," Goreth informed the turtle.

Stepping through the fanged break, he recognized a haphazard arrangement of boulders. This scattering worried him; they might be some kind of eggs. In his dreams they sometimes hatched.

Tiptoeing past, the pallet sweeping the floor behind him, Goreth joined Mordafey at the threshold to the brothers' hidden home and pointed to a boulder propped against the back wall. "Secret door," he said.

A blur of motion and a clopping din startled them. Goreth dropped the prize pallet and drew out his sword, but Mordafey had already cornered the rock goat. The long-haired, long-eared animal, which had probably wandered in looking for an escape from the winter winds, did not even manage a bleat of alarm before Mordafey tore out its throat.

Suddenly agitated, the tree turtle on Goreth's head stood up, turned, and groaned as if realizing it would take months to journey back to its tree. Goreth patted the turtle until it withdrew its head and sticky feet.

The brothers made a quick meal of the goat. As Goreth gnawed into bone, Mordafey shoved aside the boulder, disappeared through the opening, and let the stone fall back into place with a hollow *fummmm*.

Goreth set the tree turtle down among the goat bones. "Stay here, Turtle. Guard prizes. I'm going down. More food. And sleep." He patted the shell again. The turtle would not stick out its head. Goreth whined softly. The turtle's silence only increased his frustration at the absence of his twin. He could not remember a time when they had been apart for so long.

Goreth woke, hot as an ember, curled beneath heavy layers of muskgrazer skins on a shelf in the den wall. The boulder that blocked the door was rocking back into place. He blinked, listening. It might be Mordafey leaving, or returning. He was not sure.

Try though he might, he couldn't remember how long ago he had climbed into this hole to sleep. It might have been days. He did not remember Mordafey setting the fire that crackled in the pit.

A raspy *crawk* from the corner told Goreth that Mordafey's braggle was still here, tethered to her perch. He crawled from beneath the skins and peered at the grand, fire-lit cavern and its ceiling of stalactites. He saw the large predator bird, and the bird stared back with enormous, lidless eyes. He saw no sign of Mordafey. But then he heard something like a scuffle on the entry ledge high above.

A massive shape hurtled down from the ledge and slammed into the ground before him.

A dead rock lizard, legs splayed and limp, stared blankly at him, tongue lolling out over yellow teeth. The impact forced a mighty blast of air through its nostrils. Goreth breathed in the scent of the lizard's last meals—dead insects, rotten reptile eggs, and fish. The feathered shaft of a Bel Amican arrow jutted out from beneath the lizard's jaw, and Goreth could see it continued on up through the mouth with its tip undoubtedly buried somewhere in the animal's brain. "Time to eat," he laughed. Looking back up to the ledge, he asked, "What else?"

While the braggle beat its wings and screeched, Goreth watched Mordafey wrestling another shape to the edge of the ledge. Whatever it was fought back. But Mordafey overpowered it, and the shape flew into the open space, landing hard in the bonfire, which exploded in sparks and ashes.

"Same Brother!" Goreth rushed to Jordam's side, rolled him over, and pawed the glimmering embers and ashes from his cloak and fur. Jordam's eyes were closed, and he growled through his teeth.

Jordam had suffered quite a beating—a gash in his leg, blood-crusted stripes around his limbs and chest, and bruises all about his face. His woodscloak was cut through in several places and heavy with dry blood.

"No help for Jordam," Mordafey hissed, and he leapt down. "Not until he explains. Jordam failed. Almost ruined the plans."

"Did. Not. Fail." Jordam forced the words out. Clutching at his belly with one hand, he reached into the ashes with the other and flung a shower of black dust at Mordafey.

"Where's Young Brother?" Goreth asked.

"rrCaptured." Jordam's eyes opened. "Bel Amicans took him. They had dogs. Arrows, poison. rrTraps. But I got away. Jorn...not smart enough." Jordam turned his attention to Mordafey. "Must go after Jorn soon. Or give him up."

Mordafey paced a ring around the twins, his club firmly in his grip, waiting for Jordam to say something worthy of punishment.

"Send me back," Jordam suggested. "I get Jorn out."

Goreth grabbed Jordam's arm. "Same Brother, don't leave again!"

"Jordam won't go anywhere unless Mordafey has him on a leash," Mordafey barked.

"rrBrothers need Jorn," Jordam insisted. "For Mordafey's plan."

"Hrrmph." Mordafey stalked away down a tunnel. He returned and tossed dry branches onto the coals, and smoke snaked into fissures high above.

"Mordafey...I've seen the creature." Jordam spoke with passion, and Goreth knew he was trying to turn his older brother's anger toward some new target. "Still there. In the trees."

Mordafey stared into the smoke. "Brothers will hunt big creature after Essence," he muttered, lifting a heavy battle-ax from the ashes. "After Essence and after Abascar."

"Abascar?" Goreth laughed. "Abascar's gone."

Mordafey brought the ax down to cleave the rock lizard's side. "Abascar people hide in Barnashum." In strike after strike, he carved the dead reptile into wedges of syrupy meat, his vigor suggesting he was not just cutting out slabs to roast but imagining a siege. "After brothers get Essence, we go to surprise Abascar people. Kill them all. Take Cal-raven's prizes."

"House Abascar? Older Brother, you said four brothers would attack the chieftain. You change the plan?"

"Abascar"—Mordafey smiled—"is part of Mordafey's plan. After we go to Core, after we get Essence, brothers surprise Abascar people, steal prizes, take prisoners. Take it all back to the Core, to Skell Wra." Drool spilled down through his beard. "Skell Wra will be surprised. Four brothers back again so soon! He'll send us to the Sopper Crone. Brothers will have so much Essence, no Cent Regus will be stronger." He took a spear from the array of sharpened weapons set on jutting wall stones, lifted a wedge of reptile flesh, and held it over the fire. Blood and fat spat and sizzled, dripping into the flames. "Mordafey get Skell Wra's throne. Brothers be helpers. Strongest, richest, best."

Goreth struggled to grasp Mordafey's implications. "Take Abascar prisoners? Take Abascar prizes?" His lower lip quivered. "Four brothers do this?"

"Mordafey has more than brothers," he murmured. "Brothers will see. Everyone will see Mordafey's plan."

Goreth's senses were sharpening now that his twin had returned to the caves. Sucking on a slab of sliced lizard tail, he watched Jordam clutch a small bundle to his chest and crawl toward his den. His tattered cape hung down around him.

Jorn's presumed suffering amused Goreth, but something awakened when he saw Jordam hurt. Phantom jolts of pain jittered through his own body. "Same Brother, how did you get away?" he whispered.

"Remember the bloody gorrel trick?" Jordam laughed through a crimson grin, and then he made his way into his own hole in the wall to sleep.

"Bad day for Jordam," Goreth sighed. And then he said the name again. "Jordam." Strange—water ran from his eyes as he said it. "Jordam. My brother Jordam. Jordam is back."

Everything hurt—the wound of the Bel Amican dart, the trap's lash lines, the bruises from Mordafey's beating.

Beneath the skins in his own burrow, Jordam faced the wall and wished he had stayed at the glen. Already he missed the blue light, the smell of summer. Here in rank darkness, with that maddening bird rasping in the corner, he found color only when he closed his eyes and watched flares brought on by want of Essence.

Afraid that Mordafey would come searching for him, Jordam had crawled homeward, leaving the glen behind. Painstakingly he had crept across patches of ground crowded with Bel Amican snares, for where there were traps, no guards would be walking. He would find a way to slip back to the glen on another night. *Like sneaking off to O-raya's caves*, he thought.

On the stone pillow beside his head, he unfolded a large leaf and drew out two souvenirs. The golden vial of oil and the gloves that the Bel Amican woman had left beside the flower-crowned well, stained with the bitter juice of bruised flowers.

"Can't come back," he whispered, lifting the vial so the glass glittered in the firelight. "Not yet."

On the hook of a claw, the cork came loose, and the vial spoke an "oh" of surprise. A wave of warm perfume wafted across his face. He shoved the cork back to stop the scent from flooding the cavern. The fragrance filled his nostrils and lungs. Suddenly he understood.

He was drawn under the surface of a deep sleep. The plunge frightened him, and he seized the woman's gloves as if to take her hands.

12

CAL-RAVEN'S BARGAIN

Atop a wind-blasted hill in the Cent Regus wasteland, three vawn riders in ragged skins and feathers rode up to a crescent of ten tall stones that stood like worried watchmen.

King Cal-raven of Abascar dismounted, handed the reins to his guardsman, Tabor Jan, and spat out the bitterleaf he'd been chewing to keep himself awake. He surveyed the stones and the uneven blocks of an ancient platform that supported them. "This will do."

"I don't like it, my lord." Tabor Jan also took the reins of Jes-hawk's vawn as the archer jumped down to join Cal-raven. "They might recognize us. Better to stay invisible. We hunt so we don't have to trade."

"We trade because there's nothing to hunt." Trying to appear nonchalant as he shouldered a saddlebag, Cal-raven narrowed his eyes and watched the three strangers on the other side of the platform. Two merchants—blond-braided and scribbled with tattoos—wedged wooden blocks around the wheels of their wagons, while a white-wrapped giant stared at the Abascar riders who had hailed them. Then Cal-raven smiled broadly, and falsely, waving as the strangers fitted feedbags to the noses of their horses. "And we have an advantage," he added. "They don't know our secret."

"You're a stonemaster." Tabor Jan smiled. "And that's a stone foundation."

"If they threaten us, they'll sink knee-deep in molten rock." Cal-raven nodded. "Scharr ben Fray's favorite trick."

"So long as we can keep them on the platform," said Jes-hawk, reaching over his shoulder to count the feathered ends of his arrows. "And what if they have armed help hiding in those wagons? It could go badly."

"Or"—Cal-raven shrugged—"what if the wagons are heavy with valuable cargo? No, we watched them all night. There are only three. It's a fair fight, whatever happens. And this is Cent Regus country. I'll bet they want to get out of here as much as we do. Picking a fight would attract attention. And vultures."

He did not want to be here. Hungry Abascar survivors were hoping the riders would return to the Cliffs of Barnashum with a substantial catch. He had brought his two most resourceful hunters. Together they had moved north to the Cragavar forest and skirted its western edge through what was once Cent Regus farmland. Here in the haze and stench, the riders had hoped to catch small scavenging animals.

Instead they found the trail of this caravan. Surprised that anyone would lead horses through such a perilous region, Cal-raven decided to investigate, in hopes of making a trade or some other helpful discovery. When the merchants stopped for the night, Cal-raven kept his company a safe distance behind them.

Just before daybreak an unexpected prize stumbled into their camp. Now that prize was wrapped securely in a bundle on the back of Tabor Jan's vawn.

"If we play this game carefully," he told his companions, "we may go back with wagons, horses, cargo, and the merchants as well. Let's find out what they're doing here."

"You're not going to tell them who we—"

"It'll be just like the last time. You hold back. Stay in the saddle. We're just desperate Abascar hunters hungry for a trade. Do your best to look...you know..."

"Dangerous."

The standing stones, once supports for some Cent Regus fortification, provided no protection from the elements. The wind prowled around the hill's crest, whispering news of an advancing snowstorm through the sea of brambles.

The decorated strangers, a man and a woman too young to be seasoned merchants, stepped onto the twig-strewn foundation and introduced themselves as a husband and wife—Fadel and Anjee Tod. They appeared simple and unthreatening, despite their secretive glances.

But the giant—a pale traveler wrapped in winding white rags like burial clothes—did not follow them onto the stone dais. Instead he sat down on the dead grass, leaning against a wagon wheel. His unblinking eyes were fixed upon Cal-raven. The Abascar king shivered. Surely he would not be recognized here, so far from Abascar, clad in this primitive hunting garb of skins, feathers, paint, and leaves. Nevertheless, he felt exposed.

Borrowing names from the list of Abascar's honored dead, Jes-hawk introduced himself and his companions as Staub, Spohr, and Gregor. He declared that they were frustrated hunters seeking goats and deer for Abascar survivors. The merchants showed little interest, quietly spreading their warecloth on the stone blocks and eying the saddlebags on the Abascar vawns.

Jes-hawk laughed. "We have only a few treasures to offer in trade. But they are valuable indeed."

Cal-raven quickly tired of the display. His people had no use for precious stones, vawnskin boots, or bejeweled bracelets. Abascar needed food, supplies, and strength. But his mind began to drift when he caught sight of the sculpted stone ring on the young woman's hand.

The ring distracted him for reasons that his present company could not guess, kindling memories of a ring he had given to Auralia, that mysterious orphan girl in his father's dungeon. By Abascar tradition, the ring had represented a pledge of protection. But nothing could have saved Auralia from the Abascar cataclysm. He would never see her again.

The woman noticed his stare, and twisting the white beads in her long braids, she elbowed her partner. "Fadel. Husband. I don't think they want what we've got. Fold up the goods. Time to go."

But the man pressed on with forced friendliness, desperate to win a trade. "You like Anjee's ring? You can have it for a price." That set the woman to ranting.

Cal-raven gestured to the black clouds bearing cold cargo across the Cragavar forest. "You can see what's coming," he said. "Winter's not over. I'll go straight to our offer: Come with us. Join the Abascar survivors. King Cal-raven offers safety, shelter, food, and work. We're growing strong. When winter's done, we'll set up a proper house again. All we ask is that you contribute your wagons, your food, your horses, and your service."

The merchant woman smiled, amused. "Fadel and I have no desire to plant ourselves in some unknown house. Nor to bear the burdens of desperate people."

"Our honorable passenger," said the man, "has promised payment enough to keep us safe and warm for many seasons."

"Ha!" The sharp laugh from the bizarre stranger slapped Cal-raven to attention. "These dimwits have already forfeited half of what I promised them. And their compass is faulty. They'll lose the rest if they don't deliver me to Tilianpurth before those storms arrive."

"Tilianpurth?" Cal-raven's confidence faltered under the giant's hot, penetrating gaze. "That old Bel Amican bastion? Isn't it falling to pieces?"

"Come find out, why don't you?" The giant spoke oddly, as if unaccustomed to his own tongue. The corners of his smile quivered with effort, cracking the bone-white paint that caked his skullish face.

"Where'd you find such inspiring company?" Jes-hawk asked the merchants.

The man grimaced, and the woman explained. They'd found him wandering near the Cent Regus wilds on foot, and his story was suspicious. Returning from House Jenta on horseback, he had narrowly escaped when a powerful tentacle of some subterranean Cent Regus beast sprang up from the ground, seized his horse's leg, and snapped it. Fleeing on foot, he wandered into unfamiliar territory. "Or so he says." The woman's upper lip twitched. "Whatever the case, we saved his life. And trouble's all he's paid us for it."

Nevertheless, they had agreed to carry the disgruntled giant to Tilianpurth, cutting across these Cent Regus lands, for his promise of a generous payment upon arrival. "For two days he's complained." She clearly wanted sympathy. "And why? We're Fadel and Anjee Tod. The Tods have a long tradition of secure passage and reasonable trade. We're not the Fast Jandies."

"No, we're not the Fast Jandies," the man agreed. "Jandies would get you where you want to go, sure as there's water in Deep Lake. But they drive their horses so hard you'd be bruised from head to toe. And they don't stop for meals or rest. What sense do folks get of the country when they travel with the Fast Jandies, we ask ourselves?"

"They get *no* sense of the country," the merchants agreed in two-part harmony.

"A sense of the country?" the stranger hissed, his harsh smile never faltering. He pulled a bottle from his sleeve, sniffed vapors from it, sighed, and concealed it again. "What good is that if you make me late? And if my belongings disappear along the road?"

"It's rugged ground, old man." The woman waved her arms. "Bags fall out of wagons. And the birds in this wilderness are thieves."

"What have you lost?" Jes-hawk gestured to the vawns. "We're hunters and trackers. We find all kinds of things in the wild."

"Find my belongings." The smiling giant gave the order as if these were his servants. Then he buttered his tone, as if testing another sort of persuasion. "If you can restore them to me, I'll repay you with more rewards than you'll find in a hundred hunts." Seizing his polished walking stick, he rose and looked down on them all, wobbling on legs that seemed new to him. "You have the word of a Seer from House Bel Amica."

Yes, of course. The eyes. He had seen the Seers when they visited House Abascar as ambassadors from Bel Amica. They always arrived in elaborate costumes and detailed makeup, not these white shreds. But they stared with the same penetrating gaze.

The Seer stepped up to a tumbleweed and produced a crystal vial from his ragged wrap. With the curling black nails of his spindly fingers, he withdrew the cork and let one drop, red as a ruby, fall. The tumbleweed sparked into flames. The crackling tangle surprised the merchants' horses; all five whinnied into their feedbags and took anxious steps forward so that the wagon wheels strained against their blocks.

"A Seer of Bel Amica!" Tabor Jan shouted from the vawn. "What luck! Seems we've been bargaining with the wrong people. House Abascar would thank us if we brought back potions like that."

"I'm not a Seer *of* Bel Amica," said the painted man through his manic smile. "I am a Seer *in* Bel Amica. Seers do not belong to any house.

We go where our counsel is valued. House Bel Amica listens well, and Queen Thesera thrives." He clucked his tongue. "House Abascar didn't listen, and it's a shame what happened after we were sent away. Perhaps we can offer counsel to Abascar's new king."

Furious, Cal-raven almost came to his feet, but Jes-hawk reached out and grasped his arm.

Tabor Jan answered in haste. "Abascar's last king lacked good counsel, it is true. But Abascar has a new king now. This king has a vision all his own. It has saved him from despair and rash mistakes. He has united a people once divided and given them hope. I'll tell him of your eagerness to help. Tell me your name."

"My name?" The Seer hesitated. His large eyeballs swiveled to fix upon Cal-raven. "We Seers keep our true names to ourselves. But in the order of the Seers, I am called Pretor Xa." He pronounced the name as if casting a spell, exaggerating the last syllable for effect—*kZAH.*

Tabor Jan played the part of the high-ranking hunter all too well. "Honorable Pretor Xa, if you provide House Abascar with help, we would be in your debt. We can offer you gratitude in advance. Let us tell you something about your colorful escorts."

The merchants, folding up their ware-cloth, looked up in surprise.

"These merchants—they've lied to you. They have not traveled these lands for many years as they claim. Nor are they husband and wife. They're deserters from Abascar."

In the stunned silence that followed, both merchants drew their weapons.

The merchant's face went red as a rash. "We're not Abascars, Anjee and me!"

"*Generations,*" the woman blasted. "The Tods have spent *generations* on this road."

"You think we don't recognize you?" Tabor Jan dismounted and strode forward. "Fadel and Anjee Tod are musicians, alive and well among Abascar's people. You're Damyn and Lira, son and daughter of two notorious Abascar thieves. I arrested your father, Filup, myself and cast him to the Gatherers years ago. When Abascar fell, you were seen with him, looting and making off with all you could steal."

Damyn dropped to his knees. His dagger clattered to the ground. He clutched his chest, wheezing.

"Have a care!" shrieked his sister, running to kneel beside him. "Damyn's breathing is a mess."

Cal-raven nodded. "I'm sure. Many took in too much smoke and dust when House Abascar collapsed. You stayed in the rubble too long."

Damyn's face purpled with rage, but he could only cough out feeble objections.

The Seer scowled. "I've searched the wagons. My precious belongings are nowhere to be found."

"Listen to them," sneered Lira, clinging to her brother as if he were a piece of wreckage in the sea. "Abascar's last king poisoned our great house. Vision? It was all lies. And now they're trusting his son?" She turned to the Seer and pointed at the Abascar vawns. "Search their saddlebags. I'll bet *they* stole your precious jewels. While we were camped."

"We may not be rich in resources," said Tabor Jan. "But we are rich in honor. Why bother stealing when it's so much more fun to catch thieves?" He reached to the heavy bundle on the back of his vawn and untied the rope that bound it. "Here's something you might recognize." The bag fell open. Another blond-braided man tumbled out. Tabor Jan hoisted the rope-bound captive onto the stones and rolled him like a fire log toward the merchants.

"Father!" Lira leapt to her feet and ran forward. "You've killed him!"

"Oh, Filup's very much alive," laughed Tabor Jan. "Last night, thinking he was getting away with the treasure, he stumbled into our camp, startled the vawns, and got his face smashed by...that." He gestured to his vawn's clubbed tail. The reptile snorted. "And there, beside him. That's what fell from his hands."

An ornamental wooden box lay beside the vawn's foot. Glittering, crystalline crumbs spilled out.

The Seer hissed through his grin. He seemed even taller now, and Cal-raven flexed his fingers as the giant stepped up onto the stone foundation and stalked across it, his eyes on the box.

"They probably plotted this trick before approaching you." Tabor Jan scowled down at the captive. "They sent this fellow on ahead in the dark."

"The stones, the dust...we don't know what they are." Cal-raven watched the Seer carefully. "They're cold as ice, but they don't melt. They're important?"

"They have...sentimental value." As the Seer knelt to scoop them up, the hostage woke and struggled against his restraints. "They're from my homeland. A long story, actually." Standing, he addressed Tabor Jan with a gentleness more unsettling than any snarl. "You'll have an extravagant reward." As if this were some ceremonial vow, he struck the platform with the polished silver ferrule on the end of his staff. The shiny metal cap sparked against the stone, and Cal-raven was surprised to feel a ripple of power spread through the ground beneath his feet.

"In twelve days," the Seer announced, "on this very hilltop, I'll bring House Abascar a caravan full of supplies. Your people will call you heroes."

Cal-raven held his breath when the Seer turned that broad, bright grin toward him and spoke with the gloating tone of someone who has gained an advantage. "Take these words of counsel back to your king. Bring all the wagons you can. I will provide all that you can carry back to your hideaway. And bring your best defenders. It's beastman country. We're bound to attract attention."

"Why must we meet here?" asked Jes-hawk. "Why not meet where we—"

"Done," Tabor Jan forcefully declared. "It's only wise to keep our refuge secret for now. Further, we know this place. We've tested it."

Cal-raven scowled. His guardsman was enjoying this too much. But he played along, worried that the Seer had already seen through their charade. "Well said, master." Then he walked to the merchants, who were crouching beside their fallen father. "The Seer's right. This wilderness is harsh. It can ruin people. Turn them into animals. But King Cal-raven's ordered us to show mercy, even in this forbidding land. The world has given House Abascar a second chance, and so we'll extend a second chance to you. You refused our generous offer. But if you deliver this Bel Amican to Tilianpurth as you promised and join our meeting here in twelve days, we'll make you the offer again. We'll bring you home."

The white-wrapped giant licked the perfect teeth of his smile. "Forgiveness for such deserters will not help Abascar survive. But I still need what these monsters can give me."

"Surely you won't travel with them now," laughed Jes-hawk.

"Oh, they won't harm me," said the Seer. His confidence was frightfully convincing. "Now that I understand them, I'm sure that I can provide proper motivation."

Tabor Jan climbed back into his saddle. "In twelve days then. Here, on this hilltop. We will meet you and—"

"And," interrupted the Seer, turning to Cal-raven, "invite your King Cal-raven to make the journey with you. I'll make it worth his while."

Tabor Jan scowled. "Our king would never risk such a journey. But…what are you offering?"

"News. News for his ears and no one else's." The Seer's smile expanded. "News about what he has lost."

"In Abascar's calamity," Cal-raven murmured, "our king lost more than he can measure."

"Oh, this loss wounded him long before Abascar's calamity." The Seer turned and tapped his staff against the ground. "I must give my attention to these three now if I am to reach Tilianpurth before the storm breaks." With each touch of his staff, the stone foundation quaked with other-worldly power.

Cal-raven watched the caravan depart, paralyzed, the Seer's words ringing in his ears.

13

AMBUSH ON THE BRIDGE

I f I run..." Wood splintered as Jordam's grip tightened around the shovel's handle. "rrMordafey will find me."

A ring of silver afternoon sunlight outlined the massive stone that sealed him alone in the den. Worry gnawed at him. Mordafey was gone, and he had taken his brascle for help on a hunt. That did not surprise him. But Goreth was missing too, and Goreth never left Jordam behind.

Jordam hoisted another shovelful of lizard bones and carrion into the old bone cart. The stench filled the den, oozing from the rotting remains, maddening the frenzied flesh-flies. Mordafey usually bullied Jorn into clearing the den, but Jorn was gone.

"Like being in another snare," he said.

Jordam had never been so frightened by Mordafey's temper. Mordafey had no patience left, no capacity to listen. He was growing desperate—they all were. If they did not go to the Core for Essence soon, they would lose their wits and turn against each other. But there was more to Mordafey's rage than thirst. Jordam suspected it had something to do with the plot to move against the Abascar survivors.

Jordam gave the bone cart a shove, and the wheel began to turn. He stopped halfway up the ramp, set the cart down, and shook out his mane. His wits were still half-asleep in the fog of the Bel Amican slumberseed oil. He wondered if the woman had gone back to look for it. Or to look for him. He wondered if she would ever find him there waiting for her.

Reaching the entrance, he shoved the boulder aside. Cold sunlight blasted in. He pushed the cart out under the high dome of the entry cave. Something shifted against the wall, and he jumped with a bark.

Wrapped in a woodscloak, Goreth sat in the shadow, rocking and staring at an object cradled in his hands.

"Goreth, you hurt? rrMordafey beat you?"

"Turtle." Goreth choked. Forlorn, he pawed at the object. "Turtle."

Jordam dropped to all fours. "Show me."

Goreth held two pieces of a turtle shell that had been torn open and cleaned out. "I tried to follow Older Brother. He got angry."

Jordam reached for the shell halves, but Goreth snarled and jerked them back. "*My* turtle!"

"rrMordafey. Where is he?"

Goreth scratched at his side with his hind foot. "Brothers are leaving me. Young Brother, gone. Dead maybe. Older Brother gone too. Same Brother..." Goreth cast Jordam a suspicious glance. "Where do you go now?"

"Dumping bones." Jordam thrust the cart through the maze of egg-shaped stones, out into the daylight to the edge of the chasm. He dumped the remains over the edge and heard them clatter in the dry creek bed far below. Goreth had followed him. "Where's Mordafey?"

"Gone. Angry." Goreth slumped down and stared through the brightening rock formations across the chasm. "Told me to watch you."

Jordam knelt beside him. "rrWhat did he say?"

Goreth swatted at invisible pests and grabbed his shoulders as if wrestling with himself.

"rrWhere's Mordafey? rrTell me, or I go find him myself."

Goreth's whimper twisted. Quick as a snake strike, he pounced on Jordam. The back of Jordam's head hit the ground and rang like a bell. He opened his eyes and stared into Goreth's crooked fangs and felt pressure on both sides of his skull as his brother sought to smash it between his hands.

"Essence!" Goreth screamed, foam flying from his lips. "Thirsty!"

Jordam jerked his knees back to his chest and, splaying the claws on his feet, launched Goreth skyward. Limbs flung wide in surprise, Goreth plunged past, and his fingers caught the cliff's edge.

Leaping to the precipice, Jordam broke a bulge of stone free and raised it high. He saw his own threatening silhouette reflected in Goreth's wild eyes. "Never fight me," he roared. "rrRemember? Never fight Same Brother, or he'll clean out your skull." *Like...* Jordam glanced to the halves of turtle shell at the edge of the precipice. He cursed the slumberseed oil for deluding him and slammed the stone down on the edge beside Goreth's grip. "Where's Mordafey?"

"Gone. To break Young Brother free."

"Jorn? Mordafey says brothers must fight together. Not go off alone." He bent to clasp Goreth's wrists and pulled him back up to the edge.

Goreth fell at his feet and folded like a frightened cub, holding his head. "Older Brother says we make too much trouble. Jordam keeps secrets. I forget too much."

"Secrets?" Jordam pointed out into the canyon. "Mordafey runs off. Mordafey leaves you and me alone." He took Goreth by the ears and pulled him to his feet. Leaning in, he knocked his broken browbone against his brother's. "Think, Goreth. Same Brothers stay together. Same Brothers don't hurt each other. We help each other. But Jorn hates us. And Mordafey keeps secrets."

"Older Brother is strong," Goreth whispered. "Older Brother hurts us."

A ruckus rose from the canyon below—a riot of scissorjaws fighting over the carrion that Jordam had dumped into the gorge.

"Want Mordafey to stop hurting us?" Jordam gestured to the wire lines crisscrossing his arms and chest. "Bel Amicans have bad traps. All around their fort. rrMordafey doesn't know. If he goes to get Jorn, bad traps will catch him. No more plans. No more Essence. But if Same Brothers help him, then no more angry Mordafey. No more beatings." Jordam shook his twin by the shoulders. "Think, Goreth. After we save Mordafey from traps, then what happens?"

"Older Brother takes us to chieftain."

"Essence. So much strength."

Goreth forced a smile. "Rockbeetles."

Jordam eyed the pallet of loot near the entryway. Bundles of spears, blue-edged cloaks, firestarters, harnesses. Prizes from the ruins of Abascar.

Brass breastplates and battered helmets stripped from the slaughtered Bel Amicans. *Deuneroi.* Jordam cringed at the thought of Mordafey creeping into the glen where the woman would be waiting.

"We run. Together." Jordam strapped a bundle of Bel Amican cast-arrows to his leg. "rrFaster than any Cent Regus."

Shoving his arms through the sleeves of the largest soldier's cloak, he stretched and tore the seams. The brothers, unlike many beastmen, boasted in the uniforms of their kills, wearing them as trophies while never daring to admit any pleasure taken in the warmth, the protection, the concealment. He tightened a length of rope as a belt.

"Are you fast, Goreth?" Jordam looked at the empty bone cart. "Ready?" He seized the cart and flung it aside as easily as if it were a bone from a meal. It exploded into wreckage against the wall, and the wooden wheel fell and rolled in widening, wild circles until it toppled and spun on its hub.

Goreth lifted the halves of turtle shell and examined them, face contorted somewhere between rage and revulsion. Then he threw them hard at the wall, roaring as they shattered. "Ready now." He crouched, muzzle wrinkling in gleeful anticipation. "I'm faster than Same Brother."

Jordam grinned. "Try to keep up."

Goreth's tail slapped the stones behind him. "But we stop if I smell honey."

Mordafey's tracks were obvious and careless. But Jordam's concern turned to amazement when he and Goreth stumbled across a patch of disturbed ground.

"Many Cent Regus." Goreth's brows bunched in bewilderment, the blue scar on his cheek squirming. "Moving together."

The power of so many Cent Regus working together with Mordafey among them terrified Jordam. *Mordafey has more than brothers. He said so. No signs here of a fight. He's gathering an army. Without us.* He traced the jumbled tracks further, then stopped at an unfamiliar print. *Or someone else gathers them. Someone tells Mordafey what to do. That explains his frustration.*

"Did Older Brother go with them?" Goreth stared off to the southeast.

"rrNo. Here. Mordafey goes north. See? Tracks. We ask him. When we catch him."

"When I catch him. You're too slow."

They were off again, lumbering along like weary bulls, following a faint scent that came clearer as they left the trampled ground behind. As they moved into thick brush, Goreth found tufts of Mordafey's brindled fur in the bushes.

Soon the smell of a river—a thin tributary of the distant Throanscall—drew them off course in pursuit of a drink. Silent and deep, the river moved through a time-smoothed gully. They were near an old bridge where travelers who still risked this territory often crossed.

Twirl-bugs descended from overhanging boughs, spinning as they dangled beneath netlike wings that sifted the air for prey. Eight-legged clutchers, hairy and black, huddled under fallen trees and waited to pounce on unsuspecting birds. Jordam had always admired such stealthy hunting. He prowled along the bank, hungry for prey.

While Goreth drank, Jordam looked up to the top of the gully, to the dead trees swaying in slow circles on the steep banks, their needled boughs intertwined. *As though holding each other up.*

Beyond the trees he saw Mordafey's brascle hovering, high enough to be only a speck. But Jordam knew brascles could see a flea on a mouse at that height—perhaps even smell that flea as well. The bird had stopped in the air to mark a target for Mordafey. A strike would ensue. "Mordafey's close, Goreth."

A tailtwitcher, fat in its winter coat, clung upside down to a branch and lashed its bushy tail in code to another nearby. Snowbirds sang garbled tales to each other, keeping their distance. Ice cracked in the shadows.

Jordam lowered his head to drink and spotted a fat-bodied eel writhing along the riverbed. It was not what he would have preferred to hunt, but his belly demanded he catch whatever came along. He braced himself for a dive.

"Better?" asked Goreth. "Taste better than well water?"

"What?"

"Well water in a bucket. Blue flowers. A Bel Amican woman." Goreth lowered his voice in caution. "You talked in your sleep. Older Brother got angry."

Jordam's heartbeat broke into a run. "rrWhat else did I say?"

"You shouted. Tetherwings."

Jordam's grip tightened on a stem of shoreweed, and he slowly uprooted it. "Dreams, Goreth," he whispered. "I was dreaming."

A breeze, brumal and swift, wrinkled the surface of the water as it swept upriver, bearing the aroma of bread, spices, strange perfumes, the sweat of horses.

Goreth and Jordam drew back into the brambles. An eel was food, but horses could be a feast.

Jordam moved forward stealthily, the hunter awakening. Only wealthy travelers moved in carriages built for rugged roads. And those who did knew better than to drive horses across dangerous lands. These were fools, an easy catch. Maybe deranged survivors from Abascar. Or thieves.

Caught in the horizontal beams of evening—two wagons hitched together, drawn by five horses, had come to the edge of the bridge. The wagons, covered with stretched canvases of sun-bleached skins, appeared unguarded. The massive, muscular horses were desert mounts, built like boulders, the sort of animal that could withstand the sandstorms of the south.

Goreth arched his back like a predatory cat. He fingered the hilt of the Abascar sword. The kill-fever was setting in, fueled by a trace of Essence still in the blood. Jordam touched the hilt of the knife strapped at his calf. "Might be many blades inside. rrMight be archers. And scouts." He unsheathed the knife and licked the blade clean. "I'm hungry."

The hooves of the foremost horse clopped onto the bridge, and the first set of wheels creaked along behind.

"Who drives the horses?" Jordam whispered.

"Can't see. Maybe nobody."

Just as Jordam tensed to spring, a shadow fell across him. He turned, whimpering, to stare up at the looming woods. The tremor in his heart was as familiar as it was frightening. He had felt it when that massive monster rushed up to him as he stood over O-raya. But this time he did not see the Keeper. The shadow was only a cloud of sailbats taking flight from the trees, moving as if directed by a single mind until they scattered in chase of duskflies.

Jordam looked back toward the bridge and blinked, his thoughts divided.

His appetite surged, just as it had when the Bel Amican woman stepped into the glen. But his thoughts fought against that impulse. A sense that something was watching him lingered.

As the second cart's wheels touched the stone span, the brothers watched a shadow come loose from underneath the bridge, gripping one of the stones along its lower arch. Mordafey swung himself up onto the span.

One of the horses tried to bolt, slipped, and went down with a scream. Goreth bounded to the bridge in seven strides, sword in his hand.

Jordam hesitated and then, afraid to be seen holding back, joined the charge. With every stride he gave himself to his fiery instinct. His knife in one hand, he unsheathed a cast-arrow with the other.

Mordafey attacked from the front, killing the lead horse to stall the parade. Goreth attacked from the rear, leaping into the second wagon.

A woman with long yellow braids clambered out from the front of that wagon. She took one look at Mordafey, screamed, jumped to the bridge, and dove into the water. When she surfaced, caught in the river's freezing grip, she was still, head bloodied, limbs splayed, borne away without resistance.

Jordam lunged at the canvas drape on the front carriage and slashed through to get at the cargo within. He found no cargo. Instead, he found himself standing between two passengers.

A giant of a man, bundled in white strips of cloth, regarded Jordam from where he sat. His pale head was wrapped in a green headdress. He held a bloodied rider's whip in one hand, and a long, polished walking stick in the other. Seated with unnatural calm, the passenger regarded Jordam as if annoyed.

Across from him a man wearing a plain brown sack, with bloodstained yellow braids and crimson stripes whipped across his tattooed arms, lay slumped on the floor of the wagon, gagged and bound. When he saw Jordam, he struggled to his knees and tried to stand.

"You see," the giant sneered to the man, "you've scorned those who showed you the way to safety. And now the beastmen have come."

The smell of blood scattered Jordam's thoughts. Only impulse remained. He leaned in close, as he had so many times before, to let the hostage see his teeth. With a swipe so swift the man never saw it coming, Jordam neatly carved a line from one ear to the other, breaking both joints of the man's jaw. Then Jordam hooked him between the ribs with his knife, lifted him, and cast him out through the torn canvas. The man hit the bridge wall and bounced back between the wagon wheels as the horses lurched forward.

Jordam turned, and the giant struck him directly in his forehead's shield bone with the gleaming silver ferrule on the end of the walking stick. The rod looked dull as a tree branch, but something flared from its tip. The jolt of it splintered through Jordam's bones like lightning. He fell through the canvas, struck the bridge wall, and rolled back underneath the wagon. His knife scudded out of reach.

The giant jumped out of the wagon, his boots landing near Jordam's head. He thrust the walking stick through the spokes of the rear wagon wheels. The horses struggled to pull their cargo. Jordam crawled out from behind the wagons and saw Mordafey battle-ax another blond-braided man who must have climbed from the second carriage. This one was muscular, shirtless, and covered in tattoos. But he was already dead as Mordafey drove him back against the wall. He fell over and down to the river in pieces. Somewhere high above, the brascle shrieked in delight.

Mordafey grabbed Jordam by the throat, his face contorted with rage. "Fool! Why follow? Mordafey needs no help!"

"You said brothers can't go off alone," Jordam snarled back. "Too dangerous, you said. Stronger, better if four brothers stand together!"

As the horses strained, the carriages began to edge forward.

"Jordam failed Mordafey. And Jorn failed Mordafey. And Goreth, he forgets everything. Mordafey is finished with brothers. Mordafey will make his plan alone."

"Alone?" Jordam sucked in a breath, then took a gamble. "We saw them, Mordafey. Many Cent Regus. Helping you."

Mordafey's eyes flashed.

"But I am strong, Mordafey. rrFastest Cent Regus alive. And Goreth— nothing stops Goreth when he has a blade. Jorn? Jorn frightens everything. Four brothers cannot lose."

Mordafey hesitated, considering. "You still want to be part of Mordafey's plan?"

"rrYes. Four brothers stay together," said Jordam.

"Go get Jorn. Bring Jorn back. Fast. Or Mordafey goes to Skell Wra for Essence and leaves Jordam and Jorn behind."

"Me? Go get Jorn? Alone?"

A quake rocked Mordafey's body, and Jordam felt a spark pass through them both. Mordafey's eyes rolled backward, his head fell forward, and his browbone collided with Jordam's. The giant had struck him in the back of his head.

Mordafey shook himself to his senses, eyes wild and wide, and scrambled backward along the bridge.

Like a crab, Jordam thought, lying still. He had never seen this expression on Mordafey's face. Surprise. Terror.

Mordafey addressed his attacker, much to Jordam's surprise, in the language of the weakerfolk. "You," said Mordafey. "You."

The smiling giant raised a small wooden box in his hand, shaking it like a rattle. "You should find out who you are hunting before you decide to strike."

"Mordafey made mistake." Mordafey held up his hands in surrender. "Mordafey...not recognize—"

"Cent Regus fool. So zealous." Sneering, the man struck again, and tremors racked Mordafey's frame until he lay limp against the stones. "You wanted power so badly. Look what it did to you when you found it."

Jordam had felt the lightning from that walking stick. It shook him to see his unbreakable older brother reduced to whimpers. He lunged, struck the giant in the side, and toppled him into a storm of white strips. The wooden box skidded to the base of the wall, spilling a crystalline dust. The man scrambled after it.

Jordam rose, hoisted Mordafey's body over his head, then staggered to the bridge wall and dropped him into the water, knowing the shock would revive him. Mordafey surfaced, thrashing and cursing.

The giant found his feet and spun toward Jordam, eyes lodged sideways in his head, teeth of his blaring grin falling loose in his mouth. Jordam sprinted to the horses, and the icy spear of the giant's voice ran right through him, a shriek unlike the voice of any man or beast.

He heard a crash and glanced back. Goreth had unlatched the second wagon and turned it on its side. This distracted the giant. Jordam shouted to warn his twin, and Goreth yelped and dove off the bridge. In the water he helped his stunned, splashing older brother reach the shore.

Go get Jorn. Bring Jorn back. Jordam seized on Mordafey's order and turned north and east toward a vast region of trees that cowered beneath a mountainous, imminent storm. He had no time to test the horses' tolerance for a Cent Regus rider. He had one hope. He was fast.

The giant came for Jordam.

But Jordam ran.

Unleashed, he could not be caught or slowed by anything but his own thoughts. So it was that while he left the bridge, the gully, the territory behind, bounding into the Cragavar forest, questions gave chase like wolves. Questions about Mordafey's tracks among those of a Cent Regus mob; about the dangers of breaking into the bastion for Jorn; about the white giant, that specter made of pieces that did not quite fit; about Mordafey's astonished recognition of that very stranger.

He felt as if he were slipping between shifting plates of stone. Above, the storm's swift clouds sealed off all sight of stars, the heavens readying winter's final assault. Below, the ground began to quake with a new season's burgeoning life. He was caught in the tension, swept along like a fallen leaf, lost and vulnerable. The woods would be full of dangers—traps, soldiers, arrows, and, most dangerous of all, a quiet distraction.

Go in fast, he told himself. *Find Jorn.*

14

OUT OF THE PRISON PIT,
INTO THE FIREPLACE

The ale boy studied his shoes and wondered if he could eat them. The leather made him think of sausages Obsidia Dram had boiled for his supper in Abascar's Underkeep.

Fainter all the time, he imagined ghosting between the bars, past the guard, and ascending without touching a stair. Slipping into the towerhouse, he'd find a kitchen and fall into the kindness of the dark-haired sisterly, she who had brought him a bread roll, cheese crumbs, and apples neatly sliced on the first day of his confinement. Full and satisfied, he would drift out the front gate, escape the valley of whitegrass, surprise Rumpa, and spirit away to Auralia's caves. Unless the Keeper deigned to point him to some new task, he would sleep beside a small fire and listen for voices to visit him from the flames.

Anything—even a delusion about shoes made of sausage—was better than worrying about the answers he had given to Ryllion's interrogation and waiting for more punishing questions.

"A witness." That's what Ryllion feared. But a witness to what? The boy could not dispel the soldiers' suspicion. Days in this muddy pit had given him time to wonder if Ryllion knew his mind better than he did. Maybe he *had* seen something important out there in the Cragavar. But all he found worth recalling was the sight of young Wynn and little Cortie moving ahead through the trees into the care of Abascar's guards, who descended from highwatches in the trees near Barnashum. After that there was only the long, lonesome ride through grey lands. If he remained in this prison pit much longer without a meal or warmth, there wouldn't be any-thing left in his head for Ryllion to investigate.

Meanwhile the prison guard could find nothing better to do than empty the pockets of his gravy-stained uniform. On a thick woolen mat he had spread across the soil, he scattered a collection of picked-this-up-somewhere and can't-remember-what-this-is. "Kramm this mud pit," he muttered. "Dirt walls. Dirt floor. This place needs some heavy work."

Through the fog of his delusion, the ale boy surveyed the guard's col-lection, and before his eyes it was transformed. He saw an array of new inventions sent by Auralia herself. A candle embedded with shell fragments from the flotsam of Deep Lake. A necktie of dried seaweed. Keys carved from prongbull horn. A door knocker—a purple crab shell with a round stone tied between its pinchers.

But when he blinked, they were ordinary objects again—coins, game pieces, a sharpening stone, buttons, the keys to the prisoners' cages, and a blunt tusk which the guard held up in the red torchlight.

"Can't wait to show this to my boys," said the guard.

The ale boy studied him again. The officer seemed too young to be a father—too arrogant to be a good one, anyway. The fellow had a face like a yellow squash and skin wrinkled as if he slept facedown in bathwater. His nose had been broken, and there were spots like bruises under his eyes.

As if sensing the ale boy's doubt, the guard went on, "My sons have yet to arrive in the world, mind you, but they'll get here. My lady, Kyntere, back at the sovereign house by the sea, she's got a brand-new apple that's ripe and ready to scream." He patted his belly. "When spring comes, I'll go back home to my brand-new baby. I got a bet with old Bauris. Told him it's a boy. Gonna name him Garbal, just like the man who made him. I'll give him this." He ogled the tusk as if it were treasure. "Recognize it? Know what it is?"

The beastman ran his pink tongue across his own tusks.

"My lady's a netter. She nets fish, grease-eels, sea greens, everything. Being loaded with Garbal's boy hasn't slowed her down a bit. So here's the story—she snagged this sea boar by accident one day. It's a danger. I hap-pened to be standing there. Wrestled that boar down. Took this souvenir.

That pretty much settled it." Garbal sneered garishly. "Maybe I'll give him one of your tusks instead."

The beastman laughed, brash and defiant, pacing like a panther. House Abascar's Gatherers had claimed that some beastmen were smart enough to understand the Common tongue. This prisoner had somehow recognized the heiress, and he had known how to crush her spirit by shouting out a name. *Deuneroi*. The boy wondered if Auralia's beastman had ever spoken to her.

"Look at those chompers of yours, you flea-infested freak. You're part boar, aren't you?" The guard pocketed the tusk and slapped the knife sheath at his belt. "Shall we cut you open, find out what else you're made of? Teeth. Bones. That's all my boys will ever see of Cent Regus filth. You're less than human, all those critters mixed up in your blood. When Ryllion's a captain, we're gonna clean out the beastman house for good." He threw a nutshell at the beastman and spoke through a conspiratorial grin. "The Seers are going to help him, he says. He's going to trick the Cent Regus."

The beastman dug at the brittle ground with his hind feet like a bull pawing before a charge. Soil sprayed against the back wall.

"The Cent Regus are so blind and stupid that they'll play right into Ryllion's hands. But you won't live to see that, friend. You're just a little stinger-fly who tried but couldn't sting. Something we swatted on our way to smash the hive."

The beastman hunched down as if to spring right through the bars.

The ale boy cleared his throat. "Officer Garbal?"

Garbal recoiled as if he'd just been addressed by a pile of potatoes.

"I just wondered, wull...if you would talk with me instead."

"You wondered."

"I have stories you'd find interesting. I could tell you a few. About Abascar, or the Keeper, or beastmen if you like. "

"The Keeper? Ballyworms, boy, you think I want to hear about your superstitious notions? I thought you were tired of questions. You should keep quiet and count yourself lucky that Ryllion's distracted today."

"Distracted?"

"Since the heiress's crew arrived, Ryllion's been spreading more traps for beastmen. So I get to watch you like some kinda nurse in a baby room." The guard launched a nutshell, and it bounced off the ale boy's cheek. "You're a waste of my time. An Abascar leftover. Ryllion says he found you carrying some kind of crazy scarf. Probably belonged to your mother, yes?" He rested another shell on his knee and flicked it. One of the cell bars pinged. "Tell me that story, boy. Did you try to pull her out from under Abascar when it all caved in?"

The boy turned his attention to the beastman, whose claws were carving deeper ruts into the earth. Then a hind claw snagged for a moment on a stone deep in a rut. Before the ale boy could grasp the danger, the beastman jerked the fist-sized stone from the earth and threw it.

Garbal lay still for a moment. The rock fell back out of his face. Beneath the brim of his helmet, where his eyes and nose had been, blood poured out. His legs began to kick. His teeth clacked together. Then he stopped kicking.

The beastman turned to the back of the cage, reached through the bars to the wall, and dug furiously until his fingers curled around a long, winding, petrified root. He tore it out, slapped it against the ground as if killing a snake, then flung its forked, torn end outward to Garbal's mat. He fished at it until he hooked the cage keys.

As the beastman's bars swung open and a gruesome clamor erupted, the ale boy pressed his hands to his ears and clenched his eyes shut.

Keeper, aren't you watching? Won't you come and fly me out of here?

When the only noise he could hear was the thunder of his pulse, the ale boy opened his eyes. The remains of the beastman's feast were strewn across the floor, glistening and strange.

The boy also saw the keys. The beastman had dropped them and fled, forgetting all about him in his hurry. They lay within reach.

The ale boy floated across the cell. He ascended the stairs without touching a step. Or so he would swear to anyone who heard his tale in the days to come.

He drifted into the night air, every moment of freedom in Tilianpurth more surprising than the last. He sang quietly to himself the Early Evening

Verse of House Abascar as he passed through the dormant garden patches and a stand of brittle beanstalks.

The front gates were open, probably to bait the beastman out of hiding with the promise of escape across the moat. But the boy could see the nervous guards crouched along the wall above the gate, arrows to their casters. If he could see the trap, surely the beastman could.

The guards had reason to be afraid and infuriated. As the boy had emerged, he'd seen soldiers, wild-eyed and shaken, carting away the bodies of the prison pit guards. Two pools of blood reflected torchlight in the frosted moss. He turned away, too weary to acknowledge such horrors.

His capture was imminent, so he felt no urge to hide. He only hoped to find some food before the Bel Amicans caught their fugitive.

Passing through the stables, he offered a timid smile to a trembling stablehand, a boy his own age who held a manure shovel as if it were a weapon. "Don't be afraid," said the ale boy. The stablehand ignored him, watching for the beastman.

When the ale boy snatched a pear from a feed basket and took a bite, a blanketed mare, just out of reach, sighed. The boy handed it over. "Were you hoping for this?" He was surprised at how gingerly she plucked it from his hand.

He removed his travel-worn tunic and plunged his head, shoulders, and arms into a water barrel. He jerked back out, amazed that water could be so cold without freezing solid. That woke him up. The dust and sweat of his recent ordeal dripped away to the straw-strewn floor, and he climbed back into his shirt.

Torches drew their soldiers along, flames blurring into streams of light like comets across the sky. He walked through the riot of activity as if he were a drunkard lost in the midst of a dance.

Creeping around the back of the towerhouse, he gazed up at the tower. Each window framed witnesses to the courtyard chaos. All of Tilianpurth was caught up in the drama of the beastman's escape. Beyond the tower a new threat expanded to fill the sky. Even if he could talk his way out of this bastion, how would he endure the imminent snowstorm without his faithful vawn?

He approached the door at the back of the towerhouse. An explosive cough distracted him. A guard sat in the shadows beside the door. The boy forgot his strategy for a moment, startled by the unusual uniform. The man wore a bedbag over his armor, the kind of cushioned sack that soldiers crawled inside when they slept out in the wilderness, and he had pulled it up to his armpits as a defense against the cold.

"Won't it be difficult to run if the beastman comes after you?" the boy asked, surprised by his own voice.

"I am the one who asks the questions here," the guard responded without looking at him.

The boy waited for questions. But the guard sank back into silence, blinking with the world-weary eyes of an old tortoise.

The guard swelled to fill his armor like bread rising in too small a pan. He had a face of fleshy cheeks, a nose like a hairy brown sprout, and a scowl supported by a jutting lower lip. A growth above one eye looked like it had been polished, round and shiny as a grape.

As the boy reached for the door, another congested wheeze burst from the man. "Bring me a bottle, would you? A bottle of something that burns."

The boy almost laughed. The guard's request seemed like a voice from Abascar's Underkeep. "It would be my pleasure, sir. Tell me your name, and I will fetch it straightaway."

"My name? They shout it all the time, but it's easily mistaken for a curse. *Caroon* this, *Caroon* that. Who do you call to accomplish a job that a bag of apples could do? Wilus Caroon!"

The boy had observed enough soldiers to guess that this one was kept in the dark on important matters. "Sir, there's a beastman loose in the yard. Seems to me you're doing a good thing here, guarding the towerhouse."

"All the young busters get to chase that villain around. I get stuck by the back door." He laughed, a sound like a rockslide. "I don't mind. I've chased plenty of Cent Regus monsters and carved up those I caught. But now I keep the old sword handy just so I can scratch those hard-to-reach places down the back, you know?" Absently, he scratched at a patch of insect bites on his neck. "You'll be old soon," he said. "One day you'll get shoved into a dark corner behind a pile of bricks. You'll want to ride away and start over, but your joints will ache. And you'll itch in so many places that you need to sleep on a bed o' nails."

This talk made the ale boy anxious. It was far too early to think about getting old. "Beggin' your pardon, sir, but why's everyone out here at Tilian-purth? Is there a battle coming?"

"Bel Amica's strong as a mountain. Now that Abascar's outta the way, this land is wide open for the taking. But first, we're gonna exterminate those beastmen." He paused, then roared with a gale-force wind of amusement. "That," he finally scoffed, "is what they tell us, anyway. What they say and what really happens, well, them's two different kinds of business."

"They? Who's they?"

"The bony grins." He hooked his cheeks and drew them wide to bare his teeth, and the boy wished he hadn't. "The chalky giants. The tricksters. The white...outfits. The Seers have plans for Bel Amica, oh so many plans. But the heiress would rather save the beastmen. Even that one." He gestured to the open yard.

"She wants to...*save* the beastmen?"

"That's what I hear. Next she'll train poisonous snakes to play with newborn babies." Caroon turned suddenly to take full notice of the boy for the first time, one side of that crooked mouth turning upward in a boastful smile. "I don't recognize you. And I suspect if I ask questions, I'll learn things that mean I have to stand up and bother with you. Neither of us wants that. So get me some ale, and we'll both be happier."

The boy bowed. "Thank you, Officer Caroon."

Caroon swung his elbow back and clubbed the heavy door open just enough so the boy could slip sideways into a tunnel.

The tunnel led to a crowded supply room, where servants were hiding and arguing about how the beastman had escaped and who was most likely to catch him. As the boy pushed through, his long-dormant training in Abascar woke within him. What had once been drudgery suddenly seemed a pleasure. He turned, fought back through the hubbub, and surprised Caroon again. "Dark or sunny?" he asked.

Caroon choked. "Huh?"

"What kind of ale?"

As he passed back through the crowded supply room, the ale boy tossed a scrub-towel over his shoulder, grabbed a mop and a bucket of soapy water, tucked his chin low, and stole along past an ornate lift cage toward the wine cellar.

He did not step inside. Ryllion was there, sword drawn, stalking about and searching the shadows between the wine barrels. There was nowhere for the boy to run but up. So he stepped into the lift cage, shrank into the corner, and pulled the cord.

The cage rose from the lowest level to the main floor of the towerhouse. He quickly stepped out and dashed down the corridor toward the steamy kitchen, where he could hear the clink of glass and the clank of dishes.

The ale boy skated along on greasy stone tiles, tripping through bones, plates, and culinary casualties. Apparently the soldiers had helped themselves and shoved the wreckage aside for the staff. Fragrant casks, barrels, and bottles lay drained and dead, some still spinning or rolling slowly to a resting place.

He was surprised to find the place empty. The only sound came from a washbasin in the scullery corner, where dishes and pots clinked and bobbed as if washing themselves. Telling himself to ignore the plates of leftover lettuce, the hunks of bread and cake, and the bowls still sticky with stew that were piled precariously beside the murky washtubs, he scanned the kitchen countertops and cupboards for the sunny ale Caroon had requested.

Dishes continued to shift in the scullery tub, a steady stream of bubbles spluttering to the murky surface. The ale boy paused. Something like a snarl gurgled in the brine. The boy backed away, a clench of apprehension in his belly. A footfall on the stairs startled him. He ran back to the lift.

The gear wheels and chains hummed. The boy was already rising into the tower by the time he could see Ryllion advance from the kitchen with his sword drawn. He clung to the bars as the cage ascended through the circuitous stairway. He passed one level where soldiers, rousted from their sleep, were strapping on armor; another where sisterlies stood in hushed conference; and another where the heiress——*the heiress!*

He reached for the cord to stop the lift but pulled the wrong strand, and it kept on rising. It moved from the towerhouse into the tower and passed a few landing platforms where guards lumbered about with drawn daggers and snuffling hounds. At the top the lift locked into place. He grabbed the other cord, but a shout—"Thank you!"—dropped his hand to his side. He turned.

A golden glow teased the boy toward an open, curtained door. The sisterly guarding it nodded briskly and motioned him forward. "Sister Em told me I wouldn't have any help. You'll find the chambers empty. Give the floors a good scrub. There's ash everywhere from her sketching."

The boy held up the mop and bucket as if to say, "I've come prepared."

"Stay out of the heiress's way. She's in a terrible huff. Gone off with her guards to find Officer Ryllion. And if she catches him, he'll have scars to show tomorrow."

The boy nodded, although he could hardly absorb this flood of information. "I just saw him."

"I'd suggest you light the oil for the washtub, then fetch her a bottle of ale. Remember—she prefers ale. That'll help calm her down when she returns." Then she stopped. "Where did you see Ryllion?"

"Wull, he was in the kitchen—"

If the sisterly had been seated, she would have jumped to her feet. "There are soldiers in the kitchen?"

"Not anymore."

She put her hands on her head. "They're supposed to be searching for a beastman, not scavenging for a late supper." She stepped into the lift. "If you catch a glimpse of anything with nasty teeth climbing in the window, pull that red cord with the tassel beside the heiress's bed."

Muttering, the sisterly yanked the lift's release cord, and the lift dropped away. The boy leaned over the space and called, "I forgot! Wilus Caroon asked for sunny ale!"

Stepping through the curtains and into the firelight, he laughed. Everything glinted like treasure. There was a bed big enough for a family, quilts and pillows like ocean swells and frothy billows. Passing the washroom, he glimpsed a tub standing on sculpted eagle talons over a shallow, tub-length bowl of oil.

In the center of the room, a lantern spread a dim blue mantle over an arrangement of treasures—a ring, a crystal shard, a compass, a humble cup of clay, a man's ceremonial vest pinned with a feather, a dagger, a bowl, and a helm etched with eagle feathers. They were spread out as if waiting for something, pieces of a mystery.

He set down the bucket, propped the mop against the table, and reached for the dagger, thrilled at the thought of brandishing a blade of Bel Amican royalty. Something near his hand flopped awkwardly to life like a puppet on a string.

He had thought it a gargoyle carved on the edge of the ceramic bowl. It was a bat, and it dropped into the bowl with a splash. Milk splattered onto the tabletop. The boy stood on tiptoe and peered over the lip of the bowl. The bat, bathed in milk, blinked up at him, trembling.

The fireplace drew his gaze. Auralia's scarf, torn in two, was draped across the mantel.

"What are you up to, 'Ralia?" he asked. He held his hands out into the blaze, almost believing that his fearlessness worried the fire. "Why'd I end up here? Is somebody in trouble?"

He held the tip of a long firestarter in the blue core of the flames until it flared, then moved across the chamber into the washroom and knelt to ignite the shallow bowl of blaze-oil. It flared up green, bright hands cupping the base of the washtub. Small spots of scented oils floated like shiny coins on the water's surface, and the floral aroma reminded him of the young ladies who had pursued Prince Cal-raven in Abascar.

He ground out the firestarter's black tip in the mortar between two stones on the wall. On one of those broad stones, someone had sketched a bat.

As he walked back out of the washroom, his foot brushed the edge of a dinner tray. Without hesitation, he snatched a crust of the bread and then tipped the goblet to swallow whatever remained.

Half a goblet of ale was more than he should drink. He felt a bit dizzy immediately. "I know, I know, 'Ralia," he said. "That's not the way to enjoy a drink." He fell against the wall, his hand smearing a sketch of a viscorcat.

"'Ralia...look!" Now he noticed that almost every stone in the chamber wall displayed black chalk outlines of animals—simple, playful drawings celebrating the great bushy manes of lions; the strong line of neck, back, and tail of a vawn; the graceful curve of a weeping crane in flight. Rabbits. Gorrels. She seemed especially fond of the lean lines of lurkdashers.

"You'd like this heiress." He stepped up close again, tracing the line of a large figure. The artist had not given it any detail; it was just a silhouette. "'Ralia, doesn't this one look like your beastman? Like the one who picked me up and then let me go?"

A disturbance on the stairs. Shouts. A woman, furious. A man, insistent.

The boy recognized the voices. He staggered about, seeking a place to hide. The tablecloth did not reach to the floor. The walls bore no tapestries low enough to slip behind. He turned to the window. A climb down would be too risky, unless the stranglevine was rooted firmly.

He turned back to the fireplace. "'Ralia, where should I—" His mouth hung open. The scarf gleamed. "Oh very funny."

Finding Cyndere in his chamber, Ryllion smiled.

The heiress's rant began. "I hear that the main gate's standing open."

"We *want* the beastman to run," he replied, unruffled. "My company has spread a net of traps beyond the bastion."

"I know," she said.

"We'll be out of danger if he's shut outside the wall. But we'll catch him again. He cannot help but stumble into a snare. I'll show you how they work one day."

"That won't be necessary. I know they're going to fill up with animals that don't belong in traps."

"It's a small price to pay for—"

"It is not a small price," she snapped. "I know a good deal about those snares, how they cut deep at the slightest struggle."

"This convinces the prey not to struggle," he argued.

"Most animals would sooner lose a limb than wait for capture. They're braver than you think."

"I don't call that bravery. I call it empty headed—"

"Are you calling me empty headed?"

He blinked. "Of course not. I'm not talking about you. You're not in a snare."

"I'm not?" She folded her arms and spoke through clenched teeth. "Then why do I feel things closing in? Why do I hear that the intolerable Pretor Xa is coming to Tilianpurth?"

Ryllion shrugged. "I received word several days ago that he would stop here on his return from House Jenta to help us observe the Feast of the Sacrifice. But don't worry. He'll leave you alone…if he ever gets here."

"Maybe he tripped on a wire." Cyndere turned back to the corridor, too furious to think straight.

Ryllion followed her to the stairs. "Wait, Cyn. You shouldn't—"

She turned to bar his way. "Don't call me Cyn! You're not Deuneroi. You're not even a captain. When you catch that beastman, I want him caged, not sacrificed. I'm not finished with him yet."

"Finished with him? My lady, he's finished with you."

He followed her to the top of the stair and straight into her chamber, forgetting the appropriate pause and request for entrance. "This is an obsession, Cyndere. You would pick a stingerfly free of a spider's web knowing it would sting you. Your heart's full of grand ideas, but you need guidance to pursue them properly. And, yes, this was also true of Deuneroi."

Ryllion closed the door behind him, a gesture so audacious that Cyndere gasped. She glanced to the table. A mop leaned against it, and Deuneroi's dagger lay crooked—not at all how she had left it. She looked around the chamber, uncertain.

"I'm here to protect you," Ryllion continued. "We'll catch the beastman, and the Honorable Pretor Xa will present him as a sacrifice after the feast. Moon-spirits will help us make the Expanse safe for all of House Bel Amica to walk in the woods again, like you did when you—"

"Don't throw religion at me. I came here to get away from it."

"I know I speak beyond my bounds, Cyndere, but my passion is as fierce and noble as yours."

"Deuneroi and I wanted to help the Cent Regus, not exterminate them."

Ryllion pressed on. "You want peace with your mother, peace with House Jenta, peace with the beastmen. Where would the world be without dreamers like you? Those are beautiful ideas, Cyndere. I've pledged to protect them."

Cyndere started to reply, but Ryllion pounded his fist on the table. "Bel Amica can put your grand ideas to work, my lady. I've already set plans in motion that can make it happen. With the Seers' guidance, I'm finding ways we might help the Cent Regus. I'm learning how to lure them with what they want."

"What they want?" Cyndere laughed, incredulous. "It is not about what they want, Ryllion. Their desires are distorted by the curse. It is about drawing them to understand what they *need*." Where was her voice? What was this feeble chirp? She was Cyndere kai Thesera, whose arguments shook the Bel Amican courts. "They need to want what they need." She faced the fire.

"What about you, Cyndere? What do *you* need?" Ryllion stepped between her and the flames. "Deuneroi shared your dream. But now you're alone. You're surrounded by distraction and disturbance. You should be served. Blessed. Adored. You, above all in House Bel Amica. I can offer you safety and solitude. And more, should you desire it."

"I learned to see through flattery when I was a child, Ryllion." She walked around the table to keep it between them. "I came here to find peace. You've invited trouble. I've come to my chamber for quiet. You've barged in uninvited and closed the door behind you. You forgot your station when you climbed those stairs. I'm marking every step you take."

Ryllion quieted, looking to the window. "You're right. I am not Deuneroi. But I am true to my word. As he died, I promised him that I'd protect you. I won't fail him there. Let me honor my promise." He reached across the table and put his hand on the hilt of Deuneroi's dagger. "If you like, I could take this for the ceremony. When we catch the beastman, I could use Deuneroi's own weapon and avenge—"

A shape lunged from the milk bowl to Ryllion's arm. He screamed and flung the dagger away. Staggering back from the table, he waved his right arm, trying to shake free the grey mass bound to it. Then he lurched toward the fireplace.

"No!" Cyndere shouted.

The bat came free, striking the wall and falling to the floor. Stunned, it tried to crawl, and then went still.

Ryllion fell to his knees. "That...that thing bit me!" He unsheathed his own knife and raised it.

Cyndere, having pulled the alarm cord beside her bed, leapt between the soldier and the bat. "Don't hurt him!"

"Don't hurt him?!"

"He's injured. If you haven't just killed him—"

"What about me?" Ryllion all but shrieked. "What about..." He began to shake. "What's happening?"

The bat wriggled back through the crack in the wall. Cyndere took the cloth napkin from her dinner tray and wrapped it tight around Ryllion's wrist. "Get down to the healers. Those dark lines spreading around the wound... That's not good."

Ryllion's eyes bulged. He dropped to the floor.

An urgent knock, and then Emeriene appeared in the doorway. She hurried inside, followed by soldiers she had brought with her to investigate the commotion.

"Take him to the healers. He's been bitten."

After the soldiers carried Ryllion out, Emeriene demanded that one stand guard outside the door. Then, closing it tight, she blustered about the room. "I'm staying with you tonight," she muttered. "There's a beastman loose. And a bat, apparently." She snatched a robe from its hook and brought it to the heiress.

Cyndere pulled at her hair. "The noise, Em. I've got to get out of here."

Emeriene stopped, crumpling the robe into a ball. "Should I leave?"

"No, I need your help. With the beastman loose, we already have one too many threats in Tilianpurth. We have to spoil the Seer's visit. If Pretor

Xa crawls in, he'll win over anyone vulnerable to his potions. He'll spy on me. He'll follow me. He'll lecture me about the moon-spirits. I need a plan, Emmy."

Emeriene looked at Cyndere for a long time. "Promise me you won't go anywhere without me," she whispered.

"Em, you know you can trust me." Cyndere paused. "Remember that night several years ago, soon after Partayn died, when I helped you slip out of your window so you could steal away and meet someone?"

Emeriene sat down on the edge of the bed. "Yes. I was out of my mind."

"But I trusted you. And you didn't come back for two nights."

Emeriene looked into the folds of her robe, where her hands were trembling. "That was…that was a long drop to the ground. And it was a mistake."

"Perhaps. Perhaps not. You've never explained. But I've never asked, have I?" Cyndere began to straighten the items on the table, even those that had not been disturbed. "Trust me, Em. If a Seer moves in, my days will become the worst kind of hide-and-seek."

"We can deal with them, Cyn. You and me."

"I know you're far from your children. I know your husband's neglectful. I know you lost Partayn. But I can't replace them for you. I came here for a reason. And if I have to put on a false smile so you'll stop fussing over me, I'll scream."

Her face a mask of puzzlement, Emeriene stumbled to her feet. Her lips shaped words her voice would not deliver.

"You're trying to send the sun back around the other way, to take us back to childhood. It's not going to happen. Too much has changed. I came here to let go of Deuneroi and his dream, but now that I'm here, I find I'm not ready yet. He's still with me. When I last visited the glen, I felt him close by. I need to go back and see this through…whatever it is. And I can't take you with me."

Emeriene walked out of the chamber, pulling the curtains down over the entryway, and slammed the door behind her.

Cyndere fell sideways into her chair, and its arms held her like a child.

"I need a friend, not a shadow." She scanned the room from the wild new flames to the wavering curtains, to the washtub, to the tiny break in the wall.

She sat up and leaned forward, calling quietly toward that dark space in the wall. "It's all right. I won't hurt you. I promise. It's safe here. I'm your friend. You can come out now."

As if in answer, a boy clad in blackened tatters fell down the chimney and stepped out of the flames.

15

A ROYAL SCRUBBING

When Cyndere's cold hands took hold of the ale boy's wrists, he gasped. In his progress from the stale chill of the cell to the warm swirl of scented oil and smoke, he had imagined he was a ghost. So many steps. So many doors. So many encounters, and no one recognized him. But now he was seen for what he was.

She stared straight into him. Her anger slowed to a simmer, then calmed into amusement.

"You're not going to call for soldiers?" he whispered.

"Should I?" Cyndere looked at her soot-smudged hands. "I don't understand it. You should have died." She walked to the washroom, and he thought she was disgusted, that she was rushing to wash herself. But she came back with a steaming white towel. "Hold still. You're a mess."

Holding still was easy and better than answering questions.

He tried not to stare. But he could not help himself, for kindness and pain met strangely in Cyndere's countenance. Her face was like a picture hanging crooked on a wall. One side presented a proud, impetuous girl, and while he could not find the dividing line, the other bore stains of deep suffering.

"Do you need help?" he whispered. "Is there anything I can do for you?"

Her eyes flickered with anger. Then she shook her head. "No, there isn't. You're the one who's in trouble. I had planned to come down and visit you myself, but I've been so...distracted. That beastman scared me. You saw it all, didn't you?"

"He's gone. They won't catch him," he said, even as he wondered at his own rash claim.

She began to wipe ash from his face. It seemed that the more she drew him out of the ashes, the more tender her touch became. She looked at him the way old King Cal-marcus had studied his scrolls. "Tell me directly. Did Ryllion have good reasons to lock you up?"

"I was on my way to the lake. To Auralia's caves. I took a shortcut. Didn't know anybody was here."

She touched his brow and scowled. "You have no eyebrows."

Auralia had touched his forehead in much the same way, with her small, bramble-scratched fingers.

"You should have died in that chimney. Why didn't—" Cyndere stopped, found a clean corner of the towel, and dabbed tears from his eyes.

"I've made it through lots of fires. I think the Northchildren did it to me."

"Northchildren. That's an Abascar superstition, isn't it? They believe in curse-bearers who come from beyond the Forbidding Wall to kill us and drag us away, right? In Bel Amica we used to believe in ghosts. Until the Seers came and told us to stop being childish."

"Northchildren aren't dangerous. They touched me, and since that day I've never been burned."

"You must be a descendant of Tammos Raak. You're a firewalker."

He shrugged. "All I know is that the Northchildren are real. I've seen them. They helped me out of a fire, and now that's what I do. I help folks out of fire and trouble. It's what I'm for."

"It's what I'm for." She smiled. "You sound like Deuneroi."

As he looked closer, he realized that what he had taken to be purple makeup on her face was actually darkness born from sleeplessness. The whites of her eyes were shot through with red, irises like tarnished copper. Pain had hollowed her out, and the space had become a reservoir of unshed tears.

It was her turn to flinch. "I'm from Tammos Raak's line too, but I somehow seem to be born without a blessing. I'm not a firewalker. I can't speak with animals. I'm not a stonemaster."

"Scharr ben Fray, he's a stonemaster. And he can speak to some of the animals. He visited me at Auralia's caves. He gave me a vawn and told her to obey me, and she does. She's waiting for me." He gestured to the window. "Out there."

"Scharr ben Fray." She sat down on the edge of her bed and smiled. "You may not be dangerous, but you keep dangerous company. What are you called, anyway?"

"Folks call me ale boy. That was my job in House Abascar."

"Ale boy." She laughed quietly. "So are you a dark ale? Or sunny?"

"Hmmm." He looked at the blackened towel. "S'pose I'm dark today."

"You're not dangerous," she sighed. "Ryllion's a fool to think you're a spy. He's afraid of his shadow these days."

"He thinks I've seen something in the woods, something he doesn't think I should have seen. Do you know what it is?"

"Ryllion's broken. He's been through a horrible ordeal I can't imagine. He failed to save Deuneroi, so he's frantic to save everybody else." She stopped. "So...that's why you climbed up the chimney. You were trying to hide from Ryllion."

His legs suddenly shook and staggered. She caught him by the arm, and a worry creased her brow. "I'm as bad as Ryllion, interrogating you while you're half-starved and exhausted. We'll clean you up and get you fed."

The ale boy watched her walk to her bath closet to wring out the towel and soak it again. "I'm sorry," she called back to him. "You're the second young man I've caught trespassing tonight. But you're so much better company than the first. I almost climbed up the chimney myself."

He tried to resist as she scrubbed at his ears. "I know what I'm doing," she insisted. "I've helped Emeriene clean up her boys after they've made a mess of themselves on the beach." Slowly she swabbed the soot from his knees. "When I take you back to House Bel Amica, I'll introduce you to them. Maybe you can be friends."

"Bel Amica?" The boy turned his face toward the window. "Oh no, my lady. I promised Auralia I'd take care of her caves. And if I find more folks in trouble, I have to take them to King Cal-raven."

"So it's true." Cyndere stood up. She sat down. She stood up again. And when she spoke, he could hear her struggling to conceal the eager hope in her voice. "Cal-raven's alive?"

"He's helping hundreds of survivors, my lady."

She leaned against the table and looked out toward the falling snow.

"Some said they all died. I've heard rumors, but..." She turned, took a corner of the tablecloth, and wiped the hilt of Deuneroi's dagger clean. "My husband died in Abascar's ruins, trying to help people." She cleared her throat. "Tell me more about Cal-raven."

"He's a good king," he said, gripped with a sudden fervor. "He takes care of everybody. Housefolk, Gatherers, orphans—everyone. He'll bring House Abascar back again. But it'll be different this time."

"You do have a head full of secrets," she said. "Ryllion just asked the wrong questions."

The soft towel, the steam, and her warm hands—he was suddenly sleepy. He reached out without thinking and leaned against her shoulder, resisting an impulse to wrap his arms around her and weep. It embarrassed him how much he cried these days. But he was not wrung out of tears, not yet. "I should go. I told Auralia I'd take care of her caves."

"Did you say...*O-raya?*"

"Auralia."

"Someone else...mentioned her name to me."

"She was my friend. You remind me of her." Through half-closed eyes, he looked again to those sooty lines on the stone in the wall, to the familiar silhouette. "She cared about beastmen too." He felt as if he were falling into dreams as he described the day he had seen a beastman come to Auralia's caves. He told her about Auralia's concern for the creature and how he had been drawn to the colors, calmed by them. "That's where I live now. And I've got to go back."

"This girl, Auralia...she survived her encounter with the beastman? Where is she? Maybe I could find her."

"You won't find Auralia." The boy wavered on the surface of sleep's rising tide.

She touched his forehead. "What am I going to do about you, ale boy?" She pinched his wrists. "Besides getting some bark back on those twigs of yours, of course."

"You could let me go," he whispered.

"Maybe." She pulled off his shoes—he almost protested, but her tenderness was welcome—and draped a heavy blanket around him as soft as feathers and warm as a hot bath. "I know a thing or two about slipping out of Tilianpurth by night. But first, sleep for a while. You're all out of sense, you poor tired boy." She led him to her bed and helped him climb up into those billowy quilts. He wanted to argue, for it seemed out of place for him to lie down on the bed of an heiress. But the pillows had a strange gravity.

"When you've slept and eaten, I have a job for you." She rose and squared her shoulders. "Ale boy," she said with exaggerated self-importance, "I bid you go to King Cal-raven of Abascar. He is to convey exactly what his people will need to endure the winter. I, Cyndere kai Thesera, heiress of House Bel Amica, descendant of Tammos Raak, pledge to deliver those things." And then she laughed, dropping the dramatic pose.

"You pledge all that?" He sat straight up, clearing away sleep's half-spun web.

A diamond slid down her cheek. "For Deuneroi," she said. "You'll have a vawn and whatever else you need, if you agree. I'll let you go. You'll have to give Cal-raven the warmest of greetings. Not from House Bel Amica...from me. We've met, you know. When he was a young soldier-in-training, he visited Bel Amica with some ambassadors. He is..." Her voice dropped. "He's welcome if he ever wishes to come to us."

"Rumpa's out there waiting for me." He threw back the covers and swung his feet over the side of the bed. "Poor girl. Probably worried sick. All I need's a vawn whistle. I'd like to go now, if you please."

"A vawn whistle? That's easy." Cyndere walked to the window. "But that's where the easy parts stop. If Ryllion sees us, the game's over. And I won't let you go until you've found that vawn. You're not trudging off into the snow alone and on foot."

With a hint of sudden mischief, she said, "I've been myself all day—an intolerable grouch. But at night I turn into something else. A shadow. A secret. You'll see." Scuffing her silvery slippers, she rushed back to the bed and reached for his hand. A spark flickered from her fingertips to his. They both jumped. And laughed.

Hours later, near midnight, the ale boy found himself sitting on a tall kitchen stool at the edge of the long, blue-tiled counter, swinging his feet, chewing on strips of dried fish, and watching the heiress of Bel Amica pretend to be one of her own attendants. He wore a long green coat, made of such cushiony cloth that he suspected he could survive a fall from the Cliffs of Barnashum. It had a fur-lined hood that he pulled up as soon as the heiress dressed him for the journey. He had never worn such a thing. After fetching a vawn whistle from the supply room below, Cyndere stuffed it into one of the coat's deep pockets.

The ale boy watched the corner washbasin warily. The dishes were still. But he kept checking, just in case.

The frantic search for the beastman had calmed to an organized investigation. Teams of soldiers continued to scour the yard, searching for clues, while the bastion guards, helped by Emeriene and a team of sisterlies, made a thorough inventory of the towerhouse chambers. Ryllion remained in the healers' care, apparently sedated by their potions, for the distant echoes of his curses had gone silent.

But this did nothing to calm the heiress, and her anxiety was contagious. Dressed in a sisterly's gown, the hood pulled over her head, Cyndere hastened about the kitchen in half a panic, glancing up whenever she heard a soldier patrolling the corridor and turning her back when that soldier paused to investigate the late-night activity. The boy swung his legs and leaned back, watching for any suspicious approach.

"Have you had enough to eat?"

He nodded, holding up the empty plate.

In House Abascar the ale boy had watched as soldiers, servants, and errand-runners came down to the kitchens of the Underkeep for food. Nothing had ever been prepared especially for him. He ate what he could grab during his errands and sometimes happened to be in the right place to sit down with other errand-runners—the news girl, the leaf bagger, the cracker kid, the kindling hauler, the soot sweeper, and the washers—and eat simple meals of peppered vegetable broth, hard cheese, and crusty leftover bread. Sometimes he had lingered outside the king's kitchen, listening to the din of the clattering dishes. Occasionally a cook's boy would see him there and toss him a dry roll, a few strips of fatty bacon, or dried berries.

But he had never been served by royalty.

Cyndere murmured to herself as she cradled globefruit in a towel, then scooped up crackleseeds combed from the thick stands of whipgrass and popnuts plucked from the yellowskin trees. She tied each of these into separate cloth pouches and then wrapped wedges of three different cake-sized cheeses in starflower leaves.

"Red plums. Dried red plums. Now, where have the sisterlies stashed them?" She dropped the pouches into a brown bag woven from reeds, then tied off that bag with a strand of twine. "And there it is. But be careful. Predators can smell the food. Best to drop the bag in a stream or bury it somewhere when you're finished."

The wall of shelves sprang away from the wall, pivoting on a concealed hinge. The ale boy dropped to his feet and walked into the cool breeze wafting up from the darkness.

Cyndere pulled on a heavy woodscloak hanging on the back of the secret door and lifted a woven basket. "Emeriene's going to notice that I'm gone anytime now. She won't be happy. We'd better go."

There was something new in her voice, an eager mischief beyond her interest in sending a message to Cal-raven. He hesitated, sensing her desire to steal away. Suddenly this venture seemed more dangerous than before.

Glowstones pressed into the steps of the long descending stair glimmered, flickering along the winding way that opened through a maze of massive subterranean boulders and ridges of stone.

The earth seemed a living thing here. Rocks and roots and the dripping damp—it was so unlike the dry husk of Abascar's labyrinth. The Underkeep had been hollowed out of stone and dust, a complex network of forgotten empty waterways in the rock, but this was ground that breathed, restless, supporting grand old trees on its shoulders.

In one hand Cyndere carried the basket and in the other a rain canopy, its broad canvas folded around the long wooden handle. She used its tip to sweep the space before them and knock away cobwebs that had crossed the tunnel since the last travelers.

Not even Ryllion knew of this passage, she explained. King Helpryn, a man whose ambition left no room for fear, had found little use for secret escapes. But earlier generations of Bel Amican royalty, going back to the days of the beastman wars and even before, had installed escapes within escapes. Their existence was just one of many secrets preserved by the descendants of Tammos Raak. Not even the Seers could gain access. False escapes were designed as bait for traitors who would stumble into traps. Cyndere would not tell the ale boy how she had opened the door, and she would never bring him back this way. She was breaking ancient laws, she said, by bringing him along.

Even as Cyndere narrated the history of this bastion, the ale boy pushed the fur-framed hood back so he could better attend to the whispers of the earth around him, the bubble and ooze, the grinding of burrow-worm teeth, the scuttle of rats. He shoved his hands deep in the pockets of the long green coat, clutched the vawn-whistle, and shuddered. He did not want to worry the heiress by suggesting that someone might be following them. When he paused, the faint footfalls behind him ceased, and he wondered whether they might just be echoes.

"Why," he asked, "would Emeriene try to stop you from going this way?"

"Emeriene thinks I'm being reckless." Cyndere glanced back at the boy. "But Em keeps some rather scandalous secrets all her own. Or at least she *thinks* they're secrets. But she has no idea why I'm going back to the forest."

"Neither do I," the boy said quietly, but she did not hear him. He could almost believe she'd forgotten him as she all but ran into the tunnel ahead.

They sped along through the silences, arriving at another long stair, a chain of dim glowstones. Cyndere led the way, her woodscloak sweeping each stair and brushing up clouds of dust.

A muckmoth bumped its cold belly against his face, and he batted it away. Just ahead of him, Cyndere had parted a curtain of vines and was motioning for him to step through into the snowy woods.

"Take this." She gave him a glowstone the size of an apple. "It will help you find your way in the dark." He tucked it into a pocket, and then she opened his hand and pressed pale blue flower petals into his palm. "And take these. They'll bring you comfort when you're lost. Breathe in their perfumes. There's something to them, these blue flowers. I'm going to gather more tonight, before I return."

"You're going flower picking? Tonight?"

"Yes. Only for a short while. It's nothing I haven't done before." So this was what drove her, these mysterious flowers. "But mind the path. Traps. Ryllion set them to catch beastmen. I'll test each step before I take it, and you should follow me closely until we get as far as the perimeter guard."

"Then what?"

"I'll figure something out."

After a few steps he paused. Something moved in the trees alongside them. He was sure of it. It ducked behind trees. It whispered to itself. With every fleeting glimpse, he became more certain that a Northchild was tracking their passage. It was all he could do to keep himself from calling Auralia's name.

He stumbled into a depression in the earth. He stopped to trace its shape, hands shaking. He could not be sure, but it might be one of the Keeper's tracks.

"Please," he whispered. "Show me where to go." He heard the heiress's footsteps and saw her shadow climbing to the top of the next rise and standing against a soft blue glow. In her eagerness she had not noticed him falling behind.

A few frantic moments of searching, and he found a similar print in the wide space between two towering cloudgrasper trees. "I don't want to leave the heiress alone," he whispered. "But this is what I've wanted. A sign. A direction." He addressed the treetops around him. "I will follow. But please, watch over the heiress."

And so the ale boy followed the rugged ground through the freezing woods, out of the trees, and up through the snow-covered field of whitegrass. As he did, he gained confidence that these were indeed the Keeper's tracks, and he forgot the heiress's instruction to test every step.

The tracks led him safely to the edge of a camp where Bel Amican guards talked excitedly among themselves and crowded together with torches.

He saw that a team of vawns, saddled and restless, stood ready and facing the slope down toward Tilianpurth. The largest vawn bore a giant of a man in long robes and a magnificent green headdress.

The boy did not stay to learn more.

A creature of ice crystals and fog, he moved back into the Cragavar woods, where he hoped his vawn, Rumpa, was waiting for him.

Emeriene limped from Tilianpurth's kitchen, down the corridor, to the lift. Fuming over the second mess she had found in the kitchen tonight, she pulled the cord and set the lift to rising. This night had been the worst since her arrival. So many interruptions. So many crises. It was time to make her way back to Cyndere, to muster an apology for her angry departure. Maybe this time she would, at last, confess the details of that night, years ago, when she had slipped out the window and run into the arms of a secret admirer.

She found Cyndere's door unlatched and pushed it open with her shoulder. "We've got to talk, my lady," she declared, stepping inside. "I've just received word that the Seer has arrived at the edge of the valley. And—by the bones of Tammos Raak!"

The floor was strewn with ashes and soot. One of the heiress's towels lay twisted and soiled on the floor.

"What happened here?" she asked, calling toward the steaming tub.

Cyndere's gown lay on the bed. And the headdress waited there as well.

Emeriene turned, looked at the hooks made from pronged seashells on the wall. Cyndere's woodscloak was gone, her slippers missing.

Emeriene ran to the window. "No," she said, her voice breaking. "Not tonight."

She grasped the window ledge and stared up at the breaking storm. Then slowly she sank down into a chair. Sunrise was still hours away. No, sunrise would not come at all, not so long as this storm lasted.

"Everybody," she shouted at the window into the flurry. "Everybody leaves me."

Partayn. Cesylle. Even the one I loved in secret ran away. If you go, what remains? Winter reached in through the window, clutched her in its cold hands. "I've pledged to protect you, so you're leaving me no choice."

She walked out of the chamber, each step heavier than the last. She chose the stairs instead of the lift. It seemed the stairwell was darker than before.

16

BEL'S REQUEST

Drumming his black claws against the metal of a broken fangbear trap, Jordam stared at the fragments of bloodied skin still stuck in its silver jaws.

Jorn.

So this is how the Bel Amicans had caught his youngest brother—not with those wire snares, which were stacked alongside it, but with a simple clamp. As much as he hated Jorn, the idea still enraged him. He wanted to slay those trappers. But his concealment in this Bel Amican wagon at the edge of the wood was his only chance of penetrating the bastion walls for a rescue. He would have to stay silent until they returned from their late, snowy work.

The trappers still hoped to catch him out there. And since the wood was likely to be strewn with these deadly devices, the wagon was Jordam's best chance to escape them. The tiny pinging of his claw tips against the metal provoked the horses outside to murmur uneasily. They had not seen him crawl down through the whitegrass, using their hoofprints as a guide through the traps, nor had they heard him creep up behind, stealthy as a gator, and slip beneath the wagon's canvas cover.

Taking a wire cutter from the floor, he severed the coils of unset traps, one by one, just to prevent any more from impeding his progress. Outside, icedust spilled in a rattling rain down from the keening boughs. Nevertheless, he heard footsteps crunching through frost.

His appetite surged, but he resisted. "rrJorn," he reminded himself. "Get Jorn." His thirst for Essence outshouted all ordinary hungers now. A web of burning cords wrapped around his belly and coiled up his spine. He would follow Mordafey's orders. He would bring Jorn back and go with his brothers to the Core for satisfaction.

He could hear the trappers' voices. He peered out from under the canvas.

As if the storm had imagined them, three soldiers materialized. Hunched beneath the weather, they led a flustered, complaining vawn. Snow tumbled down their stormcloaks—cloaks like those folded beside him. They had, he suspected, been moiling about in the snow since sundown. They were rank with sweat.

His frozen fingers stubborn and stiff, he fumbled with one of the folded cloaks. Better these hunters saw something familiar in this storm than something strange. From a distance he might just pass for a soldier.

"Only one catch," a guard sighed. "That's all we need. Then Ryllion will have an offering for the ceremony, and he'll stop driving us so hard. He's half out of his mind."

"You talk like Ryllion's a villain."

"What's that? The silent Officer Falaroi speaks? Of course Ryllion's a villain. In his vain imagination, he's already promoted himself to captain. But Bauris is Tilianpurth's senior officer. Why's he letting Ryllion order us around?"

"Because Bauris knows Ryllion deserves to be a captain. And we should help him, Myrion. Poor fellow, he fought to save Deuneroi from the beastmen, and he failed. Now he's haunted. An event like that can light a fire in a man. He's going to change things. And take care, because with his eyes and ears, he's probably taking note of us right now."

"I don't care. It's about time he heard something better than 'Yes, Officer Ryllion' and 'Whatever you want, Officer Ryllion' and 'Are you comfortable, Officer Ryllion?'" Shaking snow off his stormcloak, he grumbled, "There was a time we caught beastmen to protect ourselves. Now we catch them for sport or ceremonial sacrifice. Remember what Deuneroi always said? 'They were people once.'"

"Keep talking like that and people will think you've been stealing away to Cyndere's room. Have you already forgotten what Deuneroi's sympathy earned him, Myrion? There's no cause more noble than wiping out the

Cent Regus. Pity's a weakness. Do you want to hand them another round in this game?"

They sounded weary and careless. Calmed by O-raya's colors, Jordam might have understood such rough speech. But tonight the animal within him roared with too much force, and the din disrupted his concentration. He lifted the fangbear trap, imagined clamping it over a trapper's head.

"The drink's half gone, Myrion! I was taking it to the stable girl. She's always thirsty for cider." Jordam heard the scrape of snare wires.

"Don't you think she's a little young?"

"Too young, too old, already married—doesn't matter. The spirits have given me a sacred longing, and I must fulfill it. I think I left another bottle in the wagon."

Jordam heard the word *wagon*, and he understood. He slipped out the back and dropped to crawl beneath, then took hold of the undercarriage and lifted himself off the ground. The trappers took no notice. He heard a cork pop free of a bottle as the horses moved forward.

While the wagon wheels trundled, he held on as long as he could. The horses took a crooked route through the trees, the trappers steering them around concealed traps. But the rugged ground scraped against Jordam's back. He let go, and the creaking of the cart and the crush of its wheels masked the sound of his tumble into the bushes.

Walking in the wheel ruts to stay free of traps, he began to plot his escape. He would have to come back along this very trail. That would be easy enough for him. But Jorn—even in flight he meandered, despising any suggestion of direction. Only Mordafey frightened Jorn enough to restrain him.

In a moan of wind, Jordam thought he heard a voice calling—"Boy. Boy." He turned, caught the scent of a coil tree's oily bark, and in the dark of his misery, memories of color and light dawned. He hesitated. The wagon moved off through the trees. *There it goes,* he thought. *My only chance of getting in.* He could not let them get out of sight.

But the throb of thirst clouded his thoughts, and he veered off the path, stalking gingerly through the bushes. O-raya's colors would not take away these turbulent waves of desire for Essence, but they would raise him up so he could keep his head afloat and breathe. Moving carefully up and over the ridge, he stood beneath the coil tree.

Curtains of fog brushed his face and closed behind him. The soft light was stronger than the fear, and he let himself be drawn in. The colors had given him relief before. A dalliance here would not disrupt his mission, he decided. He crawled down the steep incline.

The cloudgrasper tree hung heavy with more pieces from the woman's strange collection. Fresh kindling circled the tree in bundles, a nest of dead brambles. *She was here while I was gone. Did she look for me?*

He took a branch and tested the ground alongside the fallen apple tree. He reached the well, knelt on a patch of petals, breathed their pungent spice, and leaned in to bask in the flowers' blue light. For the first time he wondered, *Could I steal these painted stones? Could I put them back together somewhere safer, close to home?* The hammers of appetite slowed their punishing blows.

"You came back."

In the grass beside the Bel Amican woman, the tetherwing basket was silent, unopened. She held a strange, cloth-wrapped rod like a sword in its sheath.

"I thought I would be ready to face you again," she said. "I'm not."

Jordam leaned on the broken branch as if it were a walking stick. Worried he might frighten her away, he moved to the edge of the clearing.

"Jordam," she said, and his name in her voice surprised him. "That is your name, isn't it? Jordam?"

He nodded, amazed.

"I need your help." She lifted the tetherwing basket and walked behind the crumbling wall, testing the ground with the rod.

Help. She was asking for help again. He watched her watching him. "Help?"

"There's a boy, alone. Out there somewhere. He ran away. If he steps in a trap, it'll be my fault. Did you see him?" She held her hand flat under her chin. "This tall. In a green coat."

"rrBoy?" When Jordam stepped further, tapping snow-dusted grass, the woman did the same with the rod. Coming around the far end of the wall, she took two steps toward him. She waited. He took three cautious steps toward her. She laughed, a small bell in the quiet. Snowflakes drifted around them, melting into the mysterious, summer-green grass. He could almost reach her.

But it was she who reached for him. She set down the basket and opened her tiny hand. It was empty. He grunted, confused. "I'm sorry. I'm in a fit. Too hasty," she said, and she knelt down beside the basket. "You don't even know what I'm talking about."

She reached inside, but instead of a tetherwing, she brought out a large bowl of cold stew. He smelled roast muskgrazer. "For you," she said.

He dropped hard to his knees and took the bowl, and her fingertips brushed his hand. He sniffed the stew suspiciously, then drank it all in one gulp. It was only a bite for him, but he savored the unexpected spices.

"Thank you," she said. "You saved my life from the snare."

Wind shook the boughs that covered the glen. A clod of falling snow smashed into Jordam's head. He barked, shaking out his mane, and snow slid down his face, while more white bursts plummeted from the canopy above.

Laughing again, the woman offered him the wooden handle of the rod with the strange canvas cloak. "A rain canopy," she said softly. "It shelters you."

Grumbling, he accepted it. Unsure what this gesture was supposed to mean, he offered her the broken tree branch in return. She shook her head. "No no," she said. "That won't do me any good."

As she stepped forward to kneel alongside him, the animal within him shook, eager to seize her. But she closed her hands over the rain canopy and lifted it. "Look closer," she said. She twisted the wooden handle. Jordam let it go, astonished, for the contraption transformed before him. Small branches expanded from the rod, stretching the cloth canvas to form a broad dome. As it unfurled, green light beamed out from beneath it, for the rod was bejeweled with tiny glowstones. She lifted the canopy over her head, shading herself from the drifting flakes.

He took it back from her and examined its construction.

"See?" she said. "It's simple." Reaching forward, she placed her hands over his, showing him just how to twist the handle to open and close the sheltering span, how to hold it over his head and escape the falling snow. Her small, cold hands warmed against his. "It's a rain canopy," she repeated. "If you go to find the boy, it might help you."

He held it over his head as she had demonstrated. "rrRaykapee." Snowflakes gasped faintly as they settled on top of it. Fog from the well rose up and gathered under its span. The rain canopy was not broad enough to shield his shoulders, but he understood it now.

"You learn quickly," she said. And then she shrieked as a load of snow shaken loose from the high branches smashed across her head.

Jordam gave her the rain canopy.

Such strange cargo the weakerfolk carry, he thought. *Always making things.* His brothers had only ever bothered to make weapons. Reaching into his woods-cloak, he pulled out the golden vial of slumberseed oil. "rrLook," he said, using her own word.

"I left that behind, didn't I? Did you open it? I'll bet it knocked you flat." She drew another empty bowl from the basket. "Look closely." She took a small stick from her pocket and snapped it in two. It sparked into flame. She dropped the fiery halves into the bowl, picked a blue flower from the well-stones, and plucked its petals over the flames. A small coil of white smoke ascended in widening rings. "Breathe. Incense. You'll like it. It's not quite so powerful as the slumberseed oil."

The smoky aroma intrigued him. *Like honey,* he thought. *Goreth would like this trick.* "rrIn...sense." Tension in his brow began to ease.

Breathing in the incense, she closed her eyes. When she spoke again, the urgency in her voice had faded. "I played here when I was small." She spun the canopy slowly like a wheel over her head. Its glowstones cast green light against one side of her face while the flowers shone blue against the other. "These wellstones—they were not so colorful then. Did you paint them?" She touched the purple, the gold, the blue. "These colors. Was it you?"

Careful to arrange the words of the weakerfolk, he said, "O-raya. Paint. Colors."

"It's true, then." The Bel Amican woman looked out into the trees. "The ale boy told me about a girl," she said. "Auralia. Some kind of artist. She had a visitor, he said. A Cent Regus stranger. Like you."

She then spoke many words in Common and so easily. She spoke of the boy, a vawn, a message, and something about Cal-raven of Abascar. Could she know what happened to O-raya?

Struggling to collect her eager words, Jordam swayed, dizzy with hunger and exhaustion. The colors calmed him, but they did not erase the ache in his belly, and the fragrance of the burning flowers gave the ground a stronger pull. He growled, rose, and walked to the well. Seizing the rope within the well, he drew the bucket, tipped his head back, and gulped a bellyful of the warm water. As the dizziness subsided, he sat on the edge of the well. "O-raya," he sighed. He wondered what would happen if his brothers tasted such water, breathed incense, absorbed O-raya's colors.

"Auralia charmed you." She joined him at the well and let the bucket plunge back down. "How did she do it? Was it the colors? Was she some kind of witch?"

"rrBlue. Caves." He gazed into the darkness, eastward, thinking of Deep Lake, searching for words in Common. "O-raya, gone." He looked up through the treetops toward the faint outline of Tilianpurth's tower. "There?"

"No." The woman sounded worried. "Auralia is not with us at Tilian-purth."

"Who?" He gestured again to the tower. "Who?"

"Do you see an owl?" she laughed, following his gaze. "No, the woman in the window is not Auralia. That's..." She bit her lip, then said, "That's Cyndere. Daughter of the queen of Bel Amica. Cyndere."

"rrSin-der?"

"Yes." She pulled up the bucket and propped it on the well's edge, then cupped her hand and lifted a sip to her lips. "Cyndere is here because she is sad. Her husband...he died. Killed. By Cent Regus." She gestured to the decorated tree. "It's an old Bel Amican ceremony. I'm helping Cyndere. We're saying good-bye. Good-bye to Cyndere's man. And to Cyndere's brother...and her father. All dead. You hang their belongings in a tree, you summon them, and you set it alight. The ghosts come. They gather back all the memories in those things. At least that's what the old stories say."

"rrSin-der's man," he repeated. "Brother. Father."

"I also gather these blue flowers. When Cyndere eats them, they draw the trouble out of her. They bring her some comfort."

Jordam leaned forward, listening.

"Cyndere and her husband slept here in the blue light. They sang, dreamt of children, talked about House Cent Regus." She walked around behind the ruined wall and raised a thorny vine. "They ate these." The berries were still red, even in winter. She pulled some free, ate one, and then she tossed them to his feet. Bright jewels against the snow-dusted grass. "It's a strange place. Summer in the middle of winter."

He stuffed the berries into his mouth. They were tart and sweet. But they were not what his belly demanded, and they set it to rumbling.

"Cyndere's man was Deuneroi," she murmured.

Jordam choked, spitting out berry juice onto the snow. An image flared up, torchlit in memory—a severed hand and Mordafey's gloating grin. He turned away from her, but she strolled around to face him again.

"If Deuneroi could only see us here."

"rrDeuneroi." Jordam lifted the name as if trying to pry his way out from under a heavy stone.

When he looked up at her again, the sadness was gone from her small face. She spoke through clenched teeth, her voice low and quiet. "Do you know about Deuneroi, Jordam?"

Fear prickled across his skin. *Go get Jorn,* he thought, slumping down to sit on the fallen tree. *Get Jorn out. Otherwise. . .Mordafey.* He dug his fingers into the tree moss.

"Deuneroi's gone. Cyndere hurts." The woman gestured to the tower. "Cyndere hurts." She touched her head, then folded her hands at her breast.

He gazed into the blue glow. "O-raya gone. Jordam hurts." He folded his fingers together and pressed them against his chest in the same way.

"Jordam." She smiled. "It's a good name."

"Jordam," he agreed, marveling. Gesturing to her, he asked, "You?"

She narrowed her eyes. "Call me Bel."

"Bel."

"For Bel Amica. *Bel* means good. *Amica,* will. Good will. It was the name of the woman who started our house. A daughter of Tammos Raak."

"Bel," he repeated. "Bel hurts too? Like Sin-der?"

"When Cent Regus kill, yes. Just as you hurt because Auralia is gone.

Maybe Auralia will come back. But Deuneroi, he is…" The woman looked down into the bowl of incense and stirred it slowly, breathing in deeply. "Deuneroi won't be coming back."

A distant sound snapped Jordam's head around, his ears pricking sharply.

"The ale boy." Bel sounded suddenly urgent. "The boy who told me about Auralia. Do you know the boy?"

"O-raya's boy?" He sniffed the air, then gestured toward the tower. "O-raya's boy?" He stood up. The boy he had let go… Was he nearby after all? Would he know where O-raya had gone?

She scowled. "Jordam, would you hurt Auralia's boy?"

He pounded his chest, filling with pride as he said, "rrJordam let O-raya's boy go." With each word he understood and used, he could think more clearly, as if stepping into brighter light.

"Jordam, listen to me. If you hurt Auralia's boy, you hurt me."

He scowled, trying to make sense of that. "No hurting O-raya's boy."

She touched her lips. "Good words, Jordam. Now you can help Auralia's boy again." She spoke fiercely. Like merchant women instructing children. "He's out in the woods, Jordam. You have to find him."

He gestured southward. "I…I go to Cent Regus House." The words, the words. What could he say to explain the Essence to her? "Want. Strong blood. Strong food. Cent Regus strong."

"You won't help the boy?" Her face fell.

"Drink. Strong."

"No," she said. "Do not go back to the curse, Jordam. That isn't strength. If you go there, you cannot return to this place."

Her words confused him.

"If you go back to Cent Regus, you hurt me. You hurt Cyndere. You hurt Auralia's boy."

He did not want to hear these words. They clouded his intent, delayed his return to the chieftain's lair.

"Jordam, I have two hands." She held them up, palms open to him. "I can take hold of this with my left hand." She lifted the rain canopy. "With my right hand, I can hold this." She raised the dagger from her belt. "But my heart—I have one heart." She put the dagger and the canopy down and folded her hands over her breast. "Your heart can only hold one thing, Jordam. Your heart has one hand."

Imitating her, he pressed his fist to his chest, to the center of the thirst. "One hand," he growled, struggling.

"Cyndere's heart…it holds to Deuneroi. Your heart holds to Cent Regus power." Bel touched the well. "Hold to this instead, Jordam. This is better." She lifted the bucket, offering it to him. "Light, color, water. The things that remind you of Auralia. Hold on to those, and good things will come to you. But reach for the Cent Regus, for power, and more good things will disappear. Like Deuneroi. Like O-raya. You'll hurt yourself. You'll hurt me." She picked up the dagger and threw it aside. "Let go of the power, Jordam."

The dagger gleamed in the dirt. It frightened him to let it lie there. Jordam paced to the edge of the clearing. His nostrils flared, discerning a familiar scent on the frosty breeze. His lips drew back from his teeth.

"Jordam, what is it?"

"rrJorn." He turned to the woman. "Jorn. Dangerous. Brother."

"Brother?" She glanced down at the dagger. "Ryllion's beastman. He's escaped. Is he your brother?"

"Jorn."

She walked boldly to his side and grasped his arm. "Jordam, Auralia's boy is lost. Lost in the trees. You must go and find him. Do you understand? Help him. Help O-raya's boy. Don't let your brother hurt him. Protect him while he goes to Cal-raven."

"Help." O-raya's boy was out there. Alone. In the trees. He needed to be found. Protected. Taken to Cal-raven. Might O-raya be there, where the people of Abascar hid?

"Cyndere will be glad," she continued, her voice soft and reassuring. "Cyndere will stop hurting if you help the boy. Protect him. Stop Jorn." She held out the rain canopy. "Take this. For the boy." He accepted it. "And this too. Something I forgot. Give this to Auralia's boy so he knows I sent you."

She pressed a cloth into his hand. He held it up, let it unfurl like a flag. "rr O-raya!"

"Yes. It belongs to O-raya's boy. Tell him the colors are for Cal-raven. A gift, from Cyndere."

"Sin-der."

"Then come back. Come back to Auralia's colors." Unable to grasp such a large hand, she squeezed two of his fingers together. "Come back to me."

He stood quiet in the flurry, his gaze fastened to hers. *Come back to Bel, like a tetherwing,* he thought.

17

SHELTER

The ale boy sounded the vawn whistle until the snow-blown world spun. If that shrill call failed to pierce the wind and reach poor Rumpa, he would stand no chance of finding shelter, nor would he live to deliver Cyndere's promise to Cal-raven.

He rehearsed his message for the Abascar king as if the words could burn a tunnel through the snow. "The heiress of Bel Amica. Wants to help you. And I believe her. She's kind. She's generous. She's not like. Other Bel Amicans. She'll bring you whatever. You need. For the winter."

Moving southward through sparse patches of the Cragavar, he had ventured into knee-deep drifts. He still wore the padded green coat with the fur-lined hood that reached to his heels. But sleet pelted him from all sides while snow clouds converged in a conspiracy to bury him alive. Using curses he'd picked up from the prison guard, he punished himself for wandering away from Cyndere into this impassable trouble.

His feet stayed warm. The ale boy had gathered baskets of Auralia's work as he traveled through autumn and winter—remnants of her cloth; sculptures of eggshells and feathers edged with translucent insect wings; outrageous hats and other jokes; deep clay bowls that, when filled, reflected things the water remembered. Until he could return to his hiding place, this pair of shoes was all he had left of her.

And he would have chosen nothing else. The shoes had been folded in a blanket in the cave. He had stuffed them into a basket, intending to give them to an Abascar survivor whose feet were the right size. But during a rain-storm, shivering and anxious, he tried them on. They had remained on his feet ever since. He even slept with his shoes on, which had served him well in sudden flight from trouble.

Here in the snow, his feet snug in their warmth, he was moved to thank Auralia, and not for the first time. But when he spoke her name, the words that followed were not what he had intended.

"Auralia, where are the tracks?" He puffed his way, one laborious step at a time. "I can't. Find them. The Keeper's. Forgotten me. And I think. You have too."

He stumbled, thrusting his hands out to catch himself, punching a boy-shaped print into the snow. Rising, he blew the whistle again. The wind swallowed every shrill signal, and he heard mockery in its howling. He hoisted the heavy pack that Cyndere had prepared for him.

"Keeper," he said, fighting onward another few steps. "Keeper."

He fell forward again at the top of a long slope, then slid down as the snow loosened around him. Soon he was caught in an avalanche, encompassed in white, crashing past the snow-draped stones he had seen on the way up.

When the continent of sliding snow smashed against stones at the bottom, he felt as if he too was broken. He could not feel his hands, and his face was a frozen mask. "I've got no problem with fire. Why can't I have a gift for surviving cold?"

A rise in the ground swept upward and outward to create an overhang. Shelter. Not much, but perhaps enough. He staggered toward it.

Seconds later a bolt of lightning pierced the storm, and he saw a flower of smoke bloom beneath the outcropping. A dead tree, scorched and blackened by the blast, flared into a blaze.

If he had been any less desperate, he might have been astonished. All he could do was drag himself between the wall and the fire, hold out his arms, and welcome the waves of heat. Thawing, his fingertips stung. Eventually he could open and close his hands. He unbound the snow-covered pack he had strapped across his back and stuffed a strip of dried huskbeast into his mouth.

"I'd give my shoes for a bottle of hajka," he said, rubbing his hands together.

A few moments later, hunched over toward the glow, he was asleep. But this time, he did not dream of the lake or the Keeper. He dreamt of the fireplace in the heiress's chamber and tasted dark ale on his lips.

In Jorn's snowstorm dreams, that mysterious, dragonlike beast loomed, the same creature the brothers had tracked through the woods. Fearsome beacons of light beaming from unfurling wings. From its jaws, fire.

He woke up at the edge of the Cragavar forest, smelling smoke.

Jorn had followed the boy from Tilianpurth through the woods, through the whitegrass, and into the Cragavar. He had waited until the Bel Amican soldiers were far behind him. And he knew he was close to his prey.

He uncoiled, springing up onto the snow's crust, his skin as white as the world around him, his claws out for any traveler who might be huddled at a campfire. Loping lopsided, awkward as an injured gorrel, he pushed through sideways sleet, tracing a trail of swirling darkness through the blizzard. He watched for any flicker of fire, any sign of life there in the lee of that dark overhang.

Colors wavered against the rocks at the base of a column of smoke. Relief. Fire. Heat. And even better—hot blood. The boy would fill his belly, and shelter would save him from the storm.

Crouching, he considered his approach. He licked his arms, which still tasted of the murky brine in the Tilianpurth washtub where he had hidden from the soldiers. He had leaped through a kitchen window and concealed himself there in a soup of gristle scraps, fruit rind, seeds, bits of bone, and traces of gravy. An overturned pot floated on top, and he had shoved his snout into it, breathing air rank with the burnt residue of stew. It had kept him alive and hidden until he dared to creep out and escape. He raised his head just in time to see the secret door closing behind the cabinet, and he had followed his nose, stalking along behind a woman and this boy as they made their way out of Tilianpurth by night.

As he closed in at last, the great shelter took on definition. He slowed. He stopped.

Jorn cursed the dream that had fooled him. He was not awake after all. This was not the real world. He was trapped in his nightmare. The gargantuan creature watched him, eyes glimmering, fangs sparking with lightning. How could it see him? Jorn boasted in his capacity for concealment, but those eyes were fixed upon him, running through him, sharp and strong as iron spears.

The creature held one enormous wing against the storm, sheltering the boy beneath. The boy was not afraid. Jorn was not even sure the boy knew it was there, for he was hunched at the fire, his hands held close to the flame. Jorn looked again. The boy's hands were thrust *into* the fire.

Jorn suddenly changed his mind about the hunt. He knew he could not fight this creature. It was mighty and unhindered by the elements. It could swallow him the way Mordafey swallowed mice. It would probably do just that for the boy, who seemed to be cooking himself in willful sacrifice.

Then the nightmare took a bewildering turn. The creature, never shifting its gaze, unfolded another wing from its rough, bristling side. That wing hung like a curtain against the wind, creating a second shelter, a cave. A third wing rose up from its back, offering more protection around the bend, and yet another unfolded beyond that.

Some unfamiliar emotion sparked faintly within Jorn's heart, but he growled, snuffing it out. While it seemed the creature was offering refuge, Jorn knew better. He was a Cent Regus hunter. This monster would make an easy meal of him, just as it would surely devour the boy. What is more, to accept would be a sign of weakness.

In a surge of pride, Jorn began to back slowly away, then turned and bounded into the storm.

When the ale boy opened his eyes, the world was white, the storm's mission complete. He did not know how long he had slept. The pearly light gave no clue as to the sun's position.

He got to his feet and stared up the slope he had sought to climb. The dark overhang that had sheltered him was gone, as if the storm had carried it away. The only trace of his salvation was the smear of ash on the snow before him. He got to his feet and surveyed the landscape.

"When a rocky hillside disappears, where does it go?" he asked. He turned and stared back toward the Cragavar, which was invisible in the fog.

A beastman appeared, striding across the snow.

The boy collapsed. "Why?" he whimpered. "'Ralia, why? Why is it ending like this? After all you told me, I'm going to be supper for a beastman?"

He narrowed his eyes. The approaching figure looked just like the beastman Cyndere had sketched on the wall. The one who had let him escape.

18

The Watcher and the Ruined Farm

Skating an imperfect circle on the frozen sky, a black-winged brascle haunted the ale boy's progress. "I'm not your prey," said the boy to the bird, for if the predator could see him from that height, surely it could hear him.

With the vawn whistle tight in his purpling fist, the ale boy walked across drift after drift, taking four steps for every one of the deep prints punched into the snow by his gruff, gigantic guide.

The more he fell behind, the more he was tempted to wander off on his own. This very beastman may have come to Auralia's caves, but he had also sought to slay Wynn and Cortie on Baldridge Hill. Deepening the mystery, the same monster claimed that he'd been sent by someone named "Bel" to protect him.

He saw the beastman pause awhile and stare up at the circling bird. "They probably know each other," the boy mumbled. He remembered watching brascles swoop low over the Cragavar trees near Abascar, remembered how Captain Ark-robin had pointed out that brascles in the air meant beastmen in the trees below.

Later, during their journey southeastward through the Cragavar, the brascle chittered, annoyed, and wheeled off to the west. The boy did not feel as relieved as he wanted to. The country they traversed was still old Cent Regus territory, haunted and unpredictable. Snow-cased jags might have been piles of stone or, in the boy's numb delusion, gigantic beastmen huddled and lying in wait. His protector, wielding a rain canopy as if it were a talisman, guided them through a maze of disconnected fences made of ice-prickle brambles.

The beastman had not touched him or conveyed any threat. Instead, fumbling with Common words, forcing them together like a fool attempting carpentry, the beastman had pledged to protect the ale boy all the way back to Cal-raven in the Cliffs of Barnashum. To prove his claims, the beastman produced a familiar length of cloth—half of Auralia's scarf that the boy had seen in Cyndere's chamber.

The boy had agreed without hesitation. He feared upsetting the creature, whose conviction had a desperate quality.

"The colors are helping him," Auralia had whispered. "He comes for the colors. He stays. He sleeps. Sometimes I think he cries. They're leading him somewhere. I wonder where."

"I wonder where," he huffed and puffed. "Whatever happens. I hope he slows down. If it snows again. His tracks. Will fill. Right up."

When the heavens descended so hard, fast, and white that all signs of his guide were erased, the boy slumped down into the snow, only his head above the surface. The beastman came bounding back, growling. "Run," he said. "rrRun, O-raya's boy."

"I can't," he gasped. "You're a hundred times stronger. I travel by vawn, and my vawn's gotten lost."

"Bad bird," said the beastman, pointing at the sky. "rrBad bird sees. Tells more Cent Regus. Maybe they come." He tilted his head as if puzzled. "You...cold?"

"Aren't you?" the boy answered, a little too angrily perhaps. He brushed snow from his shoulders. "I'm so tired." He held up the whistle. "Can't even. Blow the signal."

The beastman snatched the whistle away and blew with such force that the boy felt it like a cold pin run up through his spine. Then the whistle burst into splinters.

"Very helpful," muttered the boy.

They waited, their snowy shells thickening. No sounds, no shapes— nothing emerged from the white void. The boy tried to ignore the thought that Rumpa might be trapped in one of Ryllion's snares.

"No vawn," the beastman shrugged. "rrRunning is better."

Before the ale boy could protest, the beastman lifted him up and bore him on his shoulders. The boy grasped the black mane with one hand, the rain canopy with the other. Without another word, they were off. Accustomed to the vawn's jolting pace, the ale boy was astonished at the ease of the beastman's stride across snow. The rhythms and the rush lulled him into a daze. They moved through the frozen world, all color sealed away.

The sun reappeared, a burning coin, as the beastman brought them out of the snowy rills and dunes into rockier land. The world took on definition again in thorns, ruins, and the blue glass of frozen ponds. A flock of peskies, each bird the size of the boy's thumb, sprang up from the shallow snow at their approach and hopped along behind them, cooing and chirping the same hopeful syllable.

When the beastman slowed, he asked for direction, but the boy grew more and more reluctant to reply. He feared he would lose his resolve, fall for the beastman's trick, and reveal Abascar's hideaway. As they paused, the peskies caught up to them, flitting and hopping all over their shoulders and heads. The boy saw the beastman fighting the impulse to grab their tiny, puffy bodies and swallow them by the handful.

To distract him, he offered his protector some of the Bel Amicans' dried meat. The beastman sniffed it, pinched it, and when he finally ate, he grumbled. "rrBird. Bird meat. Old." He stared off westward, clutched at his belly, and released a weary groan.

The boy said, "It will be dark very soon. And colder. Much colder. We should keep moving. Like Bel said. To Cal-raven."

The beastman carried him up over swells that bore catastrophes of wood and stone the way ocean waves carry shipwrecks—farmer shacks and shepherd houses from the early, uncursed days of House Cent Regus. Some were great carcasses, all jutting ribs and spines and rags; some, tent frames without canvas; some, small stone fortresses with towers tilting or leaning. But each one had eyes and jaws, and some of the structures moaned.

"There," said the beastman, pointing to the top of the highest rise. "Rest there. See far."

The barn and shack seemed a luxury compared to the rest of the ruined neighborhood. A small, wheezy structure slumped against a large, sturdy box of a building. Windows whistled, but the roof appeared sealed and sure. Sleet lashed the travelers, persuading them to hurry.

With each step up the hill, the beastman crushed patches of whiskbrush buried beneath the white crust.

"What's that black stuff hanging all over the barn?"

As if surprised to be noticed, the wavering dark moved. It caught on the wind and lifted in scraps from the barn roof.

They were snow herons—enormous black birds with long sharp beaks and beady eyes. Rasping and croaking like giant toads, they filled the sky with a cacophony of wingbeats. As they scattered, the wind from their passage sent icedust swirling in all directions. The flock of hopping peskies shrieked and burrowed into the snow.

"Someone's watching us. Through the window. At the top of that collapsing house," the boy whispered. "In armor."

The beastman snorted, unconcerned. "rrSoldier. Alone. Dead."

"You sure?" He could have sworn that the silhouette in the window turned its head to watch their progress. He could see the faint shining line of a soldier's helm and the gleam of a weapon unsheathed. But the watcher's features were shadowed.

"rrWe go in."

"Can't we find a different shelter?"

"Stay here. Up high. See far. See them if they come."

"Them? Who's coming?"

As the beastman had no interest in answering, the boy decided it was better not to know.

With a quick glance up at the window, the beastman said, "Weakerfolk afraid. Always afraid. Even when they fight. You?"

"Afraid? No." He laughed for the first time since Cyndere's chamber. Two days after sleeping in the bed of an heiress, here he was, carried by a curse-twisted monster through a merciless storm to trespass on haunted property. "Only one thing scares me. The Keeper. It scares me when it appears and scares me worse when it's gone. You know about the Keeper?"

The beastman lifted him off his shoulders and set him down, planting his feet in the snow. "rrKeeper?" The ale boy raised his arms like great wings, roared, and stamped about in wide steps, pointing back at his deep tracks. The beastman's eyes widened. He nodded. "Keeper."

"You've seen the Keeper?"

The beastman glanced about as if suspicious that the creature might be waiting around any corner. That was as good as an answer. He took the boy by the arm and led him stumbling around the side of the barn, past the pieces of an old plow, an overturned feed trough. At the back they found a section of wall missing. Snow drifted in across the floor of what had once been a workshop with brace tables, hackers, shavers, chippers, and a rack for hammers.

Though the barn was open to the elements, the leaning farmhouse was still walled up. The beastman lifted an unhinged wooden door and set it aside. He told the boy to stay by the door while he searched within. The ale boy waited for the clash of swords, for screams and commotion.

At the beastman's tremendous roar, the boy thrust the canopy out before him like a shield and readied for a retreat. But silence followed, and the beast-man appeared again. "rrNothing scared," he said. "Nothing moved. Nothing ran. Empty."

Inside, the boy found walls that seemed to have wept, stained with blurred hues. Inhabitants had sought to seal cracks and strengthen warping wallbeams with whatever was available to them—metal scraps, bundles of branches, spans of canvas and leather. Straw and rotten leaves made a carpet that rustled as tiny rodents scurried underneath. Sticky blackness glued the debris to the ground in random patches. Even the beastman avoided the stuff.

A round, black iron stove, just big enough for baking bread, stood near the wall. Its tall chimney pipe reached up through the ceiling. The boy pulled, but the latch remained fixed. "Guess there's no cooking tonight."

The beastman touched the latch, and it snapped loose.

The stove coughed a black cloud. Sootmice bounded out, squeaking, abandoning their nest. The beastman snatched two of them, and the ale boy tried not to listen to the crunch.

"Mind if I make a fire?"

"rrNo smoke. Cent Regus close. Must hide, O-raya's boy." The beastman looked at the weathered wooden ceiling beams. Bird droppings had seeped through over the years, gluing shut the cracks. Finished with his cursory inspection, the beastman suddenly shuddered, swayed, and slumped to the floor.

"Are you all right?"

"rrStrength," the creature snarled. "Need Cent Regus strength." The boy almost thought he saw an apology in those simian features. "Cent Regus get tired. Cent Regus hurt. Everywhere." He gestured to his feet, his knees, his chest, his head. Then he lay back, jaw sagging open, and was suddenly asleep, sprawled on the floor.

The ale boy closed the rain canopy, sat down with his back against an old barrel, and glanced nervously at the ladder that rose through the ceiling. That ladder could take them upstairs or let someone climb down.

As the room went dark, so did the ale boy's attention.

A commotion woke him, a sound like someone sweeping snow with tree branches. The world was dark, save for a faint blue at the windows and the pinpricks of stars in the sky. The storm had passed.

He reached for his bag and pulled out the Bel Amican glowstone. The light found the beastman crouched at the window, staring out.

The boy joined him, looking out at the starlit snow. "What is it?"

"Feelers."

"Feelers?" He watched the moonlit snowdrifts, and a disturbance caught his attention. Something slithered beneath those sparkling waves.

"Feelers. Looking for you, boy."

Repulsed, he asked, "What are they?"

"Don't know. rrDangerous. Feelers crawl on Cent Regus land. Underground. Come up. Catch animals. Trees. People. But not Cent Regus."

The boy did not like anything he was learning from the beastman. To shake off the thought, he began to walk about the space. "I need to get back to my work," he said. "I don't like this hiding. It's not doing anybody good." He tried to right an overturned table, but it had a broken leg. He picked up a long wooden stick with a splintered end, what might have once been a rake. Propping it under the table, he said, "Looks like we're too late to help these people. But it was a home once."

"rrOld Cent Regus. Long, long ago."

"A child lived here. He marked his growth on the wall. Perhaps once a year. He made notches, see? He made a number by each one. When he was seven, he was this tall. And here, eight."

The beastman came to stare. He pointed to the space above the tenth mark. "Stopped growing?"

"Yes, it stops there." The ale boy's face crumpled in worry. He touched the tenth mark, as if it might tell him some secret history.

"You." The beastman put a hand on the ale boy's head. "No stopping."

Surprised, the ale boy looked up. Feeling awkward, unsure how to respond, he patted the beastman's hand. "You either."

A rustle of snow outside caught their attention. And then the structure groaned a bit, as if suddenly burdened.

The ale boy checked the beastman's face. "Feelers?"

"rrNo. Big black birds. Came back. Sleep on rooftop."

"Maybe they'll block the wind. Or seal in some warmth."

The beastman stood against the wall, took his knife, and made a mark high above the tenth mark.

"I suspect you're finished growing."

The beastman scowled.

"Well, maybe I'm wrong." The ale boy smiled. He began to walk along the wall, examining the wood splinters, the piles of droppings, the scattered leaves, looking for more clues.

"Boy, did O-raya...stop?"

The ale boy kicked at a loose floorboard, then knelt and lifted it. "Auralia...changed," he said. He pulled a wooden box up from the space beneath it. "She changed very much. And then the Keeper took her away." He opened the box. It was empty.

"Keeper?" growled the beastman. He sank down to the floor again, holding his head. "Keeper took O-raya?"

"It saved her. Carried her away. Oh, I don't know." The ale boy turned toward the window and said, "I sure haven't seen any signs of Auralia or the Keeper for a very long time." He threw the box out the window.

"Must find O-raya. Must find colors. Had them. But bad Cent Regus took them. Colors...stop the hurt."

"Yes," said the ale boy. "Yes, I know. I've been sharing Auralia's colors with people from Abascar. And from Bel Amica too. To stop the hurt."

"No colors to Cent Regus. Don't go." The beastman leaned forward as if the ale boy had suddenly become interesting. Two bright points of the glowstone's light sparkled in his large, dark eyes. "O-raya...call you?"

"What did she call me? She called me ale boy."

"Ale boy."

"Yes. What did Auralia call you?"

The beastman thought for a moment. "Hairy."

The ale boy's laughter began like a trickle and then burst into a stream, rushing across the room and splashing against the walls. The beastman looked toward the ladder. The ale boy clasped his mouth shut.

"Go up now," said the beastman. He gestured for the boy to follow.

Climbing the ladder, which complained at every step, the beastman stopped halfway when the ale boy asked him, "May I call you Hairy too?"

He seemed burdened by the question. "No," he sighed and went on up through the ceiling. "Jordam. rrCall me Jordam."

Emerging onto a feeble floor of rotten beams, they found a spell of unsettling silence.

Then a frantic flock of pearbellies, flung by shock from the rafters, collided and careened into flight. Grey feather tufts filled the air. The ale boy sneezed, remembering pillow fights among Gatherer orphans.

Each step he took creaked underfoot, and he was reluctant to continue. But if the beastman could, surely he should follow.

The watcher in the chair may have been waiting for someone, or perhaps this view of the path that had led here was a subject of regretful contemplation. Whatever the case, the riot of birds did not disturb that profound reverie.

The boy tiptoed up behind the figure, raising the glowstone, and he saw that this was a Bel Amican soldier who appeared to be asleep, kneeling. But as he moved between the watcher and the window, he could see that the shoulders did not rise or fall. He guessed this had been a woman, from the long and wisping hair, the narrow bones of her wrists. Her eyes were vacant caves. The helmet rested on a skull wrapped in papery remains. Arms thrust forward, the skeletal fingers of one hand were wrapped around the hilt of a sword turned inward, the blade running straight between the breastplate and the belt.

"Dead."

"She killed herself."

Jordam prodded at the uniform looking for something useful. Thrusting his fingers through the eye sockets to hold the skull in place, he pried the helmet off. It broke free with a smacking sound, and the boy turned away. The beastman tried to put the helmet on, but his head was far too large. When he offered it, the ale boy choked.

Most Bel Amican soldiers would rather fall on their swords than die at the claws of the Cent Regus, or so Abascar's Captain Ark-robin had scornfully remarked to his men. Bel Amicans were proud and certain of superiority. Rather than give anyone reason to boast at having slain them, they would call out for their moon-spirit and then leave their attacker an empty shell.

This shell had once belonged to a swordswoman, and part of an elite company from the looks of her ornate blade that remained as silver and intricately detailed as the day it was forged.

The ale boy knelt before her. "When somebody dies like this, I wonder if Northchildren come to unstitch them and give them a new skin. Like they did for Auralia."

Jordam had pulled the head back, leaving her vacant visage etched in moonlight as if in a posthumous prayer.

"Look." The boy reached for the swordswoman's left hand that curled loosely like a dead spider. "She's holding something." He pinched the parchment free from its cage of finger bones, pulled its crisp folds open, and began to read. The runes were fancier, more dramatic than Abascar writing. But he could recognize enough to try to piece together the message.

He read aloud to the beastman, who stood and stared out the window. She was a guard, part of a Bel Amican caravan attacked by Cent Regus. The boy struggled to translate what had happened but made very little sense of it. Apparently the soldiers had been slaughtered, and the passengers had been dragged away by the Cent Regus.

"'They have taken Partayn,'" the ale boy read. "'Partayn is gone. I write this so you know. I did not see him die. He will suffer'...something I can't read. Something bad probably. And then...'in the Cent Regus den. A slave.'"

The boy pulled the parchment closer to his face. "'I have...failed.'" He read excitedly now, tracing the frail letters with a fingertip. "'Moon-spirits will punish me, if I live. I give up my life. As an apology. To the spirit.'" He stopped. "Partayn. Ballyworms! The prison guard...he talked about how Partayn died when beastmen attacked a caravan. But this guard, she says they killed everyone but the passengers. She says Partayn was dragged off to be a slave. You hear that, Jordam?"

A faint sound began, a faraway rhythm.

"Horses," said the boy.

"Brothers," Jordam sighed. He pressed his hands against his head again, as he had when the boy told him about Auralia's departure. "Brothers coming."

"Brothers? You have brothers?"

A deep unsettling growl rumbled in Jordam's throat. "Bad. Brothers. Found me." He looked at the boy. "rrBad, Jordam and boy coming here." He pressed a clawed hand against his chest, rasping something the ale boy did not understand. "One...hand."

"How did they find you?"

The shelter shook, and dust showered down as the predators' approach frightened the snow herons and sent them scattering. The first faint lines of morning glowed through cracks across the ceiling, and the ale boy backed into a shadowy corner, wishing he could pull the darkness in around him.

Jordam stood and pointed to the ladder. "rrWe go back down," he said. "Plan. Jordam makes a plan."

Like thunder before storms. That was the simple thought that rumbled in Jordam's mind as he stared down the snowy slope.

He cursed Mordafey's brascle for spotting him. He cursed Mordafey for coming so far to track him down. He would never get the boy safely to Calraven now. Either Mordafey needed him for that secret plot, or he meant to punish him for failing to fulfill the orders. Jordam had never been forced to imagine fighting all three of his brothers at once. He could imagine it now. It would not go well.

As Mordafey approached, whipping the horses, sitting on the driver's bench of the lead Bel Amican carriage, Jordam could see the brascle, large-eyed and dark-feathered, its black beak glinting in the cold light. From the bird's beak hung a strip of red meat, reward enough to keep that scavenger bird loyal.

Jordam wondered what had happened to the white-clad giant with the fiery staff. Then he marveled that Mordafey had not slaughtered the horses for food. Perhaps they were to be added to the stock of prizes for the chieftain. More Essence—everything increased Mordafey's desire for more Essence. Everything became part of the game.

Jordam would gamble on that.

Mordafey raised the bird high, and the brascle flapped its wings. Mordafey laughed, boasting some kind of victory.

Bel, Jordam said to himself. *Remember Bel.*

"You!" Sneering from his place beside Mordafey, Jorn sat wrapped in a flowered blanket, his skin painting itself with the patchwork pattern. He had wrapped the merchant woman's shawl around his head as if he was trying to disguise himself as an old Bel Amican woman, but Jordam knew that his hairless brother was just trying to stay warm. Long strings of yellow dangled from Jorn's houndish snout, and his eyes were red. Through his bruises, he grinned wickedly at Jordam, and Jordam understood. Somehow, Jorn had blamed his captivity on him.

Goreth glanced out from the carriage, and before Mordafey could launch whatever rant he had planned, he leapt out and climbed the slope to greet his twin.

"Same Brother, you've been gone." The brusque sound of Cent Regus speech was welcome to Jordam after so much struggle with Common. He would have to be careful, though, with his own words. "Look!" Goreth opened his hand, proudly displaying an array of bloodstained teeth, recently gathered—probably pulled from the merchants they had slain on the bridge. His grin seemed forced, frantic, and his laughter recklessly free, while his tail wagged and slapped against the snow. "Brothers took horses, wagons. Now we go to see the chieftain and the Sopper Crone!"

Jordam watched Mordafey's face. "rrWent to rescue Jorn. You see now. He was gone. Got away."

"You've been gone." Goreth's face crumpled, and now a wave of anger swept over him. He raised his hand to strike.

Jordam backed away, barking, "Goreth! rrRemember? I told you—strike me again, and I'll finish you."

Goreth retreated. "Right," he mumbled, sullen. "Young Brother was caged. By weakerfolk somewhere. Can't remember."

"Where were y-y-you?" Jorn stuttered, eager for confrontation. Clutching at the flowered blanket, he jumped down from the driver's bench and accused Jordam with a long, clawed finger. "M'trapped in Bel Amican sssstinkplace? Got out on m'own. Where were y-you?"

From the driver's bench behind the horses, Mordafey gestured to the shambles of the abandoned merchant dwelling. "Jordam's got a new life alone? Abandoned brothers at last?"

"No. I tried to get Jorn. But Jorn was gone. Storm came. I found shelter. Heavy storm." Jordam shrugged. "You said, 'Get Jorn.' I got past Bel Amican guards. rrBut Jorn got loose and ran. Like a gorrel."

All three brothers blinked, uncomprehending. A moment passed before Goreth said, "Young Brother's not a gorrel. Gorrels are small."

Mordafey leaned forward as if he might leap over the horses in his rage. "Jorn—bleeding Jorn—got back to the caves. Jorn got through the storm."

"But Jorn brought you no prizes," Jordam ventured.

"Prizes!" said Goreth, failing to grasp the tension between his brothers. Tail wagging with gladness, he gestured to the wagons. "Did you know? We have prizes from Abascar. Deuneroi's bones. Deuneroi's hands. Deuneroi's weapons."

"I remember," Jordam growled.

"Prizes from merchants too! Jumped them on a bridge."

"I remember, Goreth. I killed one." He watched as whorls of steam massaged the horses. *Like smoke,* he thought.

"Who's in the barn??" asked Mordafey, smiling. "You kill him too?" He leapt down, seized Jordam's mane, and pushed his head down toward the ground. "Plotting with someone else now?"

Goreth kicked a spray of snow onto his twin's woodscloak. "Bird says Jordam runs with someone. Says two stay here."

Mordafey unsheathed a stabbing fork from his belt and pushed it up under Jordam's chin. "Tonight three brothers go to the Core. Time to get the Essence we have earned. Tomorrow we go inside, where Skell Wra gives us strength. Then we get ready. For Abascar. Mordafey killed Deuneroi. Remember? Now three brothers make a better strike."

Let them go, said a voice within him. *Let them go, and do what you promised Bel you would do. Protect the boy.* But another voice fought back. *If they go without you, you will be cut off. Those who are not with the brothers are enemies of the brothers. They will hunt you.*

He had no choice. He had to take a terrible risk.

"Prize," Jordam muttered. "I brought Mordafey a prize."

"What"—Mordafey twisted the fork, cutting into Jordam's throat—"prize?"

Jordam laughed. "You thought I couldn't. But I caught him."

Mordafey let him go. "Caught...who?"

As the brothers approached the shack, Jordam seized the unhinged door and planted it in the snow against the wall. Jorn shoved his head inside and shrieked, "Keeper's boy!" Hysterical, he limped back down to the wagons and dove under the canvas.

Mordafey stalked through the door, growling in suspicion at the boy bound to an empty feed barrel in the center of the room, a strap of leather tying his mouth shut.

"The boy," Jordam boasted. "Ran away from Baldridge Hill. Remember? You said I let him go. But I caught him. For the brothers."

Mordafey clasped Jordam's arm and laughed softly. "Good. Good catch."

"Run!" Jorn's voice howled from outside. "Fire monster watches th'boy! Run!"

Mordafey scratched a line across the boy's forehead. The boy's eyes fluttered open, and he shrank back, whimpering, then cried out as the brute seized his ear.

Protect O-raya's boy. Jordam dared to seize Mordafey's wrist and pull him away. "rrWait. Listen, Mordafey. Keep the boy. He's an Abascar boy. Hide him here. When the brothers come back from the Core, we take the boy to Abascar. rrRemember the old trick? Use the boy. Bait."

"Bait," said Mordafey, nodding. "Bait." He turned to Goreth. "Lock the boy in that stove."

"Stove?" Jordam and the boy shared a bewildered glance.

"Brothers come back for the boy later," said Mordafey. "Mordafey's tired of waiting. We go to the chieftain now. Today. Together. Four brothers again."

As Goreth broke the boy's restraints, he smiled admiringly at his twin. "Same Brother," he said, "I think this is the boy who ran from Baldridge Hill."

The horses moved down the old rugged road, Jordam trudging along behind as if chained to the back of the second wagon. Only a few paces along, Mordafey cursed at the horses for dragging the wagons into a snow-draped marsh, the wheels sinking into the soft ground. He lashed at the steeds while Goreth and Jorn tried to lift the front of the wagon frame.

Jordam stepped behind the wagon to raise it, then cautiously peered beneath the canvas at the loot. He pulled out Deuneroi's bloodied woods-cloak, which bundled together his bones and treasures. As the others hauled the wagon out of the sunken ground, Jordam dropped these prizes into the marsh and kicked snow over them, burying them out of sight.

19

A Seer Comes
to Tilianpurth

Ryllion woke to the sound of the ocean and the smell of salt.
A deep ache throbbed in his right arm, and he remembered the bat
fastened there, the bite in his wrist. He wondered if he had been rushed to
House Bel Amica for attention from special healers. *If it gets me home, it will
be worth it.* He tried lifting his arm, but the cast was heavy. He opened his eyes.

"Do you hear it, Officer?"

Emeriene sat at a table before the window of his chamber in Tilianpurth's tower. He was not home. The scent of the sea and the roar breathed
from a large, spiral seashell propped next to his head.

Emeriene laughed, stirring something steamy in a clay bowl. Broth—
he could smell it now—most likely a foul green brine, some weedy soup
without a scrap of meat. She would swear it was healthy for him. He wanted
a prowlfish steak.

"Kramm," he muttered. "I was having such a lovely dream. You drowned
in a shipwreck."

She applauded. "I thought the bat might have bitten off your tongue,
but there it is. Moon-spirits be praised. Come and eat, child. The ordeal has
sapped your strength."

Her dark disheveled hair, her voice scratched and deepened by pipe
smoke, the ties of her robe loosened just enough to tease him—so she
wanted his attention, did she? If this conversation continued in such a con-
genial tone, the injury might prove useful after all.

"Since you asked so nicely," she said, "I'll tell you."

"I didn't ask."

"The sisterlies pumped a powerful antidote into your veins. But apparently your heartbeat runs stronger than most. From head to toe, the bat's venom discolored you. You'll be in bed awhile, and your arm will be slow in healing. But you're lucky the damage stops there."

His gambling cubes lay scattered across the floor. As he counted them, he noticed her slippers by the door next to a heap of rumpled cushions. She had slept here, watching over him. He was about to pry this admission from her when she volunteered that very truth, describing how he had required attention to his seizures during the night.

He asked who had caught and killed the beastman. "That privilege is still available," she replied. "Our prisoners seem to have slipped away. Both of them."

"That bratty little Abascar spy?" he growled. "No matter. We'll catch him again. But that beastman—we needed him. The ceremony is coming fast."

"It's tomorrow."

"I've slept a day, a night, and another day?" He began shouting questions, which Emeriene answered calmly.

She had doubled Cyndere's guard, yes, and the heiress's chamber had been thoroughly searched. While no one had seen the beastman run for the open gate, the search had produced no clues. They had buried the slain guards in the yard. Everyone else was accounted for.

"But not everything is in its proper place," he mused, eyes fixed on her face. "There's trouble in those pretty eyes."

"You always trouble me."

"But I am a jealous tormentor. And something—or someone—else has put a wrinkle in your voice."

She stirred the broth.

"You want to go back, don't you? To Bel Amica. To your sons."

"I need to see my boys. They'll have caused all kinds of trouble by now. Out here I forget who I am. I start treating other people like they're my children."

"Is that what you're doing? Mothering me? I hear I'm incorrigible. So please, don't stop."

"You're beyond help, child."

"Har, har." He picked up the seashell and raised it as if he would throw it. She folded her arms defiantly, and he put it back down. "Let me give you some advice."

Her eyes narrowed.

"Tilianpurth is a different world. Quieter. Simpler. It gives us opportunities to catch new visions from the spirits."

"Don't get religious on me."

"I'm serious. Since the queen ordered me to do some good around here, I've had new adventures. You could too. You might indulge yourself a little. You might become something more than a sisterly and a mother. What desires have dusted you during the night, Em? What has your spirit whispered in your ear?"

"I *am* something more than a mother." She let go of the spoon and tapped the tattoo on the back of her hand.

"Ah yes. How could I forget?" Her glare pleased him. He pressed harder. "Tell me, if Cesylle cares so much about his wife, why has he not come out here to be with her?"

"The Seers need him in Bel Amica."

"You've got it backward. Cesylle needs the Seers."

"They're training him to use skyscopes and farglasses, to interpret the moon colors and read the moods of the spirits. He says he'll show me wonders someday." As she poured water from a pitcher into a clay cup, her casual tone began to sour into resentment. "He used to say that *I* was a wonder."

Ryllion scratched around the edge of his cast. Her voice was edged with a new, reckless sense of trust in him as a listener. Something had knocked her off balance. "Cesylle's forgotten the treasure he has."

She dared to meet his gaze, but only for a moment.

"We noticed you on the same day, Cesylle and I. Did you know that?" He laughed. "Don't ever tell your husband I told you this."

"Told me what?"

He rose from the blankets, and she turned to the window with a noise between a laugh and a cry, for he was naked. He casually wrapped himself in a sheet and sat down at the table. She pressed her lips together and stared intently at some unremarkable place in the grey sky, red rising up her neck and tinting her cheeks, while he seized the bowl and gulped the broth.

"Ambitious youngsters, we were," he said as if they spoke like this every morning. "We had a round of cubes." He nodded to the game pieces on the floor. "Cesylle won. He got to invite you to the king's feast."

"You had a round of cubes." She shook her head and laughed bitterly. "Before the king's burial feast? Oh, that is just pristine. It explains so much— that I was Cesylle's prize in a game. And then he moved on to play other sorts of games." She tapped the windowsill. "You couldn't even grow a beard yet. Do you think I would have accepted your invitation to the burial feast if you'd won?"

"Let's call it by its proper name—it was the Feast of the Reward. A celebration. King Helpryn heard that coveted call, the blessing that the moon-spirits grant their most faithful servants. He was carried from the deck of his ship to the moon. He never died. He was taken straight to his reward."

"And thus, King Helpryn's people were blessed. Is that what you think?"

"He impressed the spirits, and he continues to petition them for favor. Thus, his family is blessed. House Bel Amica is richer than ever. We should learn from his example and risk everything—everything, Em—to pursue the desires that seize us."

"Where are Cyndere's blessings?"

"Deuneroi wasn't a blessing?"

"You call their short-lived marriage a blessing?" Her laughter lacked any note of humor. "That kind of loss is a wound that doesn't heal. Believe me. I know."

"You're talking about Partayn, aren't you? You think Cyndere's brother was your only chance for happiness. So you settled for Cesylle."

"It's none of your concern," she snapped. "And, no, he wasn't. There were other chances. But why trust my desires when they're always spoiled?"

Perhaps there was more to Emeriene's pain than Cesylle's neglect. "Let me tell you what the Seers tell me." After an awkward pause, he cleared his throat. "Sometimes what I desire is lost. That's not my fault. The world is a tangle of many hearts, many desires, and not everybody gets what they want. But the desires are still sacred. They're a compass. If we don't indulge them, we'll never find the one that brings us happiness. I hear it in your voice, Em—the longing. You haven't given up. I think I can help you."

She took the dull cheese knife and pretended to threaten him. "Notice my weapon of choice in resisting you."

"You feel too bound to the old ways, the contracts. They get in the way of your sacred—"

"You think it's my faithfulness to Cesylle that makes me unhappy."

"There's something you think you can't have. I understand that." He dropped both hands onto the table, his cast thudding down hard, causing the bowl and the bread plate to jump. "But I won't let the expectations of others get in my way. I don't even tell the Seers the full nature of my desires. If I did, they'd meddle and make my quest more difficult."

"Oh, you think we don't see it. But everybody knows your quest, Ryllion." Taking her cheese knife by the blade, she whacked his cast with its handle. "Is this what happens to people who reach for what they really want? You want to be a captain. You want Cyndere. And then you'll get to be king someday."

"That's the Seers' understanding," he sighed. He lifted the bowl and drank it dry.

She handed him a piece of bread but put the lid on the dipping bowl. "No syrup for your bread. Not until you start speaking plainly. What quest are you talking about?"

"I'll give you a hint if you'll give me the syrup."

She watched him for a moment, then lifted the lid.

"Deuneroi wanted to tame the beastmen." He lowered his voice, dipping the bread. "And to make it up to him, I'm pursuing that dream. But I'll need help. So tomorrow, at the Ceremony of the Sacrifice, I will make an offering that will dazzle the spirits."

"How is killing a beastman honoring Deuneroi's desire to save them?"

"Under that watchful green moon, I'll gain the spirits' favor. They'll see that we are united in our desire to rid the world of the Cent Regus scourge. And they'll lend us power. But my plan is to conquer the beastmen by luring them into a choice—either obedience to Bel Amica or destruction. If we can compel them to follow orders, to fight for us instead of against us, we can tame them."

"And how long have you been planning this?"

"I've had a lot of time to think during my stay. And one of the Seers has been learning to manipulate the beastmen."

"The Honorable Pretor Xa."

His smiled vanished. "How did you know?" He leaned forward. "Did Cyndere tell you? He's on his way to join us here?"

"He's here," she said sharply.

Ryllion's knees bumped the table as he rose, and the syrup jar skidded to the edge. Emeriene caught it, pushed it back onto the table, and put the lid on it, a smug smile on her face. "Now, now, child. Don't make a mess."

"Why didn't somebody wake me?"

"I told Pretor Xa that you'd been bitten by a rodent and weren't in any condition to take visitors."

"You enjoyed that, didn't you? Humiliating me before one of the Seers. You've embarrassed me three times now. When Cyndere arrived, you let me go on speaking like a musker's backside when you knew she was listening. And now I wake up to find myself wearing nothing but the bed blankets. I suspect it was you who wrapped this bandage too tight." He picked at the edge of his cast.

"We had to get you out of those clothes." She absently poured more water into her cup, forgetting that she had already filled it, and it splashed onto the table.

"We?" He wrapped the sheet tighter around him. "How many sisterlies were part of this wicked endeavor?"

"There wasn't time to waste." She stifled a smile. "The last thing you need is flattery. But the so-called privilege went to... Well, there was this game of cubes, you see."

She leaned forward to cast a cloth napkin across the spill. He caught a glimpse of the fiery purple moon-tattoo that showed at the base of her throat, and he wanted, just for a minute, to give up his perilous plans. To abandon the ceremony he had arranged for the evening. He wanted to take her away and flee back to Bel Amica, to the familiar games of wit and flirtation. "You with your leg in a cast. Me with my arm. We're quite a pair, you and I."

"We are not a pair," she scoffed.

"Let me tell you what caused this injury, Emeriene." He knocked on his cast. "My father and grandfather labored in those shipyards for Bel Amica. They trained me to seek advantage. They told me that I should take one small step every day toward a greater opportunity. That's why I'm within reach of Cyndere's hand. The Seers encourage my ambition. They want me to be king. But, Emeriene, my moon-spirit knows my heart better than anyone. She knows something even the Seers don't know."

"And what's that?"

"Something has complicated my ambition."

"Cyndere's refusals."

"No," he declared, bringing his fist down on the table. "It's true, I approached the heiress. I made a scandalous suggestion—that she allow me to fill the void left by Deuneroi's death. But that's what the Seers want. It's not really what *I* want. I see that now. My moon-spirit punished me; she made the bat attack me. I was straying from my true desire."

"Your true desire." Emeriene put the cup on the table, tracing its rim with her fingertips.

"Cyndere's heart belongs to Deuneroi. But you knew, even before we arrived at Tilianpurth, Emeriene, what my heart now understands."

He reached for her hand, but she jerked it away. "Don't say those things out loud! This is an open window."

"You see?" he said. "No bat jumped out of the shadows. I'm speaking the truth. You haven't thrown the cup at me. You haven't mentioned Cesylle's name."

"You haven't asked about *my* desires!" she shrieked, flustered.

"You're sad and lonely. You sat in my chamber to watch over me. What does that tell you?"

She rose, red as sunburn, and walked past him toward the door. "You presumptuous fool. I haven't told you why I'm here."

"Then what?"

"I'm here because I needed to speak with you before that meddling Seer starts hovering over you. I need your help, Ryllion." Anger flared in her voice. "And I don't know where…" The anger broke into something more unstable, something like grief. "I don't know where to turn."

"It's Cyndere, isn't it, Em?"

"Don't," she whispered, "call me *Em*."

"She's hurt you."

"We used to share everything. When she had secrets with Deuneroi, I could trust her. Because I trusted him. But now she has new secrets. Dangerous secrets. Something else is taking her away. She's shutting me out. And it's only going to get worse. I'm afraid she'll run away. Away into her secret."

"She can't run away." Ryllion moved toward her. His arm pulsed like a violent alarm, and he caught the bedpost to keep from falling. "There's nowhere she can go. She'd need a soldier's help, and no one here would risk spoiling other officers' trust to help her. Not while I'm nearby. I see everything." *But I had better look again,* he thought.

Emeriene walked to the bed and sat down on the edge, her shoulders shaking. "She's lost so much. She's so lonely. But she's not the only one. Can't she understand that?"

He sat down next to her, watched their reflections in the mirror that faced them. "You don't have to be lonely," he said softly.

"You want to help me?" she said, wiping her eyes on her sleeve. "Post a guard in the kitchen. All night."

He took her hand gently and squeezed it. "Done. I'll post guards in the kitchen, at the lift, at the stairwell, if you're so sure."

"Just be watchful."

"Listen, Em. *Emeriene.* I want you to have a seat on the balcony tomorrow night during the Feast of the Sacrifice. It will do you good. Watch what happens. I'll give the people a picture of what is to come." She looked up and started to protest, but he touched her cheek with his fingertips and said, "Shh. Trust me. I'm ready for this. I'll slay a beastman in the Ceremony of Sacrifice. That should release the anger that has built up within Cyndere since Deuneroi's death. It should release the anger in all of us. The spirits will be pleased. And then. . .imagine it. We'll go out and strike fear into their hearts. And tame them."

"Before an audience?" She pulled her hand away. "You'll kill a beastman in front of Cyndere? You know how she feels—"

"I also know how she feels about losing Deuneroi. A beastman killed him; a beastman must die. The ceremony will do so much more to encourage the people than those few token beastman skulls I've sent home. Those who watch will have a sense of participation. It will move all of us toward healing."

She cast a doubtful glance at his reflection.

"Listen, Emeriene. The Seers have shown me that if people unite in a desire, moon-spirits overcome their differences and strive to bless us all. Together we can begin to break the scourge of the Expanse."

She closed her eyes and squeezed his hand with both of hers. "I should go," she said. "I shouldn't be here. The other sisterlies will talk. I'll call for the Seer to help prepare you for the ceremony." She moved to the door, paused, and looked at him in the mirror hanging there. "I'll be there on the balcony to watch you tomorrow. And, Ryllion...strike true."

"If I know you'll be waiting for me when it's over, I will strike the truest blow Bel Amica's ever seen."

The white sun hung in the white sky the next day, and the stone whistle that Cyndere had found inside the oceandragon's skull gleamed like a jewel in her hand.

She thought of the stonemaster who had sculpted it. She did not trust Scharr ben Fray, but she was drawn to the idea of someone out there wandering and pursuing the mysteries of the Expanse. Oh to be so free.

"I've met a mystery for you, old man," she said, turning to look at the likeness she was detailing on the wall. "He's a beastman. And he's healing." She put the whistle down and took up a lump of burnt firewood. Clearing a patch of wallstones, she began to sketch the ale boy's face. "And there's someone else. A young firewalker. Out there in the snow. I hope they've found each other."

Emeriene crept in as if wanting to remain unnoticed and dutifully gathered up the woodscloak that Cyndere had brought in from the wild the night before. The sisterly had stopped asking questions. Cyndere knew that her friend was angry and that she resented these solitary excursions by night. She also knew that Emeriene would sound an alarm if she guessed what was happening in the glen.

"Emeriene," Cyndere called to her friend, who was heading for the door. "It is…it is helping. Walking in the woods at night. I can't explain yet. But I will someday. You don't have to worry. You won't lose me. I—"

"If I cannot be a part of your new life, I'm losing you already." Emeriene pulled the door shut hard behind her.

The sound was like a slap, and Cyndere felt the sting. She went back to the incense bowl by her bedside, sat down, cupped her hands and drew the aroma of those crushed blue flowers to her face. Drawing it in deep, she felt the calm come over her. She looked about the room. She was tired of this space. She wanted to emerge from hiding. Conversation with Jordam had invigorated her. She would go back to the glen every night until he returned.

"An honest beastman, Deun. I've found him. I'll speak with him just as we practiced. I'll teach him. He has so much to learn." She stepped to the window and lifted an empty cup, pretending to raise a toast. "I wish you were here. We could celebrate." She glanced about, but the sisterlies would not bring wine until evening. "It's too early for wine. Let's go find something special."

She took the stairs and strolled a leisurely circle around each level in the tower and the towerhouse below. The soldiers—those resting from their night patrols—were a cacophonous concert of snores. One man, creeping in his bedblankets from the bunkroom of the women's chamber, turned white with fear and then red with embarrassment as the heiress smirked.

Then it was down to the main level, where she wandered to the open doors and gazed out at the snow path that ran to the gates. A warmer wind had set the icicles to dripping from windowsills above her. Fog rose from the snow. Wilus Caroon was slumped in the guard chair, snoring. Spittle drooled from his bulging lower lip, and when he choked on a dream, his eyes opened, rolled, and fixed on her. "It's up to no good," he rasped. "You watch for it. Up to no good, I tell you."

"Indeed," she laughed. "What's up to no good? The beastman?"

"It's after us," he said, still deep within delirium. "All of us. Wings, fire. A big black thing, flying straight for my face. But I shooed it away, and it was gone."

"Are you dreaming about the Keeper?" she whispered. "Lapsing back to childhood in your old age, are you?"

The sound of a plate breaking drew her back into the corridor, then to the bar in the kitchen, where she surveyed the bustling crew. "So is anyone going to offer me a bottle of berry juice?"

They all changed direction in midstep, scrambling to answer her request, and in the process, two more dishes broke.

"Such attentive helpers," said a deep, resonant voice.

The Seer swept into the kitchen, his robes a whirlwind about him. He came to the bar to share Cyndere's view.

Cyndere took a step away from him. Pretor Xa had departed House Bel Amica long before she had come to Tilianpurth. By way of explanation, the Seers had announced that the philosophers and historians of House Jenta in the south had summoned him to aid them in revising their histories of the Expanse. Whenever the Seers offered elaborate explanations, Cyndere immediately sought for clues to the truth.

Speaking as if from a throne to an assembly—an annoying habit of the Seers—Pretor Xa explained that his stay in Tilianpurth would be brief. He was late, for beastmen had slain the merchants he had hired to bring him home and stolen their horses and wagons. Two days he had walked in the storm. But he knew that they needed him to lead the Ceremony of Sacrifice, and he would stay to share the feast before his return to Bel Amica.

"It is good to see the heiress up and about," said the Seer to the air. "I hope that her moon-spirit has granted her the healing that she sought here after such terrible losses." His perpetual smile sickened her, and he seemed especially pleased with himself.

"Why would moon-spirits bother to heal a wound that they allowed me to suffer in the first place?"

"Softly, Heiress." The Seer's voice took on a patronizing tone that made her teeth hurt. "You would do well not to offend the moon-spirits."

"It must be too late for that. I pursued my heart's desire, and they let him die."

"You're distraught over your loss, but lift your eyes. Look about. We're all wounded by what the beastmen have done. Tonight we will assemble to ask the spirits to put aside their differences and bless us."

"Please, Pretor Xa. What you would do in response to Deuneroi's death only shows how little you knew him."

The kitchen staff was scattering.

"When you perpetuate this false hope of redeeming the beastmen, you prolong your suffering, Heiress. Let go of Deuneroi's dreams. You'll find it easier to let go of Deuneroi himself. The world will be a safer place with one less savage in the wild."

"You spit upon all he strove to achieve. And didn't you hear? The beast-man Ryllion planned to kill—he escaped."

"Didn't you hear?" the Seer replied. "They've caught another."

Cyndere pressed a hand to her breast.

"Oh. They didn't tell you? Yes, before the sun rose, they caught one. Clearly, Ryllion's moon-spirit heard his plea. And this beastman? He boasts of Deuneroi's murder."

She began backing toward the door, suddenly terrified by the Seer's painted face and his lipless grin. "Whatever he boasts, I do not want a beast-man killed here. In a battle to defend ourselves, yes. To save a life, yes. But to settle a score, no. I came here to find peace."

How she hated their faces. Their elaborate tattoos and paint obscured any hint of expression, save for that mad smile.

"Heiress of Bel Amica," he said in his singsong fashion, "you may not need this closure, but your people do."

"This beastman." Cyndere put a hand out to steady herself against the bar. "What does he look like?"

The Seer's white eyes rattled in their sockets. "Why?"

Cyndere turned and fled back up the corridor. "Deuneroi," she whispered, "help me." She thought of the woods. If she disrupted the Ceremony of Sacrifice or found some way to escape it, her mother would punish her for offending the spirits.

This time it would be different. If she ran away, she would have to keep running.

"Honorable Pretor Xa," Ryllion murmured in his empty chamber, "forgive me. I have been false with you."

As he stood chest-deep in a steaming soaktub, his reflection in the full-length mirror stared back at him. He posed several expressions of humble resolve. "You assumed that my desire was for the heiress. I did not contradict you. It seemed the obvious path. But while I am called to lead the people of Bel Amica someday, I cannot sustain this notion any longer. I have wounded Cyndere too deeply already, and my true desire is for someone else. My spirit tells me that Emeriene will stand beside me as I take the risks that lie ahead."

He raised his hands as if his listener might interrupt. "Yes, yes, I know that her husband is your faithful student. But Cesylle neglects her. And he is not a descendant of Tammos Raak. I am. And when I make my move for the throne of House Bel Amica, as you have prepared me to do..."

He heard footsteps, and he bent his knees, sinking into the hot water of his soaktub. The water closed over him, sealing off all sound but his strangely accelerating heartbeat. Here, submerged, he could safely trace the lines of his plan without any fear of spies.

Tonight Pretor Xa would tell him how many beastmen were willing to trust them, willing to take orders. The people of Bel Amica would protest if they learned that the trap involved conspiring with the Cent Regus. But these maneuvers were necessary in order to bait enough beastmen into their plot and to find a way to penetrate their lair and tear down their chieftain. By slaying a beastman in a sacred ceremony, he would convince influential Bel Amicans of his resolve against the Cent Regus and gain momentum in his mission to win the allegiance of the people back home.

He exhaled the deep breath he had held beneath the water, emerging into the air and blinking in the light of early afternoon. A pitcher of water and a cup had been placed on his windowsill. The blankets of his bed had been smoothed. Servants had done their work and left, all the while unaware that he was holding his breath beneath the water.

He laughed, then paused to admire the beastman tusk he had strung over the knife-sharp pinnacle of his shard-shaped mirror. He submerged himself again.

One thing was certain. He was tired of waiting.

He would have to be careful. Best to focus first on the fight, to ensure a quick and thrilling victory. He pictured the beastman. Pictured it charging at him. Pictured the dodge, the lunge.

He burst up from the water, gulped air, and shouted in challenge. A wave drenched the Seer, who staggered away from the tub with a curse, robes darkening and dripping.

"What are you—"

"It is good to see you, Captain Ryllion," said Pretor Xa through his teeth.

"Captain? I'm not there yet, and you know it." Ryllion sank down to his shoulders in the water, alarmed that one of his meddling overseers had been watching, had caught him unprepared. "Why are you in my chamber unannounced?"

"You didn't expect me? The Ceremony of the Sacrifice. So little time to prepare. And you are injured."

"I expected you. You just…startled me. I am ready. As we discussed."

"Rumors are spreading. Everyone believes our new captive was carrying Deuneroi's emblem."

"Clever. They will be ecstatic when I cut him in half under the green moon. Trust me. Now, if I you'll grant me a few moments alone to dress…"

"First, I'll apply a potion." The Seer drew out a small clay vessel, lifted the lid, and stirred the steaming oil with a finger. "You must dazzle your observers. You must shine against the night sky like a moon-spirit embodied. News of what happens here tonight will run like a chill through the beastmen of House Cent Regus. They will whisper about Ryllion, the fearsome beastman slayer."

Ryllion leaned on the edge of the tub. "If you say it is so. But every day it becomes clearer that this will not impress the heiress."

He might be ready to face a beastman, but, no, he was not strong enough yet to tell Pretor Xa the truth about Cyndere and Emeriene. Not here. Not now. The Seers had taken great pains to improve his chances of winning the most powerful woman in Bel Amica. They would not understand a man with his potential having such affection for a sisterly. He could not risk losing their favor, not after giving up so much. He would have to keep his secret until a better time.

"Tonight when you come out to make the sacrifice, Cyndere and the rest will see the two extremes of being—the accursed and the ideal," said Pretor Xa. "Your spirit is pleased. And our desires align with yours. So do not hesitate to tell us anything you might sense your spirit saying to you. We will help you."

Ryllion scowled at his reflection. "My arm hurts. I want it to stop."

"We have what you need. You'll feel no pain tonight. Anything else?"

"I'm young, but my hair already recedes. And it's yellow, unremarkable. Deuneroi's hair was black and shiny as crow feathers. Perhaps if I looked more like Deuneroi..."

"Your hair can be as dark and bold as blacklode," said the Seer, leaning over the water again. There was something beyond admiration in Pretor Xa's wild eyes.

The Seer tipped the oil out of the bowl and let a thread run down into the water. When it touched the surface, Ryllion felt a faint charge spread through him, and the ache in his shoulder faded.

"What...was that?"

"A little something to make you strong. When you fight tonight," said the Seer, "you will find resources you did not know you had. You'll destroy that beastman. And you won't feel anything at all."

"Good."

"I've learned a great deal in my travels. You and your patrols have become famous among the beastmen. With a little encouragement from me, I think we'll have an obedient army, Ryllion. They're disgruntled. Their chieftain is stingy with his resources, the essence of their power. They're ready to follow someone who can give them what they want. Can you imagine? They're playing right into our hands."

"Deuneroi," Ryllion insisted. "Deuneroi would be impressed. Beastmen ready to talk with Bel Amicans."

"Of course he would, Ryllion," Pretor Xa laughed. "Of course."

"Now let me ask you something. Seers don't sleep. Isn't that right?"

"Seers never sleep."

"Then perhaps you can help me. I've been asked to post a guard in the kitchen at night. Someone's been making mischief there and needs to be...discouraged."

"There is nothing I'd enjoy more," said the Seer. "Let's bring order to Tilianpurth."

20

THROUGH THE CLAWS

hrough the stench and haze of death, Jordam returned at last to the Core of House Cent Regus. But for him it was not so much a return as a revelation.

House Cent Regus had flourished once, hundreds of years ago. But disease had conquered the land. He noticed this now as he compared it to the woods and the glen. *Nothing ever smells like summer here.*

To Jordam, it seemed now that the sickness was spreading from the center of their land. *Like ivy draining life from a tree. Like the poison from the arrow spreading through me.* The closer he came to the Core, the more color seemed leeched from the landscape. Forgotten farms succumbed to mold, rot, and decay.

The Cent Regus who were strong slunk out to hunt, seeking plunder that would gain them reward. But many still lingered here, appetites enslaved to the source of their power, their bodies too distorted to travel far. They staggered crookedly, clawed at the weeds, licked at snow, and sipped from polluted streams until they inevitably crawled back to their chieftain to plead for a visit to the Sopper Crone. *Like muckmoths flapping into campfires.*

Jordam had never considered such comparisons before. Finding O-raya's colors in the glen, learning that his favorite blue came from a fragile flower there—this had given him new eyes and exposed his own world for all its unfruitfulness.

"Go back," he whispered to himself. He longed to return and release the ale boy. He longed to deliver him to the Abascar survivors as he had vowed. He envisioned the Bel Amican woman waiting for him at Tilianpurth.

Jorn, meanwhile, cackled and guffawed, narrating for Mordafey how he had terrified the heiress, how he had sneered Deuneroi's name at her.

Jordam's fury flared, wondering if Bel had been there to see the heiress so shaken. He knew that he would have done the same without the influence of O-raya's colors. And he knew the danger that he would become when the Sopper Crone served him Essence. Promises, conviction—these things would burn away. *Like dry leaves.* He would lose all resistance. Essence would boil in his belly, spread out through his veins, climb his spine. He would thrill with stronger sight, smell, jaws, and claws. He would pose and strut. He would need to batter something into submission. And even that would not be enough.

He thought of the Bel Amican guard who had fallen on her sword, and he put his hand on the wooden grip of his blade. He wondered if he could muster that same strength to save Bel from what would come.

By the power of the Essence, the Cent Regus had ruined this land. He wondered now, for the first time, what it might have been—vivid fields, blue streams bearing golden fish, bee-crazed berry patches, generous orchards. The roots of everything had been corrupted by spreading contagion. The region appeared to be ravaged by wildfires, but the fires burnt within—slow, imperceptible. Subterranean disturbances opened crevasses that filled with something like tar. Silos, stables, mills, and metalworks were tended by ghosts. No Cent Regus cared about those settlements anymore, for they despised their ancestors as puny and weak. They did not call anything home. Generations of families had disintegrated into a world of hunters, seekers, and plotters.

Jordam knew a little about Cent Regus history. He had heard about farmers struggling through hard seasons and the arrival of strangers offering relief. These newcomers had established a farm near the center of the region, tapping into a resource they promised would bring abundance where rain and sunshine did not. Their livestock pulled heavier plows, laid larger eggs, gave richer milk, and ran faster.

The people were curious what this concoction could do to enhance their senses. They called it "Essence," an elixir that pleased like wine even as it made the farmers' bodies stronger. The strangers promised it contained nourishment that would enable those who drank to surpass ordinary people in their ability to hunt, kill, and survive.

Those who drank soon bragged of scaly skin that shielded them from the elements. They could see in the dark and labor without the need for sleep. Some grew forceful as fangbears, others fast as viscorcats. Some gained a brascle's eyesight. And they strengthened themselves against the other houses, for as their capacities grew, so did their suspicion and fear that others would try to seize their advantage and turn it against them.

The strangers left their reservoir in the care of the chieftain, but by then it was too late. Through him, the people continued to indulge in the Essence, unable to control what it compelled them to do. Each new wave of creatures was weaker of mind yet stronger in body, fiercer, hungrier. Many died of the distortions forced upon them by the lawless mutations.

When a Cent Regus creature died, the hunger in its blood survived, seeping into the grass, soaking into the roots.

Remnants of this curse swirled around him, scraps, shells, and dust, a constant clatter against the decrepit structures. Coughing, Mordafey threw the reins to Jordam, then leapt down. He snarled at any who leered at them from the shadows, watching the wasted spaces that provided passage through the maze of the ruins. Jorn skulked along behind, still telling his story of hiding in the Bel Amican washtub. And Goreth, murmuring in the madness of his dreams, starved for Essence inside the carriage.

The wheezing horses' steps became stumbles. Occasionally they stopped to bite at dead weeds. This territory still teemed with life, but life in varying stages of affliction. All that rose from the earth labored in excruciating strain. Gardens became feeding grounds. Farms lost all order, monstrous alterations of one crop turning to invade the next. Ground grew and congealed, thinking it was vegetation. Vegetation crawled, thinking it was animal. Animals were infused with enough sense to be miserable and bitter with jealousy.

The curse had flourished. In constant flux life swelled and sank, branched and collapsed. And still the Cent Regus embraced this parasite, convinced they were stronger than other houses, reveling in the fear they inspired.

But now Jordam could see that he was not so strong as he had thought. Even if he willed otherwise, he could not turn away. When he tried, cords tightened around him. He was not powerful. He was the servant of something greater, more powerful than Mordafey. He cursed himself. He had come from this place. It was within him. It went out from him. And if he replenished his strength, then returned to the glen he so longed to see again, he would destroy it and the woman who waited for him there.

As the beastmen neared their goal, Jorn grew more excitable. "Th' Claws!" he barked, attracting glares from the sullen watchers in the bushes and up in the dead pricklenut trees.

"Yes," said Mordafey. "Four brothers have reached the Claws."

Once the walls surrounding the center of Cent Regus society, and a habitation in itself, the Claws remained a multilevel ring of tunnels, chambers, and windows. It stood as a shield around the chieftain's village of storehouses and prisons and the palace itself. A fungus like damp clay that spread in clusters, cakes, and columns, crowded and spongy, steadily consumed its structure. Devouring detail and gnawing away distinction, this mold stole from memory anything it besieged. It carved a void in the air.

Creatures passed above a narrow gate on a crooked arch, anxious as if they had forgotten why they were there. Others slumped along the road, half asleep.

Tilting back his birdlike head, a worrier—a guard of the dens—let his grey, fleshy throat expand, opened his gull-like beak, and emitted a long series of descending cries like a squeaking wheel. The cry was taken up by the next worrier on her perch on the avenue's opposite side. Soon a flock of flightless worriers crawled on sharp-nailed hands and taloned feet across the Claws, lunging about on stiltlike limbs with the agility and aggression of spiders.

As the brothers emerged from their passage through the Claws, they entered a neighborhood that had once housed Cent Regus counselors. The brothers could see fragments of the original structure—sections of crumbling brick, disheveled wooden planks, windows boarded up or sewn shut with silken webs. Breaks in those same walls framed the glittering eyes of watchers from secret worlds within.

A musclebound giant known as "the Usher" stepped in front of them. Wire stitched his mouth shut to keep visitors from asking questions or conspiring, and he had lived so long empowered by Essence that his leather uniform had merged with, and become, his skin.

The Usher led the brothers toward the great crown, a dome of decorated tiles that had long ago lost their luster. "I see," said Mordafey. "Jordam, you see? Here is where Skell Wra now hides." The chieftain rarely stayed in the same place for long. He moved his throne about within the border of the Claws, seeking to confuse those who sought to overthrow him. This dome sagged in one hemisphere, like a fruit with a spreading bruise.

But the Usher suddenly veered off the path, and Mordafey steered the carriage into an alley between two derelict brick storehouses. There was always a surprise. These tactics were so familiar that Jordam knew what would happen next.

A deranged challenger hoisted himself from the gutter, a creature rather like a man of monumental girth, growling through a flattened snout, standing on the knees of legs fused together in his mutation. He sloughed himself into their path and opened his mouth to give the usual threat in the coarse Cent Regus language: "I kill you, take your loot, get your reward. Unless you take me with you."

The worriers and the Usher gathered above and beside to watch the clash.

It lasted as long as a gasp. Mordafey moved forward, running the carriage past the blade-hewn pieces of the challenger heaped like firewood on the side of the path.

And so Jordam walked with his brothers into the shadow of the Longhouse.

At the Longhouse, Cent Regus counselors had once assembled the managers of every farm in the territory. The farmers had submitted their best offerings, and the council honored them with banquets prepared from that superior stock, lavished on tables so long they fit one hundred chairs to a side. The farmers so reveled in these celebrations that they sought even richer rewards the next year. These feasts inspired rumor and legend, remembered among the other houses but long forgotten here.

The same bland clay that encompassed the Claws had besieged the Longhouse, breaking apart the seams and swelling like bread. It raised the roof at one end so that the structure resembled a gator's open jaws. The brothers stepped under that shelter, but guards prevented their progress.

Beside the open maw of a massive pipe, a structure of nailed-together planks passed for a stable. The stable reverberated with the impatience of horned steeds—mighty prongbulls, white as ash. They scythed the air with red horns, fire roiling in their heads and smoke gusting from their nostrils. Shaped by the chieftain's experiments on the grand old bulls of Cent Regus farms, their bodies were not the burdensome bulk of cattle, but bundles of muscle and sinew, steeds for privileged hunters. When the chieftain's subjects sought to escape his wrath, he sometimes let them run just for the drama of watching the guards ride the prongbulls in pursuit to trample and gore them.

Mordafey offered a greedy smile. "Look." The prongbulls' keepers held long, barbed whips as powerful as coil-tree branches. "Maybe brothers' treasure earns us a prongbull."

Goreth, bleary-eyed and panting, thrust his head through a flap of the wagon's canvas. Mordafey seized his mane and dragged him into the dust. Jordam helped him up, growling, "rrDon't speak."

Guards glowered and hunched about on long, multijointed legs. Their faces were human, but their bare chests had grown armor like the shiny shells of beetles. Their arms sprouted bunches of wriggling fingers and pincers that flexed toward the carriage as if itching to snatch the loot for themselves.

Gesturing to the open passage, the Usher raised a hammer and smashed the battered bell pinned to the pipe. It rang out low and long.

Blind carrion owls fluttered above the carriage, their thick wings disturbing shafts of pallid light.

Then a parade of rickety wooden carts appeared, pushed from the pipe by the chieftain's servants. These mindless drones, spindly with hunger, were animated by Essence but not enough to prove powerful or dangerous.

Beneath the brims of polished helmets, the guards watched everything. To entertain them and assert his dominance, Mordafey kicked Goreth's belly and mocked his weakness. The guards purred, pleased, and thumped the butts of their spears against the ground.

Slaves lifted the wagons' treasure and piled it into smaller wooden carts, moaning jealously over what they carried. Mordafey strode before his brothers as they pushed the prizes along through the maze of corridors in the chieftain's new hiding place.

As they left behind the din of the guards and the laments of the slaves, the brothers sank into the dark, and the crooked wooden wheels trundled up a rhythm of drums.

"Be ready," said Mordafey. "When Skell Wra is pleased, the Usher will bring Mordafey back. Then down, down, down. Brothers will go to the Sopper Crone."

"For Essence." Goreth laughed in a manner indistinguishable from weeping.

"Drink and drink and drink," said Mordafey in what he considered a whisper. "Don't lose a drop. Brothers need strength for the plan."

When they stopped, a dry clucking rasped from a guard's tortoiselike beak, and he prodded Mordafey forward through a curtained archway and into the throne room.

"What plan?" whispered Goreth to Jordam.

Jordam shrugged, leaned close to Goreth's ear, and muttered, "Mordafey doesn't trust Goreth. Doesn't trust me. rrEven after we helped him gather all these things." His hope of turning Goreth against Mordafey was running out of time.

Jorn watched them, eyes narrow as sweat dripped down his brow and spilled across his wolfen nose. "S'time," he hissed, "I will be strongest. S'time I be strongest."

Jordam listened to the distant clatter of prizes being unloaded, displayed. He waited for Mordafey's roar. He thought of Deuneroi's woodscloak, shield, and sword buried in the snow, and wondered if he would ever have enough sense to take them back to Bel. As he closed his eyes, the pulse of his thirst conjured a dream of distant pounding—the ale boy kicking inside the iron stove.

"W'go take Abascar prizes soon, yes?" Jorn asked. "Y'think Abascar queen is still here? Still alive?"

The queen. Jordam looked at his laughing brother in surprise. He had forgotten the rumors.

"Abascar queen stuck in a cage. *Hel hel hel.*"

Stories of Jaralaine, queen of House Abascar, had spread and evolved. Some said the chieftain had made her drink Essence, shaped her into some unrecognizable Cent Regus creature—a rodent, reptile, or flightless bird. Others claimed he had preserved her, uncorrupted, to better flaunt his victory over Abascar prisoners.

Sudden notes from some stolen Bel Amican instrument rang out dissonant and strange, the chieftain exulting in a souvenir that no one in this realm would know how to play. The sound dissipated. Guards grew restless. Their claws looked sharp, the plating across their chests looked strong. They would not expect an attack, especially from only one of the brothers. If he struck, the defenders would turn against all four brothers, and that might be to Jordam's advantage.

But then? Alarms—bells, roars, whistles. Worriers would seal paths through the barrier. He would have to disappear, lose himself in the labyrinth, emerge elsewhere—perhaps among the slave horde. If his brothers survived the initial riot, they would join the pursuit.

If he managed to escape, the glen would not offer refuge for long. Sleeptalking had spoiled his secrets. Mordafey would seek him there. He could retreat to O-raya's caves—the brothers had never discovered them. But Mordafey would still hunt him at Tilianpurth. He would find the well. And Bel.

The thud of a club on a table startled him from worry. Mordafey's audience with the chieftain was over. The blows echoed down the long hall informing all who could hear that these hunters—yes, all four of the notorious brothers—would receive generous draughts of Essence.

Run. Run now. Before Mordafey comes back. His claws emerged. He ground his teeth. He steeled himself for the strike. *Remember,* he thought. "rrRemember," he said.

"Remember? Remember what, Same Brother?"

But when the oldest brother returned from the throne room, the Usher escorting him wide-eyed and impressed, Mordafey did not look at Jordam. Instead he pranced and beat at his chest.

"Chieftain is pleased," groaned the guard, who could speak intelligibly. The others, disappointed they would not be skewering their visitors, surrounded the brothers. Together they followed the Usher down through the tunnels toward the Essence pit. When Jorn began to laugh hysterically, Mordafey raised him by his back leg and slammed him against the wall.

"Jordam, help Goreth."

Jordam caught Goreth's arm as he collapsed, draped it over his shoulders. Goreth whimpered, and his eyes were wide and blind. "Where are we, Same Brother?"

They gathered in a circle in a hollow of black, polished stone. In the cracked, black mirror of the floor, Jordam could see another self staring up between his feet. He looked closely at his face, seeking any change that might betray his new understanding. No, he looked as monstrous as his brothers.

Torchlight danced in red flares around the brothers. The walls reflected myriad images of everyone in the chamber from the front, the side, and the back. Jordam gazed into reflection upon reflection. The glinting torchflares, the huddled circles of thirsty Cent Regus—they stretched on around him infinitely, offering no hint of escape, only the same scene playing out as far as the eye could see.

In the center of the floor, a hole opened, and above it a metal cage swayed on frayed ropes. Jorn scampered about the cage, squealing like a newborn hog, reaching out and touching the metal as if he might draw strength from it.

"Jordam first," said Mordafey. "Put Jordam in the cage."

Jorn complained, but Jordam did not step forward. "Goreth," he argued. "Goreth is weak and sick. Goreth goes first."

Mordafey growled at the suggestion that he was not in charge. But Goreth could not even lift his head, moaning, "Where am I going, Same Brother?"

"Essence, Goreth," rasped Jordam, his voice heavy with despair. "Essence."

At the entryway two guards pulled a barred gate down from a slot in the ceiling—a safeguard against Essence thieves. *Now.* He could dive beneath it, run up the corridor, gain ground in the pause between surprise and response.

A million Mordafeys bristled their golden manes, grinning and gloating.

The guards latched the gate shut with a sharp *clang* of finality.

21

CEREMONY OF SACRIFICE

"Our dear old protector." Emeriene stood beside the high-backed, decorative chair where Cyndere sulked, and she reached behind it to touch Bauris's arm. "It's so good to be back here with you again. Even though times are different now."

Under a dimming sky of scattered clouds, an assembly of soldiers, sisterlies, and staff had gathered with Cyndere on the towerhouse rooftop. While they turned their attention to the tower, which stood illuminated in the rays of a cold sunset, Cyndere's gaze remained downcast. On this night of solemn ceremony, she had invited Bauris to stand at her right hand and Emeriene at her left. Despite the honor of such a request, Cyndere knew that Bauris accepted only out of a sense of duty. He would have preferred, as Tilianpurth's senior officer, the privilege of participating in the ceremony on the top of the tower. She knew that he wished to stand beside Ryllion and sharpen the ceremonial blade. But she needed someone close at hand whose love for her surpassed mere formality, someone who would respond predictably to the charade she was about to perform.

Emeriene, meanwhile, had reluctantly accepted, making noise about an earlier invitation from Ryllion to sit at the front of the assembly.

"I remember," Bauris was saying. "You ladies were trouble back then."

"Oh, we're still prone to the same troubles and rebellions," Emeriene remarked, and Cyndere did not miss the note of bitterness at the end of the line.

"Remember the stories my brother always asked you to tell out there?"

"The legend of Inius Throan," Bauris nodded. "Partayn loved to hear how Tammos Raak freed the children from captivity beyond the Forbidding Wall."

Emeriene scowled. "I used to have nightmares about the curses that bound those people in the north. I still sometimes get a chill, thinking about those phantoms in your stories, the figures that creep down from the mountains. Snatchers, you called them. Northchildren."

"Such a terrible thought, captivity," Cyndere murmured. "Out here we're so free."

"What's that?" Bauris asked.

"Emeriene doesn't like the forest anymore," she said, and she drew her arm across her brow. "Is it very warm tonight?" To escape the cruel grip of this pageant, she would have to make a scene.

Emeriene watched the tower, anxious. "No, I didn't say that I don't like the forest. I only said that the woods have become dangerous. Everybody knows that. I'm fond of memories too, my lady. Perhaps you remember that you used to treat me as a faithful friend."

"I'm surrounded by faithful friends," said Cyndere. "So faithful, they ignore my desires and decide what's best for me. They place guards at every door so I cannot walk where I please. Like last night . . ."

The guard's long, grey mustache did not conceal his deepening frown. "You do still bicker like arrogant girls. I remember those days. You'd argue and compete to win Partayn's attention or mine. Nothing's changed." He glanced at the eager audience. "He was always more interested in music than games. I remember the day he blew those first seven notes on a shiny new hewson-pipe. It was like he'd been waiting to play them. He took hold of that line and played it over and over. Haunting, really. I wake up thinking of that little song."

Emeriene and Cyndere were stricken silent, sobered.

"Now, pay attention. This is going to be exciting. For the good of our house, Ryllion's going to make his appeal to the moon-spirits and sacrifice a beastman. How I wish he'd let me take the first shot. I've never yet fought one, you know."

"Here's a tip," snapped Cyndere. "Ryllion's decided to post a guard in the corridor beside the kitchen. Perhaps he suspects the beastman will raid the cupboards. You should look into it."

She let her hands drift into the folds of her gown where she had concealed a bottle of pepperdust, taken from her midday meal. "It's the cold," she said. "I shouldn't be out here at twilight. I'll catch a plague."

"You're as safe as the rest of us. We're all here, Cyndere. Everyone in Tilianpurth, from Bauris to the greenest of the stablehands." Emeriene, furious, strode to the front of the assembly.

I'm depending on that, she thought.

The night before, she had learned the extent of the rift between her and her devoted sisterly when she tiptoed down the stairs and discovered a guard lurking in the kitchen. She had to find a chance to slip past him and get back out to the forest in case Jordam returned. It might be her only chance to put Deuneroi's plan into action. It was what she had left to do. Giving that up, she would be trapped in the path leading to her mother's throne and the Seers' constant surveillance.

Pretor Xa leaned over the battlement atop the tower, gazing down like a predatory bird. Magisterial, he waited until the gathering quieted in a reverent hush. On either side of him at the corners of the tower's crown, torches flared orange against the grey. Beneath a dark ceremonial headdress, his chalk white face looked all the more skullish. He seemed absorbed in thought. He raised his hands, and the people trembled, for it was as if he had choreographed the skies himself—the green crescent moon emerged from behind a cloud in the space of sky between his open hands.

In a soft voice that somehow reached each soldier, sisterly, and privileged servant on the rooftop and those gathered in the yard below—servants, stablehands, and soldiers—Pretor Xa led them back to the simple glories of House Cent Regus before its miserable decline. He brought them to those famous feasting tables. He recited poetry about their fields and farms.

Then he showed them the first signs of disintegration. The Cent Regus farmers, he explained, had failed to acknowledge their moon-spirits. They had not offered sacrifices, as the people of Bel Amica would this cold night. Fearful of violating their traditions, they had not pursued new dreams with passion. But the spirits, he reminded them, demand respect.

"The spirits are pleased when we follow our hearts. We must not be swayed by pity for those who made the wrong choices. We must not try to interfere. The Cent Regus have brought the spirits' punishment upon themselves."

Bauris blinked. It was a strange declaration. He was puzzling over it when something fell against his side.

Cyndere was slipping from her chair, clutching at her throat. "Help me," she whispered. Her eyes were blood-red and streaming with tears. Her face flushed, beaded with sweat. "A fever."

Bauris helped her lean back into the chair. She pressed her hand to her breast, and her breath came in gasps. Around her, the sisterlies in ceremony robes were wide-eyed in alarm, as distressed by the disruption of formalities as by the heiress. Emeriene, near the front of the assembly, had not noticed.

"Tonight we follow our hearts," Pretor Xa declared, clearly enamored of his own eloquence. "We lift up a sacrifice to let the spirits know what we, in unison, desire. And when they see a picture of this, the spirits will put aside their own disputes and deign to grant us our request. They've taken land. Treasure. They've taken the heir to the throne, and they've taken Cyndere's consort. For our sacrifice we offer up a beastman."

Even though they knew it was coming, the people responded noisily, with anger and eagerness for justice.

"In some of us goodness grapples with corruption. But not the Cent Regus. Contrary to what some, in their compassion, would tell you, there are people bad to the marrow."

"Watch, my lady," Bauris whispered to Cyndere. In the dimming light, Pretor Xa loomed like a puppet in a shadow play. "You'll feel better when you see the abomination receive his just—"

Cyndere dug her nails into his arm, and her crimson, crying eyes stared into his. "I can't see." She fell forward onto her knees. With a collective gasp, the sisterlies crowded around her, their dresses sliding across the floor with a rush.

"Take her inside," Bauris growled through his teeth. "Quietly."

The silhouette on the tower paused, then continued with even more drama, determined to hold the crowd's attention. But he had all the help he needed, for Ryllion had taken the stage.

The stout and naked beastman facing Ryllion seemed a musclebound soldier in costume, with shaggy white hair like thick trousers on his legs, hooves black as boots, and a hooded snake's head. His eyes glittered like polished black beads.

Sword in his right hand, Ryllion snapped the fingers of his left. No one in the audience below would notice the signal. Nor would they witness the response—a tile on the rooftop lifted, and a guard thrust his head and arms out from beneath it and swiftly fired a tiny pin from an arrowcaster directly into the beastman's thigh. The creature winced, hissing. His leg buckled. His forked tongue lashed. As Ryllion advanced, the archer dropped down, and the hatch closed over him.

The bolt's poison would confuse the beastman for a while, but it would not finish him. Ryllion wanted the satisfaction of the kill. He was confident he could slay the creature in a fair and open fight, but this was not meant to be a contest. It was a ceremony, symbolic. There was too much at stake here to risk having anything go wrong.

He raised his sword, raised a cheer from the crowd. Then he sheathed it and drew a smaller, ornamental blade instead. Deuneroi's dagger. The better for ceremony.

But as his hand closed around the blade, he hesitated, his gaze drawn to a glimmering figure on the edge of his vision.

In that instant the beastman hissed a harsh stream of viscous venom into Ryllion's eyes. He threw his arm across his face, staggered sideways, and cried out. The beastman howled. Ryllion felt a blow to his chest from both of the beastman's hard hind hooves. He was cast up, away, over the low south wall into open space.

For an instant he saw the green moon. The four torches framing the square where he had fought. The crowd on the rooftop, the assembly in the yard. Stars emerging from dusk blue. The long drop to the grassy yard below. And the ground rushing up to meet him.

Cyndere lay on her bed, her head sunk into pillows, biting her tongue while the pepperdust burnt. She felt as if she'd inhaled the whole bottle through her nose. She could only see blurred images of her sisterlies scurrying about.

One of them cast a cold, wet towel across her forehead and her eyes. Another clutched her hand and appealed to her moon-spirit, asking for healing and intervention. She heard another draw back the heavy curtains, felt the rush of cold night air, smelled candle smoke and oil—they were placing spirit bowls on the windowsill in hopes of drawing the spirits' gaze.

She tried to ignore their chatter, gathering her strength and courage and thinking through her plan once more.

"What is in this incense bowl?" one of the sisterlies asked.

"Blue flowers. Her favorite incense."

"Light it then."

Cyndere felt her tension ease as she breathed in a cloud of calm, blue light. Her determination grew. She felt poised for a daring jump.

"Bring me a pile of clean towels," she said, her voice scorched by the pepper. "Quickly. Then you must return to the ceremony at once. Moon-spirits. . .they'll be troubled to find you absent."

"But, my lady—"

"I need the towels to wrap myself in perfumes and drive away the plague. But first I'll pray here. Beside the window."

The sisterlies crowded together, frightened pearbellies with ruffled feathers. And then they scuttled from the room, drawing the door closed behind them.

Slowly the details of the room came into focus. Clean towels rested just inside the door. The basket of tetherwings, undisturbed, waited in the closet. The bag packed with strips of dried meat and fruit. The woodscloak. Everything she needed.

"It's time, Deuneroi. This is it."

Without thinking, she began to hum the seven notes of Partayn's pipe song.

After a moment of silence, the beastman on the tower trilled a triumphant cry.

"Bauris." Emeriene ran to him, her hands on her face. "Bauris, it's killed Ryllion." She looked about for Cyndere. "Where…where is she?"

Bauris stepped out from the row of terrified observers and unsheathed his sword. "Kill it! Somebody kill it!"

The riot of the distraught crowd echoed across the roof of the towerhouse. Further dismay rose in chorus from those in the yard below. Soldiers shouted frantic orders. And then at a sharp command, their arrows crowded the air, sharp tips catching the last rays of the setting winter sun and glittering like sparks before they rained down on the tower. The beastman dodged, darting about in his limited range. He strained at the end of his chain, trying to reach one of the torches mounted on the tower's edge.

Emeriene turned away. Gasps of disappointment told her the shots had failed. She saw three guards break from their formation around the crowd and enter the tower for a quick ascent, hands on sword hilts.

They appeared at the top of the tower. One man held the base of a net. A man and a woman held corners and advanced.

Crouching, the beastman let them sweep it over him. Then he seized the net's strong strands and pulled fast and hard, catching the guards by surprise. One stumbled backward against the wall. The other tried to let go, but his hand caught in a tangle. The beastman pulled and pulled, drawing the desperate guard in like an animal in a trap. Emeriene saw the guard raised up and thrown down. The beastman seized the guard's sword.

Stunned onlookers watched the net thrashing. The beastman looked like a giant spider killing its prey in the middle of a web.

The soldier who held the base of the net released it and unsheathed his sword. But the beastman bounded toward him, dragging the net along, and cast the stolen sword forward, neatly pinning the soldier to the low wall of the rooftop.

The last remaining guard unharnessed her arrowcaster from its strap on her back and leveled it at the approaching monster. But a new roar tore the night. The crowd went silent.

A familiar silhouette stood against the moon. Ryllion. Dagger in hand, he advanced toward the beastman as if he had never been cast down.

"How?" Emeriene gasped. "How'd he get back up there?"

"Moon-spirits," whispered Bauris, awe-struck. "His moon-spirit saved him. He's alive. He's alive!"

Like a predator defying others to come near, Ryllion turned upon the guardswoman with a searing command. She dropped to her knees. Then he advanced toward the net-tangled beastman.

Forked tongue flicking in and out, the creature fought with the net, trying to reach the edge and climb free. As he did, he backed away from the transformed man until he reached the extent of his chain.

Ryllion stopped, held his left arm straight, as if measuring some distance, and then cast Deuneroi's dagger skyward like a spear.

The beastman watched it soar, reach the apex of its flight, turn, and plunge tip-first back down. The creature jumped from its path, and into Ryllion, who had anticipated the move. The soldier had lunged the moment he cast the blade, snatching two fallen arrows, one of which was now wedged deeply between the creature's ribs.

Hissing, the beastman tried to spray venom at his attacker, but Ryllion drove the other arrow up to pin the creature's mouth shut. Then he uprooted the first arrow, and air from the creature's lungs whistled out through the puncture. Ryllion threw him down.

In that moment, as murmurs of amazement rippled through the crowd, Ryllion felt he could conquer anything. Anything. He snatched up his dagger and slashed at the air, wishing he had another beastman to fight. A strange fever had seized him, and he knew that if he chose to leap down from this great height into the crowd on the towerhouse roof, he could do so and laugh at their bewilderment. The wind moaned, and a torch at the edge of the tower fluttered in its current. He seized it from its hold and waved it back and forth in the sky as if to write his name there.

A cheer from the crowd on the towerhouse roof caused him to look down. Pretor Xa stood at the edge of the crowd staring up with that ever-present grin.

A chill ran through him, driving out the fever of his pride. He felt suddenly awkward, as if waking from a vivid dream to find himself standing on a stage. What was he doing here prancing around like some sort of conqueror? Bewilderment choked him, and he looked down at the fallen beast-man. He remembered venom spraying his face, and he could still feel flesh burning around his eyes. He had taken a hard hit from those powerful hooves. He remembered the fall. But the impact—he could not recall landing in the yard. And then he was climbing, climbing up the tower in a blur of motion, as if some invisible line were raising him up through the air. Something had carried him, something within and yet beyond him.

His hands began to throb in their grip on the dagger's hilt and the torch.

This had not been Ryllion's plan. This was not what he had invited the people to witness. The sacred Ceremony of Sacrifice was meant to inspire Cyndere and the people of Bel Amica with a taste of justice. He had meant to quiet his own conscience. And above all, he had intended to lead his people in a unified plea to their moon-spirits, demonstrating a shared desire to vanquish the abominable Cent Regus and gain sovereignty over the Expanse.

Instead, here he was, laughing and savoring the uproar. Posturing like some brutish bear-tamer in a Bel Amican circus, he found himself waving as if to goad the onlookers to praise him.

He shifted his stance, pushing his arms back out to show refusal of the praise. He raised the torch again. "For Deuneroi!" he howled, anxious to steer the ceremony back to its proper course.

An awkward silence fell over the assembly. The torch flapped and licked at the air. A cloud passed in front of the moon.

One voice answered him. He recognized it. "For Deuneroi!" Emeriene was shouting. "And for Partayn!" The edge of anger in her voice told him that she was not merely echoing his tribute. She was glad. She was satisfied.

More sisterlies' voices answered in chorus. And soon the crowd raised the two names—Cyndere's husband and her brother—in a chant of remembrance.

While the chant ran on, Ryllion leaned back, arms spread wide, and stared into the face of the moon. Tears slid back from his eyes into his hair. "Was it you, Spirit?" he said. "Was it you that saved me? Did you send me the strength? I'm ready, Spirit." He turned and gazed southward. "I'm ready to carry out the plan. To claim the vision that the Seers have shown me."

"Sir," said the swordswoman, backing away from him, "you should get down to the healers."

"I'm not bleeding. Nothing's broken."

"Your eyes. They're…they're not right."

Tilianpurth was full of mirrors, but there were none at the top of the tower. Ryllion raised the dagger and tried to discern his reflection in the blade, but the pale green moonlight was not bright enough to show him a clear image.

He did, however, notice his gloved hand where it gripped the hilt. He turned his gaze to the hand that held the torch, and he saw the same alarming change. His hands had grown. His battle gloves were splitting at the seams. "What is happening?" he whispered, dropping the dagger. He hid his hand behind his back and looked to the swordswoman, trembling.

"Sir?" Bauris had arrived on the top of the tower. But he stopped short when he saw Ryllion's face and turned away.

"The heiress." Ryllion cleared his throat, desperate to conceal his confusion. "Is the heiress pleased?"

"Sir, the heiress fell ill. She had to leave the ceremony."

"What?" Ryllion spun around to scan the towerhouse rooftop. "Cyndere wasn't there? She didn't see the sacrifice?" His grip tightened around the torch. "The spirits will be offended. We were to stand together." He reached out to steady himself, and Bauris rushed to his side.

But Ryllion pushed the soldier away, growling as that feverish zeal spread again and silenced his self-doubt. The surge had carried him up the wall of the tower in a rage, like a hound bounding along even ground in a hunt. Now it carried him forward again, and he brushed Bauris aside, snatching up Deuneroi's dagger. "Let's find out what's really ailing the heiress."

Emeriene pounded on the door of Cyndere's chamber. She was shaking, terrified of all she had seen and even more afraid of the way Ryllion's feat had inspired her to cry out in exultation. The sisterlies crowded in around her, a worried flock of whispering robes, until she scattered them with a curse.

"There's no answer," she said. "Who's in there with her?"

"No one, Sisterly," said one timid attendant. "The heiress commanded us to return to the ceremony."

"She gave you orders? She's in there alone?" Emeriene turned and pressed her forehead against the door. "Idiots! She was pretending. She's angry with me for spoiling her midnight adventures." Emeriene struck the door with both fists. "Cyndere! Heiress! My lady! Forgive me. I'll call off the guards. You can do as you please. Run away. Mope around in the woods all night. I won't get in your way."

No voice, no footstep—there was nothing beyond the door.

Emeriene felt a twinge of fear. "Not again." In her mind she was back at the doorway of Cyndere's chamber in Bel Amica, discovering the heiress crumpled in a pool of blood with Deuneroi's dagger in her hand. She had come in time that day.

"I think," she said with new urgency, "that we have to open this door."

"I'll do that," snarled a monstrous voice. "Get out of the way."

Ryllion walked toward Cyndere's door as if it were wide open. He did not stop. Emeriene gasped when she saw his face, the dark scars around his eyes. She leapt aside with a cry. He kicked the door so mightily that it ripped off its hinges, skidded into the room, and fell flat with a crash.

The candle flames in Cyndere's chamber leaned away from Ryllion. A faint hint of the blue perfume swirled in the air around them and faded.

"Ryllion!" Emeriene hurried inside and seized a fireplace poker, ready to strike the soldier squarely in the back of the skull. But then she saw the rope of many towels tied together and crossing the span from the bedpost to the window.

The fireplace poker clanged against the floor. "She's hanged herself." Emeriene's heart leapt to her throat. "What have I done?" She ran to the window. "No," she whispered.

Ryllion joined her at the window, gazing into the darkening gloom. "She hasn't," he scoffed. "She just climbed out the window."

The swaying strand below ended a fair distance from the ground. Emeriene turned away, leaned against the sill, and noticed that Cyndere's woodscloak and the oceandragon whistle were missing from their hooks. She fought to regain her breath. "She's not dead," she whispered. "She's not dead."

"No. But the rope stops beside the window that opens...to the kitchen." Ryllion glanced about the courtyard. "Didn't you tell me to keep Cyndere out of the kitchen?"

Emeriene bowed her head. "She planned this." As tears fell to the floor, she laughed. "She's fooled us all. There is no stopping her."

"Why didn't she just take the stairs?"

The answer was so plain to Emeriene that she clutched at her stomach. "She...she did not want to risk being seen." But that was not it.

"What are you hiding?" Ryllion growled as if he had only just noticed her.

"Why are you speaking so harshly? Cyndere's my problem, not yours. I'm responsible for her."

"You forget. I was responsible for Deuneroi. If the heiress disappears while I'm here, who knows what they'll think? They'll never let me come back to Bel Amica."

She went back to the window and tried to untie the towels that were bound together. She worried at the first knot, which had tightened from the weight that strained it. "She asked me to trust her." She clawed at the knot. It would not come loose. "And she...she trusted me. Once."

Ryllion seized her wrists, pried open her grip, and pushed her away. She spun around, catching herself against the wall, smudging one of Cyndere's sketches.

He took the towel, cut through it with one clean swipe of Deuneroi's dagger. He held out the slashed end to Emeriene. His eyes were fiery red in the midst of deep red burns.

Begrudgingly she accepted the strand. Her gaze strayed toward the fireplace, to the lonely half of the scarf that Ryllion had given to Cyndere. The other half was missing. Emeriene let go of the cord. Its falling weight drew the end to the window, and it disappeared over the edge. She walked to the window, peered over the sill. It lay in a meandering line, ending suddenly, broken and frayed.

"The heiress is delusional," Ryllion ranted. "Can you imagine being so crazy that you'd climb out a window to run away when you know you'll get caught?"

"Imagine?" she whispered. "I can remember."

"You wouldn't behave this way for your Cesylle, would you?"

"Oh no," she laughed. "Not for him." She looked to the woods, where the stark line against the dusking sky blurred. "But for someone." She lifted the bowl of oil with its dancing wick and blew out the flame. Then she drew the heavy curtain across the window.

"Who is it?" Ryllion seized her by the arm, and the oil bowl fell, splashing across the floor. "Who's making her behave like this?"

Emeriene struggled to wrest her arm from Ryllion, frightened at his fierce grip. "It's her compass, Ryllion. Isn't that what you called it? Except that she and Deuneroi shared a compass, one that works differently than ours. She's being called out."

"And where does that lead her?"

"I don't know." Emeriene smiled through tears. "I don't understand, and I don't have to. Not today. I choose to trust her."

She moved toward the door, but Pretor Xa pushed his way through the sisterlies and stepped in to block her way. He cast a questioning smile to Ryllion.

"Back to the kitchen!" Ryllion shouted. "I think Cyndere's up to something. Kramm those old Bel Amican kings... There's probably a secret room or a passage she knows."

The Seer stared daggers through Emeriene. Then he turned, his gaze scouring the walls for clues. He stopped in front of a particular sketch, as if he recognized the likeness. "She's in the woods," he hissed.

Emeriene stepped between him and the drawing.

"In the woods?" Ryllion ran to the window and pushed back the curtain. "Why? And how did she get out?" He turned to Emeriene. "Is she so determined to relive old times with Deuneroi?"

"It's harmless, really," Emeriene said, desperate. "She'll be back anytime. She only meant to light up a burial tree and raise her last wishes to the ghosts."

"No," said the Seer. "There's something else out there. Prepare riders, Ryllion. The heiress is in danger."

"If we lose her too," Ryllion shouted at Emeriene, "it won't be *my* fault. Not this time."

Compelled by new courage, Emeriene limped to the fireplace poker and thrust it into the flames. "Out! Out, both of you!"

They did not stay to test her resolve. The Seer slammed the door, shutting her in.

Emeriene walked back to the wall, to the illustrated stones. "Tell me they're wrong," she whispered. "Tell me he's not dangerous, Cyn."

The heiress had sketched intricate details into the silhouette. Dark, sad eyes stared back at Emeriene from a face framed by a bristling mane.

She scowled. "My secret stranger...he was much better looking."

22

JORDAM'S DESCENT

The Usher turned the crank. The cage rose, swinging into view like some spider's capture.

At first Jordam thought it housed a different passenger than it had carried down. When the guards opened the cage, Goreth leapt out onto the black mirror, larger, laughing with deep strength. Dark syrup ran from his beard to the floor, blotting out patches of the reflection. The teeth of his triumphant grin were inky with the broth that the Sopper Crone had served him. His eyes swelled in their sockets, aligned again, burning in fierce focus. He shook out his mane and slapped his shaggy tail against the floor.

Jordam knew what Goreth felt. *Like swallowing a fistful of rockbeetles*, he thought. *But the beetles don't stay in the belly. They crawl out the arms. Crawl out the legs. Spreading fire. Spreading strength.* He wanted to look away. In this intoxication, Goreth would strive to indulge any impulse and unleash his burgeoning power. Mordafey would direct him, and he would be deaf to any hint of caution or restraint. He would have no patience for second thoughts.

"Good," murmured Mordafey. "Strong."

"Strongest!" Goreth laughed.

Mordafey cuffed him. Essence splashed from Goreth's beard to spatter Jorn's face. Jorn licked it up, ecstatic, leaping about like a young ape. Grasping Goreth by the throat and lifting him up, Mordafey proved to all observers that he was in control here and that even in their fever of new power, his brothers would not resist him.

As Goreth choked an apology, Jorn interrupted the reprimand. Inspired by that slight taste of Essence, he had lost all patience, shoved aside the guard who held the cage door, and jumped inside, desperate for his turn. Enraged, the guard spun around and pressed his spear into Jorn's chest. Jorn squirmed, whimpered, and called Mordafey's name.

Mordafey dropped Goreth to the floor. "Jordam is next. Come out."

But Jorn did not dare move with that spear tip digging in against his ribs. His gaze shifted to Jordam and burnt with jealousy. Jordam remained where he was, searching again for a way to delay his descent.

The guard waited as if hoping for permission to impale his offender. Then he stepped back, grunted a warning, and barked a question into the abyss. When a shrill note answered, he closed the cage on Jorn. As Mordafey hissed in protest, the Usher took hold of the crank.

Mordafey stepped forward and seized the bars. "Crone will serve you. Be fast. Mordafey is thirsty."

"Hel hel hel." Jorn laughed all the way down.

Mordafey turned to Jordam, furious. "You next."

Jordam knew that when he returned from that abyss, he would not be so capable of questioning Mordafey's orders. He would not be free to refuse. He remembered that troubled patch of ground, where Mordafey's footprints had veered off from a crowd of Cent Regus. He wanted to understand Mordafey's intentions now, before the Essence set his appetite ablaze and overwhelmed his thoughts.

"The plan," he murmured to Mordafey. "rrFour brothers start tonight?"

Mordafey's brow crumpled. He nodded slowly. "The plan already started," he said carefully. "Tonight Mordafey will tell the brothers. You will know everything. Then we run. Far and fast."

The guards' pincers squeaked, bone scraping bone. Jordam wondered how much they understood. He leaned close to Mordafey and whispered, "rrBrothers take Abascar's weapons. Yes? rrFinish Abascar's king. Finish Calraven like you finished Deuneroi."

Mordafey stifled a growl. "Not here, Jordam." He glanced at the guards. "Too many ears. Skell Wra already interferes. Stole prizes from our wagon."

"Stole prizes?" Jordam growled.

"Deuneroi's treasure." He seized Jordam by the beard and spit out his rage. "Deuneroi's bones…missing from our wagon. Skell Wra took them, or somebody stole them. Sssneaky."

Jordam flung curses to affirm his brother's rage, relieved that Mordafey did not suspect him. "rrBrothers will get Abascar prizes soon. No one will steal them."

Mordafey hesitated, unsettled by Jordam's sudden surge of interest in the plan. "Yes," he admitted, but guardedly. "Four brothers will take Abascar. Cal-raven is mine, like Deuneroi."

"But the tall one?" Jordam ventured. "The white giant? With the firestick? Will he go with us? Help take Abascar's prizes?"

Mordafey cast anxious glances at the guards, then snorted. "The white giant thinks he tells Mordafey what to do. But Mordafey will laugh at him."

"rrWho is the white giant?" Jordam put a hand on his brother's shoulder. "Four brothers have no secrets."

Mordafey pulled away and glanced at the pit. "Jorn is late. The Sopper Crone gives him too much."

Jordam persisted. "We may be strong, but Abascar has many fighters. Will the white giant with the fiery staff help us?"

Mordafey lashed at the air with his claws, barking at Jordam in a fury. But Jordam was astonished, for the words his brother spoke were Common—"Mordafey's found help. The white giant made promises, gathered many Cent Regus to take orders and fight together. Mordafey leads them."

Goreth and the guards gaped as if Mordafey had been seized by some enchantment. Only slaves spoke Common in the Core.

But Jordam understood. And Mordafey, knowing this, pressed his browbone against Jordam's and murmured an explanation. Passing on the white giant's promises of reward, Mordafey had mustered a force of fighting Cent Regus—a swarm—larger than the Expanse had seen in generations. Under the direction of that fearsome stranger, Mordafey would lead the pack and lay siege to Abascar, wiping out the survivors and looting their hideaway. This would prove his quality to the white giant, who had promised even greater conquests upon their success.

"rrBigger prizes than Abascar?" Jordam swallowed his other questions hard.

"He says so," sniggered Mordafey, continuing in Common to keep the guards in the dark. "But whatever happens, Mordafey will surprise the white giant. Mordafey will lead the swarm to take down Skell Wra."

"Mordafey," Jordam whispered. "The white giant will trick us. The white giant will take our prizes and—"

"No," said Mordafey. "White giant has promised. Many prizes. So much Essence." Then he turned to the abyss, which was strangely silent.

"I can bring help too, Mordafey." It was a risk, but Jordam lunged for an advantage. "Let me go. Now. I can bring you help for the swarm. A power I found. Fixes what gets broken. Stops bleeding. Stops hurting. I go now. rrBring you that power. I will go—"

"Jordam won't go anywhere. Brothers stay together now. Tonight we run to Abascar." Torn between aggravation with Jorn and misgivings about having revealed his secrets, Mordafey turned and tugged at the dangling ropes. Far below, the cage rattled against the floor of the Sopper Crone's chamber. The guard prodded Mordafey back from the chasm, but Mordafey snarled, "When Jorn drinks Essence, Jorn gets…dangerous."

"Let me go," Jordam pleaded in Common. "I'll bring back more help for the brothers. Goreth comes with me. That way we can bring you more power. One brother cannot carry enough."

"Four brothers go together!" Mordafey's voice shook the chamber. The guards lowered their spear tips toward him. "Jorn!" he shouted at the chasm. "Jorn!"

Jordam found Goreth staring at him with surprise and dismay, and he realized that his conversation in Common had left his twin feeling abandoned, cut off. Brusquely Goreth huffed, turned, and rattled the bars of the chamber's iron gate, eager to hunt in the rush of new power.

"Jorn!" Mordafey throttled some imagined enemy in the air before him. As if persuaded, the gear wheels pinned to the wall began to turn at last.

When Jorn reappeared, he shuddered as if his body had broken free from his mind. Essence ran from his head and hands. His eyes swept the scene as if he were surveying the frenzy of battle.

Guards unlatched the gate, swung it open, and Jorn crawled forward on all fours, painting the floor with a swath of pitch. He pulled himself into a corner where a fit of choking seized him. Essence spread around him in a puddle as if oozing from his flesh. Jordam's nostrils flared. Something wasn't right about Jorn's scent. Was he wounded?

"Too much," Mordafey laughed. "Too much for Jorn."

"You." One of the guards raised a claw to Jordam. At first he stiffened, thinking he was being accused. But then the guard pointed to the lift.

"Drink deep, Jordam," snarled Mordafey. "Strength. Strength for the plan."

Jordam's feet felt nailed to the floor.

"Go." Mordafey seized Jordam's mane and dragged him to the cage. Stumbling inside, Jordam heard the cage door latch behind him.

The Usher began to turn the crank.

"Rockbeetles." Goreth smiled at him with blackened teeth. "Strength, Same Brother."

"Strength."

As he plunged into the dark, the ropes sang to the end of their reach. The warm oily fragrance of Essence intensified as if he were sinking into a pool. A mouth behind his ribs opened, demanding to be fed. His hands shook. He dragged his tongue across his lips.

The cage rattled as it touched the ground. Jordam waited for Kreanomos the Sopper Crone to lift the latch and invite him to her cauldron. He groped about for a last-minute revelation, an unlikely escape. Perhaps he could just pretend to drink. No, the Crone would punish him if he spilled Essence on the floor. Moreover, he knew that he would have no power to reject it when it came within his reach. If the Sopper Crone lifted that large iron ladle, he would drink.

Perhaps he *should* drink, he thought. Perhaps he could receive that strength and control it, break free from the brothers forever. Perhaps he was stronger than other Cent Regus and could use this power to achieve something good.

He turned, reached through the bars to unlatch the door, and stepped out to face Kreanomos.

All across the walls of the Essence chamber, bulbous tendrils of a foul weed wriggled, a plague of devouring vines. In previous visits Jordam had taken them to be part of the construction, a sort of reinforcement. But now he observed they were a species of parasite, destroying whatever they touched. Where they had once been only sparsely spread, now the entire wall was consumed by them, and they had come alive. He recognized them now. Feelers. These were the rootlike predators that dug up through to stone and soil, snakelike arms invading the ground, seizing and dragging down anything uncorrupted by the curse. He wondered if the tendrils that had troubled the snow near the merchants' barn were anchored here, so far away.

But the feelers did not hold his attention. Bulging from the ceiling like a tumor, a dark, fleshy sponge seeped an oily brine, which spilled down into a smoking cauldron.

Warily he stepped forward, licking his lips.

Jordam remembered Kreanomos. She was not easy to forget. An ancient female with a long curved snout like a turtle, her wide milky eyes ran perpetually to clean away the glaze of steam from the cauldron she guarded. She stood between the cauldron and an apparatus of rusted metal that bristled with levers, a heavy wheel-crank affixed to the top. Her back, shoulders, and neck bulged with muscles to support an array of spindly arms—six knobby spans of bone wrapped in papery flesh. With some of her hands, she worked the levers and the wheel, controlling the flow of murky pitch from the sponge. With the others, she stirred and ladled out the portion for her visitors.

"Strength," she would say quietly. "Strength for all Cent Regus."

But today Kreanomos did not stand and work the machine or trouble the contents of her cauldron. Her ladle lay on the floor as if she had cast it down in a tantrum. Jorn must have given her trouble. She reclined on the cushions, the bed where she slumbered between the visits of hungry guests. Her six arms splayed wide, her knees bent, and her beak sagged open. Her translucent eyelids, which allowed her to see with her eyes closed, slid slowly up and down.

She did not greet him.

He reached for the ladle, but as his hand closed over its sticky iron handle, the skin of his fingers tasted Essence. He felt a slight charge, and it shook him. He smacked his lips together, and the cauldron pulled him forward. He stepped onto the stone block that supported it, reached over the edge and broke the roiling surface with the ladle's bowl. It was all he could do to keep from plunging his face into the stew. He lifted the ladle to his lips and drew the hot soup into his mouth.

As the Essence took hold, he glanced nervously at the Sopper Crone. She made no move to assist him. He paused. Was she testing him? Perhaps she waited to see if he would follow the rules. Perhaps he was, right now, failing that test and ensuring the brothers would be punished. He spat the Essence to the floor, staggering away. A trickle of pitch drew a hot line down his throat, and a presence throughout his body awakened and raged like a hungry infant, demanding more.

Jordam waved the ladle in the air. "Crone," he gasped. "Serve me."

Kreanomos answered with a gargling cough, and Jordam smelled that strange, rancid air again, the foul vapor that Jorn had brought out of the pit.

He stepped around the cauldron, and the matter became clear to him.

The Crone's belly was open, gaping.

The ladle fell from Jordam's hand. "Jorn," he muttered.

The Crone examined what had happened to her as if for the first time. Her hand reached out, trembling for the spoon. "Strength," she rasped, tonguing blood. "Help me."

Help me. Jordam thought of Bel. So much the same. So different altogether.

The comparison shook him. The cauldron. *Like the well. But, no, not like the well at all.* The Essence, pungent and enervating, while the perfume of O-raya's blue cast a spell of calm. This cavern, a cold and colorless ache in the belly of the earth—the glen, alive with summer.

He pressed his hand to his chest. "Let go," he groaned. His steps heavy, he staggered back into the cage and tugged at the ropes. "Mordafey!" The cage did not rise. It was too early.

Jordam climbed out of the cage, jumped on top of it, and began to climb the ropes. A lightning storm sparked and flashed in his head, and the pit below pulled at him. Striving to release his hold on the Essence, he could feel that the Essence had a grip on him. He strained, dragging himself up through the abyss toward the platform. Halfway, he paused to catch his breath, suspended between the source of his power and his waiting brothers, and he realized that his chance had come.

As if sensing his plot, the walls began to move, tendrils prying themselves loose in an effort to seize him. Jordam flung himself up the ropes like a frightened gorrel scrabbling up a tree.

When he burst up through the fanged maw of the floor, the confusion amongst his brothers and the guards threatened to break into violence.

"Nobody to serve Essence," he shouted. "rrJorn finished the Sopper Crone!"

Mordafey shook his mane in confusion. The guards twitched, clacked their pincers. One uttered a guttural clatter, and the others looked to Jordam.

Jorn, who seemed to have swallowed more Essence than even Mordafey could safely stomach, blinked silently, crazed and disoriented, until Jordam's accusation sank in through his confusion. Seized then in a sniveling fit, he lunged, shrieking, "Y'liar!"

Jordam ducked, caught Jorn in the air, and flung him against the gate of the chamber. Jorn sprawled on the ground, slipping on dripping hands.

"Say again, Jordam." Mordafey stalked up to Jordam and pushed him to the edge of the abyss. "Say again."

"Sopper Crone's dead," he replied, cautiously subservient. "You can smell it. Not just Essence, but the Crone's blood on Jorn's claws."

Mordafey stared deep into Jordam's eyes as if to sift his mind for a lie.

"Older Brother," Goreth whined, leaning against the gate. "Your turn."

Mordafey roared with such wrath that Jorn leapt straight up, clubbed his head against the rugged stone of the ceiling, and then shoved himself against the bars of the gate.

"No escaping, Jorn," said Mordafey.

Jorn whimpered, turned to Jordam, and hissed, "I run up behind you. You no see me. An' I finish you next." In a surge of power that stunned everyone, Jorn bent the bars of the gate and opened a gap. Before Mordafey could stop him, Jorn wriggled through, knocked down one startled guard, and flattened another who was marching down the tunnel. Like a bushpig in a charge, he fled.

Mordafey sprang after him but could not fit between the fractured bars. "Skell Wra will punish brothers unless...unless we catch Jorn." His silhouette trembled, volcanic, and his eyes glowed red as embers. "Skell Wra will kill us all."

The guards fumbled at the gate latch and sent it crashing up.

"I go after him," Jordam growled.

"What?" Mordafey barked. "You said that before."

"rrThis time it will be different," Jordam promised quietly. "Watch. I'll surprise you."

Mordafey took a moment to grind his teeth, scorching Jordam with his burning gaze. Then he shouted at the guards. "Jordam is fast. He'll catch Jorn and bring him back." Their glimmering eyes did not blink, but they lowered their weapons and waited, seeming to understand. "Then..." Mordafey turned to Jordam. "Then you have your Essence."

Jordam clasped Goreth's bristling shoulders and looked into that baffled face. "Remember," he said, his voice suddenly faint as if it were disappearing entirely and forever, "I'm your Same Brother. I'll come back."

Goreth stared back without expression.

Jordam forced himself through the gate, making a vow as he went. If he could escape this power, his twin could learn to leave it too. He would find a way to draw Goreth away from the others someday, to break him of the curse's hold.

Goreth hated the Cent Regus guards. He hated their hairless arms. He hated their joints—the shrill scraping sounds they made sent chills ripping up and down his bones. He hated how they moved in fits and pauses like the hard-shelled pests crawling on the bottom of Deep Lake. To be held under their guard made him want to smash their shells.

"Let me run too, Older Brother."

"Jordam goes alone," said Mordafey. "You stay."

He wanted to run with Jordam. To run and to keep running. The urge grew within him. The thrill of the kill had become complicated. Mordafey demanded more and more, and Jorn twisted everything into anger and blood.

Only Jordam made him feel at ease. Goreth felt like a reflection, an extension of his brother. He wished it could be the other way, that Jordam would seek to be like him. But in moments of crisis, it was Jordam who took charge. Jordam could deflect Mordafey's tantrums through clever words. Goreth admired that.

But Jordam had been absent lately. And now he was leaving Goreth behind again. Jordam always found ways to break away from the brothers, even if he knew Mordafey would make him pay. Goreth wanted to break free as well. He found himself imagining what it might be like to venture away from the four brothers' den, to hunt and kill by himself. Some beastmen hunted alone. They did not need Mordafey's permission to feast upon their kills. They did not have to cringe.

Unaware of his fidgeting, he began to whine like an anxious hound. The guards stared at him and flexed their pincers. He wanted to kill them. But that would make Mordafey angrier.

So it was with trembling alarm and a sob of dismay that he received Mordafey's instructions to stay there. "Wait. Jordam will bring Jorn back."

"But you will stay here?"

Mordafey stared up the tunnel. "Mordafey's earned his Essence. Mordafey will take it before they find another Crone. And then the plan, Goreth. Four brothers follow the plan."

Seizing the ropes, Mordafey descended through the hole in the floor.

The Usher, caught by surprise, grumbled at the guards through his stitched lips. One reached out and severed the ropes. They dropped and disappeared. Far below, Mordafey crashed to the floor.

Goreth's breath hissed in, out, in, out. Paralyzed, he stared at the hole. He waited a very long time.

When Mordafey finally returned, climbing up the walls with ease, unstoppable, he was soaked from head to toe in Essence, and Goreth did not like the change in his eyes.

Nor did the Usher and the guards. But their worries were brief, their deaths quick and sure.

23

RUNAWAYS

E merging from the throat of the Longhouse, Jordam remembered the brascle. If he ran, Mordafey would turn that wretched bird loose to pursue him.

He smelled the dust stirred up by Jorn's escape and the guards' pursuit, but the scent of fresh blood surprised him, and he turned. The brascle's perch was bare, a ruin of feathers strewn beneath it. At every turn of his escape, Jorn was blazing the trail for Jordam's escape.

In dread of Mordafey's rage, Jorn had run for that narrow gate through the Claws. He would escape. Jordam knew it. Even though alarms had reached the worriers, and Jordam could hear them laughing, Jorn would force his way through. He would survive their hail of arrows and spears. Outrunning the guards who pursued him, he would bolt away through the wasteland, unstoppable for the surfeit of Essence. A long chase would begin.

Such a show of strength would impress Mordafey. Although Jorn would earn frightful new scars, Mordafey would terrify him into submission and whip him into obedience. Jordam would have to run farther, burrow deeper.

The ramp guards were gone, drawn into pursuit. Two of the prongbulls' keepers emerged from the rickety stables—hissing females with shields pockmarked from the bulls' heavy hooves. Slyly they poked at the absent guards' preyboxes, sniffing the live contents of those cages. But when they saw Jordam unattended, they rose and lumbered toward him.

"rrStupid brother," Jordam snarled, "trying to escape. Killed the Sopper Crone. I'm to catch him."

"Killed the Sopper Crone?" the bullmasters seethed, confounded.

"rrChieftain calls you." Jordam pointed back down into the pipe. "He'll make one of you the new Sopper Crone."

The bullmasters climbed over one another, each declaring herself most deserving, all the way down the pipe.

Worrier cries warped from bloodlusty howls to challenges of furious intent. Jorn had reached the gate.

Rattling heavy chains, the last bullmaster—a brute of human features and crocodilian skin—muttered crude commands as he unlatched the harness lock of the first prongbull in the line. He meant to climb astride the monster and join the chase.

With the eyes and ears of the Cent Regus Core intent upon Jorn's disruption, Jordam grabbed a torch. When the bullmaster's key snapped in the latch and he dragged the chain free of the prongbull's tether, Jordam slammed the torch against the back of his head. He fell face forward into the bull's feed trough but held the bullwhip fast. Jordam pressed his foot to the bullmaster's elbow, grabbed his wrist, and snapped the arm like a branch. Screaming, the bullmaster let go of the whip.

The bull bolted, a plume of ash and dust rising behind him.

Enlivened by the thought of a chase, Jordam felt that slight swallow of Essence simmering beneath his skin. He clenched his teeth and ran, each step making his retreat through the Core indelible, irreversible. He hurtled forward as if driven by a gale. In six long bounds he leapt and landed astride the charging bull.

The bull bucked and jerked, carving the air with its sweeping horns. But Jordam, fueled by new strength, gripped the whip in his teeth, wielding the torch in his left hand and holding the bull's mane with the other. As the bull turned circles, kicking up cakes of earth, Jordam pressed the flaming brand into the animal's side. Protests deepened to groans. Jordam dropped the torch, took the whip, and let the creature know that he meant to control it. The kicking stopped. The animal stood still, venting gusts of hatred through its teeth. Jordam pulled at its mane.

Never, the bull's temper rumbled.

"You," said Jordam evenly. "rrGreatest prongbull in the Expanse. No more stables. Go free. Show them you are fastest. Strongest."

The bull, confounded, chewed on that awhile.

"Are you slow?" said Jordam. "Can't catch the runaway?"

The bull coughed something like an arrogant laugh.

Jordam turned it toward the alley, and it obeyed.

When Jordam and the bull charged the gate, worriers threw themselves aside and clambered up the walls to their perches. They did not recognize Jordam until he passed beneath the arch.

He caught up to Jorn and found him bleeding and panic-stricken, clutching a spear, skin already fading into the ash-grey of the dry riverbed. As the bull gained ground, bellowing a victorious cry like a horn, Jorn reared up and aimed the lance at the steed's low crown.

Jordam turned the bull abruptly and felt the spear sail past his ear. Bringing the animal back around, he caught his brother's bewildered expression. Jorn's face was lined with black veins thick as strands of ivy. He bent his knees, ready to leap in attack. Jordam recognized that savage courage. He knew how it felt.

The bull bore down on Jorn, picking up speed. Jorn raised himself to his full height, arms outspread, and roared as if to intimidate the bull. Jordam could see right down his throat. One stride away Jordam pulled the bull's mane sharply.

"Show them now," he barked into the bull's ear.

He left Jorn standing there, frozen. The bull galloped away from the Core and through the maze of farmland ruins.

"I run up behind you!" Jordam caught the trace of his brother's hysterical cry. "I finish you!"

Wind combed Jordam's mane. He rode against it.

The boy. The Bel Amican woman. They gave him a simple plan, a map of his strange new future. *Like two moons shining in a dark sky,* he thought.

Upon his arrival back at the snow-blanketed hill on the edge of the Cent Regus wasteland, Jordam tied the bull to a patch of bramble. "rrRest," he said. "Run more later. Get stronger. Go back so strong. Make other bulls afraid." The bull relapsed into a bluster of hateful rants, but those blasts seemed less fervent now. No one punished it. No chains held its hooves to the ground. It could breathe wild air instead of stale dust, watch trees and sky instead of stable walls.

Jordam climbed the hill to the collapsing farm shack.

Snow herons scattered. The old barn groaned. Outside, all remained as he remembered. But inside, the black stove lay on its side, the stovepipe bent like a broken limb on the floor. A hole in the ceiling spoke of the force that had ripped the whole thing down. The stove's hatch door hung open. In its ash-dusted hollow, Jordam found only a crumpled, cracking scrap of parchment.

He dusted it off, held it up to the grey glow of dusk. It was the message that the boy had pulled from the grip of the dead Bel Amican guard. "Partayn," Jordam remembered. "Partayn."

He set the stove on its feet in the center of the floor and propped the scrap of parchment on the top, a sign marking the place where someone had been lost. An expression of failure and desperate hope.

Searching for anything he might leave as a sign in case the boy returned, he found the half of O-raya's scarf that Bel had told him to give to the boy. He whimpered, the pain of his failure worsening as he drew it from the pocket in his woodscloak and set it on top of the stove.

After a few moments he took it back.

Outside, on the old road where Mordafey had run the foremost wagon wheels into a rut, Jordam scooped away piles of snow until he uncovered Deuneroi's woodscloak, the emblem, and the rings, and bundled them together. The bones he quickly covered in snow.

Back inside the shelter, he scanned the hillside below, the dark sprawl of the Cragavar forest to the east. Something had taken the boy away. A search could take days, and the trail might lead to a dead child. Meanwhile, his brothers would reunite and plot their pursuit. The prongbull was fast, but it left an unmistakable trail. Mordafey would catch up.

Jordam felt the pulse of new Essence coiling about his mind. His senses surged, searching for signs of prey. Smoke. A camp, nearby. Hunters, most likely, or mercenaries. Few beastmen built fires, even here. He could hunt and eat tonight.

But he had talked in his sleep. Mordafey would make his way to Bel.

He crawled out into the snow, pressed a handful of powder to his forehead, ran his fingers about the base of his shattered browbone, then drove that broken horn into the cold ground. The freeze burnt through the bone, and blue light flared behind his eyes.

Jordam made his way back down into the bushes and found the bull uprooting the bramble patch in a fury. He won the bull's attention with a crack of the whip. The bull answered with curses, and Jordam waited until the animal stood panting and confused.

"rrBull goes back to stables? To masters' beatings?" he said. "No, not you. You're the strongest bull. You run wild tonight."

The animal shook its horns in pride, then lowered its head.

On the eastern horizon, the moon gleamed like a bright green claw.

Deep in the night, the frozen valley of Tilianpurth glinted in green moonlight.

Jordam bound the exhilarated prongbull to a tangle of roots. Standing at the forest's edge and gazing down across whitegrass, he knew he would have to be quick. He would plant a warning to scare Bel back within the safety of the bastion walls.

Flares ringed Tilianpurth, torches burnt along its walls. And there, atop the tower, a blaze of light. The Bel Amicans were busy tonight.

Hearing a shift in the snow, Jordam punched through the frozen surface, pawed through the powdery layers beneath, snatched up a sluggish yellow viper before it could flee, and wolfed it down. Then he reached into the tangle of twiggy boughs above and ripped a branch away. He began to probe his way down toward the trees.

Seven soldiers stood in the green and blooming glen beside the well. Three saddled vawns shoved their snouts into the verdant ground, snorting and snuffling for insects. In hushed, conspiratorial tones, the soldiers muttered about *ceremony, runaway, search, secret, heiress.* No tetherwings perched in the trees; no one expected a beastman here. This was a search not a hunt.

Jordam's hunger intensified. The bullwhip grew restless in his hand.

But when he shifted his gaze to the well's blue light, the Essence within him recoiled. He choked as if someone were jerking an invisible leash to drag him away.

A horn blast shattered the silence, sonorous notes echoing all around the valley. Dogs bayed somewhere in the trees. Jordam bared his teeth and waited. They did not come. *They're on leashes,* he thought. *The traps. They're worried about the traps.* He crouched lower, crawling halfway about the glen's circumference, and came upon a familiar wagon, unhitched this time.

As he approached, a soldier climbed out from the back of the canvas. Jordam slipped silently between the front wheels, cloaking his footfalls by matching the soldier's steps.

"Heiress?" the soldier whispered warily. Jordam heard a sword slide from its sheath. "Cyndere, is that you?" He watched the soldier's boots. The soldier walked around the wagon. "My lady? We only want to take you back inside, where it is safe."

Jordam backed out between the rear wheels and glanced up at the tower. They were searching for Sin-der the heiress? Out here in the trees? Would Bel be out here too?

His heel came down on a brittle root that snapped.

The soldier stopped. "My lady?"

Jordam seized the back of the cart and shoved it forward with all his might, knocking the soldier down hard. The man's voice rose in anguish.

Hounds barked. Soldiers in the glen shouted, scrambling up the rise.

Jordam dove beneath the fanning leaves of a dragonfern. When the searchers gathered around the groaning soldier, distracted, he leapt out and bounded into the glen and across it.

All around him the forest awakened with noise.

The vawns shrieked, reared, and separated at his approach. Jordam paused only long enough to seize the bucket, which rested on the edge of the wellstones. Only a splash of water remained there, but he swallowed it. Then he bolted after a tall, black-scaled vawn that had paused to sneeze soil from her snout. He leapt into her saddle. She tried to buck him free, but Jordam had grown accustomed to the frantic, kicking prongbull. He whipped her, triggering her three-voiced howl, and spurred her up the glen's slope and into the wood. When she veered toward the bastion, Jordam punished her and drove her out toward the edge of the wood.

She ran a long while, dodging trees and tearing through curtains of ivy. In his haste Jordam forgot one of the dangers. Near the edge of the wood, the sound of twanging wire stung the air. The steed lurched, screamed, and fell.

Jordam tumbled free of the collapsing vawn. When the world stopped spinning, he found himself face to face with a wide-eyed gorrel. He recognized it. The gorrel yelped in disbelief, sprinted up a tree trunk, and vanished.

The vawn struggled while the wires tightened around her powerful legs. The yellow saddlebags had fallen free. Jordam saw the broken buckle, the flap flung back, the contents.

He stuffed the bundle of Deuneroi's garments inside, slung the heavy saddlebags over his shoulder, and stumbled through the trees toward the whitegrass, risking traps with every step. As the vawn shrieked, dogs barked and advanced.

Another cry rang out, and everything changed. Jordam turned. "Bel?"

A Bel Amican woman in a soldier's woodscloak stood halfway across the thick, snow-frosted field. She stood still, grasping at her leg as if a snake had seized her.

Jordam bounded through the grass, carefully following her path. Her blood smelled sweet. The woman suddenly straightened and aimed an arrowcaster directly toward his chest.

"Stop!" she said.

He stopped, not from the command, but for recognition. "Bel!"

A gleaming wire twisted about her leg, and she did not fight it. One foot was clad in a tough slipper of glittering sea-gator scales. The other foot was bare. "Jordam," she said, her voice softening.

"Bel," he said.

She lowered the caster. "Help me."

Jordam crouched down, parted icy strands of whitegrass, and found the heavy metal pin and the powerful coil of retracting wire. He dug his claws under the edge, pried it out. "Free?"

"Not yet. I've got to leave, Jordam. We've got to go away from Tilian-purth. Where can we go and be safe?"

He glanced back at the trees. Any moment now, hunters. Arrows. Dogs—all teeth and claws. "Came to find you," he said. "Trouble coming. rrBrothers. Cent Regus." He found the trap's switch, which disengaged the springs, and the line went slack. With curved claw tips, he pried the wire free from the layers of a towel she had tied around her legs. Wire had split the cloth, but it had not broken the skin anywhere but her ankle. His heartbeat raced as he pulled the wire away. "You can run?" he asked in Common.

"Not fast enough." She laughed a little, a response that bewildered him, and then she rose shakily to her feet.

Back in the trees, the vawn's cries increased in a sudden frenzy and then went quiet.

"We go up," said Jordam. "rrForest. I have help."

"Ryllion came to the well to find me. The Seer came with him. They know. They want to kill you and lock me up. Nowhere is safe now."

Even that slight smear of blood on her foot distracted him. He bit his tongue. "We go," he said, forcing himself to look back at her face. "rrSome-where far. Safe."

"Heiress!" The men were out of the trees, marching forward, holding the strained leashes of the hounds. One of the dogs squealed, snapping up the lost silver slipper from the snow and shaking it like captured prey. The guard took it, showed it to the others.

Jordam saw the soldiers pause. Their faces changed when they saw the woman in the grass. They would not understand. They would see a woman and a beastman crouching over her.

He growled, tensed, stood up, and cracked the bullwhip in challenge. Echoes of its sharp report clapped around the valley.

Her hand gripped his arm. "No. You'll be killed. I can't bear it."

"rrWe go now. I carry you?"

Trembling and wild-eyed, she gripped his arm with both hands and nodded. He turned his back and knelt. Her arms folded around his neck, her legs about his waist, her bloodied heel pressing into his belly.

"Heiress!" The soldiers were running now.

He turned his head, amazed to find her chin resting on his shoulder. "You. Heiress." He breathed in the traces of incense in her hair. "Sin-der. Bel. The same?" There was a mystery here, but he had no time to untangle it.

"I was afraid you'd treat me differently if you knew. I lied. I'm sorry."

"Heiress!" One of the soldiers was shouting. "Don't!"

"You'll keep me safe?" she asked quietly.

"Safe."

The hammer of the prongbull's stride punished Jordam's aching head. He began to wonder if the Essence would kill him for his defiance. Waves of pain dissolved his thoughts, and something stronger took over. Memory. Memory of safety. Of rest.

He knew where he would take her.

Before him on the prongbull's back, the Bel Amican woman braced her feet against the yellow saddlebags. He showed her how to hold the whip so that its barbed tips clattered next to the animal's ear. This freed his hands to grasp the prongbull's mane and steer the animal through the forest.

Even if winter unleashed another blast, a prongbull's trail would be impossible to hide. Jordam would have to send the steed away, take Bel, and disappear. He drove the animal eastward, up the rising slopes of the forest, to the bluffs high above Deep Lake.

"Where have all the animals gone?" the Bel Amican asked, turning and shouting to be heard. "These trees are empty."

"rrHigher," he answered. "Higher ground." He gestured eastward and then to the north.

"To get away from something?"

He thought about that, then nodded.

"Away from what?"

He could not explain the feelers. He did not understand them, how they grew so quickly underground, how they knew what to seize and what to let go, or what they did when they dragged their prey underground. And he did not expect the heiress would like such a lesson. She repeated the question, and he shook his head. "rrNot now."

When the prongbull's hooves clattered on the bare stone of familiar cliffs, Jordam pulled him up short. The great white steed snorted, eyes ablaze, tail thrashing.

Jordam climbed down, drew the woman into his arms, and set her on her feet, then removed the saddlebags. He told her to stay with the bags at the edge of the trees. Seeing her shivering there on the bluff, he wondered what the wilderness felt like for someone so small, with such a short yellow mane, hairless limbs, and delicate hands and feet. He removed his woods-cloak and cast it about her. As it enfolded her, she wrinkled her nose, then smiled faintly in gratitude.

Jordam steered the prongbull back into the trees and to a place where the ground spilled in a perfect river of snow that ran northward into another patch of lower forest.

He grabbed a firm hold on a tree branch and lifted himself from the bull's back. As he did, he shoved the bull's back with his heels. "Go."

The animal stayed, glancing back at him uncertainly, confused by any gesture that lacked cruelty.

"Go. Free." He brought the whip down in as hard a blow as he could strike, raising a deep red stripe across the bull's flank. The animal launched, bellowing, leaving Jordam to swing from the bough behind, and charged away, staining the snow with a trail of plowed earth. The brothers would have no reason to suspect that the rider had abandoned the steed.

He concluded that the bull would find his way back to the familiar pun-ishments of the Cent Regus Core, knowing nothing else. All Cent Regus creatures returned there eventually, no matter how many scars they showed for it. Groaning beneath the burden of freedom, Jordam would take a dif-ferent path.

24

What Became of
the Boy in the Stove

A nut in a nutshell buried in the snow," muttered the ale boy. It was a scrap of a verse that Obsidia Dram had sung to lull him to sleep many years ago.

The last thing he had seen before the door of the black iron stove closed was the gloating grin of a beastman who looked just like Jordam. The last thing he had heard was Jordam's small, striped brother laughing, *Hel hel hel.*

Jordam had promised to protect him, to keep Mordafey from dragging him off to Cent Regus enslavement. "rrSleep," had been the order, and the ale boy had feigned unconsciousness. Jordam tied him with loose knots so he could make an escape after the confrontation. But none of that mattered now.

Flaming wagons on Baldridge Hill. The fireplace in Cyndere's chamber. The storm-lit blaze in the midst of the blizzard. Now here he was, folded in an oven without any fire, sucking air through a chimney too narrow to climb.

The boy strained for some sign from Jordam, some indication he would not be forgotten. Only the wind visited him, whistling through the vent in the hatch, but then it departed in a flourish, slamming the shack's wooden door shut behind it.

"A boy who walks through fire," he sighed, "found dead inside a cold, dark stove."

He could turn his body, but there was no room to unfold it, and even a twitch loosed fine black dust into the air. Try as he might to wipe soot from his eyes, he only spread grit with his filthy fingertips. He pulled out the scrap of Auralia's scarf that Jordam had brought him and pressed it over his nose and mouth. Concentrating on the faint shimmer of those colors, he felt the beginnings of calm, breathed evenly, and slept. Asleep, he was free in immeasurable space, in a world of steaming hot towels.

When he awoke, the muffled sound of distant wind had ceased. Silence was worse.

"How'm I s'posed to look for the Keeper's tracks now, 'Ralia?"

The sound of his voice was some small comfort. He kept talking. He told Auralia stories. He described recent dreams. "I'm on my raft, floating on Deep Lake. But I've lost my oars. There's no wind to move me. I'm stuck. I watch for a ripple and listen for a splash. But the Keeper doesn't come. All I hear's an echo from far away. A song."

He hummed a bit of the melody just to fill the silence. He had never enjoyed singing. He did not like the feeble timbre of his voice, which betrayed his uncertainty. But here, in the midst of this darkness, soot cleared from his throat, and the song began to sing itself, each note like a footprint leading him along. The sound made the stovepipe hum. He recognized the song—House Abascar's Midnight Verse, which the watchman sang to mark the deepest point of night.

A thump interrupted his song. Something had bumped against the shack's wooden door.

He waited. Silence settled.

Then the sound of splintering wood. An explosion. A heavy crash. Wind rushed back in, and the boy closed his eyes to the swirling ash.

In the stillness that followed, he pressed his ear against the vent. As soon as he could open his eyes, he peered intently out.

Whoever or whatever had come carried no torch. As the intruder shuffled about in the damp, dead leaves of the space, the boy turned his face from the hatch so nothing would notice his white eyes staring through.

A gust of foul air puffed through the vent. The iron box rang, struck by something like bone, but the stove did not budge. The ale boy held his breath and tried to be a piece of firewood.

Another crash shook the stove. This time it rocked up off two of its feet, and the stovepipe groaned and clanged as it bent, warped, and tore free of the ceiling. The stove teetered. Old layers of chimney soot crumbled down over the ale boy's head. He coughed and spluttered, knowing even as he did that his presence was revealed.

The stove lay on its side. The boy saw the shadows of two massive legs against the faint light from the door. He heard a snuffling, then a frustrated growl. The stove spun, struck by a tremendous blow.

The boy shook his head, trying to clear it of debris, choking on clouds of grit.

A guttural voice sounded at the vent. The latch scraped against the door. Bit by bit the intruder was prying it open. The boy heard it snap free. Then nothing. Just the faint rush of cold wind. He blinked against the burn of the soot in his eyes.

A sonorous, three-toned blast filled the farm shack.

The boy thrust the hatch open and pried himself free. "Rumpa!"

His vawn shrieked in dismay and staggered back. But he opened his arms. "It's me! It's me! I...oh." He understood. The vawn was looking at him but seeing a monster made of coal.

The vawn's muzzle, like a duck's bill fused shut, sniffed him through three small nostrils. He reached up and gently stroked her scaly neck. She trumpeted in sudden recognition, knocking him backward.

"How did you find me?" The ale boy climbed on top of the overturned stove, finding the vawn with his hands and embracing her. "You followed me, didn't you? The beastman, did he scare you? Did you hear him break the whistle?" He patted the bony ridges on her head, tightened his fingers around the brush of her narrow mane. "How did you find me? Was it the song? That old Abascar song?"

Rumpa whimpered with glee, trotting in a circle around the shack, kicking wooden crates aside, and knocking out one of the struts that supported the upper level so that the ceiling sagged, split, and dumped piles of old straw and showers of bird droppings into the air.

The boy felt his way on all fours until he found the wall, then stood and leaned against the doorframe. A faint glow drew him to the green winter coat that he had cast aside to cover the Bel Amican glowstone. He held the stone and illuminated the wide-eyed, boastful vawn and the disarray all around them. The boy laughed and ran out into the light snowfall. "We're going to King Cal-raven, Rumpa. He needs to hear Cyndere's message."

Outside, flakes alighted on his sleeves, and he would have been no more delighted if stars had lodged in the folds of his coat or alighted on his cheekbones. The air burned in his lungs, and he coughed blackness onto the snow. Waving his arms about, he danced like a drunken fool. Fire had tested him. He had survived. A blizzard had sought to bury him. He was alive. Beastmen had captured him. His spirits were high again. He was not the boy he had once thought he was. He threw himself down in the snow and rolled across its unblemished blanket, leaving a smear of soot behind him, then waved his arms and legs until he swept a snowbird's outline like he'd seen the Gatherers' orphans do.

The vawn, not quite so eager to rejoice in beastman territory, knelt down and grunted, urging the boy to climb into her saddle. Shaking off the snow, he wrapped his arms around her neck, buried his face in her bristly mane, then climbed on her back. "Rumpa, sit!" he shouted sharply. She sprang into a full run, and they left the Cent Regus farmland behind.

He tried to steer the vawn southeast to make for the Cliffs of Barnashum. Much to his surprise, Rumpa resisted. He wondered if she might have a grudge, but her step was sprightly enough. Her mind was made up. She would take him due east into the southernmost reach of the Cragavar forest.

"You're s'posed to obey me," he murmured. "And there's only one person who can change that."

The vawn looked back at him, eyes narrow and intent.

"Ah," said the boy. "Very well, then."

Vawns were not horses; while their two powerful legs were just as muscular, the ride was rough and jarring. But Rumpa was fast, and they traversed miles in minutes. When they brushed against frozen quill trees, shivers of ice slid down the boy's neck, and the branches tapped their fingers with crystalline tones that reminded him of strings lightly plucked on a perys.

Thoughts of music took him into the caves of Abascar's survivors. He had, at times, crept into those passages, as inconspicuous as he had ever been in the Underkeep. He had watched as people he guided to that refuge found their place and shouldered responsibility for others. He had crawled into hollows and listened to the songs that brought them together. Had he stepped into the light and revealed himself, Cal-raven's people would have drawn him in, and failing to understand his mission, they would have made him stay. Better to remain on the edge of it all—a rumor, free to venture out under the night to search for those in trouble whom no one else could reach.

But tonight, as icy roses dissolved on his face, he yearned for a warm fire. A hot meal. Kind voices. Maybe even laughter. With no sense of where to go, no tracks to follow, he wondered if it was time to return to House Abascar, to become the ale boy again. What did they brew in Barnashum?

Rumpa paused in a clearing high on a hill and glanced back as if to confirm that her passenger remained in place. She snorted in surprise, and he laughed, for now he had become, to all appearances, a sculpture made of snow.

Making her way to the edge of a steep slope that stretched down between trees tall enough to scratch the stars, the vawn stepped out and shoved hard with her feet, dropping down flat on her scaly belly. She sledded down, down, down toward a circle of trees.

In the center of those trees, a campfire flickered. Crows sprang from the figure they had settled upon and merged with the shadows above.

A man engulfed in heavy furs watched them approach, sipping from a steaming bowl before a swell of stone, a hand-sculpted oven.

Rumpa skidded to a stop beside the fire.

"Magnificent, Rumpa!" The mountain of furs rose, the small man inside them taking the reins from the boy and looping them about the low branch of a cloudgrasper tree. "You found our little firewalker sooner than I expected. Now all of us can get some rest." He grinned at the ale boy. "After all, we'll be traveling together tomorrow. A fair distance, I suspect."

The ale boy recognized him at last.

25

AURALIA'S BLUE ROOM

S*he is like me*, he thought. *Hunted. Alone.*
  Jordam slowed his passage through arcades of trees and landed lightly on a high branch. The air was dry and cold, but Bel was not shivering anymore. She stood at the cliff's edge, leaning forward into the view—Deep Lake, with its floating icedrifts, its mirrored constellations sparkling through rips in the clouds. She seemed to dare the wind.

The recent storms had scoured the sky, and the stars seemed closer, brighter. They reminded Jordam of the mysterious lights strung from threads along the high ceilings of O-raya's caves, suspended in delicate balance. The Expanse felt small in view of that light-dusted space so full of unknowns.

He held back, one foot on this strange new path, the other in memory. From this vantage point, he could look back and see the tree where he had struck a fleeing boy from his horse. And there, where Bel stood, was the very spot where he had stalked a singing girl, where his world had changed. He shivered, shaking off a premonition that his brothers would find her soon, that he would not be able to save her.

Climbing down, he brushed snow, twigs, and leaves from his mane. He tightened the belt of the tattered soldier's tunic and made sure his weapons were sheathed. He crouched beside the Bel Amican saddlebags, then cleared his throat. He dared not frighten her.

"Bel," he whispered, stepping into the moonlight. Then, "Sin-der. Come. Hide. Safe."

She did not respond right away. After tearing strips from the lining of her cloak, she bound up her ankle where the wire had cut deepest. She pushed her hood back, ran fingers through her short, strawgold hair, and looked up at the sliver of moon. He heard her whisper sharp, bitter words but could not make them out.

Turning to face him, she said, "Show me."

Cyndere followed Jordam along the cliff's edge to a place where it split open as if someone had cut into it with an ax. She thought he would lead her around the crevasse. Instead, he stepped to the deepest point of the break-age, carrying the saddlebags over his shoulder, and walked down onto a steep crumble of rock that sloped to a dizzying drop.

She hesitated. "We'll fall into the lake."

He crouched, swept away debris, and lifted a series of wooden planks like fence posts from where they lay under the dust. This opened a deep shaft like a chimney. "Down," he said, pointing into the pit. "O-raya's door."

"What am I doing?" she muttered.

She looked down inside to see him descending a long ladder. In the faint moonlight, she saw him beckon. She followed.

At the bottom they stood in a cave where rivers of air crisscrossed from adjoining tunnels like cold blood through a heart. She was too weary to fear anymore. She followed him through one of the narrow passages. This was not what she had imagined when she and Deuneroi dreamt of making con-tact with Cent Regus. She had envisioned herself healing them and teaching them her own ways. Instead, she felt herself being drawn into Jordam's sur-prising world.

Metal buckles of the saddlebags clanked and scraped against the walls of the narrow space ahead.

"How did you find this place?" Her whispers echoed close and far away. "Are we safe?"

The walls were wet from the seeping snows, soft with burgundy lichen and hanging moss. She heard watery murmurs from distant places, cavernous spaces. Just when it seemed they had left the light behind, they would pass a glowstone embedded in the wall like a lantern.

Eventually the passage grew larger and wider. She ran her fingers along a meandering line of gold drawn on the passage wall. The colors stained her fingers. "Someone painted the stone," she concluded. "It's like…"

They stepped into a room where the walls were painted from floor to ceiling with the same colors that she had seen lining the wellstones of the glen.

"Auralia," she whispered.

She wanted to stay, but Jordam led on, showing her a tunnel where the walls were lined with shelves. Most of them were empty, but in one corner there were hollows in the wall stacked high with scarves, capes, stockings, and bundles of yarn. She withdrew a heavy shawl that smelled of mildew and shook it loose of mothwings and webs, marveling as it rippled with intricate lines of radiant green.

"She did all this?"

"All night O-raya makes colors," he answered in a reverent whisper. "No sleeping."

"You can't be the only one who knows about this," she said. "Won't we be found?"

"Safe here. rrNo one comes." He paused, twisted strands of his beard, then shrugged. "Ale boy comes. And…cloud people."

"Cloud people?" She puzzled over that, picking up a broom from the floor. "So. This really was her home. And you and the ale boy, you were her guests." She swept dust, debris, strands of thread, flakes of falseglass, fragments of shells, and chips of paint. "How is it that both of you came to me? The Expanse goes on forever, but we found each other." She propped the broom against the wall.

Jordam paused, his shape stark against the blue promise of the next tunnel. "Strange forest," he replied.

The neighboring chamber was spacious, like one of the moon-spirit observatories in Bel Amica. Cyndere stepped in and heard a fluttering as their entrance disturbed some shadowy life in the high recesses of the cave. But before she could discern what kind of creatures they were, another mystery stole her attention.

Jordam stood before a wall thinly curtained in rippling water that shimmered and spilled away through cracks in the floor. Behind that quiet, glistening sheen, blue constellations pulsed and glittered intermittently, like faint notes of music.

"How?" Her own voice surprised her in chorus as the word flew about the great space and returned. Moving forward, she felt like she was falling into a night sky. "The snow…it's melting."

Jordam watched her approach, and she saw something like jealousy in his eyes. "rrNever showed this," he whispered, half growling. "Never."

She touched the wall, opening a tear in the cascading water, which flowed around her fingertips. "It's beautiful." The blue light enveloped her hand through the water, and she did not know what moved her more, the ghostly lights or the dark spans between them. "Spring's beginning. At last."

"rrBlue from flowers." He set the saddlebags onto the larger of two broad boulders in the middle of the floor, then climbed up to sit back against them. He folded his legs beneath him and rested his chin on his hands.

"Yes," she said. "Yes. She took the blue from the flowers and painted this wall."

"O-raya made blue," he said. "She gave blue to me. I climbed the wall. Put the blue there, there, there." He reached out, touching places in the air as if reliving the work.

"You did this?" Jordam looked down at her, his eyes so wide she could see white around the dark irises. A smile spread across his face as she exclaimed, "You did this!"

They stood together staring into the blue.

"O-raya," he said, his voice like small stones cracking under a great weight. "O-raya."

"What does the blue make you think about?"

He narrowed his eyes, tapped his claw tips on the stone. "Like…windows. Windows to good places."

She sat down on the floor, leaning against the boulder, and tilted her head back to look up at him. He hunched forward, looking into her face. "What was it, Jordam, that changed you? Was it Auralia? Or the colors?"

"Yes." He touched his browbone absently, then pressed his hand to his chest.

"You're sad. Sad she's gone. You miss her."

"Miss her. O-raya gone to Abascar. I searched there. Found the colors, but then"—his voice curdled—"rrCent Regus took them."

"Cent Regus came here?"

"No. They took O-raya's colors from Abascar." He lay back and stared up at the ceiling, his head on the saddlebags. "Someday I get them back."

He continued, the words coming with greater ease as he relaxed. He described the days he had spent here, wounded by his fall but enthralled by O-raya's colors. O-raya had brought him fish, apples, water. "Good water. Deep water," he added. "Brown cup."

"From the lake?"

"No." He gestured back to the adjoining passage. "rrWater from caves. Deep. Like the well."

Cyndere liked the sound of Jordam's voice here. It had lost its jagged edge, resonating instead like those sad bass horns in the bands that once played for the departure of ships. She could almost imagine what he might have sounded like had he been an ordinary man. He was taking time, she noticed, to become descriptive. The colors calmed him, gave him a safe place to remember and piece things together, to give his feelings shape.

"Once, I look for O-raya," he continued. "Crawl through many caves. No O-raya. But water. And lights. rrMany lights. Lights on the water. Colors grow there, on the water. Like weeds. Like leaves. Like blankets."

"Colors growing in secret caves." She shook her head. "I've never imagined it. Every question answered asks another." She saw his eyes searching about, trying to interpret her words. "Why did you leave Auralia? Why did you go back to your brothers?"

Jordam explained that he had departed Auralia's caves for fear of his brothers—especially one called Mordafey. And he was drawn away desiring power and strength. She knew he was speaking of the Cent Regus curse.

"But you came back here."

He spread his hands in the air as if searching for something, then dropped them to his sides. He was quiet for a time. Flies buzzed about his nose and lips and crawled on the crooked line of his browbone. His face was so strange to her. It was as if a man were trying to escape an animal that had consumed him.

"You can stay here, Jordam. You don't have to go back. There are probably plenty of fish in the lake and birds in the wood. Not to mention berries and roots. You could live here." She thought of the speeches she had rehearsed with Deuneroi, pleas to help the beastmen find their way to healing. "You could sleep here." It was so different from what she'd expected. She had assumed she would have to persuade him. But he had made his desires known, and now her words came easily, for she was answering a friend, and he was listening. "You could be the first. A new Cent Regus man."

He closed his eyes and winced. His massive chest rose and fell. He flared his fangs in a yawn.

"Those blankets in the corner. Who slept there?"

"Ale boy."

"You haven't told me, Jordam, what happened to him."

The beastman did not answer. She heard his breathing deepen.

She stood and found that he had stretched out on the rock, calm and quiet, just as her viscorcat basked in the heat of a fire back home.

While Jordam slept, Cyndere wandered through Auralia's caves, eating wedges of dried sour apple from Tilianpurth, passing rooms full of gems, shells, and tree cones. She began to imagine a small hand tucking a nest of red thread or puffgoose down into the silver whirl of a snail shell or the empty glossy cup of a nutshell. She was content to leave signs of Auralia's work where they lay, moving deeper into the labyrinth.

She thought she heard the patter of feet. At first she told herself they were echoes, for when she paused, the sounds stopped. "Cloud people," Jordam had said. She thought of the apparition she had seen at the well. Her father's courage awoke within her.

"Mother would say you're a moon-spirit come to study my choices." She began to walk slowly to show that she was not afraid. "House Abascar...they would have called you a Northchild." She watched the path before her, every corner cast in a glowing sphere of a different hue. "I don't know what to call you. I only know what I wish you were."

The footsteps began again and seemed to be just around the bend, leading.

"Deuneroi would have loved this secret palace. He would have told elaborate stories about its history. They would go on and on, and I would have no idea where he was taking me. He wouldn't either, probably. "

She began to whisper a song, one that Deuneroi had often asked her to sing. As she passed a curtained chamber, the echoes faded entirely. She stepped back and looked at the curtain. It was woven from strands of inkblack weeds. Unlike the other chambers, the space gave no evidence of light beyond. The curtain wavered in a flow of air. Something shuffled in the distance behind it. She drew it aside, and cold engulfed her, spilling out from the dark. She took a cautious step into the opening.

"rrStay out," said Jordam. He was standing behind her.

She looked back, but she did not let go of the curtain. Something within her needed to go on into the dark.

He cocked his head, then gestured into the blackness. "Stay out. That place is bad."

She opened her mouth to protest, but the cave's deathly air seemed to suck all heat from her body and leave her aching and tired. "I think...I think I need to sleep."

"rrStrength," said Jordam. "Sin-der needs strength." He stood aside and let her walk back down to the cave. She wanted to tell him to leave her alone. But he did not follow. She walked into Auralia's blue cave and over to the ale boy's bed.

She pulled the frayed, damp blankets over her head, cocooning herself in darkness. "Again someone else decides where I can and cannot go." In her dream she crept back to the door of that void and leaned in.

"Eat," Jordam gruffed.

As the cave came into focus, Cyndere saw him standing in a flourish of daylight in the passage beyond the cave. She heard pebbled shores murmuring in the lake's wavering shallows. She smelled smoke. And fish.

She blinked, rubbed her eyes, and sat up. "You cooked for me?"

She found coals crackling in a pit under a mesh of stripped branches on the shore near the entrance. Resting on those branches, three large shells emanated steam and a strong aroma of seared meat. He lifted one of the hot shells and placed it on a painted clay plate before her.

"Beastmen put their food on plates?"

"O-raya's way." He gave her sharpened twigs to use in prying apart the shell. Then he broke another with his bare hands and consumed all of its contents in a gulp.

She prodded at the shell. "Thank you."

"rrThat cave. Dark cave. Trouble," he said.

"What's in there?"

"One day O-raya gone. I looked. Found her there." He shuddered to imitate her condition. "Carried her out. Something bad happened there." His hands were shaking. "Then later O-raya gone. Did not come back."

"How long have I been asleep?" she asked.

"Sun down. Sun up."

"They'll be in a panic at Tilianpurth. Poor Emeriene." She tried to stand, but her legs shook.

"Stay." He sounded distressed. He watched her pick at the meat with the twigs. "Good," he said.

She peeled one of them until it was sharper, then speared a piece and put it in her mouth. She chewed thoughtfully. "You should bring your brothers here someday. Maybe the colors would help them too."

"Mordafey comes, bad. Jorn comes, bad. Goreth comes... rrGoreth is like me."

"Bring Goreth. Cook fish for him. Show him the colors."

Jordam seemed to think about this. "Danger," he said.

"I'd like to speak with Goreth the way you speak with me. Maybe we could help the rest of your brothers—"

"rrNo," he said flatly. "Brothers finish all people. Cent Regus. Bel Amica. Abascar. They finish anything that runs." He grasped a stone and flung it. It landed far out in the lake with a *plup.* They sat and watched the ripples expand and then disappear as if nothing had disturbed the water. "Goreth is like me," he sighed. "Not so fast. But someday."

She thought about that as he brought her a fat yellow fish. She took a small knife from her bag and skinned the fish on the stone. He watched, fascinated.

"Would it hurt you if your brothers killed...I mean, if they finished me?" she asked softly.

"Yes. You helped me." He opened his hands. "Would you hurt if...?"

"Yes," she said quietly.

"I am Cent Regus."

"Yes."

"rrCent Regus finished Deuneroi."

"I know, Jordam. But you did not hurt Deuneroi. Remember? You told me so."

"Would you hurt Cent Regus who...who finished Deuneroi?" He would not look at her.

"Yes. No. I..." She put the fish aside. "I am very angry. It is not good to do anything when you're angry. Cent Regus who kill people should be stopped. But they are born under a terrible curse. They will kill unless they have powerful help. Look at you, Jordam. You found help. You're growing stronger all the time."

"Grow?" He seemed surprised by the word.

"Yes," she agreed. "I think we're both growing."

A black bat skittered over their heads and disappeared into Auralia's caves, retreating from the brightening daylight and moving up the passage. Cyndere smiled.

Jordam pushed pebbles and debris over the coals to squelch the smoke. "Are they close?"

He shrugged. "No. rrMordafey must have gone away. Plans."

"What is he planning?" She hugged her knees to her chin. "Is it bad?"

Jordam expression was pained. "Would you hurt if brothers...finished Cal-raven?"

"Why? Why do you ask this?"

"Cent Regus. rrMany Cent Regus hunting Abascar people." He gestured toward the south and east. "Cent Regus finish them. Take weapons. Treasure. Clothes. Everything." He sighed, held his head. "rrMordafey hunts Cal-raven. Soon."

She got to her feet. Her answer was forceful, urgent. "Yes, Jordam. I will hurt if Mordafey finishes Cal-raven. We must stop him."

"Can't," Jordam barked. "rrMordafey too strong. Many Cent Regus help him."

Cyndere took the platter of fish and threw it out onto the rocks. She got up and walked down to the water. She could feel her heartbeat pound out an alarm.

"rrCome back," he snarled. "Sit here." He bent to pick up the pieces of her meal, trying to reassemble it. "I catch more fish for you. Talk more. Talk of everything."

"I want to talk with you, Jordam. About everything. But not yet. We don't have time." She was punishing him, even as he tried to serve her. She knelt to help him pick up the pieces. "I'm sorry, Jordam. But I'm angry. I want to help Auralia's people escape this attack just as you helped me escape the snare. If we get there before your brothers, we can warn them."

"rrCent Regus will finish me."

"You're stronger than they are."

"No. rrMordafey."

"Could Mordafey have rescued me? Could Mordafey have run away from the Cent Regus strength? Could he have caught me a fish and cooked it without eating it himself?"

Jordam carved up fistfuls of stones and crushed them in dusty explosions. Then he slapped his hands over his ears, dusting both sides of his face. "Lost O-raya," he groaned. "Lost colors. Lost ale boy. rrJordam loses too much."

"We'll both lose much more if we stay, Jordam. If you won't go warn Cal-raven, I'll find a way."

"No." He waved his hands.

"Would Auralia hurt if your brothers finished Cal-raven?"

He looked back into the caves, and she thought she heard him stifle a whimper.

"Find Cal-raven, Jordam. You can. Tell him we want to help him."

"You want this?" he asked.

"I want this," she said. "This is how we show that we are strong, Jordam. We do what is difficult. This is what Deuneroi was trying to do when he was killed in Abascar. Help people in trouble."

He turned away and walked down the pebbled bank to the edge of the lake. The shores were quiet as if the lake were listening, waiting for him to decide.

She followed, watching water swirl around his legs. She searched for another appeal, but he strode further out, deeper, deeper, until he was submerged. The waters stilled.

"Deuneroi," she whispered, "can you hear him learning to speak with me? Can you see him?"

Jordam broke the surface and strode onto the shore, water streaming from his savage expression. He splashed up toward the caves. "A plan," he said. "rrJordam's plan."

She started to follow him, but he barked a refusal. "Too dangerous," he said. "Many Cent Regus."

"I'm tired of being told to stay!" she shouted.

"Dangerous. Mordafey has his plan. rrThis is mine. Help people in trouble."

"Then what is mine, Jordam? I have no plan. Am I to sit in this cave or go back to the tower and wait while you never come back?"

"I come back," he assured her. He described how he would have to run to reach Cal-raven in time. She would be safer here, he insisted, in Auralia's caves.

She grabbed his arm, closing her eyes. "I'm sorry. I know you'll come back."

He looked up at the cliff face. "rrStay inside. Hide."

"Wait. I have one more thing for you to take." She led him back into the caves and reached into the pocket of her woodscloak. "Keep this." She opened her hand, revealing the stonemaster's whistle. "If anyone comes, I'm going to hide deep within the caves. But if I hear the whistle, I'll know it is you. And I won't be afraid."

It was a stone, but someone had troubled to sculpt it in the shape of a reptile's remains. For a beastman, a bone was something worthless, a scrap, something to cast aside. Jordam stared at the whistle as if Cyndere had handed him an empty nutshell.

Cyndere blew softly through the cavity at the back of the skull. A resonant, mournful tone sang through the eyes of the whistle, filling the caves and continuing, the earth becoming an extension of the instrument.

Color all around her blazed in response, as if Auralia herself had come home to a welcome. Deep beyond, the echoes went on and on and on.

26

SCULPTING A FUTURE

"Don't look," said Tabor Jan to himself, forcing a harvest cart up the ledge from one tier of Barnashum's cliffs to the next, just a stumble away from a dizzying drop. Others had assured him that the fear would pass. But he found no fondness for heights, and this rickety cart that groaned under the weight of winterroots made every step seem more precarious.

"I don't know what will kill me first," said Brevolo behind him, "harvesting roots or eating them."

"Complaints are what'll kill me," he shot back. "We've come this far today without any. Don't spoil it."

"Let's go hunting, Tabor Jan. I'm so hungry, I'd roast a Cent Regus cow."

"If the Cent Regus had cattle, the cattle would be hunting us."

"I could do with something dangerous. I'm a swordswoman. Slashing vegetables loose from their stems just doesn't scratch the itch."

"So you want to go pick a fight."

"I'd rather find them before they come for us," she snapped. "We're not ready. The first siege of Barnashum will be the only siege of Barnashum. The hungrier we are, the clumsier we become. We're spilling out on these cliffs in full view of anyone paying attention." She struck a fighting pose, spun her spear swiftly in one hand, and pretended to plunge the dull end between Tabor Jan's chest shield and belt. "How will our king defend us when our enemies come? Will he scare them off with a blast of unspeakable beauty?"

To Tabor Jan's relief, the ledge broadened and led them to the edge of a dusty hollow, a stone bowl that bulged out from the cliff like a balcony.

Down inside, Cal-raven, king of Abascar, sat on the back of a massive stone animal that he was sculpting with his bare hands. Notes from Lesyl's string-weave rose like fireflies, and five children sang quietly along. Guards on opposite sides of the bowl tossed a tree branch back and forth, teasing Hagah, Cal-raven's hunting hound. One of them saluted the newcomers.

Brevolo passed Tabor Jan and glowered down at the scene. "*That* gloomy song again? Why can't she sing about something hopeful? Who wants to hear all that droning about descendants of Tammos Raak?"

"*They* do," said Tabor Jan. "They *are* descendants of Tammos Raak." He gestured to the three children who were busily carving intricate details into the statue's right foreleg. "Cal-raven's a stonemaster. And who would have believed our only batch of triplets would manifest that same gift."

"He should be teaching them to defend themselves, not how to play with clay. Maybe they can sculpt us some rocks to throw at beastmen. Seriously, Captain,"—she thrust an accusing finger toward the statue—"are we safer when our king daydreams? Where's the proof that such a creature even exists?"

Tabor Jan set the cart down, grabbed a winterroot, and sat with his back against the rock wall, relieved to be farther from the edge. "You have better ideas?"

"Here's one." Brevolo knelt down beside him, grabbed a fistful of his long, ragged hair, and pressed her lips to his so fiercely that he dropped the root. She did not stop until they were both out of breath. He was wide awake in ways he had forgotten during months of anxiety.

As she let him go, she cocked her head back. "When I get an idea, I'm shy at first...and cautious. But when I'm ready, I turn aggressive." She unsheathed a dagger. "I don't like waiting. I like to act. I'm ready to turn these cutters into swords. Abascar should stop hiding."

Tabor Jan rose and grasped the handles of the harvest cart, more to steady himself than to move on. "That...idea you just shared with me. Was that a genuine proposition?"

"This endless winter's made me impatient. I'm in the mood for a gamble. And I've got a proposition for the king as well." She pranced down into the bowl and did not look back.

Tabor Jan brushed his beard with the back of his hand. His lip stung where she had bit. "This should be worth seeing." He followed.

Hagah barked at Brevolo and Tabor Jan, pink tongue lolling and eyes smiling through the bunches of flesh in his face.

"Tabor Jan." Cal-raven was out of breath, shaken from the exertion that his stonemastery required. From his position on the statue's head, he had reached down to sculpt the subtle contours of a frightening but noble face. "Good. I was about to send for you."

Behind him, the span of the statue's sweeping wings spread out, providing shade for Luci, Madi, and Margi, his freckled apprentices. The triplets now stood on stacks of wooden crates, reaching up to illustrate feathery details beneath those magnificent wings. Their faces upturned to scrutinize their work, they resembled three baby birds waiting to be fed.

Nearby, the orphans, Wynn and his sister, Cortie, carved their own version of the creature with hammers and chisels from a section of a dead tree. Since their arrival, Cal-raven had kept the orphans close, comforting them and sifting their memories for details about their travel and about their remarkable rescuer.

The sight of the children cheered Tabor Jan. They kept everyone focused on progress. And Lesyl, leaning over the cords of her beloved string-weave, also pleased him. When she sang, the king seemed less prone to fretting and biting his nails. The captain had arranged an armed caravan to set out during the night for their risky rendezvous with the Seer from Bel Amica. He needed the king to be calm and careful.

Before Brevolo could drop to one knee, Cal-raven slid down from the statue, clapped dust from his hands, and gestured for her to remain standing. "My king," she said, "we've brought you more winterroots for your next glorious feast."

"More rocks for Yawny's stone stew, I see. Thank you." He slapped the statue's foreleg and laughed. "Don't say any more, Brevolo. I know you disapprove of my...my recreation."

"I know you love stories of the Keeper, my lord." Brevolo, stepping closer to the creature, ran her finger up the veined surface of the neck. The statue's eye seemed to stare down at her. "And your stonemastery is extraordinary. But—"

"You think I'm wasting time when there's so much that we need."

"I'm your servant, my lord. We owe you our lives. You sculpted figures in the Hall of the Lost. To honor the dead, you said. I understand that. When I walk among those statues, I remember what we were, what we lost, and our responsibility to learn from mistakes. But this—something from children's stories while we're fighting to survive? Is this helping us move forward?"

The king scratched at his unshaven face. "I'm glad you understand the Hall of the Lost, Brevolo. Some don't. But you're right. We must move forward. The future needs a shape."

"It's a heavy burden, my lord. I have no doubt."

"I'm supposed to protect you, to provide. And to dream. Without a vision for Abascar's future, I can't lead." Cal-raven pondered the statue a moment. "My father exiled Scharr ben Fray for encouraging me to dream about the Keeper. My mother told me the Keeper was nonsense. They liked things they could explain and possess and control. Anything mysterious, anything more powerful...worried them." He tapped his forehead. "This notion of the Keeper, it's child's play. Make-believe. But it haunts my dreams. Yours too. Don't deny it."

He turned to the apprentices. "Luci, Margi, Madi, what did you dream about last night?"

"The Keeper!" they exclaimed together, their identical gap-toothed grins beaming.

"Wynn, Cortie, what about you?"

Wynn scowled and looked back at his work, but Cortie nodded, enthused.

"And was it a good dream?"

In a celebratory chorus, they agreed.

"Why?" he asked.

"Because..." They stretched the word out like a long spill of honey, then trailed off, uncertain. "Because when it's there, I'm safe," said Madi.

"The light in those wings," said Luci, and she could not complete her sentence, seemingly lost in the memory.

"The stones under its feet sound like music," Margi mumbled shyly.

"That's where I want to take us, Brevolo. Not just away from here. But somewhere safe. With beautiful light. A solid foundation. Music. Somewhere high above these troubles, where the wind is not so punishing, where we don't have to hide, where beastmen never come." He brushed his hand along sculpted scales. "Is the Keeper real? Does it look like this?" He shrugged. "Wishful thinking, perhaps. I wake from those dreams with an urge to search. I've collected a lot of clues in my investigation, although I still haven't found it. And if it's not there in the shadows and luring me on to understand more all the time, then I can't explain what I've seen...all these wonders that whisper about what's broken and what's best."

He touched the band of colors about his neck. "Auralia testified that the Keeper sent her to Abascar, and she brought colors we've never seen. She knew something we need to know. That boy called Rescue—he swears he found survivors by seeking the Keeper's tracks. He knew something too. Think what it would mean for House Abascar if we all set our minds on finding what they've found, if we believed as they believe."

Brevolo kicked at the scattered stone fragments. "I agree that we can do better than these caves. And your vision...it sounds lovely. But if I may be so bold—"

"I hope you will be."

"Abascar's weakening. We might be wise to seize something good rather than go on reaching for something better, lest we collapse. I'm hungry, my lord."

"And I'm hungrier," he sighed. "And restless. But when House Abascar leaves the Blackstone Caves behind, it will be at our tremendous peril. We need a plan worth the risk. Every day we're closer. We're preparing tools. We're studying maps. Tonight we ride to gather a generous gift of supplies that one of Bel Amica's Seers promised us. And this work, this *play*—it sharpens my vision for that journey."

He walked along the statue to the ridge that would soon become the Keeper's tail. "I must admit, at the end of a difficult day, when I feel as though I've failed, there's something deeply satisfying about doing this." He took up a long-handled hammer from the dust and brought it smashing down.

Crystal shards scattered everywhere, glinting in the afternoon light. "I've struck mirrorstone!" Hagah ran at Cal-raven and barked at the hammer. The children dropped their tools and scrambled to gather the shards. Cal-raven bowed low so that his beaded red braids brushed the ground. "You see? Sometimes there are rewards for such play."

Brevolo stared at her reflection in a mirrorstone. "Can we eat crystals, my king? Or use them to arm ourselves?" A note of bitterness tainted her voice as she added, "That Bel Amican had better keep his promise." She turned abruptly, crossed the hollow, and disappeared beyond the rising ledge.

Tabor Jan opened his mouth, but the king silenced him. "I wish more of us cared as passionately about Abascar's future as Brevolo does. And...by the severed arm of Har-baron, Tabor Jan, I fear your lip is bleeding." As the captain felt his face begin to burn, Cal-raven laughed, "Is there something you want to tell me?"

Hagah woofed after Brevolo, then at Cal-raven to remind him that the time for his dinner was at hand.

Cal-raven leaned against the statue. "Wynn, take the children back down to the tunnel. It's time to burrow in."

Wynn dusted off his sister and beckoned to the three young stone-crafters. As the children moved off, Tabor Jan directed one of the guards to follow. Turning to the king, he asked, "What is it, my lord?"

"I saw a beastman today. At the edge of the wood. Staring in our direction."

"You can't see so far, my lord!" Tabor Jan laughed. "Or do you have other gifts besides stonemastery?"

Cal-raven took a wooden cylinder from his pocket. "A farglass. Fashioned by young Krystor. As fine a scope as any my father ever used from his tower. Climb up to the edge. Look fast to the forest. It's getting dark."

Up among the stone teeth, Tabor Jan peered through the farglass and scanned the edge of the Cragavar. The land seemed to rush at him. He lowered the glass. "I could swear Scharr ben Fray enchanted this glass. Cal-raven, I..."

The king was gone.

Tabor Jan understood at once. "Brevolo." The captain climbed back down to where Lesyl sat tuning the string-weave.

"You'd better leave them be," she muttered. "The king thinks that Brevolo's angry. He doesn't understand women very well. She's baiting him. To speak with him alone."

"On the whys and hows of women, I bow to your wisdom, Lesyl. But I think you might be wrong this time." He licked the congealing blood from his lip. "The king of Abascar can't go running off unguarded. That's bad behavior he learned from his mother. And I intend to break him of it. Especially with beastmen around."

Perhaps he had been too harsh with her. Perhaps he was just too weary to spend another night plotting ways to mend torn threads. Whatever the case, Cal-raven felt compelled to catch Brevolo.

Everyone hiding in Barnashum had despaired or lashed out at one time or another during this long, punishing winter. If the flaring tempers of Abascar's survivors had given any real heat, ice would have fallen from the cliffs. Cal-raven learned to ask questions carefully, and he prepared himself to dodge violent replies. Too much had been lost, too many days had been cold and hard for him to expect better. Patience and good humor were in short supply. Like food. Like garments. Like tools and weapons.

He tried to ignore the other feeling that had drawn him after her. Jealousy. Cal-raven had been careful to conceal his own feelings for Lesyl, which were growing stronger by the day as her music sustained him. This was too fragile a time to make himself vulnerable to heartbreak. With a similar concern for Tabor Jan, he wanted to warn Brevolo. Surely she had taken leave of her senses even as she knocked the captain out of his own.

He paused. Ahead the ledge split into two paths, one leading up to the next tier of the cliffs, the other continuing on. Brevolo had already disappeared. She might have run up, taking the hard route in order to discourage pursuit, find solitude, and nurse her pride. Or if she hoped he would follow to continue their argument in private, she probably would have stayed on the level path.

"She is a woman," he sighed. "Whatever I guess, I will guess wrong." He made a decision and dashed forward. To his left—two tiers of high cliffs towered above him, grey and dull in the winter glow, with squawking precipice birds picking at their wings and preparing for their night flight back to the forest. To his right—a sheer drop to what people called the Red Teeth, intricate spears of blood-colored rock as tall as cloudgrasper trees, sharp as razors, impassable except for the surefooted rock goats.

He paused before a cave that opened into the cliff. It was quiet, but the dust just outside the cave mouth had been disturbed. "We need more guards," he muttered, remembering that he had made his way into the survivors' hideaways through breaks in the wall at the back of this hollow.

Something moved inside the tunnel.

"Brevolo?"

He saw eyes. Jaws. Claws. And then the Cent Regus beastwoman pounced on him.

27

THE FIGHT IN
THE HALL OF THE LOST

They grappled at the edge of the frosty precipice, House Abascar and House Cent Regus, a man and a savage.

Cal-raven tumbled back, his head and shoulders hanging in open space far above the Red Teeth. The beastwoman pressed her knees into his belly and clamped a powerful clawed hand over his mouth to muffle his cry. As the grip tightened, four claws ran through Cal-raven's cheek and scraped the edges of his teeth. Blood filled his mouth, and he choked. Rocks broke away behind him, the jagged edge receding under the pressure, and after a long fall they shattered among the sharp stalagmites below.

Cal-raven clapped his hand to his thigh and flicked a concealed knife free from its sheath, then plunged it into the beastwoman's side. The creature threw back her head in a howl, kicking herself free. But her powerful thrust turned Cal-raven over and spun him around—his legs flailing over the cliff's edge, his chest pressed to the failing ground. He clung to the rock, blood pouring from his face and his mouth.

The creature's roar warped into a laugh. She sprang back to her hind legs and removed the knife.

Cal-raven looked at the beastwoman. But for the feline mouth, gangly white-haired arms, and lashing black tail, she might have been one of his own soldiers. The torn, bloodied Abascar soldier's jacket she wore—that was just mockery.

"You won't get out of here alive," he spluttered through blood and dust, feeling a flicker of regret that he had left his alarm horn on the Keeper's statue.

The beastwoman bounded forward, just like a predator cat.

Cal-raven closed his eyes, took a deep breath, let go, and fell away from the cliff.

He caught hold of the creepervine that his foot had found below. The vine held, and he hung there, taking in a sweeping view of the darkling plains. He pressed his other hand flat against the cliff face and felt for a handhold. As if in response to his attention, the rock shifted under his fingertips.

"I am a descendant of Tammos Raak," he whispered. "I will not die at the hands of a common Cent Regus animal." He waited for the monster to look over the edge and readied himself.

When the beastwoman did appear, she was not crawling but standing. She spat, and Cal-raven dodged, fearful of venom. The creature knelt, reaching down to pin his arm to the wall with his own knife.

Cal-raven knew he had no choice but to drop and hope for another line of creepervine to break his fall. But as he glanced down, he heard a grunt. The beastwoman above him somersaulted out into the air, screaming. As she fell past, she clutched at the wall, digging Cal-raven's knife into the stone. The knife caught, but she could not hold on and fell. The sharp stone blades neatly sliced her to pieces.

A figure appeared at the cliff's edge and extended a hand to help him. Cal-raven reached up, then jerked back in surprise.

A beastman—one with a wild, black mane, a broken bone protruding from his forehead, and a face of rough, porous skin—offered him a leathery hand lined with bristling red-brown hair.

"rrNo fear!" the beastman barked. "rrHelp you. Give message to Abascar king."

Cal-raven looked down again. The fall seemed a better gamble. But then Brevolo might be up there. She might be dying in the cave from which his attacker had lunged.

Before he could decide, the beastman thrust his hand down farther, seized Cal-raven's arm, and with strong, clawed fingers pulled him up and set him down on the dusty edge. Cal-raven spat out globs of blood.

"rrFind king of Abascar," the beastman continued. "Give him a message."

His voice was hoarse and his accent thick and strange. But the words were unmistakable. This beastman was speaking in Common. "Cyndere. Bel Amica. rrCyndere sends message."

Cal-raven pushed himself up onto all fours, panting. He shifted his attention from the silent, dark cave before him to the massive feet of the creature standing over him.

"rrMessage," said the beastman. "For Abascar king. Cent Regus come. They come for Abascar."

"Thank you," Cal-raven answered. "And this...is for you." He plucked out his knife and thrust it down through the beastman's hairy foot, jerked it out, and plunged it through again. Then he rose and sprinted forward into the cave.

Behind him, the beastman muffled a roar. Sending power through his fingertips, Cal-raven drew a sharp stalactite from the ceiling, held it like a sword, and channeled more of the magic to mold a hilt from its broken end. Then he fled like a rabbit through the warren that opened beyond this cave.

The beastman came after him. With every corner he turned, Cal-raven led his pursuer further into the network of Abascar's hideaways, looking for an advantage.

Jordam limped into the cave, painting a stripe of blood along the ground. As shadows sharpened in detail, revealing a narrow break in the corner and a round window high on the back wall, his ears twitched, and his nostrils flared. The survivors of House Abascar were hiding in here.

His ears flicked backward as he advanced. The man wanted him to follow, probably to lure him into an ambush. Every instinct within him screamed retreat. But this man could reach King Cal-raven of House Abascar. And Jordam hated the thought of failing Bel again.

A voice called out, baiting Jordam. "I'm right here, Cent Regus. You think you can trick me. But Cal-raven is a good king. He remembers the hands that shed Abascar's blood."

Jordam leaned against the wall, listening to the voice emerging through that high window. He wished for a drop of that Bel Amican poison, just enough to erase the feeling in his wounded foot. Growling against the pain, he climbed through the window and down into a hollow, then scrambled on all fours after the flicker of shadow in the narrow crevasse ahead.

He emerged into a cavern where stony platforms rose to varying heights—giant mushroom columns of stone growing into and out of each other. He surveyed the myriad hovels and holes.

"You say Cent Regus are coming?" the voice continued.

The question surrounded him, ricocheting from walls, whispering in the mouths and eyes and ears of the cave. Jordam stepped forward, clearly visible to the man, wherever he was. And then he saw it, a faint cloud of breath emerging from a space between pillars on the far wall. A rope ladder rose from that place to a vent near the ceiling.

"rrFire," he barked. "Animals make no fire." Jordam edged along the side of the cave and wrapped himself in shadow beneath a stony overhang. "Cent Regus saw torchlights. rrTorchlights in caves. Scouts come. Plan to hunt Abascar people. I followed." He leaned back against the stone, dizzy and weak, and ripped off a long strip of his woodscloak to tie around his bleeding foot. "Message for Cal-raven. Help Abascar." He tightened the strip, then beat his fist against the ground, for the resulting wave of pain made it feel as if the knife had gone into his head.

"I will not take you to Cal-raven," said the man, "unless you tell me more." His voice came from higher up the wall. He was climbing toward an escape. Jordam could smell his sweat and blood. But he could smell something else as well. Incense. Flowers. He was still being led toward something he could not imagine. The trap was not yet sprung.

"rrCyndere Bel Amica sends message. Many Cent Regus. Hunting Abascar. Here on these cliffs. Soon." With that, Jordam ran across the crowded cave to the hanging ladder and began to climb. The man was already gone, but there was blood on the floor and splashed across the wall where he had spit.

Reaching the top and worming his way through a hole, Jordam emerged into an even larger cave under a high, arching dome. What he saw there almost scared him back into the hole.

Before him stood a host of stone people. There were hundreds. Crowns of flowers encircled their heads. Small curls of incense wafted through the air from bowls at their feet. Their stony skins were painted. Some were detailed, with sculpted faces, while others were abstract and simple. He recognized soldiers, children, shepherds, harvesters, miners. Some had cloaks of woven grass and leaves draped about their shoulders, as if to warm them in the cold.

"Do you see this?" The man stood at the far end of the host, standing between two regal figures and leaning wearily on their shoulders. One of them, a thin and stately statue costumed as a king with a shield slung over his shoulder and a sword strapped to his side. The other, a proud queen with a sweeping gown and wildflowers in her hands. Behind the statues, a crude stair rose to lanternlight.

"Abascar," said Jordam. "People of Abascar. Dead."

"Yes. Many are dead. Some were killed by Cent Regus beastmen. But no more." The man drew the sword of the king's statue and advanced toward the beastman. "I plan to even the score."

Jordam raised his hands and backed away. "Come to warn the king. Abascar, danger!"

The man did not slow down.

Jordam got down on his knees. "rrI protect Cyndere Bel Amica. Cyndere says Cal-raven will listen if I say 'O-raya.' If I say 'ale boy.'"

The man stopped two paces away, teeth flaring white through his blood-masked face.

"O-raya helped me. Colors...colors made me better. Now I help Cyndere Bel Amica. She wants to help you."

"I don't believe you." The man lifted the sword and brought it down. But he swung too hard, his reach too far, an awkward strike driven by rage and confusion. Jordam easily dodged it, falling forward to embrace the prince, bringing him to the floor. They tumbled together. Jordam seized the man's wrists and squeezed to the point of breaking the bones. The sword fell free. Jordam released him, picked up the sword, and cast it to the wall. As the man waited for a killing blow, Jordam retreated into the rows of statues.

He sat down behind the proud figure of a high-ranking soldier, noting that this distinguished figure had three fingers on a hand that was raised to his brow as if he were searching for a threat.

He could hear the man searching for him among the statues. He held still. The footsteps moved farther away. Jordam stood up to risk a glance. The man, having recovered his sword, ascended a stair on the far wall toward the open ground at the top of the highest cliffs.

"No games," the man shouted. "You know about the ale boy. You know about Auralia. But you're a beastman. And a liar."

Jordam risked one more glance and then bolted down the row. The man saw him, leapt from the stairway, and landed running to meet him. Jordam reached the statue of the old king, and he had just enough time to seize and lift the ornamental battle shield from the statue's shoulder and bring it around to block Cal-raven's strike.

Cal-raven smashed the sword into the shield again and again, and Jordam blocked each blow. The cave clattered with their struggle.

"Drop my father's shield."

The words hit Jordam even harder than the heavy strikes of the sword. "Your...father?"

The man barked a defiant laugh, lunged, and scraped the edge of Jordam's ankle. But this time Jordam did not just block the blow—he jabbed his assailant with the edge of the shield and sent him reeling backward with a bloody gash on his forehead.

Nostrils flaring, Jordam growled with the hunger rising within him. The king of Abascar lay before him, and the opportunity kindled his pride and bloodlust. He clutched at his chest as if he could seize the Essence and tear it out through his skin. And then he pounced on Cal-raven and pinned his sword arm to the ground with the edge of the shield.

Seething into the man's face, he sprayed desperate words. "Again, I could kill you. rrBrothers...would kill you. *Will* kill you when they come. Cent Regus kill Abascar's people. But not me. rrNot Jordam. Not today."

He reached for Cal-raven's throat to silence his voice. "Listen." He commanded himself to continue, to restrain his appetite and finish his mission. His fingers closed around Cal-raven's broad, woven neckband and tore it free.

Beads scattered from it and rolled across the floor. "O-raya." Jordam held up the broken band.

"Yes," Cal-raven sneered. "The ale boy gave it to me."

"I...watched her make colors."

"You are a liar."

"rrLook." Jordam held it close to him. "Look." He waved the frayed edge in front of Cal-raven's face, then tugged at a tangle of his own black mane. "O-raya cut this."

Cal-raven furrowed his brow, tugged at his pinned arm, and shook his head. "But you're a beastman."

"They come in two nights. Many Cent Regus."

"I don't believe you," said Cal-raven, but his resistance was slackening.

"rrThey swarm in the trees. I saw them. They watch Abascar. Lights. Shadows. They know where Abascar goes in, where Abascar goes out."

"You cannot fight together. You're crazy animals."

Jordam did not understand crazy. But he caught the point. "rrMordafey brings many Cent Regus. Mordafey promised them reward. Big stranger, white rags...leads them." He pointed to himself. "Jordam got away. Come to tell you. For Cyndere. rrCent Regus come, not tonight. Tomorrow night. Hide away, Abascar people."

Cal-raven lay still and speechless.

Jordam lifted the shield and stood.

When the king spoke again, each word was burdened with uncertainty. "How do we stop them, Jordam?"

"Don't let them get in. They bring...dangers. They get in, all goes bad."

"That's Cyndere's message?"

"More. Cyndere tells Cal-raven—don't trust Bel Amica. rrTrust only Cyndere." Jordam felt a rising sense of relief with every word he conveyed to the helpless Abascar man. "Come to Cyndere. She will help."

"We've received an offer of help from Bel Amica. From a Seer."

"Cyndere helps Abascar like O-raya helped me. Makes good what hurt. rrGives Abascar a safe place. Food. Help."

Cal-raven laughed and laid his head back, reaching out his splayed left hand and pressing it against the stone. "I will listen to Cyndere. I won't trust anybody." He narrowed his eyes and smiled. "And that includes you."

Jordam felt the floor ripple beneath him. What was stone became sand. His right foot sank into the hot, disintegrating floor. As he fell, he lunged forward with his left foot, but that punched through the ground as if he had stumbled into a bog. He looked up at Cal-raven and gasped, "Help."

The king's face purpled with exertion. Sweat ran down his brow in rivers. His arm trembled. Spreading out from the points where his fingertips met the floor, the stone softened until the ground all around Jordam's feet sank into sand. Jordam clawed at the molten floor, seeking a hold on the firmer ground where Cal-raven lay. But he could not reach it.

Instead, he groped for something to seize the king's attention. "Abascar queen!" Jordam gasped, but in his panic, he spoke in the crude beastman tongue. Frantic, he sought for a word in Common to inform Cal-raven that the former Abascar queen was imprisoned in the Cent Regus lair.

Cal-raven twisted, his left hand fixed to the floor, and put his right hand alongside it. "We will bury you. All of you." As if he were smoothing out a blanket, Cal-raven shoved the ground, projecting a wave that liquefied the floor before him. Jordam's last glimpse of the king was a fierce, contorted grin of triumph before the floor closed over his head.

Jordam sank fast in a fall of sand. And then his kicking feet broke through into open space. He wriggled like a fish and fell.

In a rush of falling debris, Jordam plunged into the cavern beneath the hall of statues. He plummeted toward a stone pedestal, and the edge of it struck what was left of his browbone, cleaving it from his forehead. The blow tumbled him like a falling twig through the high boughs of a forest. He crashed to the top of another stone mushroom, bounced down to another, which caught him in the ribs and knocked his breath out. Flailing, he fell the rest of the distance to thud against the hard floor, where mounds of falling, liquefied stone plastered his face before his wounds could bleed, burying him half alive.

"Kramm." Cal-raven tried to see through the hole he had opened in the cavern floor. It was too great a distance to jump. Leaning on one statue, then another, he made his way across the cave to the crevasse in the wall, anxious to learn the fate of the fallen beastman.

He had meant to cut the magic short and let the stone solidify, trapping the beastman in the floor. The kill would have been easy then. Scharr ben Fray could have done this without much effort.

He lightly touched the scabs along his cheeks where the beastwoman's claws had pierced his face. If she had pressed those claws to his temples or his throat, things might have gone differently. He touched the spots on his neck where Jordam's claws had barely left a scratch. But the neckband that the ale boy had sent with a message—"Do not let the people forget about Auralia"—was gone. The band that Auralia had woven with the hair of a beastman.

The king of House Abascar hesitated, fighting to regain his breath. The room spun, the ground's pull almost irresistible. It was the stonemastery. Night after night he had endured his sleeplessness by working himself to exhaustion manifesting likenesses of Abascar's fallen in the Hall of the Lost. Once they began to emerge from the stone, what had begun as an impulse became an obsession. With each face, each name, he renewed his promises—to make something strong out of broken pieces. The dead of Abascar stared back—some expressionless, some proud, some blank, some lifelike—a question in their stillness. They wondered if he would finish what he had started or if he would leave them like this.

During a few short days that lied about spring's arrival, he had found a sculpted message in the forest—his old teacher, Scharr ben Fray, was alive and would meet him soon with counsel. The message had inspired him, bringing back the stories he had first learned from the old man's lessons. So he had sought a blank canvas on which to shape a new figure in the open air. In a surge of longing, he returned to that shape he had crafted over and over again in his childhood but this time on a larger scale. He shaped the outline of the Keeper until he was so exhausted he could hardly think.

Unleashing that blast against the beastman had called up strength he did not know he could muster. He had strained every sinew, and something in the back of his mind had burnt out. He clung to consciousness, but sleep's grip was powerful. Sweat began to chill down his back, across his brow. He needed dry, warm clothes. Bandages for his wounds. And strength.

But there was a beastman down below. In a cave not far from chambers inhabited by Abascar's people.

Cal-raven urged himself down the narrow stair, which seemed so much longer than before. Clambering down the rope ladder, he cursed the alarms that blared in his shoulders and back. He scanned the shadows, hoping to find some sign of the creature.

Ribbons of blood trailed out of the cavern, into the crevasse, and pooled below the window in the entry cave. Then they continued out the open mouth of the cave and into the dusk, blurring into the scene of their struggle on the ledge. The creature had dragged himself out on all fours.

At the edge of the cliff, the battle-scarred shield of Cal-raven's father rested against a boulder. The king touched six new scars on its shining face, cleft by his own sword. "I'm sorry, Father." Draped over the edge of its shining disc hung the broken strand of his neckband. The colors gleamed as if mirroring a sunset from a world where it was summer.

He gazed down to the Red Teeth and then looked up to find Tabor Jan trying to make sense of the scene. The captain's eyes ran across the ripped-up ground, the blood splatter, and the sight of his battered king. He unsheathed his sword.

"Just in time!" Cal-raven coughed. Then, regretting that, he changed the subject. "Where's Brevolo?"

"What happened?" Tabor Jan crouched to survey the ground. "A beastman!"

"Two. One dead. The other...probably dying."

The captain stood, pressing his hand to his brocaded shieldvest. "I've failed you. I should not have let you—"

"The fault's mine. I wandered off without guards. But Brevolo—"

"Safe. You didn't catch her, so she came back to the statue. My lord, you're unarmed!"

"One Cent Regus killed the other. Then he ran away." Cal-raven sank down, leaned against the boulder, finally crumbling under the weight of realization. "I was careless. I almost lost myself. I almost lost all of us."

"Are we safe?" The guardsman paced the ledge.

"No. More beastmen. And soon." He shouted in surprise as if some invisible hand reached into his belly and squeezed. Gasping, he doubled over.

Tabor Jan eased him to his feet. "We're going to see Say-ressa."

"Everyone," he rasped, "must burrow in. Deep. Double the night watch. Assemble the defenders. We've much to do before tomorrow's sunset."

"Then you already know," said Tabor Jan. "You know what I've seen."

"The farglass," Cal-raven muttered. "You saw more than one beastman. Kramm." He watched two circling brascles, drifting feathers of shadow against the sky. "Their spies are here already. Jordam told the truth."

"Who?"

"There's an army of beastmen, Tabor Jan. Tomorrow night House Cent Regus is coming for us. Led by someone called Mordafey. The world is changing, and we're not ready. We have to—"

"Close the tunnels. But no more. We can't fight back, Cal-raven. You know that. If we fight too soon, we'll lose those who can train others." Tabor Jan looked out to the forest. "Who told you this?"

"That's a tale for a long night with a big fire and all the ale that Abascar can brew."

"My king, our plans... We're supposed to set out tonight. The Bel Amican."

"Tonight. Of course. The Seer. The supplies. He'll be waiting, and we won't be there. By the bloody bones of Tammos Raak, Tabor Jan, it won't work. We can't go out to meet him. I need—"

"You need to sleep. You need to heal. That beastman tried to rip your face off."

Cal-raven stumbled, spit more blood into the dust. "White rags," he whispered.

"What?"

"White rags. Mordafey's working for something the beastman called a 'big stranger.'" Cal-raven looked into Tabor Jan's confounded expression. "Ballyworms, Tabor Jan. It was all a lie. The Seer...he's luring us out. Making us vulnerable. It's a trap."

28

THE SIEGE OF BARNASHUM

There were three of them this time. Stealthy as midnight mist in the forest. Ravenous.

Mordafey could see Goreth and Jorn growing agitated as they approached Baldridge Hill in the southern Cragavar. They were uncomfortable with this revelation—that their older brother had conspired with others behind their backs. "Others will fear Jorn and Goreth," he assured them. "Others do what three brothers say. But three brothers take the reward."

"Only three brothers?" Goreth grumbled. "Where's Same Brother?"

Without breaking his stride, Mordafey uprooted a pricklebush and thrashed it against the trees until the plump young heads of unborn flowers flew off. "Forget Jordam." It had always unsettled him, this mysterious closeness between the twins. With Jordam falling away just when he needed him most, Mordafey was tempted to put Goreth on a leash. "If Jordam comes back, three brothers punish him."

This set Jorn to drooling and laughing. Departing the Core unchallenged, Mordafey had chased his youngest brother down, enraged at how he had nearly turned all of House Cent Regus against them. He wanted to kill him, but he stopped at chewing off one of his ears. Jorn would not turn against him, not with the Abascar slaughter ahead of them. And Mordafey needed the wretched creature's speed and savagery. "Jorn will do what Mordafey says," Mordafey had declared, "or next time Mordafey bites off his head."

As they moved down a dry riverbed, the brothers saw Mordafey's conspirators skulking among the Cragavar trees. Their isolated, predatory existence had sharpened their edges, curdled any sense of kinship. So they spread apart, suspicious, baring their fangs and flaunting their weapons. Some crept along the ground, some leapt through the treetops. Soon it seemed the trees themselves were scratching and flexing, restless.

Slipping away from his brothers throughout the autumn, Mordafey had sought these hunters. Their instinctive enmity began to slacken as he baited them with the white giant's promises. If they proved their power against the Abascar survivors and salvaged treasure from the Cliffs of Barnashum, the giant would reward them with new conquests, richer spoils. They'd overpower Skell Wra himself, break his grip on the Essence.

Inspired by such a prospect, the hunters surged into action. But in their simple bloodlust, they failed to consider what would happen after they tore the tyrant from his throne. There, Mordafey saw his advantage. He did not like the white giant or trust him. He did not like waiting to learn what that next conquest would be. But if he could seize enough power to take the chieftain's throne for himself, he would wield strength that would bend and break the giant's influence.

Mordafey leapt the riverbank to a rocky jag that jutted from Baldridge Hill like a platform. He barked to silence the others, and the myriad congealed, a clot of craven appetite attentive in the dusk.

He enjoyed their amazement as they looked around, for according to his promise he had mustered a swarm. Reptile-skinned brutes. Shaggy ram-horned men with shoulders strong as bulls. Wildcat creatures with hissing females and strutting males. Small, quick birdmen with talons and eyes like black marbles. Thick-skinned dwarves with long, curved tusks and heavy hooves like tree trunks. Yet he found himself scanning the crowd for Jordam's face. It was an itch he could not scratch, this sense that Jordam had found something more important than the brothers, been drawn to something more powerful than Essence. He began to feel that Jordam was watching him, listening from the shadows as he detailed the steps of his plan to Goreth and Jorn.

As if they were guarding a king, Goreth and Jorn stood on either side of Mordafey, snarling and beating at their chests, boasting in their priority and privilege.

But the swarm did not cower. "Where is the giant?" one wolfman sneered. "Show us this giant." Mordafey had gained their attention with a prize of distinction—the skull of a great Bel Amican leader, Deuneroi. But all his overtures involved a mysterious stranger who would lead them to power and reward.

As if in answer, a whirlwind with a walking stick appeared on the barren scalp of Baldridge Hill. A towering specter with bone-white hands and lidless eyes, he swept down the hill to the promontory and stood beside Mordafey. Goreth and Jorn cowered and crawled out of reach, eying the walking stick warily.

Translating from the stranger's Common speech, Mordafey reassured the swarm of those promises.

"Skell Wra will hear of us and be afraid," Mordafey declared. "If he tries to break us, we are stronger. We strike back."

"Who will be chieftain then?" came a snarl from the swarm.

"There will be no chieftain," Mordafey lied. "We break the throne. Everyone's the chieftain now. Essence for all."

Pride swelled within him as they wagged their heads and flung themselves about like string-bound puppets. They wanted to be unleashed at once.

While cold evening wind swept the ground and rattled the bushes between the forest and the Cliffs of Barnashum, Mordafey brought the unruly army to the Cragavar's edge.

He had observed how the Abascar harvesters withdrew, ascending ledges to the third tier of cliffs with their harvest carts and vanishing into concealed tunnels like rabbits into burrows. Soldiers patrolled the ledges and ensured that the openings were safely hidden. More soldiers patrolled the threshold through the night, watchful for any approach. These patterns were essential to his plan of attack.

The strike would begin with the combatants lurking in the brush-tangles and the trees at the base of the cliffs. When Jorn's company reached its position above Barnashum, Mordafey would unleash a wave of swift runners through the brush. They would attack the unsuspecting harvesters. The slaughter would draw Abascar's soldiers out from the caves.

Any Cent Regus onrush would send the cave-dwellers scrambling for retreat and attempting to wall themselves in. So Mordafey's plan depended on corrupting the caves, giving those inside no choice but to flee into the open and those outside nowhere to go. So far, Cal-raven's people had cleverly concealed the tunnels that let them move in and out of that great stone plateau.

But Mordafey's scouts had learned that no guards were watching the unknown territories to the southeast, beyond Barnashum. If the Cent Regus moved south, climbed to the top of Barnashum, then descended from the heights, they would have their chance to penetrate Abascar's labyrinth.

Jorn, Mordafey explained, would lead the best Cent Regus climbers. They would scale the cliffs in the near dark and creep back along the top, carrying with them a sting to bring Abascar's second ruin.

Mordafey's listeners, disgruntled and doubtful, had barked at him in challenge. How could a small pack of hunters ruin the caves? Mordafey directed their attention to the boughs above the heads of the swarm. Bundled among the branches there, like enormous husk-shelled fruits, were bags made of skin, tightly drawn, and pods made of stretched, seamless bushpig stomachs. "When Abascar's soldiers run out from hiding," he explained, "climbers drop down to secret gates. Throw the curses inside."

"What curses?" the challengers chorused.

"Bags came from the white giant," Mordafey told them. "Firestingers inside." He began to unbind one of the bags, and the hunters cried out in dismay. "Wait," he smiled, and he drew out a fragile glass sphere. The long-tailed bees inside drove themselves against the glass in a fury. "See?" He explained that the clouds of poisonous bees were raging, ready to sting whatever they touched. Firestingers liked caves, nooks, and crannies, and they would drive out anything else that occupied a space. The cave-dwellers would panic. Those not blinded by the quick stings would flee.

"Those who run will breathe this in," he laughed, drawing out another glass sphere that contained a swirling cloud. "Poison to cloud the tunnels. The white giant's poison. They fall right into us."

He reminded Jorn and the climbers that they could not linger to watch the people suffer once they had cast the curses in through the gates. Run away, he insisted. Fast. Hard. Or risk the firestingers' fury and breathe the poison. The people would spill out onto the ridges and ledges, disoriented and clumsy. Then the third wave of attackers would close in from the forest.

But the prizes, the Cent Regus wanted to know. When would they claim the prizes?

"Cal-raven and his people won't go back inside," Mordafey reminded them. "Caves, poisoned. But later, stingers settle. Poisons blow away. Daylight, we take the treasure. Bring it all to the old ranger graveyard west of Baldridge Hill. Show the white giant what we've done. Prepare for the next hunt. Better than Abascar."

As the climbers took to the trees to claim their bundles of trouble, Mordafey turned and seized Jorn by his remaining ear. "You know," he said, "what happens. Will you fail me again?"

"No, *hel hel hel*," Jorn laughed. Mordafey gave him the bag of glass spheres, and Jorn vanished with the crowd of climbers into the cover of brush.

Tabor Jan looked out at the dark spread of brush, and he shuddered. The cold breeze wheezed and moaned through the bushes, but he knew that there was more than wind at work in that darkness.

He and the harvesters had seen only a few brascles soaring in high, lazy circles and nothing more to suggest the closeness of the encroaching attackers. But he knew what he had seen through the farglass, and the people trusted their king's conviction. *The beastmen are coming.* Even now that dark line of trees stood like a dam on the verge of breaking, ready to release bloodthirsty enemies across the brushbound plains.

And so, when the Abascar watchers—courageous and more than half crazy—sent their signal from the treetops at the edge of the Cragavar, the harvesters cast dark blankets over their hooded tunics, merging with the shadows of night's rising tide. Abandoning their harvest carts, which they had loaded with useless tangles of brambles and thistleweed, they crept back, crouching low, to the base of the cliffs.

A new break had opened in the wall, a space just wide enough to accommodate the girth of the largest laborer. Their king had carved this tunnel with his own bare hands, but that did not stop them from grumbling about being run like rats into a burrow. Giving no heed to these complaints, Tabor Jan all but shoved the last worker into the passage.

Cal-raven's young apprentices waited at the other end of the tunnel. Although he knew it would happen, he still watched in amazement as the narrow passage sagged shut, the combined powers of the stonemasters' magic sealing the wall again.

Now, only he and a few of the guards remained outside, exposed. They strolled back across the ground beneath Barnashum's steps to the harvesters' carts. They set fire to tiny scraps of oil-soaked leaves, wrapped the smoldering pods in cloth, and set these slow-burning bundles among the kindling in the carts.

One by one the guards moved to stand with backs against the cliffs as if taking their positions for the night. When ropes dropped down from the tunnels on the third tier high above, the guards seized these lifelines and turned, holding tight as strong teams far above drew the ropes back in. Tabor Jan heard them walking right up the icy cliff face alongside him, laughing quietly. But he just clung to the rope, sweat streaming down his face, fiercely ignoring the vast space opening below him as he climbed. He wished he were a stonemaster who could blast his own door into the wall.

As the horizon had faded from deep blue to dark, a widespread scene of harvesting had quieted to a barren stretch of desert. Only tumbleweeds moved about the base of the cliffs now. There would be nothing for the swift tide of beastmen to attack.

Moments later he stood, farglass in hand, at the main entrance and watched a subtle ripple of shadows surge through the bushes far below—the first wave of beastmen rushing in, blades raised, ready to slaughter weary harvesters. When the Cent Regus reached the abandoned carts, they galloped about like hunting hounds whose quarry had disappeared. They leapt away, snarling, as the cargo suddenly flowered with petals of fire and exposed them in the light. The breeze whipped the flames, painting the surroundings in gold, and the beastmen darted in and out of the glow, furious.

Some attackers turned to climb up the ledge paths. But the children, pretending to play on those runs in the afternoon, had gingerly littered them with razor-sharp shards the soldiers had smashed from the field of Red Teeth. Yelps and howls rose as the beastmen stumbled across them. Most scattered or fell. Only a few slipped past, making their way up to the cliff ledges along the higher tiers.

"How did Cal-raven know they'd come tonight?" Brevolo whispered in Tabor Jan's ear.

"He won't say." The captain glanced upward to the highest tiers of the cliffs. "Let's go. Time to throw fuel on this fire."

They withdrew through the main gate, and the strong teams of rope-pullers piled heavy boulders to fill the entrance. As the stones settled, Cal-raven pressed his hands against them, his breathing shallow, his face red with exertion, and the mysterious power in his fingers ran into the stones, fusing them into one solid barrier.

Wheezing and stooped, the king nodded to Tabor Jan. He might have been smiling, but the bandages Say-ressa had spread across his stitched face hid any expression. "Can you hear them?" he mumbled through the binding wrap. "They're here. They've dropped from the high cliffs. They're right out-side, and they're not happy."

"They'll get their welcome," said Tabor Jan. "I'll signal Jes-hawk and the archers."

Inside Abascar's hideaway, music drifted through the tunnels. Cortie, small as a kitten in a palace, wandered along barefoot, chasing zephyrs of colorful notes.

The long grass skirt she had made swished along the floor. She ran her fingers against the great, smooth cave walls, imagining herself deep inside the veins of the earth, moving toward the rhythmic heart. The thought comforted her as she moved deeper into the labyrinth, the shouts and the commotion of Abascar's defenders growing fainter behind her.

People were fighting outside the Abascar caves tonight. They were fighting the monsters that had killed her mother and father. Cortie had not spoken since that trauma. But Cal-raven had knelt down, eyes level with hers, and taken her shoulders in his firm hands. "Don't fear, Cortie. The Keeper brought us just what we needed. We're safe tonight."

At a crossroads, she waited and listened. The music danced in the air, teasing her. Taking hold of a shimmering melody, she followed where it led, not sure why her pace increased or why her spirits rose.

Around a corner she found a cave with a great wall of orange clay illuminated by lanterns. Hanging between the lanterns, a swirl of color unfurled—paint on the stone, scraps of cloth, glimmering ribbons—alive with hues she had only seen in Auralia's colors.

Lesyl sat beneath this array, tapping the cords of her string-weave with the rings on her fingers, teasing the melodies out of hiding. Cortie tiptoed around the edge of the room, careful to be silent so as not to break the spell. When she saw the tears on Lesyl's cheeks, sliding down like the long sustained notes of the song, she sat down at a distance and folded her hands in her lap.

A boy's shrill voice bounded in from an adjoining tunnel. "Cortie? Cortie? Cortie?"

Lesyl paused, the song unfinished, a note hanging suspended.

"Close it tight, Wynn!" Cortie roared. "I'm here!"

Her brother marched into the cavern, and his momentary surprise at her voice was quickly overcome. "I've told you not to run off by yourself! You could get hurt."

"I'm fine, Wynn. Listen!"

"But there's a fight, Cortie." He stood shaking, divided by fear and outrage. "There's beastmen. You can't just run away and listen to pretty music. We should be doing something important!"

Lesyl began to quietly pluck the strings again, and the song returned without hesitation. It seemed to open a warm new room in the air and lift her up into the glow.

Wynn's complaint dissolved. He sat down beside Cortie. "This is important," she whispered, leaning against him.

Song after song washed over them, and a crowd of children began to assemble, drawn along by the winding threads of notes into the mysterious comfort while the world outside erupted in fear, fire, and frenzy.

Mordafey was silent as the sentries returned from the brush, squawking their reports and thrashing their feathered limbs.

Abascar's harvesters were gone. Vanished. And the guards had walked up the cliff face as surely as tailtwitchers scrambling up trees, escaping before the runners could reach them. The carts had burst into flame, the fireglow revealing the attackers to anyone watching.

"These Abascars, they can walk on walls," one of them chattered. "Even through them. Maybe we should run."

"Wait." Mordafey stared out at that dark rise of cliffs. "Wait for Jorn. Not too late for Jorn."

When Jorn's signal had flared out from the top of Barnashum's wall, Mordafey had purred, delighted.

But as more signals flared, Mordafey began to feel unsteady. The vanishing harvesters, ascending guards, disappearing gates—nothing made sense. Stranded with their bags of firestingers and bottles of poison, Jorn's team dashed about on the high ledges, scouring the stone for an entrance. Their signals back to his spies were dismay and fury.

"They knew," Mordafey muttered. "They made tricks. They were ready."

"What now, Older Brother?" asked Goreth.

"Must find another way in."

"What's that?" Goreth pointed to the top of the cliff. "Rock goats?"

Mordafey cursed. Archers were firing down on Jorn and his hunters as they rushed along the third tier in search of safe ground. Mordafey could hear the faraway screams. His climbers either leapt from the cliffs or tumbled along the ledges, wounded and scattering.

"Firestingers," Mordafey growled. "Bags broken."

Worried murmurs spread among what remained of the swarm in the trees as they waited for Mordafey to unleash the final wave.

"Forget the plan." Mordafey glanced back into the forest, wondering if his mysterious commander had come to watch this miserable display. "Got to be a way in. Or the white giant will be angry." He barked a command to the scavengers, the hunters, the scourges. He drove them into a run. "Cent Regus are not afraid. Cent Regus are stronger. Prizes are waiting."

He bounded forward on all fours, a bear in full charge, and heard, to his relief, the horde flooding onto the plains behind him in a fierce tide of teeth and claws.

As he ran, the cliffs loomed above him, higher and higher like a great black wave ready to break over him. He felt suddenly naked. He was as vulnerable to the Cent Regus galloping up beside him as he was exposed to the rain of projectiles from Barnashum. He turned, commanding Goreth to stay close.

But Goreth was not beside him.

As the mountainous rise filled their view, a hundred fires sprang to life at once across the tiers—like stars exploding in gold and red.

The swarm divided into swirling eddies. Some defied the lights, dodged the arrows that needled the air around them, risked the wayward firestingers, and fought their way up the bloodied ledges, intent on those gleaming points of flame where they were sure to find soldiers hunkered down with quivers of arrows. But they slowed when a new sound shattered the din.

In a cacophonous drumming, the gargantuan boulders that had lined the highest tier of the cliffs like a row of crooked teeth began to topple over the edge and crash down the cliffs as if shoved down a stairway. Mordafey ducked as one struck the tier above him and sprayed sharp splinters. The boulder bounced over his head to smash against the ground behind him, obliterating several Cent Regus runners. Islands of stone careened past on both sides, great wheels, massive jags, thunking and thumping and gouging deep holes as they fell.

He looked up again, half-expecting to see an army of giants hurling the slabs. Wedges of crumbling cliff slid down and sent ascending beastmen leaping off the rockslide paths to fall into the Red Teeth or onto flat, merciless ground. The avalanche continued beyond the cliffs, boulders racing each other across the spread of brambles and brush, carving avenues of crackling ruin as they rolled into the deepening dark.

As the barrage subsided and Mordafey's swarm lost all momentum and coherence, he found himself climbing alone. Rage boiled within him. Word would spread across the Expanse that Mordafey was a fool and could not be trusted.

As he explored the shadows, details deepened his rage. The lights that flickered closest to him were unattended. They were not torches but stones, framed by pieces of glass—light and reflection. He seized these pieces and dashed them against the rocks. The apparent scale of Abascar's defense was—he now understood—an illusion.

A horn sounded from high above. Sonorous replies rang out from every tier across the wide Barnashum span. Mordafey crouched in the rocks, awestruck, for the sound seemed to come from miles around.

The horn calls increased, populating Barnashum's layers with clear, golden reports. More answered them, blasting like beacons from the forest.

As he looked back at the trees, a volley of flaming arrows fanned out through the air over his head. "Wasting arrows," he grumbled, moving further along the ledge. But then another array of fiery projectiles flew from the top of Barnashum. These bright missiles did not arc gracefully and fall like arrows. They blazed straight paths across the sky and kept on soaring all the way across the brambled plains to the edge of the Cragavar—an impossible distance—descending only then into the trees where his swarm was retreating.

"Birds," he sneered. The defenders had tied bundles to the long-feathered tails of precipice birds. They had set the bundles alight and turned those hulking scavengers loose, knowing they would fly with all their might back home to their nests in the trees, trying to outrun the flames behind them. The fire burnt through the ties that bound the bundles to the carriers' feet, and sparks showered down on the woods like falling stars.

The fleeing horde did not yet see through this charade. Mordafey cast fistfuls of stone at the birds, then turned when he heard a frantic creature vaulting down the rockslide. He leapt and caught the animal in midjump and slammed him against the earth, ready to spill blood to satisfy his temper.

But it was Jorn sniveling in his clutches. "Birds," he howled. "Birds fly for Abascar!"

"Quiet or I'll rip out your tongue!" Mordafey shouted into his brother's face. "Tricks! Mordafey's not scared of tricks!"

Jorn struggled, trying to pry Mordafey's claws from his sides. "Where's Goreth?"

Mordafey scanned the cliffs. Soldiers rushed along the ledges, making sure to pass before the lights to increase the illusion that a militant multitude were readying to descend and finish any Cent Regus who were foolish enough to remain. Mordafey wanted to stay. He wanted to surprise one Abascar soldier. Just one.

He broke away from Jorn and launched himself at the second tier of the cliffs. On all fours, he scrambled over debris and carcasses. Pausing only once, he came to a struggling Cent Regus wildcat whose paws had been slashed by the razor stones. He lifted the creature by the throat and snapped the bones like twigs, watching the runner's eyes expand in recognition as the body went limp in his hands. Then he rounded a corner and lunged down into a clay hollow, the scent of soldiers sharp in his nostrils.

He stumbled to his knees, his breath stopped short by the sight of a familiar shape looming in his path. Its wings were outlined by the glimmering moonlight. A great sweep of neck supported a massive head that hovered over him. Dust roiled about it, and the eyes shone crimson as embers. Smoke curled from its nostrils, and its front feet clutched the ground on both sides of Mordafey.

The sound that seared Mordafey's throat was one he had never uttered before, not even in the dreams where he had run from just such a colossus. But his pride fought back, stronger than his fear, and his jaws snapped off snarls of challenge. Now he saw that the eyes were red, round crystals and that burning bundles were stuffed in the nostrils. The wings were sculpted from stone.

Another trick. Mordafey carved up a handful of rubble and flung it at the statue.

A groan rose from the statue. The ground trembled. Its tail lashed high over its back like a scorpion's sting, then fell like a massive marrowwood tree to smash a rut in the stony ground. Mordafey saw that the tail did not belong to the statue at all but to something awakening behind it—a shadow with the same sweeping wings, legs like mighty stone columns, and flames in its eyes and its jaws, a creature many times larger and very much alive.

Mordafey screamed and bolted back the way he had come.

He found Jorn still gripping the rockslide, skin blackening to hide him in the night. He lifted him by the scruff of his neck and dragged him down the rubble-strewn path. As he did, a rhythmic rumble began in the forest—battle-drums.

"Run now?" Jorn's question was desperate. "Finished?"

Mordafey tore at his own mane, exasperated. "Cal-raven thinks he's beaten Mordafey. But Mordafey is not finished. Mordafey will remember."

As they made their way back through the brush, arrows clattered into the brambles around them. Mordafey pressed on, unmoved. He wanted to knock the forest down.

This was not a defeat, he told himself. This was only an interruption.

29

A Song for Abascar,
a Song for the King

Beneath the green moon that gilded the plains of icebound brambles, Cal-raven lay on the domed head of his sculpture gazing beyond the dusty bowl to the eerie glow of the faraway Cent Regus wasteland.

Everything hurt—his body, his memories, his questions. Sweat ran down his face and beneath his bandages and stung his stitches. He wondered if stonemastery burnt away marrow; every bone in his body, every link in his spine, felt charred and fragile. The cooling air was a relief to the fever that followed the strain of exertion.

But there was no help for his raw and bleeding hands. Not yet. The heat and the friction of so much stonemastery had burnt much of the flesh away. He did not understand how his hands could soften and sculpt stone any more than he understood how an impulse could direct his hands or his feet. He knew his control of that gift came from patience and rigorous discipline, and he knew the limitations of his abilities.

Somehow he had surpassed those limits in his struggle with Jordam. And tonight he had driven himself further—sealing tunnels, raising walls, melding boulders, opening passages. New windows allowed archers to fire arrows from safe chambers and freed trumpeters to blow their horns into the night until his hands sealed those open spaces. Riding a vawn up to the heights of Barnashum, galloping along the edge of the cliffs to the great pinnacles, he had dismounted to place his hands at the base of each stone, weakening the foundations with surges of power. Soldiers, waiting for his signal, then struck at the foot of each monolith. One by one those pillars toppled, hurtling down the rockslides, laying waste lines of attackers.

"You are not the king your father was," Brevolo had said, kneeling suddenly before him in a corridor during the struggle. "And I am grateful. Forgive me, my lord."

After all this, Cal-raven had hauled his exhausted body up to this high, quiet vantage with his ruined hands. They seemed like something separate from himself—fierce wonders, opening and closing. What they had wrought tonight he found hard to fathom. How many lives had been saved by the work of these hands and by those of the three girls? The thought shook him, made his stomach turn. It might have gone so differently had he not heard a few words of the beastman's truth through his rage.

He had found at last the answer to the terrible questions that had burdened him these months within the caves. Yes, he *could* bear the burden, fulfill the role of king. He could unite these desperate people, protect them, and draw out their strengths. But he had needed help. And it had come from a creature he thought his enemy.

"Don't thank me, Brevolo," he had answered. "Someday I'll tell you about the man who deserves our gratitude."

Abascar's survivors would reassemble in the grand cavern soon. Say-ressa would apply healing salve to the young stonecrafters' hands. Parents would calm their children's fears and assure them that all was well. Guards would patrol, numbering survivors, taking account of the wounded and the dead. And Lesyl would soon ask, "Where is the king?" He would go to her soon, to put her worries to rest.

Who had planned a defense so outrageous? Who had ever trusted the survival of a house to the notions of children?

Last night, as Say-ressa tended to his wounds after the beastwoman's savage attack, his apprentices had whispered at the door. The healer commanded Margi, Madi, and Luci to stay clear and let the king plot Abascar's defense, but Cal-raven invited them in. The triplets spoke in bursts of inspiration, finishing each other's sentences, their words tumbling over one another. Their proposals were ridiculous. They involved shadow puppets.

Costumes. Noisemakers. Deception. One even suggested that Abascar slip out of the Blackstone Caves, bait the beastmen inside, and then bury them alive there.

As the children blustered, each idea more audacious than the last, Cal-raven had thought of Auralia's cloak and how those colors had struck the house like lightning, breaking his father's feeble hold on the Housefolk. He remembered those beacons of light shooting forth from the girl's prison cell, illuminating the Underkeep. Beauty had made the people stand still—the poor and the powerful, the dreamers and the dangerous.

After Say-ressa politely dismissed the children, her laughter continued as she passed on a similarly ludicrous notion she had overheard from two Gatherers—the idea of setting the precipice birds on fire and releasing them to the forest. Perhaps it was delirium setting in as she tenderly threaded stitches into his face, or perhaps she'd given him a potion. Whatever the case, Cal-raven fell into a dream shot through with threads of color, each strand clutched tight in the hands of his apprentices. The tapestry forming behind them rose up, became an army. It was the host of statues in the Hall of the Lost. The eyes of each figure shone. Closed lips opened, and chests heaved with breath. Their stone shells began to break as power surged from within. Cal-raven had awakened with a gasp.

House Abascar might not have resources to fight the enemy properly. But Jordam the beastman had said that the Cent Regus had been watching them. Perhaps Cal-raven could convince the beastmen that there were too many survivors to overcome. Perhaps they could turn the beastmen's fears against them. Perhaps, he had thought, his gifts could serve in the defense of his house after all.

"Master?"

Krawg descended from the ledge into the hollow. Cal-raven recognized the former Gatherer's awkward, angular silhouette and his wheezy, rasping groan. He raised a hand in greeting.

"Master, is it over?" Krawg stood staring up as if addressing the statue.

Cal-raven tried to respond, but his throat was parched. He shifted his head to keep the bandaged side off the stone and rested his thin beard against the Keeper's head. The moonlight, the faint sparkle of snow on the distant forest, columns of smoke still rising from the ruined harvest carts, the gleaming of the glowstones shining from the cliffs in the night—it was a spectacle with all the strangeness of a dream.

For a moment Krawg wavered where he stood. "Master, are you well?"

"Still here," he wheezed. "The counting. Have you heard?"

"The counting, master? No, not yet."

"You should have seen us," Warney exclaimed, staggering up behind Krawg on a crutch. "We put on scowls most fearsome and stood our ground. No Cent Regus dared approach our tunnel."

"Warney, think for a moment of somethin' besides your own flea-bitten hide." Krawg turned and tried to kick Warney's crutch to keep him back.

"You're wounded?" Cal-raven asked.

"Oh, it's an honor to be hurt in a battle against beastmen, master." Warney held up his bandaged leg, tapped it with his crutch, and winced.

"He didn't see any such battle," Krawg snapped.

"In the morning I'll need your help again," said Cal-raven. "To retrieve arrows from the ground below. And the sharp stones too. We'll need them again. We've won ourselves some time, but the beastmen will be back. Next time they won't fall for illusions." Caught by a wave of nausea, he lay down, clinging to the Keeper's head.

"We did it. Didn't we, master? We fought a battle with light," murmured Krawg, amazed. "With string and birds and fire and stone. And horns."

"And a little bit of help from beyond our own house." Cal-raven wondered where Jordam had gone. He wondered if he would see the creature again. If he did, things would be different.

He strained to keep his eyes open. *You'll freeze to death if you fall asleep out here*, he thought. *And Tabor Jan will drink your share of the celebration wine.*

A glimmer of crystalline green moved between the stone teeth on the edge of the hollow. Cal-raven saw a ghostly figure there holding a glowstone and looking back at him. The figure raised a hand as if in salute.

"Who am I to say what's possible?" Cal-raven raised his hand to answer, but when he blinked, he saw only the glowstone set on the ledge between the teeth. He tried to lift his head, but it was too heavy. "Krawg," he rasped.

"Master?" the old Gatherer answered. "What is it?"

"Not long ago you were stranded out here, stuck on a ledge, trying to steal an owl."

"Yes, my king. I tried to adopt the blasted bird and take it inside where it would be safe. Soon as I told it so, it up and flew away! And I remember that you did me quite an honor. You helped me down. Probably saved my life."

"Well, now you can return the favor," Cal-raven laughed. "I can't move."

With a little help from Warney, Krawg helped the king of Abascar down.

Pacing in front of the fangbear's den at the base of Baldridge Hill, Mordafey watched Goreth whimper and cling to the trunk of a two-columned tree. The beating he had just given his brother had not satisfied his fury. "Where were you?" he roared again. "Why didn't you run with Mordafey?"

"Older. Brother." Goreth clutched at his bruised belly, then his bleeding head. "I forgot the plan."

Mordafey pressed his snout against Goreth's so that the browbones on their foreheads clattered together. "Forgot?" His question sprayed Goreth's face. "What were you thinking about?"

Eyes pleading, blood running from between his teeth, Goreth replied, "Same Brother."

"Sssame Brother? Jordam's a coward. A fool." He seized Goreth by the beard and raised him to his feet. "No more time for Jordam. Mordafey must plan. Goreth must help the brothers ruin Abascar."

A small pack of Cent Regus lurked about, glaring at the brothers, hoping to claim some kind of prize for their ordeal. When Mordafey stormed down into a fangbear's burrow, he heard them crowd in behind. They feared him. They feared he would hold them responsible for this defeat. And yet they were hot for revenge against Abascar or revolt against the white giant.

Frantic to come up with a strategy that might still salvage his bargain with the stranger, Mordafey began barking about weapons they should assemble for an attack at daybreak. "Cal-raven thinks Cent Regus will give up," he growled. "Mordafey is patient. Cal-raven will come out. Cent Regus will be waiting. Go. Gather lost arrows. Find cowards who ran. Bring them to me."

Mordafey's mad laughter reinvigorated the stragglers of the swarm. They pressed together to make their way out of the tunnel and hurry back to the cliffs, where Abascar's defense had quieted and the day was ready to break.

Mordafey turned to Goreth and Jorn. "Four brothers not finished yet."

"Three brothers," sighed Goreth. "Only three."

Jorn, striving to impress his older brother again, sprang after the departing crowd of Cent Regus and pushed his way out of the burrow. "Always let Older Brother go first," Goreth muttered. Mordafey was surprised by the unusual show of respect.

As they made their way into the tunnel to catch up, the sounds outside the burrow suddenly changed.

The quiet of the woods was torn by screams and the sharp song of wires snapping taut.

All about the mouth of the tunnel, across a wide swath of ground, the Cent Regus were struggling, bound in tightening snares, every attempt to break free causing the wires to dig in.

"Someone," Mordafey gasped. "Someone followed us to the burrow. Someone...someone set traps!"

Goreth scrambled down the tunnel, crying, "Abascar's come after us!"

"No." Mordafey looked up toward Baldridge Hill. "No. Not Abascar." He scanned the piles of sprawling, thrashing Cent Regus for Jorn. He found his younger brother jerking and clawing up clods of earth, his skin absorbing the color of the blood-flooded moss beneath him.

"Bel Amican," Jorn rasped as Mordafey leaned over him. "Krammed Bel Amican trap." He begged Mordafey to release him.

Mordafey yanked the pin of Jorn's trap and examined the spring-spool. Then he unearthed a heavy stone and smashed the spool until its mechanism fractured. The tension loosened. He pulled the wires free from Jorn's lacerated body. Jorn whined, crawled a few steps, and lay still, heaving for breath.

"Smell no Abascar here." Mordafey's gaze scoured the surrounding forest across all of the groaning, dying creatures. "No Bel Amicans. Something else." He knew that he had lost the allegiance of the swarm. If any of these stragglers survived, they would hunt him in their rage. He had brought them here. He had promised them everything, given them nothing. They would kill him if he set them free.

And so with a spear in his hand, Mordafey stalked about the bloodied ground and silenced every moan with swift, sure strikes, finishing the army he had worked so hard to assemble.

Then he lifted Jorn up, slung him over his shoulders, and marched off through the field of sprung traps into the trees. Goreth, staring at the steaming, wirebound corpses, stepped gingerly around them, following.

By morning the brothers reached the place where Mordafey had left three prongbulls they had stolen from the Core. Only two bulls remained.

The white giant waited there, grinning that ever-present grin. The prongbulls bowed their heads beside him, their hides branded with scars Mordafey recognized, for his own chest bore those same scars from the stranger's walking stick. He looked about, joining his brothers in sudden confusion. The third bull they had stolen was missing.

The white giant advanced, shrilling a question in the Common tongue. "Where have you been?"

Mordafey gathered what strength he could muster. He felt his brothers' attention and knew that other witnesses might be hiding in the shadows. He had no choice but to respond to this challenge with strength. His claws sprang out for the strike, but the stranger stopped, jutting his walking stick out before him. A bolt of lightning jolted Mordafey, branching through his limbs like blades springing from blades. The blast cast him backward into the trunk of a tree.

The stranger came at him again. "Now that we remember the proper order, I will be brief." He towered over Mordafey, his cape billowing about the winding white rags of his costume. He scrawled an X in the air just before Mordafey's face. Jorn snarled, yet Mordafey knew that his brother would not risk a blast from that stick. Goreth stood quiet and did nothing.

"Now hear this," said the giant. "I shall come to you again. At your den this time."

"Brothers' caves?" Mordafey cast a startled glance at Goreth.

"Don't underestimate me, Mordafey." The giant raised a small wooden box and rattled the contents, as if this were some sort of weapon. "I have powers you'll never understand. You can't hide from me. Or from the captain."

Mordafey looked up the slope of the hill. "The captain?"

"Yes, I've sent him a report of your failure. He's had enough of your foolishness. You have yet to prove to him that you can muster an army worth his time. I'll bring him to your caves, and he'll have instructions. You'll obey him. Remember what he's done for you—the sacrifices he has made. He'll not tolerate another disappointment."

Mordafey sank his claws into the tree trunk and pulled himself to his feet.

"I was going to send you off like a good dog to sniff out and destroy the one who betrayed you. But that riddle is already answered. The traitor ran right to me. Took one of the bulls before I could catch him. He looks"—the Seer pointed to Goreth—"like that one."

Goreth yelped, fearful of what the Seer might be saying to his older brother. Mordafey's scowl slowly twisted, curling back into a gleeful grin. "I know the one," he answered in Common. "And I know where he's hiding."

"I drove him off," the giant said. "He fled. On one of your bulls. You must promise to bring him back to me. Or…what remains when you are finished with him."

"Abascar." Mordafey glanced in the direction of the cliffs. "What about Cal-raven?"

"I will deal with Cal-raven. Eventually."

Jorn whimpered as Mordafey strapped him over the back of the larger bull. Then Mordafey climbed into the saddle. He wanted to kill the giant here, now, and rid himself of any worry. But he bottled his rage, saving it for another target.

"Where now?" Goreth asked. He did not approach the other bull. Something held him back.

"Goreth," Mordafey said through a smile. "Goreth is faster than Jordam. Yes?"

Goreth's tail twitched, swiping traces of snow behind him.

"Goreth is stronger than Jordam, yes?"

Goreth nodded slowly, but his scowl remained.

"Jordam set traps for us, Goreth. Jordam tried to finish us. Time to teach Jordam not to trap his brothers, yes?"

Goreth scratched at his ear. Then he climbed into the saddle of the second prongbull. The animal kept watch on the giant's staff.

The Bel Amican spun his walking stick slowly in the air. "You know where to find him?"

"Awake, Jordam lies to us." Mordafey spurred his bull beneath a leaning tree and reached up to snap off a branch that would serve as a whip. "Asleep, Jordam has surprises. Secrets."

"I remember!" Goreth announced.

Mordafey looked at Goreth. "Goreth remembers what?"

Goreth's face quivered with indecision. Then he muttered, "Always let Older Brother go first."

Mordafey snorted, assuming that his brother was confused again. But as they rode out, picking up Jordam's trail, he could hear Goreth repeating those words again and again to himself. They buzzed about him like a stingerfly he could not smash.

Tabor Jan found his king staggering down a corridor, one arm draped around Krawg's neck, the other around Warney's, and he immediately pitied the man. Anyone trapped between those two smelly old fools was worthy of pity.

But the captain's concern deepened to fear when he got closer. Cal-raven seemed hollowed out, his eyes dark, the bruises beneath them even darker. The bandage on his face was purple with old blood. His short red braids were matted with sweat, and he shuddered, racked with chills.

"Give him to me." Tabor Jan pulled the king's arm around his own neck and dismissed Krawg and Warney. The two thieves walked away slowly, as if in a dream, having just served the greatest privilege of their often unpleasant lives.

"The counting?" Cal-raven's voice was like dry leaves.

"We're still waiting," said Tabor Jan.

"Must know."

"You look terrible."

"Never looked good with a beard," said the king.

After leaning on Tabor Jan for a fair distance, Cal-raven paused at a crossroads. "I wish I could tell my father." The captain felt tremors shake the king, long-suppressed emotion threatening to erupt.

He coaxed the king back into walking, and they made their way around a corner and down a steep incline into a cave lit with torches. The walls surrounding them were strung with tapestries of interwoven blackreeds. The people of Abascar had generously and reverently displayed the gifts Auralia had given them. Many of these treasures had been returned to Abascar's people by the efforts of the boy, the one they called Rescue. He would leave them where harvesters would find them, at the base of the cliffs, in the bushes, in the harvest carts. Now they shone like flares soaring through dark skies.

Cal-raven did not have a throne room in the Blackstone Caves, although the people had offered to craft one. He refused, for they slept in crowded spaces, and every chamber needed to serve several purposes. Instead, he sanctioned a chamber for private conferences, for strategy, for heated debate. He had chosen this room, where he could peruse a display of Auralia's colors to remind him of what his father's house had lacked, what it had been offered, and what might yet be achieved.

Tabor Jan helped the king lie back against one of the cushions where the counselors sat during daily sessions. Then he moved to stand by the door and ensure no one disturbed the chamber. He watched as Cal-raven stared at the spectrum of Auralia's inventions illuminated in the torchlight. He seemed to bask in the color.

Brevolo and Say-ressa appeared in the doorway. Brevolo whispered something in Tabor Jan's ear. His eyes widened, and he looked at her in disbelief. She smiled and then leaned in to whisper more. He nodded, trying to maintain a solemn scowl in spite of the rather alluring invitation. "Perhaps later," he said.

Say-ressa started forward when she saw Cal-raven, but Tabor Jan stopped her. "Leave him be for a few moments. I'll bring him to you soon for some attention. He'll need whatever you can give him."

Cal-raven raised a hand in greeting. "I must look like they dug me out of a grave," he rasped.

"We'll patch you up, master," Say-ressa promised him. Then she and Brevolo moved away, whispering together.

"My king," said the captain.

"Stop," Cal-raven whispered. "Listen."

Tabor Jan tensed, expecting trouble. Instead he heard the faint touches of Lesyl's music rising from somewhere deep in the labyrinth.

"My lord," said the captain, "it is time for you to know."

"Lesyl is playing music for the children."

"It was your idea. You said it would calm them so they would not be afraid. So they would sleep. It's the Early Morning Verse. Don't you remember?"

"I don't. It's lovely. She can make the saddest song beautiful. And the joyful songs...oh."

Tabor Jan pressed on. "Master, I've heard the report. All have been accounted for."

Cal-raven stared into the colors, his head cocked thoughtfully as he listened. At first the captain thought that his old friend had not heard. But then the king looked at him and answered. "All of them."

"Down to the last watchman blowing a horn in the woods."

"Alive? Unharmed?"

"Say-ressa says that two of the cave cleaners, Copus and Saugus, got scratched up pretty badly when they fell on the climb down from the precipice. We should never send those two out into the wild. They couldn't boil stew chunks if you gave them a pot and a fire."

"And Krawg and Warney? They showed signs of a struggle."

"You really want to know?"

"I need a good laugh."

"Took each other for beastmen in the darkness of the corridor. Scuffed each other up good."

"That's it?"

"I'm telling you, King Cal-raven, that it's done. All of Abascar's people are alive. The siege is over."

With great care Cal-raven got to his feet. He spread his arms to find his balance, but when Tabor Jan stepped forward to help him, he waved him back. The king walked across the chamber to pause before Auralia's array, pulled the torn neckband from his pocket, and tucked the edge of it through the reeds so that it glimmered among the gallery. "Maybe something out there is watching out for us after all."

"How did you know that the beastmen were coming? How did you know when they would strike?"

Cal-raven scowled. "You're not ready to know the answer yet."

Tabor Jan's eyes widened. Then he scowled and barked, "What do you mean? I can—"

"You're not ready to know the answer, Tabor Jan. I wasn't ready."

"Try me."

"Very well, then. I will try you. I am glad, Tabor Jan, that we did not have to venture out and fight the beastmen face to face tonight. I could not have done it."

"Of course you could have, my king. You are the best beastman slayer I know. You could have taken on that whole—"

"Don't make me tell the tale tonight. It would ruin me."

Shaking his head, Tabor Jan ignored the king's objections and placed his arm across his shoulders. "You need sleep, King of Abascar. The caves are sealed. The people are safe."

"Take me to the music."

They found the cave where Lesyl was singing. Children were gathered in a crowd about her. Merya, once a Gatherer and now in charge of planning meals, stood cradling her newborn at the edge of the room, listening. Many of the soldiers, the Gatherers, and the Housefolk were assembling as well.

Cal-raven tried to quell the emotions that seized him as he took in this sight. Peace. Relief.

Lesyl sang quietly about a magnificent violet tree that had fallen in a storm. One bird tried to lift it, but her wings were much too feeble. Another came to offer help, but they were not enough. But when their whole flock descended, each bird grasping a branch, they could fly together and lift the tree, planting it back in the scar of its uprooting. As she sang the chorus again, the children of Abascar raised their tired voices to join her. She looked up and saw Cal-raven. Her voice faltered.

The audience turned, saw the two men in the entryway, and against the king's objections, they stood, every one of them, silent and respectful.

"Please," said Cal-raven. "Please, finish the song."

They remained standing, bowing their heads in reverence, and Lesyl made her way through the song, her voice shaking as her emotions overcame her craft. The children sang the chorus for her and kept on singing as their parents and guardians guided them away to sleep for the night.

Shoulder to the wall, Cal-raven thanked and dismissed the captain. "Go and say good night to Brevolo, my friend. I think you'll find it easier to rest and regain your strength if you're in her company. And I suspect she will welcome seeing you."

His face reddening in a stubborn frown, Tabor Jan departed.

Cal-raven sat down.

He saw that it was difficult for Lesyl to meet his gaze. She plucked a few melancholy notes. "I don't have gifts like Auralia," she said.

"No one has gifts like Auralia," he said. "The world would burst into flames. But you, you play beautifully. Did you look up while you were singing?"

"I don't pay attention to the listeners." She pressed the blisters forming on her thumbs. "I play to find some kind of focus in the fear."

Cal-raven smiled, sympathetic.

"When Mother and I learned that Father was dying, Father asked me to sing for him," she said. "Mother insisted that I only sing songs from their youthful days together. She wanted me to take her mind off Father's pain. But when she stepped away, Father asked me to sing songs about pain. About loss. About the world without him. When I played those songs, he would cry. It was the only way he could cry. And now it's the only way I know to cry."

"We need you to lead us in crying, Lesyl, or we'll drown in unshed tears." He gestured to the empty corridor. "Tomorrow we'll want you to lead us in celebration. There are enough songs in today's story to keep you busy for many days to come. But I would ask you to consider something else as you play."

"My lord and king."

"The people will want to jeer at the beastmen. To exult in how we deceived them. But if they saw the whole picture, it might give them pause. I want to ask House Abascar to remember the fall of House Cent Regus."

She turned her head, as if he had inspired some troubling memory of her own.

"I hate the Cent Regus," he continued. "I learned to hate them when I was a child, and I've never questioned the training that prepared me to strike them down in battle. But through it all, I've never understood them or even tried to. I don't know what they are. Or how they came to be. Abascar's in a desperate state. Who's to say we're not vulnerable to such corruption? I want us to consider what they were, what they lost."

"I once woke from a nightmare," Lesyl began, "and tried to compose a song about the beastmen in the dream." She placed the instrument back across her knees, strummed a dark and dissonant chord. "I thought it would help me overcome my fear. But instead, the music just made me sad. It's a sad story, the fall of House Cent Regus. I've never played it for anyone. Your father's counselors would have confiscated all my instruments if they'd heard me singing this song. Nobody wants to hear songs about their enemies unless I'm praising the brave men who cut them down."

"I think I need to hear that song tonight."

The notes were simple at first, harmonious and sustained, swelling into a foundation of chords over which she improvised a grand architecture of melodies and countermelodies—terror and magnificence, hunger and ruin—and lingering above it, a shimmering sadness, a heartbreak deeper than blue.

30

AURALIA'S FEAR CHAMBER

During Mordafey's failing charge at the Cliffs of Barnashum, Jordam had surprised his twin brother, stepping out of the shadows and beckoning him to follow. "Goreth, come. Follow. Run with me."

But Goreth did not obey. He stared in confusion at Jordam's stone costume, that burden of clay that had weighed him down since his struggle with Cal-raven. But when Goreth finally fixed both his eyes on Jordam's face, he smiled in relief, and his shaking stilled. "Rockbeetles, Jordam! Strange armor."

The journey from the cliffs to the Cragavar had been an excruciating ordeal. After crawling away from the caves, Jordam dragged himself into a shallow, icy ravine on the first tier of the cliffs, where he lay for the rest of the night. Abascar soldiers had climbed over him in the dark, too busy preparing Abascar's defense to notice the breathing body in the stone encasement. When sunrise woke him, he had only enough strength to clutch at bundles of loose spineweed and pull them over himself for concealment before the pain of his broken bones burnt him unconscious.

During the long day before the siege, as flies buzzed about his ears and scourge-bugs crept across his brittle shell, Jordam remained in the ravine listening to Cal-raven's people whisper and bustle about. Broad-winged brascles circled above him, harbingers of bloodshed. He could not move.

The weighty costume had cooled as the sun set. When he shivered, his brittle crust rattled with a sound like chattering teeth, intriguing a pair of crows who climbed about on his chest and pecked at him. *Live*, he had urged himself through the alarms of pain that blared from all corners of his body. *Live. To help Cal-raven. To get back to O-raya's caves.*

He woke wishing the crows would return, for he was famished. He tried to move, but his ribs were fiery lances, and his knees were broken glass. Eying the dark forest, he knew Mordafey was coming. He began to grind his arms together slowly, chipping and crumbling the shell. With a sharp-edged stone, he shaved stone-burdened hair from his mane, tearing away as much as he could.

Then, just as the Cent Regus horde invaded the bushes below and assailed Barnashum, Jordam forced himself to climb down to Barnashum's threshold. Mordafey's swarm took no notice, intent upon their siege, distracted by fiery carts and lights on the cliffs. He recovered the Bel Amican saddlebags from the bushes where he had concealed them before his ascent. They seemed even heavier as he draped them over his shoulders and crawled.

When Mordafey loped past him, eyes fixed upon the cliffs, Jordam hardly recognized him for all that the Essence had wrought in his brother's form. *Like a team of bulls. Like a fangbear. Like a dragon from the Desert of Smoke.*

In the forest Goreth gave him the old Abascar sword, and he scraped more stone away from his legs and arms. Goreth, unsteady in his fear and confusion, persisted with questions, and Jordam described a fight with an Abascar soldier. It was true enough. But Goreth was not put at ease. "Older Brother will finish you."

"rrGoreth, listen," Jordam said, dust in his voice. "You don't know Mordafey's plan. When he's chieftain, he'll kill us both."

"Not the brothers," Goreth scoffed. "Chieftain. Kill the chieftain." His face and neck were swollen, emboldened to blistering with the Essence. Treasure. Glory. The chieftain's throne. He turned his bulging eyes back toward the attack.

Jordam pleaded with him. "I found something. rrBetter than Essence. Better than treasure. Follow me."

But Goreth began to tremble, unsettled. "Can't run, Same Brother. He'll find us. He'll catch us."

"You're faster," said Jordam, changing his tone. "You're faster than Mordafey. Faster than Jorn. Faster than all...except me."

But Goreth scowled, his voice filling with menace. "Don't make trouble, Same Brother."

"Same Brothers can be stronger together, stronger than Mordafey." Jordam pointed into the darkness. "Did he tell us about the swarm? Did he tell us about the white giant? No secrets for the brothers, says Mordafey. But he lies to us."

The ground shuddered. They beheld the massive shadows of falling boulders smashing their way down Barnashum's stair. Jordam's words wisped away like bursts of vapor.

"rrGoreth, I found better prizes than Abascar. Better strength. Run with me, or you won't see me again. Gone forever. No more Same Brothers. Finished."

"Brothers are everything," Goreth whined. "Can't remember anything else."

"rrYou remember the Old Dog? Long ago? What happened to him?"

Goreth's eyes widened. "Don't make me remember."

"What happened to the Old Dog, Goreth?"

Goreth looked down, trying to escape the memory of their father lying in the den with his sons, a metal pin driven through his head. Mordafey's search for the killer had been short and unfulfilled.

"Who would kill the Old Dog, Goreth? rrWho would be stronger if the Old Dog was dead?" He seized Goreth's arm, trying to drag him away, but Goreth laughed, pulling back. "Let's run, Same Brother. Before Mordafey kills us too."

Goreth wrenched his arm free then and lifted his Abascar sword in an unmistakable threat. Jordam, backing into the shadows, said, "Same Brother goes now, Goreth." His eyes began to sting, his vision blurring. He raised his hands. "Listen. rrTonight, watch out. Step careful. Always let Older Brother go first."

Goreth started after him. But horns sounded from the cliffs. Answering fanfare rang out in the treetops. Absorbed in the chaos playing out before him, Goreth seemed to forget that Jordam had been there.

"Say it back, Goreth. Always let Older Brother go first," Jordam shouted.

"Always," said Goreth absently.

"Rockbeetles," Jordam sighed.

Jordam withdrew into the trees as Mordafey returned. He prowled in the shadows, worried that Goreth would warn Mordafey. But Goreth's memory failed when Mordafey's beating began. With every blow of the club, Jordam shuddered as if *he* were absorbing the strike.

When Mordafey led the swarm into the fangbear den, Jordam unbuckled the saddlebags. First he took Bel's gift, the oceandragon whistle, and draped the string around his neck. Then he pulled out many coils of snare wire and did what he had mustered the courage to do. "Always," he whispered, as if Goreth might hear him. "Always let Older Brother go first."

A familiar sound had spun him around. The bellow of prongbulls nearby in the forest.

Jordam clung to the prongbull as fiercely as he had grasped the branch of the coil tree, exhausted, trying not to fall. This bull was not so cooperative, and it took every ounce of his strength to steer the beast.

And then his strength ran out.

He fell into a delirium and dreamt that he was snatched from the back of the bull by a storm cloud and carried into a cold, vast space, where he floated among the stars.

When he woke, the cold was no illusion. He was floating on the surface of Deep Lake, staring up into starlight. He remembered nothing of the journey, and the shreds of his dreams slipped through his grasp. Had the bull carried him all this way? Had he slipped from its back and run? Or had a winged shadow carried him over the forest?

He had never gazed at the constellations like this before, but now they seemed merely an extension of O-raya's artistry, as if she had moved on from this world to paint the sky. He might have stayed there, floating and forgetting, but his wounds stung in the cold water, and he was weak from hunger.

As he struggled to the shore, the remaining patches of his crumbling costume weighed him down. He limped into O-raya's caves, desperate for a fire. He blew on the skull-shaped whistle. Mournful tones echoed in harmony all throughout the caves. But Bel made no reply.

The ale boy's blankets were empty. He found no sign of struggle.

He began to search the tunnels but found nothing more than Bel's footprints in the dust. Waters deep within the recesses of O-raya's caves whispered soothing promises, and he answered their call. He ripped away his tattered cloak and bathed in a deep, hidden pool. The water here was as strange and pure as what he had drawn from the well at Tilianpurth. Patches of luminous color floated on the surface. The water gave him strength and soothed his pain.

Sinking, he found glowing, translucent, eyeless fish. He caught them and swallowed them whole. They had no taste, but they filled his belly and gave him enough strength to continue his search.

Emerging from the water, he found that the remnants of stone had fallen away. He looked at his rippling reflection. His jutting browbone was gone; only a flat plate of bone remained on his forehead. His mane ragged and torn, the hair on his arms and legs shorn clean, he did not recognize himself. He looked like one of the weakerfolk.

The pain in his wounded foot still flared up when he walked, but he managed to make his way back down the tunnel toward the cave. He stopped outside that dark, forbidding chamber, and a worry closed his hands into fists. The curtain lay twisted on the floor.

Jordam stepped up to the entrance. Fear spread in tendrils through his body and chilled him. He knew before he reached the spot that Deuneroi's garments were gone from the place where he had concealed them in his worry. He had tried to stop her, tried to keep them hidden until the time was right to tell her.

He turned and clambered out of the cave. Bel's footprints led up through the tunnels to the ladder they had descended together only a few days earlier. On the vantage point high above Deep Lake, on the ledge where his journey had begun—where O-raya had slept and the Keeper had saved her—no one was taking in the view.

If Bel had found Deuneroi's belongings, she would have guessed who put them there. She would have arrived at the inevitable conclusion.

Just as he suspected and feared, Bel's footprints led into the forest, alone. His hand closed over the whistle, he stepped forward to follow her. But he had not gone far before he realized that another kind of path ran alongside Bel's faint footprints. The impressions were enormous, the stride vast...and familiar. These very marks had led him to Tilianpurth in the first place.

How, he thought again, *did I get here?*

He ran then, compelled by longing, drawn by a vision of Bel waiting defenseless in the glen.

Two days after Jordam's departure, Cyndere began to get hungry.

Lake fishing was not at all like the sea fishing she had learned as a child. She found a small, timeworn net in the caves, but it drew little more than weeds and tiny crabs with unbreakable shells. Weary of striving for a catch in the cold rain, she returned to the cave and built a fire. But currents of wind discouraged her, filling the cave with smoke and stirring the fire's appetite so the driftwood burnt too quickly.

Complaining to the silence, she found herself waiting for sisterlies to crowd into the chamber. But no one came. There was no one to hear her. A tantrum would last only as long as its echoes.

"Totally alone." She fell back into the ale boy's blankets and laughed. "At last."

Night came but offered no sleep. Long, wakeful hours were nothing new to her, but the solitude, the isolation—it frightened and inspired her. She spoke things aloud she would barely dare to think in House Bel Amica. She could sing songs, tour the caves, practice telling children's stories, wander wherever she wished without any fear of restriction or interference. She found a chalky patch of damp stone and drew versions of Jordam's outline on the walls. "Auralia would approve," she said.

She walked out to the water and listened to creatures scuttle along the pebbles—*tappita tappita tap-tap tick*—while frogs performed percussive melodies. Splinters of shadow shot up from the water and splashed back down, and she scolded the fish for eluding her net.

A paddle-tail swam across the water toward her. She could see its whiskered nose at the front of the rippling arrow. She couldn't remember if paddle-tails were dangerous and tried not to budge. When it came close and caught sight of her, it smacked its tail hard on the water to alarm nearby kin and dove to safety. She glanced about for someone who could share the moment. But it was all for her, and all the more wondrous in that these things happened in the world every night. There was nothing quite like this in all of Bel Amica. She savored every detail, from the dissipating circles of the paddle-tail's dive to the lazy glide of a fishercrane across the water, as if drinking her way to the end of a rare vintage. The ocean was a storm, but this, this was a place for rest, for dreaming.

Moonlight flickered. She watched frantic bats zig and zag, heard the faintest trace of their chatter. Wind rushed low over the water, and a cloud soared across the moon as if hunting. She scowled at that bold green disc and whispered challenges to it. She had come this far without the help of any moon-spirits.

She thought of Emeriene standing at the window and staring up at that same moon. The sisterly was probably exhausted from worry. "Forgive me for speaking so harshly, Emmy," she whispered. "I was suffocating, and I made you suffer for it. You were only trying to protect me. And now I've run out on you. You must be worried sick."

She thought of poor Night-scrap and wondered if anyone would feed him. Or if Ryllion would set a snare in her chamber.

The thought of Ryllion disturbed the peace of her lakeside idyll. She stood and walked across the pebbles, her heart heavy again. She did not want to go back home. Yet she could not stay by the lake. This place offered an appealing stillness, but only if she ignored the distant clamor caused by her absence.

All she could do was wait and hope that Jordam would return. Then she could work with him, coax the conscience within that massive, maned head. Together they could find more Cent Regus to rescue. They would need Auralia's colors, for that was what had calmed Jordam's temper. They would need the water from the well at Tilianpurth.

Back inside the cave, she heard the bats drop from their roosts and flutter deeper. In a sort of trance beyond sleep, she followed the leathery rustle up the tunnel. She listened for footsteps behind her. Nothing. Curtains in her memory stirred, opening to blackness, and she found herself standing at the mouth of the darkest cave. This time Jordam did not appear.

The braided curtain wavered, sparkling with green light from the wall's embedded glowstones. It felt strange against her hand. She pulled it back and reached her arm into the space, then stepped into the cave's cold, suspended breath. Keeping a hold on the curtain, she let in the corridor's faint green glow.

She discerned a shape, a shrouded figure, far across the chamber. The figure seemed to move.

"Is it you?" she whispered.

Moving farther in, she allowed the curtain to fall, and she gasped at the depth of the darkness. Holding her hands out, she took cautious steps forward, her woodscloak sweeping along the floor. The air was stagnant and unmoving. Her heart beat like a ceremonial drum.

In illuminated chambers she had already discovered cloaks in hanging rows. A chiming crystal. A pedestal with a pool of milk-white water. The outlines of doors that would not open, of locks that sealed up secrets tight. On an impulse, she reached out to touch the figure, accepting whatever secret Auralia might have kept here. She remembered Jordam's story, imagined Auralia's scream.

Her hands met a smooth slope rising from the floor and cautiously traced the lines, discerning a woman's shape. It was a statue. The woman wore a crown of leaves and brambles, a cloth cape draped around her shoulders. That was what had moved in the darkness—a draft had brushed the cloth.

Cyndere knelt. There was tension in the statue's legs. This woman was leaning forward, striving.

Her hands moved down the woman's wavering cape and found that it was caught, clutched tight in hands made of rough bark and twigs and something colder—bone. Cyndere drew back her hands, suddenly questioning what more she wanted to learn about this story in the darkness. After a pause she cautiously continued her investigation and found that there were many hands grasping and holding the woman's cape. The fingers were webbed with spider-strands and fused to arms that reached up from a swell of densely woven branches, like a wave of the forest's fallen. She patted her palms along that rising wave until her fingers found cold, smooth spheres. Her breath caught, and she was terrified. There were skulls here, set in gaps between the branches. Cyndere began to shake.

A ripple of air wriggled across the floor and tugged at her woodscloak, then prowled across the chamber. It shivered the curtain, letting in a flicker of light. Cyndere crouched, overwhelmed by the scale of detail that glittered around her. She glimpsed walls plastered with winter-blackened leaves, embedded with bits of bone and eggshell. Threads spun from ash webbed the ceiling, penetrated by tusks that hung like stalactites.

She knew, then, that Jordam had been wrong. Auralia had crafted this chamber. It was all her work. She had given her fears some kind of shape, screamed her secret suffering into a detailed expression, here in this private place. Vivid manifestations, appalling distortions, and colors that made Cyndere's stomach turn—this was where Auralia had wrung horror, spite, and rage from her heart. And then she had left it all behind.

This ghastly vision culminated in a sculpted wave of slack-jawed skulls and empty eyes, of arms and hands reaching for a desperate woman and taking hold of her, trying to draw her down into their miserable grave.

Cyndere wanted an ax. She wanted to hew those arms, break the hands that held the woman's cloak. Instead, she slid her hands back up to the woman's shoulders and found her face. Unlike the detail of the feet that pushed against the floor, the face—a fragile mosaic of glass fragments—had no lines or features. It seemed this figure, in the force of her attempt to escape, had forgotten herself. Auralia had not finished this work. It stayed suspended, a question. And yet Cyndere felt she knew this woman, trapped by all that pursued her.

Tears stung her eyes. She had all but forgotten the sensation. She had wept when her father died. She had cried herself sick for the death of her brother, Partayn. But months had passed, and she had not found any way to cry for Deuneroi. Not yet.

Cyndere turned, then walked forward, leaving the woman behind. "You were trying to get somewhere," she whispered. She needed to believe that Auralia had given this figure somewhere to go, some chance of escape. That mysterious, scuttling wind had to have come from somewhere. A window, a door, a passage.

Her foot came down upon a coarse fold of cloth.

She knelt.

Her hands gathered the folds of a bristling woodscloak made of skins and thistledown. It was a cloak just like the one that Deuneroi had worn. Her hands knew it so well, and she could hardly hold it for the shaking. Something tumbled loose from the folds. By the bell-like tone when it struck the floor, she knew it was the helm of his armor. She put the cloak down, felt about the stone floor, and found a ring.

Recognition burnt her hand. She forced herself to pick up the ring. Her fingertips moved back through the cloak, and she found a sharp-edged object pinned there—a brooch with an eagle-shaped jewel. With urgency, her hands ran farther, in search of an explanation. In the span that would have covered the space between his shoulders, she found it—a slit in the fabric cleanly cut by a blade.

She let go. Stillness, and then at last she felt a seam split, a barrier break. The grief rose. The flood.

Cyndere's voice shattered the darkness, displacing the bats that roosted in bones glued across the ceiling. They slapped their wings together and rushed at the curtain where they fought to escape.

She whispered his name again and again, holding the cloak so tightly to her breast that the brooch's pin pierced her garment. When the curtain rustled behind her, she waited for a footfall and whispered, "Jordam." He did not answer. He had not come. But now her solitude had been disturbed, just as it had been that night in the glen. "Jordam," she said. "No." She let the cloak fall to the floor, and she pulled at her hair.

Cyndere cursed the Cent Regus beastmen. She raged at Deuneroi for leaving her behind. She punished her brother for running away on a mad errand in search of music. She damned the vast and reckless sea for taking her father. She cursed the moon-spirits. Cursed her mother. Cursed Bel Amica and all its blindness. She cursed herself for all her failings, the loss of her hopes, the ruin of her life.

When she lifted her head again, her body ached. The hours had emptied out her grief. But through her tears, she saw an intensifying light somewhere far away.

She rose to her feet, feeble in her anguish. As she did, she saw the faintest hint of detail and realized that the woman leaning forward was reaching out toward the distant light. Cyndere fingered the sculpted arm, found her way down to the hand, which was pointing directly toward that faraway glow.

Cyndere gasped, for as she touched the woman's cold clay hand, it shifted like a lever. A rumble moved from the statue to the wall, and then a bold beacon shone in, illuminating something at the end of a tunnel.

While Cyndere could not make out the details of the spectacle illuminated there, she saw another figure standing just this side of the beacon. His arms were spread wide.

Cyndere let go of the woman's hand and surrendered to the pull of that mystery. As she tiptoed down the cold, bone-encrusted passage, expecting to enter an embrace, she began to understand. This man was not facing her, nor was he raising his arms. He was spreading wings to venture ahead. To lead the way.

"Deuneroi," she whispered.

The statue was as unfinished as the besieged woman's face. He was just an outline, as if Auralia was not quite sure of him. He seemed enthralled by what lay before him. On a smooth stretch of wall, Auralia had painted a scene. The sunlight that now streamed into this cave illuminated the spectacle. Cyndere stared. A jagged sea of green filled the lower part of the wall's canvas. Above it, a dark, mountainous line.

High above that line, over a vast space where nothing had yet been painted, Auralia had begun to sketch a mountain with white chalk. Cyndere did not recognize the place; Auralia had only swept the first brushstrokes of white. It hovered over the landscape, suspended. The figure standing beside her seemed free, eager, ready to fly, and his head was tilted back, looking at the mountain. Cyndere felt an urge to finish the painting, to fill that void with detail so the mountain would reach the ground and the man could make his way to the snowy peak.

Looking back, she could see the woman leaning forward from the mass of nightmares, from the surge of clutching hands. She approached the woman and saw her more clearly—a figure of sorrow. The surface of the sculpture sparkled as if made of salt. The strain in her posture was not fear but determination. The shadows were not seeking to drag her down. No, she had offered them her cloak that they might take hold and be drawn out of their darkness, like survivors from a flood.

"Auralia," she whispered, "where did you go? Who will finish the picture?" Cyndere turned, leaned back into the woman's robes, and shared her gaze. "And who was he for you?"

The figure in the distance blurred as tears came again. "I can tell you," she said, "who he was for me." She drew her husband's cloak about her. She wept again for Deuneroi until at last the tears were gone, her heart wrung out, his bloody cloak baptized.

31

THE MEMORIAL TREE

A few snow flurries fell as the Forbidding Wall of the north flung new blankets of clouds across the Cragavar, but by midday it had warmed into rain. Winter was finished, all its conviction lost.

Jordam ventured west from the southern end of Deep Lake through the forest, then turned north, finding clear tracks of small, bare feet. Eventually the tracks bloodied, and then their shape changed. Bel had stopped to wrap her feet in cloth. He worried. The Bel Amicans were not likely to give up looking for their heiress. Good trackers would find her.

As night fell, his hopes failed. The tracks led straight to a camp of Bel Amican soldiers. Their tents glowed like lanterns, but Jordam saw no shadows moving within them. Nor did he find any trace of Bel's scent. The men saddled their two vawns and three horses. A debate broke out over who would stand guard at the camp while others went hunting. Six soldiers, Jordam thought. But only five steeds.

Edging along the bough of a coil tree, he learned that a horse had been stolen. The soldiers argued about when the animal was taken and by whom. A watchman defended himself. He claimed that his job was to guard the tents not the animals. He insisted that a beastman had taken the horse. The others objected, saying a beastman would have killed something. "A blasted thief," argued another. "Desperate merchants in desperate times." Another blamed the missing horse on a tether poorly secured.

The argument turned to a debate over solutions, and Jordam crept away.

He picked up the horse's trail and followed it wearily as the moon ascended toward midnight. The strength that he had gained in O-raya's caves was failing. The horse traveled westward, and Jordam knew the rider was heading for Tilianpurth.

As the forest's rainsong loudened, he heard hounds and the heavy footfalls of vawns. Two soldiers had been sent to recover the horse. He leapt off the path at the top of a ridge, bounding into the treetops just as the dogs began their ascent. They passed beneath him, a streak of torchlight, a clamor of vawns and dogs.

He dropped from the trees, distracted by another glow, this one north of the horse trail. Tied around a strong white branch of a birch, a long and trailing banner wavered gold and green in the wind. He touched the familiar weave. It was a frayed and unfinished sample of color from O-raya's abandoned work.

Bel put this here for me.

He untied it from the bough and uncovered a simple figure etched into the white bark with a knife. It was the star shape of the blue flower from the glen.

Bel wants me to follow.

Her tracks reappeared beneath the tree, leading northward, away from the horse's progress. Perhaps remembering their strategy with the prongbull, she had dismounted to confuse her pursuers. She was making for Tilianpurth now.

He found her just before daylight. She was asleep, rain-soaked, huddled at the base of a tree, blanketed with enormous dragonfern leaves. She had almost reached the edge of the valley above Tilianpurth.

When he blew softly through the oceandragon whistle, she did not open her eyes or lift her head, but she spoke. "You came back. You found me."

He pointed to the way he had come, but she would not look at him. "Hunters," he said. "Close. rrMust go."

"I'm going home, Jordam. Back to House Bel Amica. I'm going back to my people. I have work to do. "

"rrWhy not go with hunters? Hunters search for Bel."

"I have to get back to the glen first. One last time, before they find me. I have to finish something." She surveyed the branches above. "Can we get there before daylight?"

He scowled. "rrLong way for you."

"I can make it." She stood and watched the cover of ferns fall away. "If you'll carry me."

He felt a burden, as if another garment of stone had been cast around his shoulders. She came forward, and he shrank back, pained, even as she raised her eyes to look at him. At first he feared she would be frightened by his changed appearance. But then he remembered that he would be only a patch of darkness to her.

She too had changed. He sought to understand what was different about her face, but he was distracted by the glint of a brooch pinned to her cloak. It was not her cloak at all. He wrapped his arms around his head as if to deflect himself from a blow.

"You were right," she said, her voice hard and cold. "Auralia's caves were full of surprises."

He searched for words, words he might have heard from her before. "I lied," he said. "I lied."

"Jordam, I'm not going to hurt you. Is that what you've come to expect? No, I'm just going to ask you why. Why are you keeping secrets from me?"

He closed his hand around the whistle, as uncertain as he had been at their first meeting. "Can't. Can't grow alone."

"You think you'll lose me. Like Auralia."

He remembered a word. "Help."

She looked eastward, into the darkest part of the woods. "That's a fear I understand." He closed his eyes, began to assemble some manner of explanation. But before he found any words, he felt her arms slide up and around his neck. "Deuneroi promised he would bring me something from the ruins of Abascar. Maybe he did come back. Maybe he brought you."

"Brothers went to Abascar," he murmured. "Hunting. Mordafey—"

"Shh." She touched his lips with her fingertips. "Hush, Jordam. I don't ever want to hear another word about it. You've changed. I'm going to help you find a future. That's my purpose now. To lead you out of the old life, to follow Deuneroi."

She leaned in, her forehead on his shoulder. "I don't want to do this. I'm worn out from depending on those I cannot trust, those who let me down. And I'm sick of being served and guarded and carried. But we have to reach the glen by daybreak." She leaned in and quietly said, "Will you carry me, Jordam?"

He lifted her. She felt lighter than before. And yet with every step he felt lighter too, the weight of fear slipping away.

As the night sky grew pale and the horizon turned a cold blue, they reached the whitegrass, which wavered, already rising again as the snow melted away. Rain fell upon the forest in dark, ghostly veils. He could smell the smoke that rose in a thin line from the tower's chimney ahead. He caught no trace of soldiers. The search for Bel had spread beyond the Tilianpurth wood.

But he was attentive for other signs as well. He was both relieved and troubled to find that the soldiers had cleared all traps from the whitegrass. He was free to move directly through the trees, but nothing would stop his brothers from tracking him to the glen.

"You...you're wounded," she said, seeing him clearly in the morning light. She touched the broken browbone, ran her fingers through the remaining shreds of his mane. "You look as if you've been flogged."

"Hard work," he sighed. "Hard work reaching Cal-raven."

"You almost look like a..." Her voice trailed off, for she was suddenly distracted by a blue glow through the trees. "We're here." She pressed her face to Jordam's mane, whispering, "Thank you."

He almost stumbled, choking as his throat tightened, his sense of shame increasing with every kindness. Bel slid from his arms and walked down the slope, then paused to unbind her feet and walk barefoot in the grass.

"Traps!" Jordam hissed, not quite ready to believe that the soldiers had cleared them all.

Bel slowed her pace and surveyed the glen. "They're gone. Jordam, look. I...I watched them. They stripped everything away."

He remembered too. The vawns had trampled the glen. The soldiers had stripped the cloudgrasper bare, the ornaments carelessly cast aside.

But this morning the bold green boughs of the cloudgrasper sapling were decked in garlands of starflowers, beads, and bells and strung with the full array of belongings that Bel had hung there to remember those slain by the Cent Regus.

Bel tenderly traced the curve of her brother's seven-stringed perys, then reached up to touch Deuneroi's bow. "Emeriene," she said, kneeling down to draw away a blanket, revealing the tetherwing basket. "She left the basket for me. She decorated the tree." She lifted her eyes to the tower, then covered her face with her hands. "She's prepared everything."

Bel searched the ground around the loose stones and uncovered firestarters. She pinched one between both hands, readied to snap and ignite it.

Jordam, frustrated at the failures that haunted him, stalked down into the glen. Bel stood up as he bent to grasp the fallen apple tree, the casualty of his escape from the snare. The branches thrashed in surprise. Roots flailed about like gnarled fingers. He tried to stand it upright, but the ground had hardened; its grip was gone.

"You can't replant a tree like that, Jordam. I'm afraid it's too late."

"rrToo late?" He cast the tree back down. While the branches wavered and went still, he slumped down with his back against it. "Too late for everything." He picked up a fallen apple and hurled it into the trees. "You should send Jordam away."

"What happened?" She walked to the well and began to pull at the rope slowly, hand over hand. "Did something go wrong at Abascar?"

"No," he sighed. "Abascar safe."

"You...delivered the message?"

He fumbled his way to words that would explain how he had warned Cal-raven, how Abascar had hastened into action, how the next night had come alive with fire and fury. "Abascar is good, safe," he assured her. "Cent Regus army ruined."

"Deuneroi would be—" She leaned back against the well, and her face was wet with tears.

"rrNot enough," he growled.

"You can't replace what's lost, Jordam," she said softly. "You were born into a curse. And you've done your part to make things worse. So have I, I suppose. But you're awake now, thanks to Auralia. All you've lost...that void can fill with purpose. We're not so different, are we?"

His hands opened and closed, as if he were searching the ruins of Abascar, digging for consolation.

Bel went back to the well and drew out the bucket. Propping it on the edge, she gazed into the well and listened to the rush of the water in faraway passages and caves. "I am waking up too," she said. "I'm seeing what must be done." She set the bucket on the ground beside him. "I won't abandon you, Jordam. But I must go home to House Bel Amica for a while. I have to prepare the way so we can draw others from the curse. Just as Auralia brought you. Just as she brought you and the ale boy to me."

"rrBel Amicans will finish me." He made a gesture like drawing back a bowstring and letting the arrow fly. "Cent Regus no good to them. No help."

She sat beside him for a long time, silent. Then she rose and moved to seize the tetherwing basket. "It's time for me to finish this." She drew out the feathered crown and broke it in two. She set half of the crown on Jordam's head and half upon her own.

The birds rose slowly and hovered about their heads. He held still as they pecked at his feathery half crown. They chirped, baffled. And then those weightless puffs of feathers spread out about the clearing, sentries rising to settle in the branches of the trees above the glen.

"Now," said Bel, "what comes next is not for me to do. I see that now. It is for you."

Jordam grunted, puzzled.

"Take this." She held out Deuneroi's cloak to him. "Take it," she said again, and her tone was far from friendly.

He cowered, shuddering. "No," he growled, "not that. Not me. Could have stopped Mordafey. Could have helped—"

"So you took this cloak from Deuneroi. And a good deal more. It's true." She draped the garment on the ground before him. "Cast it on the Memorial Tree. Give it back to him in the flames. Give him a sign. Let it go. And you'll be free."

He regarded the cloak as if it might suddenly rise and attack him.

"Stand up, Jordam. Set your regrets on fire."

Feeling suddenly ancient, Jordam climbed to his feet. He lifted the cloak, and it seemed heavier than ever. He crossed the glen, eyed the boughs of the cloudgrasper, then stretched to the high branches that had been beyond Emeriene's reach. He cast the stained and tattered cloak over the crown of the tree. The edges fluttered in the faint breeze, and rain misted across it.

"Now." Tears sparkled in Bel's eyes. "The firestarter." She took a bright white stick from the tetherwing basket, rose, and stood beside him. She held out an end of the firestarter. "Break it with me. We'll say good-bye. To my husband. To my brother, Partayn."

She sharply bent and broke the twig. Both pieces sparked into flame. She reached into the kindling she had shoved against the trunk of the tree. Flames caught hold, rapidly blackening the circle of thorns. They stepped away from the tree as smoke roiled about its base.

"Jordam, this is where his dream began," she whispered. Then she reached out, and her small, cold hand found its way into his.

The flames crackled, exuberant. The cloudgrasper's bark caught fire, peeling and curling. But only the outer skin burnt away, the greener layer beneath it repelling the flames. While the outer layer would be lost, the tree would stand bright and bold again. Eager to find more fuel, the fire climbed into the branches and moved out along the boughs.

"rrDoon-roy. Partayn," he whispered solemnly. The name seemed strangely familiar to him. "Partayn," he said again, trying to remember.

"Cent Regus killed him and all his guards as he traveled to House Jenta." Bel stared at the blaze as if she would commit every floating speck of ash to memory. "He sang. Beautifully."

The flames whipped and beat at the boughs. The perys warped and burst. When its strings broke, he felt her tense as if something within her had broken as well. Deuneroi's cloak rippled above the branches in the swelling heat.

Unfamiliar emotions quivered in Jordam's chest. They frightened him, and he looked away from the woman and her grief, then froze when he caught sight of a figure in the trees. The apparition stood quiet, watching, just as it had the first night Jordam had freed Bel from the trap. The figure raised a hand as if in acknowledgment. Compelled to see if Bel would once again share this unsettling vision, he put a hand on her shoulder. She turned to him and wiped the tears from her cheeks.

He gestured, but the figure was gone. He opened his mouth to explain, but something in the air tickled his nose, and he sneezed.

She laughed, wiping her eyes. "Too much smoke?"

Jordam sniffed the air. "Something...not good." There was more than smoke on the air.

One of the tetherwings chirped a worried syllable.

Jordam touched the half crown of feathers; it was still on his head. His ears flicked forward.

"Soldiers." Bel dropped to her knees. "Jordam, I think they're coming for me. You have to run!"

"No," Jordam said. "Not soldiers. Brothers."

Burdened with dread, Goreth trudged through the trees toward Tilianpurth as if toward his own demise.

When the brothers hunted, this was his favorite moment—the closing in, the surrounding. Mordafey, Jorn, and Jordam would fan out around a target, then move in from all sides with great stealth. Sometimes the prey would run to him, trying to escape Jorn. Sometimes the prey would slip between the brothers, renewing the chase. Sometimes the brothers would gather about the base of a tree and laugh as their prey made a futile climb. There was suspense in guessing which brother would make the kill.

But today he felt no excitement. Today there were only three brothers, and they closed in on someone who was not prey.

Jordam was like him in so many ways, but smarter. Jordam would have known what to do here. Jordam would have made a good plan.

Goreth bore his weapon awkwardly; this Abascar sword, his favorite trophy, seemed heavier and cruel. "Older Brother kept secrets," he argued. "Older Brother, he snuck out. But Jordam, he came home. Jordam told me everything. Told me to remember. Something."

Goreth stopped and clutched at his belly, which was swollen with Essence. He clenched his eyes shut, sucked in the cold air, and smelled distant woodsmoke. He scooped up a handful of slush and ate it. It cleared his thoughts for a moment, the shock of the cold rushing down his throat.

When he opened his eyes, he watched crystals dissolve in his hands, like a mystery fleeing from his grasp.

The woods were quiet. When he was still, the trees spoke only of melting snow. Perhaps the fight was already over. Young Brother had probably already found Jordam.

"Same Brother." A strange thought entered his head. Born at the same time. Born so much the same. He worried—if Jordam was killed, perhaps they both would die.

Goreth growled and hacked hard at a young cloudgrasper tree with his blade, chopping straight through its trunk. The cut was so neat that the tree remained standing, the line barely perceptible. If it had stood alone, it would have fallen. But its branches were entangled in those of its neighbors; they held it up.

Something dropped from the tree into the brush. He lunged forward and snatched it up, then laughed. It was a tree turtle, and it pulled its head and legs deep into the shelter of its shell.

Goreth looked at the turtle awhile, and his smile faded. His memories stirred, and anger swelled within him. "Older Brother has no care for Goreth," he announced. "Older Brother lies. Older Brother cheats. Older Brother makes secret plans. But Jordam always helps me." He shook himself and gripped his sword in decision. "Same Brothers stronger together."

He ran, gaining speed, and the trees became dark blurs, the snow a gleaming stream. He had run for hunger. He had run for the rush of power. He had never run for anger or raised a finger against Older Brother before. This was a strange exhilaration, rushing to protect Jordam. Together they would be stronger.

As a burning tree on lower ground came into view just ahead, Goreth paused. Jordam's last words suddenly returned to him. "Let Older Brother go first."

Perhaps he was wrong. Perhaps Jordam wanted Older Brother to find him first. Perhaps Jordam had prepared a trap, as he had beside Baldridge Hill. Or if Older Brother ran first, Goreth could always strike him from behind.

He slowed, holding to Jordam's advice. He stepped into a bed of ferns, crouching low so that only his ears emerged from the leaves. He wrapped his arms tight around himself, trying to wrestle down the surging appetite of new Essence. Another will within him roared, pushed, reached for the glen just ahead. He listened, eager for a sign that Mordafey had made his move. He dug at the soil, found rockbeetles, and ate them. A scent caught his attention. *Honey*, he thought. *Nearby.* But he stayed where he was, waiting.

A faint vibration rippled through the ground beneath his feet. It was a familiar sensation. He thought back to the last time he and Jordam had run together through the whitegrass. What had they been hunting?

He heard twigs snap. He heard leaves rustle. Something was bounding in from the left. He heard Young Brother's voice snarl, *"Hel hel hel."* Goreth raised his head. Young Brother's skin cloaked him with the colors of the surrounding trees, but Goreth could see his wild eyes, his gleaming teeth, and the shiny, jagged pike in his hand.

Young Brother pounced. "Got Jordam!" he shouted to the forest, exultant. Goreth looked down at the pike buried in his ribs. He forgot everything.

32

THE BREAKING
OF THE BROTHERS

Setting the wooden cover over the well, Jordam turned to see Mordafey snatch one of the tetherwings out of the air, crush it, and cast its crumpled form to the side of the glen.

"Now," said Mordafey, "Jordam learns not to keep secrets."

Jordam met Mordafey's burning gaze. "Older Brother," he said, surprised at how much he sounded like Goreth.

"No brother at all." Mordafey raised a broken Bel Amican trap by the pin, wires hanging down like a scourge. "You talk in your sleep. Your secrets aren't so secret. And look, you have no weapon to defend yourself."

"Jordam has something else." Jordam seized hold of the well. "rrBetter than Essence. Tried to tell you. You wouldn't listen."

Mordafey slung the trap wires about in the air and advanced. Jordam thought of tearing loose a wellstone, but here in this place he felt a hesitation. It was not just Mordafey charging toward him. It was the Essence that controlled him. In the midst of the fear, he felt a pang of sadness.

"I know your plan," said Jordam. "You don't care about brothers. You'll finish all of us when you take Skell Wra's throne. Until then you need us…because you're weak. Weak without help. Weak without Essence."

Mordafey struck. The wires striped Jordam's side. His head hit the wellstones and rang loud as a bell. "rrLook at me, Mordafey." Tasting blood, he laughed and pushed himself back up. "I'm stronger. I walk away from Essence." The lash struck again, carving lines from his face to his chest. The scene melted into clouds and shadows, save for the burning tree, lit like a pillar.

Mordafey tossed the snare aside and kicked Jordam in the belly. Jordam's knees buckled, and he fell, crushing the tetherwing basket beneath him. When he glanced up, Mordafey stood over him, gloating.

"Be afraid, rrMordafey," he gasped.

"You should be afraid. You should have obeyed. Mordafey will be chieftain."

"Not mine." Leaning against the well, Jordam closed his eyes. "rrMy chieftain...told me to stop you."

Mordafey stood up straight, sniffed the air. "Your...chieftain?"

The glen was quiet, save for the snapping of the cloudgrasper and the mournful hoots of the tetherwings. The remnant of Deuneroi's cloak suddenly fluttered like wings on the intensifying heat, rose up on escalating flames, billowing and dancing in the open space, higher and higher. The rustle of its cloth turned Mordafey's head.

Jordam looked around, but his vision was fading. He could see only the grass before his face and a glint of golden glass that had tumbled out of the crushed tetherwing basket. He crawled forward, closed his hands around it.

Mordafey turned, seized the wooden well-cover, and opened it so that the fog wisped into the air around him. He leaned over and looked inside. "Ssssecrets," he muttered, tossing the cover into the grass and grasping the rope. Jordam listened for cries of dismay. Bel had clung to the rope, her feet on the bucket, and he had let her down into the well. But now Mordafey was drawing the bucket up easily.

Jordam felt gravity's pull, felt his thoughts dimming like dying stars. He could feel tremors. Footfalls. "Keeper," he whispered as O-raya had done so many times. "Keeper." He opened his eyes and strained to see in the direction of the commotion. Then he pulled his closed fist to his mouth.

Mordafey gathered in all of the rope, sniffed the empty bucket in his hands. He shoved his muzzle into the bucket, and Jordam could hear him lapping up the warm well water. Mordafey held the bucket before him, staring inside as if to puzzle over his reflection. "Strange," he muttered. He eyed Jordam with suspicion. "This," he asked, "your...secret?"

Jordam felt a wild surge of hope. "Yes," he whispered. "Yes."

Mordafey stared at him as if suddenly unsure how to conclude the confrontation. Then he turned and cast the bucket back into the well. The taste of the water had slowed him with a question.

But then a sharp cry echoed within the well. *Bel.* The bucket had struck her, and Mordafey leapt up with a snarl of pleasure. "Can't fool Mordafey," he roared into the well. He clawed at the wellstones, breaking O-raya's painted boulders apart and shoving them into the hole. Jordam heard them splashing deep underground. He did not hear Bel's voice again.

Then Mordafey stalked up close to him. Jordam could see only the shadow and the gleam of his teeth. Mordafey leaned in close, gloating, and grabbed him by the beard. "Jordam's secret belongs to Mordafey now. Mordafey will make her a slave."

Slave. Jordam felt Mordafey's hot breath on the one side of his face that still had feeling.

He bit down on the small glass vial he had tucked into his cheek. The glass splintered, slicing the roof of his mouth. With his last flicker of strength, as an explosion of pungent perfume filled his head, he spewed splinters of glass and slumberseed oil into Mordafey's sneering face.

Mordafey fell away, clutching at his eyes and nose, trying to spit the oil from his tongue. He staggered about, fell onto his knees. "Goreth!" he howled. "Jorn! Help me!" He crawled out of the clearing, already half-asleep. After the bushes stopped rustling, the tetherwings stopped crying.

Jordam looked up into the rain. "Slave," he spluttered, hearing the ale boy's delighted cry in that snowbound shelter. "Slave. Partayn's a slave." And then the slumberseed oil drew him down into the dark.

Mordafey's mind fell asleep, but the Essence had a life of its own within him, and to preserve its host, it carried him forward until the scent of blood brought his senses surging to life.

Ahead, just beyond three trees that seemed to have fought, broken each other, and collapsed in death, he could see Jorn, blood streaking his muzzle, dancing about in celebration.

Mordafey clambered over the massive, splintered trunks, slipping in the soft, melting snow. He tried to bring himself to his feet but fell forward, claws splayed into the slush.

"Look!" Jorn shouted, holding up Goreth's sword. "Look look look what I done, Mordafey. Jordam try t'get away. But I run up behind 'im. Got 'im!"

Mordafey saw the carnage, the bloodied black mane framing a devastated face. He saw the browbone, unbroken. "Jorn," he groaned. "Jorn. Where is Goreth?"

"Goreth? *Hel hel hel!*" Jorn scampered about in the ferns. "Must show Goreth!" He stood between two trees, grabbed them, and shook them so that snow crashed down on his head.

"This." Mordafey crawled into the cold spread of dark blood and lifted the limp, hairy tail from the gore. "This is Goreth."

Jorn looked back at him, pink tongue wagging. Then his grin closed. He blinked. He whined through his teeth. "But...*urg!*"

He jerked, hit from behind, and clutched at his chest where a wooden shaft tipped with a sharp, wet metal point protruded. He reached for the trees again to catch himself as his legs gave way beneath him. He fell on all fours. "No. Jorn can't finish," he spluttered, crawling toward Mordafey.

The Bel Amican soldier standing behind Jorn notched another arrow to his bowstring. "One!" the man shouted, marching forward.

Mordafey stood up. The Bel Amican's second arrow grazed his side. He felt the sting, smelled the poison. Already dizzy from the slumberseed oil, he knew he had only moments left to escape. He ran.

"Just...an arrow," he heard Jorn groan. "Jorn is strong."

The Essence carried Mordafey in a frantic flight. He did not see the trees. He saw instead a familiar silhouette, a mountainous shape, advancing not far away, watching with crimson eyes and laughing through fiery teeth, raising wings that spread to blot out the sky.

He heard Jorn's howl and heard it interrupted.

"I'll have two today!" the soldier was shouting after him. "You cannot escape me! I am Bauris!"

Arrows buzzed past Mordafey's head, thudding deep into tree trunks. He broke out of the wood, dove into the sea of whitegrass. Blind with fear, he set his mind on his destination, the core of the world he understood.

He did not get far. Someone was waiting for him at the edge of the Cragavar.

Cyndere tightened her grip until blood trickled from her fingers down her wrists and arms.

Her father to the sea. Her brother to the beastmen. Deuneroi to Jordam's own brother. And herself...never to be found, swallowed up by the earth.

The stone walls of the well shaft were rough, and they ripped skin from Cyndere's hands as she clutched the lowest ring. Her body hung down into a large tunnel, legs trailing in the slow, warm glide of a subterranean river. If her grip failed, she would sink into the flow and be carried away on the current into darkness.

A silhouette blocked the distant spot of light above, a vague shadow through thick, rising vapor. An unfamiliar voice had echoed down the dark shaft. The bucket had suddenly been lifted from the water beside her. She let it go, too worried to risk rising into a predator's clutches.

"Please," she whispered. "Please."

If her mother were listening, she'd rejoice and announce with satisfaction that the heiress had finally acknowledged her moon-spirit and called out for help. The thought made Cyndere cringe. Still, she called out again, unable to resist what seemed an instinctive compulsion. "Take me out of here. Whoever you are. Moon-spirit. Anything. If you can hear me, get me out of here. I know what you want me to do. "

She stared into the darkness, and it might have been delirium, but she sensed the darkness staring back at her.

A beastly voice echoed down the well shaft. Then it was quiet except for the rippling hush. Something faint touched her face as she looked up. Rain.

A shadow appeared, falling fast. The bucket. It struck her shoulder, and she fell. The water welcomed her easily, and the beginning of her cry was erased by the river. She fought. Swallowing that strange, pure water, she felt strangely empowered. Her arms embraced the bucket. She drew herself up, gasping, and clung to the rope.

The river flowed. The fog swirled in the faint ray of light from the well shaft.

"Please," she said again. "Please. I have so much work to do."

Heavy wellstones plunged into the water beside her, and she clung to the bucket, bracing for the moment when the stone that anchored the rope would fall. But it did not fall. The river flowed, the well shaft quieted, and she clung for what seemed an hour.

Then the bucket jerked again. The rope began to rise.

"My lady?" came a familiar voice. "Cyndere?"

"Bauris!" she cried, incredulous. With all her might, she pulled herself up the rope to brace her feet against the bucket as it came out of the water, and she ascended into the light.

In the glen the air was full of rain. Bauris, his tears spilling into his grey mustache, took her hand. "My lady."

She stepped down into the grass and found that her feet were whole and unscratched. The slack of the rope coiled on the ground in a bundle beside a bloodied beastman who lay on his side in the grass, the half crown of feathers still clinging to his mane.

"It spoke," Bauris said, voice trembling in disbelief. "It said, 'Cyndere.' And it pointed to the well. Then it collapsed. I saw it, my lady. It fought for you."

Cyndere took the bucket and quickly began to pour the water over Jordam's mane and face. "Jordam, wake up. Wake up."

The beastman groaned, but he did not open his eyes. The grass gleamed bright green where the water melted the last traces of snow.

"My lady, you should step away—"

"Bauris." She put down the bucket and embraced him. "Bauris, you know how much I love you. But you have to trust me. This beastman is a friend. He saved me. From so many things. Please, do as I tell you. Protect this place awhile. At least until I can help him escape."

He thrust out his jaw, biting at his mustache. "We...we thought you were dead. Your sisterly, she's been pulling out her hair. We haven't been able to drag her away from your window in the tower."

"Bauris, he told me there are others. Beastmen. Here in the trees. They're not like him. They'll kill us if they can. Find Mordafey. And drive him away. You'll have a medal, I assure you."

"Not for medals, my lady," he said. "For you." He picked up his bow and fixed her with a stern glare. "But you don't have long. Soldiers are coming. And they won't trust you about...about this." With that he quickly climbed the slope past the coil tree.

Cyndere knelt beside Jordam and wept, wet hair falling across his face, her arms about his neck. When she could find her voice, she spoke softly into his ear. "Jordam, can you hear me?"

His eyelids flickered, but he could not see her. He groaned, and then his pink tongue licked blood from his lips. "Bel," he said, reaching toward the crumbling remnant of the well. "rrMordafey. Broke...O-raya's well."

"Listen, Jordam. You have to get away. Hide in Auralia's caves. Do you hear me? Wait in the caves, and stay hidden. Wait for summer. Then come back to Tilianpurth. Watch for a white flag over Tilianpurth's tower." Cyndere gestured to the monolith beyond the trees. "A white flag, Jordam. When you see it, you will know that I have prepared a place for you in House Bel Amica. Do you understand? Summertime. The white flag. Come to Bel Amica's front gate. I'll have guards watching for you. They'll know what to do. You'll be a guest in our house. But you must wait for the white flag. Do you understand?"

His hand reached up and held her shoulder, shaking. "Ffflag," he said. "rrSummer."

She released him and moved to stand up. But his hand tightened around her shoulder.

"No," she said. "You can't come with me. Not yet. You have to be strong on your own. Hold to the colors with all your heart." She helped him rise. He leaned against the well, breathing in the vapors.

The glen quieted. The sun burnt a hole in the rain cloud. Starflowers began to glow. The cloudgrasper stood tall in its new green skin. The heiress picked up the broken basket, then reluctantly lifted Jordam's half crown of feathers, for hers had been lost in the well. She whistled for the birds. Like small puffs of smoke, they returned to their center, chirping uneasily and keeping wary eyes on Jordam.

"rrBel," he said in a sad, faraway sigh. "You're going away." He looked up toward the coil tree. "There," he said. "I watched you. Was that me?"

"Trust me, Jordam. I'll summon you. I'll need your help. Be ready." She turned away, stepping forward as if into a harsh wind. "Distance," she said to herself, "is an illusion."

Finding no way into the shambles of their basket, the tetherwings hovered about the feathery crown in Cyndere's hair and circled her, bound by invisible strings.

33

RYLLION'S FAITH

Bauris tracked the spatter of blood left behind by the escaping beast-man.

He ran, knowing the creature could run faster. He ran with the nervous excitement of a dog that has snapped its leash to attack a trespasser.

He ran with an urgency he had not known since his youth.

In his hand he held the gory arrow he had pulled from the carcass of another beastman. It was more difficult to remove than he'd expected, as if the beastman wanted to refuse him a trophy. He would clean it. Hang it on the wall. Name it, perhaps. "Vengeance," he said. "I'll call you Vengeance."

Bauris laughed, for his admirers would assume they understood the name; after all, this arrow slew the beastman who had murdered Tilianpurth's prison guards. Bauris would smile and nod, knowing that it meant a differ-ent kind of revenge—a strike against those who had taunted him for so many years.

Bauris was no longer "the baby-sitter" who had guarded young Cyndere, who had grown old watching ivy climb the walls of an empty towerhouse. Now he was a hero. He had defended the bastion, fired a true shot, and avenged the prison guards. Word would spread. He was part of a story at last. Bauris, the watcher of Tilianpurth. Single-handedly, he'd faced two beastmen, killed one, and driven the other from the woods.

One beastman would be enough. Enough for today, anyway. Soon he would be relieved of his tedious duty at Tilianpurth and given a more promi-nent station. He would ride the wide patrols, respected as a soldier.

His sons. Bauris paused, leaning against a violet tree. His sons would hear about this even before he was back in Bel Amica. They would be proud of him. He had left his beastmen prize in the melting snow. A shame, really. Predators would move in tonight. Perhaps he should pry out the teeth of his victim and send them to his sons as trophies.

But there was still a threat left in these woods. And Bauris wanted to erase it.

He broke out of the trees, and his gaze found the moon. "You were on my side today, weren't you?" He stepped into the steep whitegrass, then sank low when he spied two figures at the top of the slope.

He watched them for a long time, his exhilaration evaporating.

He looked at the arrow in his hand, and a chill climbed his spine. He did not understand it, but something had changed. He had seen Cyndere beside the well, comforting a fallen beastman. And now this.

Bauris backed away and moved into the wood, aimless at first, until he came within sight of the glen and remembered the heiress. But when he reached the glen, Cyndere and Jordam were gone. The cloudgrasper's fire had gone out. Ashes lay in a dark circle around the tree, which now gleamed, its new green skin exposed to the air.

Ryllion was there, crouching over the bloodied ground in rapt attention, reading the grisly display. Bauris was startled to see him. He had watched Ryllion ride out with one of the search parties.

Bauris cleared his throat and hid the arrow behind his back. "Officer, I have news."

Ryllion rose awkwardly to his feet, as if caught in some indiscretion. His face was a fright, for a purple mask surrounded his eyes, scarring from his bout with the venomous beastman on the tower. He seemed taller, and his yellow hair was streaked with black. "Bauris, you are not at your post."

"No, Ryllion. It's been an eventful day. Sit down. Some of what I'll tell you will be hard to—"

"I will stand. Why are you here?"

Bauris brought out the arrow, trying to suppress a smile. "Sisterly Emer-iene saw smoke rising from this area. She knew what it meant. It's Cyndere, sir. She's returned. Sure enough, it was true. She's burnt a Memorial Tree in honor of Deuneroi. I found her here."

Ryllion started. "The heiress? She's come back?"

"Now you have something in common with her. Back home, plans had already been set in motion for her funeral. They'd given her up as lost. And lo, here she comes back to Tilianpurth. Just like you."

"Just like me."

Bauris glanced into the trees. "She should be back in the towerhouse by now. Unless..." He suddenly wished he had not spoken. He had been foolish in his zeal to hunt the beastmen. He had left her behind with a wounded Cent Regus savage. Now they both were gone.

"What else, Bauris? What else did you see?"

Bauris told his story.

He described how he had rushed to the glen seeking the heiress but found two enormous beastmen fighting there instead. He had lifted an arrow to the bow, only to see the larger beastman thrash the other to the edge of death. The battered beastman seemed to be trying to protect the well. Bauris had come to his feet to take aim, but the fiercer monster suddenly staggered away from the well, wiping at his face and howling. He fled. Bauris had turned his attention to the fallen beastman.

Then something unexpected had occurred. "Sin-der," the wounded Cent Regus had gasped, pointing to the well, unable to move. "Help Sin-der."

Listening to Bauris's account, Ryllion seemed to grow angrier by the moment.

"When I pulled Cyndere from the well, she insisted that I was not to harm even a whisker of that fallen beastman," Bauris laughed, still amazed. "She swore that he had saved her life. Jordam, she called him. Then she ordered me to secure the area. Told me to go after the biggest one, a beastman called Mordafey."

"Did she?"

Bauris described how he had pursued Mordafey and how he had found him with two more beastmen—one already dead, another bloodied and crazed. "I put this arrow," he said, "into the striped one. The one with a face like a boar. The one who murdered our prison guards. The same one who taunted the heiress in our prisons. My arrow, Vengeance, went in through his back and came out between his ribs."

"Did it now?" Ryllion muttered.

Bauris struggled to sustain his sense of pride. He continued his story, determined to impress this celebrated soldier.

In pursuit of Mordafey, he had come to the edge of the wood. And there—sure as the moon's in the sky—he had witnessed the Honorable Pretor Xa standing in the whitegrass at the top of the slope and shouting at a beastman. The Seer was scolding Mordafey. And Mordafey had cowered like a beaten dog. When the Seer gestured into the Cragavar, the beastman crept away, sullen and defeated.

"I know it sounds impossible, sir. I was so stunned, I felt like a horse had kicked me."

Ryllion gazed off into the trees. He did not seem shaken by this news. Only sobered and deep in thought.

Lowering his voice in solemn resolve, Bauris said, "You'd best look into this, Officer. I tell you, I suspect Pretor Xa of conspiracy with beastmen. I think we need to secure the perimeter."

"You think we should close the perimeter?"

"Shouldn't we?" Bauris's world was shifting around him. He felt as though the ground might give way beneath his feet. "Sir, there's a traitor in our midst."

"Are you sure of what you saw?"

"Clear as I'm seeing you now."

"And you'd swear to it in our queen's court?"

"I've always been an honest man, Officer. My reputation will persuade them to believe my tale."

"You persist in calling it a tale."

Bauris held up the arrow, Vengeance, looking at it as a reminder of his achievement. He was surprised by the anger that welled up inside. He did not deserve to have this taken away.

Ryllion blinked as if just waking up. Then he clapped Bauris on the shoulder. "Congratulations, Bauris. Well done. You've set things right. I enjoyed your tale immensely. Your moon-spirit, she understood your desire to slay a beastman, and she rewarded you with satisfaction."

"Yes," said Bauris, although he was hesitant to agree with anything Ryllion said about spirits. "Yes, but it's all so strange. You should've seen it. It was like getting a glimpse of Deuneroi's dream. There was Cyndere, her arms draped around a beastman. And he was tame. He cared about her. Deuneroi was right."

Blood filled Bauris's throat. The blade slipped out as soon as it had gone in. He turned, choking a question. Ryllion would not meet his gaze. The young soldier seemed sad, in spite of his clenched teeth, his flaring nostrils, and the explosive force with which he seized Bauris, raised him, and shoved him into the well.

Ryllion heard the splash far below.

He brushed off his hands, then leaned against the well, shaking. A cry broke out in a voice transformed, his own, and he clasped a hand over his mouth. Tears spilled into the dark maw.

"Never again," he said. Not for the first time.

"That's a rash promise," said Pretor Xa, striding down into the glen. "To accomplish what the moon-spirits desire, you have to make difficult choices."

"He saw you." Ryllion's hands closed into fists. "Bauris saw you talking to Mordafey."

"Bauris had to die. A small matter, Ryllion. Bauris killed a beastman today, so he died happier than he was ever likely to be again. We'll praise his bravery in Bel Amica. It will make his family proud. He died after slaying a beastman, making Tilianpurth safe for all."

"A small matter?" Ryllion shouted. "Listen to yourself!"

"I *am* listening to myself, Ryllion. What are *you* listening to?" The Seer smiled down at him, ghostly in his winding white rags. He reached for Ryllion's chin and turned his face toward the moon. "Attend to the vision that your spirit has given you. It is your sacred duty to pursue your heart's desire."

"At such a cost."

"A great future is a costly one. It's easy to become distracted by fears, by pity. But your spirit wants to bless you, Ryllion. Pursue happiness, and it will lead you to blessing."

"These…these risks. These deaths."

"You made a sacrifice for a noble cause. The Bel Amicans deserve better than Queen Thesera. They need you. We Seers see your potential. My moon-spirit has called me to help you rise and take Bel Amica's throne. Your gifts, they surpass all others. That is how you know that the spirits favor you. Even the beastmen are impressed with your strength. And while they still have much to learn, we have assembled the beginnings of a great Cent Regus army that will serve you."

"We failed at Barnashum, master. We needed those Abascar weapons, that treasure. It would have given us the advantage we needed to take the throne from Thesera."

"We," snarled the Seer, "did not fail. Beastmen failed. But even that, Ryllion, is a blessing straight from the spirits. For now Mordafey is ashamed, humiliated, humbled. He wants to prove something to us. Next time the beastmen will be unstoppable. We'll have Cal-raven's treasure. We'll equip an army. If there's anything the Cent Regus cannot abide, it is the suggestion of weakness. Patience, Ryllion. What you desire will be yours."

"Maybe my desires are changing." Ryllion scowled toward the moon. "This path—it's too costly. And the destination feels so far away."

"Far away?" Pretor Xa raised his hands, triumphant. "We're closer than ever, Ryllion. The heiress has vanished. We did not dare imagine such an opening. Of all Bel Amicans, you are now foremost in the queen's favor. You're all she has left. We may not need to seize the throne by force. We may not even need Abascar's surrender. The spirits might usher you into power without any struggle at all. With Cyndere out of the way, House Bel Amica may herald your arrival as the coming of a future king. Then our conquest will continue across the Expanse."

"Cyndere has returned."

Pretor Xa's teeth clacked together. Smiling, smiling, and yet the Seer swiveled his eyes toward the tower. "That meddling little girl."

"How will we stop her now if she has tamed a beastman?" Ryllion clasped his hands to his head. "Think of what this will do to the court. She'll kindle compassion for the Cent Regus. She'll inspire Deuneroi's allies. It's like he's watching us. Like vengeance."

The memories of that autumn day burned brighter in Ryllion's memory than anything that had transpired since.

Deep in the ruins of House Abascar, he had rushed ahead of Deuneroi toward the dungeons. The plan, so carefully designed by the Honorable Pretor Xa, had been playing out perfectly. He knew what waited at the end of that tunnel. And he knew what followed behind him.

He rounded the corner, stepping into a cave of stagnant air and a ghastly array of bones and chains. "Look, Deuneroi!" he had said, feeling as if he were both an actor in a stage play and a viewer in the audience.

Stepping in behind him, the royal consort had cringed, examining the vaulted, soot-blackened chamber, the dangling string of chains, the pit in the floor. "What was this place?"

Ryllion shrugged. "Abascar's dungeons. We heard stories about the torturer who lived here. Maugam. He was a monster." He wiped the sweat from his face. "Spirit," he said, "I cannot do this."

Deuneroi frowned. "Talking to your spirit again?"

"Master," Ryllion whispered, "I know you won't understand this. But I must confess it. While we're alone. Before it's too late."

"What is it?"

"I've let you down."

Deuneroi laughed, and he reached out to slap the guardsman on the shoulder, but Ryllion shrank away from him. "Ryllion," Deuneroi said, solemn now and worried, "you knew that we had little hope of finding any survivors."

"I've kept something from you. But I had no choice. My moon-spirit has called me to something. I've a vision for House Bel Amica, a way to bring the Expanse under control and cleanse it of corruption."

Deuneroi stopped. "You have great faith, Ryllion. Me, I have doubts. But I admire your dedication."

"It pains me, master. But the Seers promise that the suffering you and I must endure now is nothing compared to the glory that House Bel Amica will know. I have watched you in the court. I know you desire Bel Amica's success."

"Of course."

"Your moon-spirit knows your desire, master. She will fulfill it."

With a grinding of stone, the passage behind them sealed shut. Ryllion coughed, as if the closing door had cut off all air. He stared over Deuneroi's shoulder at the gigantic beastman who had shoved the boulder into place. They were trapped. Only one way out now. He had to carry out the plan.

Deuneroi turned, unsheathing his sword. "Beastman!"

Ryllion stepped behind Deuneroi and pressed the tip of his sword into his back. He knew the beastman. He had watched the Seer coerce the creature into obedience. "Wait, Deuneroi," Ryllion whispered. "Don't be afraid."

"Welcome, Mordafey." Pretor Xa rose from the pit like a dark bird, with a bright glowstone fixed at the top of his walking stick. "Do you see what we have brought you?" Grinning, he approached Ryllion, his white rags wavering even though the air was still as death. He tapped the floor with the staff's silver ferrule, then struck Deuneroi's arm. In a spatter of sparks, Deuneroi's sword clattered to the floor.

Mordafey stalked to the pit and barked a command down into it.

Ryllion sheathed his sword, then pinned Deuneroi's arms behind his back. "House Bel Amica is buying the loyalty of House Cent Regus," he half whispered. "To win their trust, we must offer them proof of our conviction."

"This beastman, he's what you dreamt of, Master Deuneroi," said the Seer, opening his arms as if to present some kind of pageant. "He listens to reason. And your sacrifice will purchase the very thing you desired—a relationship between Bel Amica and the beastmen. A beginning. A reconciliation between the children of Cent Regus and Bel Amica, those descendants of Tammos Raak."

"Ryllion," Deuneroi snapped, "open your eyes. Have the Seers deceived you so completely?"

"Quiet, master," said Ryllion around the cold lump rising in his throat. "The beastmen will fight for us now. They'll trust us. We'll conquer the Expanse."

"They're liars," spat Deuneroi. "They've appealed to your vanity."

Beastmen, like spiders from a nest, crawled out from the pit and filled the room. They lashed out at each other. They growled and cursed and spat.

Mordafey stood between them and the Seer, snarling instructions. Then the Seer spoke as if he too were a beastman, and the Cent Regus glowered back, suspicious. Mordafey turned, pointed to Ryllion, and spoke the name: "Deuneroi."

Ryllion looked at the Seer. "You do it," he hissed. "I can't."

"Do this!" said Pretor Xa. "And these beastmen will never harm you. They'll respect you. They'll be yours."

Deuneroi broke free and spun around. Then, to Ryllion's surprise, he embraced him. "The truth," Deuneroi whispered, "will be known, Ryllion. Someday it will be known. What do you want that truth to be?"

Ryllion closed his eyes at those words and nodded. "You're right. Forgive me."

Deuneroi stepped away and turned to face the Seer.

Ryllion looked at the hate-filled eyes, the cold malevolence, the alien nature of the beastmen. Fear took him. He brought the blade down through Deuneroi's wrist. Deuneroi wheeled in surprise, a fleeting question on his face. The Seer struck him from behind with the staff. Lightning flared through Deuneroi's body as he howled and fell, his long black hair spilling across Ryllion's feet.

Keeping his eyes on the beastmen, Ryllion plunged his sword through Deuneroi's back and felt it chip the stone floor. He let go as if the sword hilt had caught fire. Deuneroi pressed at the floor with his remaining hand, then strength went out of him, and he did not stir again.

The Seer pulled the sword free and tossed it aside. He spread his arms again, as if presenting the next act of the play.

Laughing in apparent disbelief, Mordafey seized the gleaming emblem-clasp of Deuneroi's cloak and tore the garment away. "That," he said, speaking Common, pointing to Deuneroi's severed hand. "I want that." The Seer bowed as a servant would bow to please a king. Mordafey reached for it, and Ryllion turned away.

"You've sworn your vow to the Cent Regus, Ryllion," said the Seer. "Mordafey will prepare them to follow your orders. He has these in his service, and he's gathering more. His brothers too. It's their turn now to prove their conviction and capability. Soon I'll lead them south to where the weak remnant of Abascar is hiding. We'll end their suffering and take what they no longer need. This will equip our army and ready us for the next conquest."

Ryllion acknowledged this with a nod, but he could not find his voice. In that moment he made himself a promise—he would destroy these creatures as soon as they had served their purpose. Each and every one of them. Vowing that, he could hope to overcome the emptiness now aching within him.

34

NEW TRACKS

Scharr ben Fray ladled herbal stew from a stone pot that hung from a crosshatch of sticks suspended over the campfire and handed the ale boy a steaming bowl.

"Most vawns will run from their masters, given the chance," he said, nodding to Rumpa, who lay resting with her legs sprawled out behind her. "But when I found Rumpa wandering alone a few days ago, she was worried." He shook his head and laughed. "She missed you."

"How'd she find me? I thought I'd never get out of that stove."

The mage gestured to the world beyond their firelit sphere. "There's an exodus happening among the creatures of the Expanse. Those that remain—birds, scavengers, rodents—they're eloquent enough. So I asked the shrillows, the gorrels, anything I could find. A black heron spoke of a beastman. A beastman hiding in an old Cent Regus farmer's house." He knelt down, binding stalks of toughreed to a branch to construct a makeshift broom. "That beastman, he had brought a boy along."

"That's me!" The boy pressed his hands against the warm bowl. "Did you really learn about me from a bird?"

"Birds don't pay much attention to the affairs of folks like us unless there are breadcrumbs involved." The old man swept the layers of snow from his tent. "But those that aren't carrion seekers despise and avoid beastmen. Most Cent Regus kill what they catch. But a beastman traveling with a boy? That is unusual. That got the birds' attention."

The boy was tempted to say that he found the idea of an old man holding conference with a heron unusual. Instead he sipped his stew, which smelled of potatoes, onions, stasiaroot, and spicy herbs.

Scharr ben Fray chuckled as if the boy had spoken after all and playfully brushed his broom across the fur-fringed hood of the boy's green cloak. Then he sat down on the other side of the fire, set aside the broom, and caught a snowflake gingerly between his finger and thumb, a trick that interrupted the boy's ponderous thoughts. He held it up to the light. "All descendants of Tammos Raak are unusual, boy. Stonemasters, wildspeakers, and firewalkers like you. If more people had the courage to discover their potential, we might find that such talents are not so rare."

The boy wondered if this was the kind of thing the mage had said to young Cal-raven in their lessons long ago.

Scharr ben Fray rose and ducked into the tent to rummage around, his voice continuing through the canvas. "The Expanse is in trouble. We're not reading the signs. Just think of Auralia."

"I always do."

"Auralia knew what was happening. Such a fascinating girl. I sent a viscorcat to play with her, sure as I brought you this vawn. I hoped that cat would help me learn more about her. But then we lost her in Abascar's fall, just when she was trying to show us something. Something we need to know."

"Does it have anything to do with the Keeper?"

"The Keeper, sure. The tales of Tammos Raak. Those annoying Northchildren. Moon-spirits. The disappearing wildlife of the Cragavar. The Cent Regus curse. Seers and all their tricks. And of course, Auralia's colors. Those mysteries are connected somehow. There's a scroll somewhere that holds the secret. I intend to find it. When I figure it all out, maybe I'll know how to save this world."

"Save the world from what? Beastmen?"

"There are dangers worse than beastmen, boy." The mage emerged with a tall red bottle. "Let's not talk about those in the middle of the night." He pulled the cork, a sound that always pleased the ale boy's ears, and tossed it into the fire. "I wonder," he mused, "whatever happened to that rascal cat."

The ale boy looked into the fire, thinking of Jordam and of Cyndere's bold hope. "How'd the beastmen get cursed?"

"Why do you want to know?"

The boy scuffed his feet and scraped at the bowl with his spoon. "The heiress...she thinks we might be able to help them get better."

"A question worth asking. All questions are. Every question I ask leads me to another. Now, let's see what you know, my little firewalker. You've seen things no one has seen. Been places no one has been." The mage paused expectantly, took a swig from the bottle, and handed it to the boy. "Maybe this will help you come up with some idea I haven't thought of yet."

"Where did you find this?" the boy exclaimed, running his hands over the glass. The bottle was almost half full. "It's Abascar wine! Some of the finest!"

"You think I'll tell you about my secret wine cellar?" Scharr ben Fray reached for the stone stewpot, scraped the remains of the stew into the fire, and then collapsed the pot in his hands, melting it into a shapeless mass that he began to knead vigorously like bread dough. "Let me ask you a question, boy. Have you ever felt as though there was a piece missing inside of you?"

"Yes," the boy answered immediately. "Yes." He thought of his childhood. He thought of his many questions about his own identity, his purpose in the world. He sipped the wine, and it was as though he had been transported into the Underkeep to sit in the breweries, tasting some of a forbidden royal vintage.

"But you found that missing piece, didn't you? Your question, it had an answer."

"Right there in front of me all along. I just couldn't see it."

"The houses were united once. Something was lost. No one seems to know what it was. No one asks. But our longings exist because there's something to them. The missing piece is out there. We catch hints of it."

"In Auralia's colors."

"Indeed. A sense of reconciliation. Harmony."

"It's like the Keeper. We all dream of the Keeper. But it's a mystery, and most folks think it doesn't exist."

"Auralia knew the Keeper, didn't she, boy?"

"Yes."

"She was wiser than all of us, somehow. Closer to the answer. I want to know the details she knew."

"What details?" The ale boy rubbed his eyes, then, without thinking, swallowed more of the wine.

"I am tracking them down. I have a journey planned."

"Where?"

"North, to Inius Throan."

"Inius Throan. I've heard of that." The boy stood and spread his arms. "It was an enormous gathering of children. Far away. It's where Tammos Raak first made his camp. After he led the escape from the north, of course."

"You've a good memory for fireside stories, boy. You're right. Tammos Raak climbed up and over the Forbidding Wall and made camp at Inius Throan, above Fraughtenwood." Scharr ben Fray's eyes sparkled. "I told Cal-raven that story when he was younger than you. Storytellers disagree about what happened there. Whatever it was, it divided Tammos Raak's gathering into four groups. All four abandoned Inius Throan. Tammos Raak slipped through the cracks of history, never to be seen again. But Inius Throan, my boy. I think it's the storybook that must be opened. It's the key. I want to find it."

"And then what?"

"That's why I came looking for you."

The boy suddenly turned. "Me?"

"I have a job for you. We'll discuss it tomorrow."

"Why tomorrow?"

"Because you're exhausted."

"I don't feel exhausted."

"And that's because you *are* exhausted." Scharr Ben Fray walked around the fire and took the wine bottle which, to the boy's chagrin, was empty. "Time for you to sleep."

"Oh no. I'm wide awake. I rested plenty inside that stove. And now that I'm free, I'm..." He blinked. "Now that I've eaten, I..."

He never finished the sentence, his thoughts melting under the weight of weariness.

Asleep, he found Auralia waiting for him, somersaulting through laughter down a bank of pillowy snow. She was older—several years older. And when she threw snowballs at him, they burst in explosions of color.

The ale boy awoke when the canvas ceiling stopped rippling, when the wind ceased its persecution of the bent and barren trees. He sat up as if the silence were a summons.

He was not aware of the dull reverberation in the ground, not until the world stilled. He did not think about the crackle and flash of the campfire outside the tent, not until the glow on the wall of the canvas suddenly went dark. He got to his feet.

"I am here," he said.

No one answered. The stonemaster's bedblanket was folded and cold, just as it had been when the boy arrived.

He pulled the tent flap aside and stepped into the clearing. "I am here," he said. "What now?"

The clouds streamed overhead in silent, twisting ribbons. The branches of the trees were empty. Nothing waited or moved between them.

Looking up as he approached the ashes of the fire, he stumbled into a sunken space. The ground within it hummed with the sound of a bow drawn across the thick strings of a lynfr, music raised by mist. He knelt and picked a few stones free of the soil, held them up to his ear, and then cast them down, incredulous. He pressed his hands flat against the dark earth and began to feel its contours, the edges that revealed he was standing in some kind of depression. A footprint.

Across the clearing he found another impression.

Lifting a forked tree branch that the wind had thrown down, he broke it into a single arm and thrust it into the remains of the campfire. Smoke surged and increased, coiling around the tip of the branch. He waited, trusting that fire still burnt in the ashes. An ember awoke. The branch sparked and flared.

He lifted the flaming brand and traced the progress of the footprints. He heard a whimper and found Rumpa hiding behind the tree where Scharr ben Fray had tethered her. Her milky eyes stared in the direction that the tracks led. She turned to look at him and gave her leash a tug as she always did when she wanted to move on.

After climbing onto Rumpa's saddle, the boy looked back to the tent and sighed. "I'm sorry, Scharr ben Fray. I hope you find what you're looking for. 'Ralia told me to follow the tracks." He looked at his shoes, which she had made. "The tracks led her into Abascar. Guess we'll find out where they take me."

With that, he gave the reins a gentle twitch. "Go!"

Rumpa fell to her knees and sighed, then snuffled about in the ferns, searching for worms.

"Rumpa, it's a simple command," the ale boy groaned. He dug in his heels. She grunted and went on eating. "Stop!" he shouted. Immediately Rumpa sprang back up and trotted into the trees.

The ale boy took the vawn southward, all the way to the edge of the forest and into the green haze that hovered over the realm of the Cent Regus beastmen. Grumbling, afraid, but obedient, Rumpa carried him down into that wasteland, following the trail.

EPILOGUE

W ilus Caroon slandered the stubborn chill that lingered in the springtime air and struggled with his crutches to climb the stairs on the inside of the bastion wall. Arriving at the top, he found the wagon-chair that waited for him and unfurled the bedbag that he had requested. He sat in the bag, a creature half out of its cocoon, and wheeled himself about on the wall, his raucous complaints subsiding when he observed the trees in their outbursts of beauty.

Tilianpurth was quiet while spring greened the lawns and fattened apple buds among the orchard boughs. Cyndere had gone home to Bel Amica. Ryllion had followed, sullen and prone to tantrums, even though a summons had come for him to return and receive a promotion to the honorable station of captain. Only a few bleary-eyed caretakers remained, setting up ladders for the tiresome task of stripping creepervine from the tower and renovating the prison pit.

Wilus watched young Pyroi the stablehand gathering wildflowers outside the gates. Continuing his ritual of honoring the lost, Pyroi scattered the flowers over new burial markers in the far corner of the bastion's north yard—tombstones for the prison-house guards killed by the escaping beast-man and for the soldiers slain at the Ceremony of Sacrifice.

Looking up, Wilus could see Bauris peering out the tower window and smiling. Tilianpurth's senior officer might have lost his movement, his speech, his wits, and his station, but he still knew a beautiful day when he saw one. Or perhaps he just appreciated the light more than anyone at Tilianpurth after spending so much time at the bottom of a well.

Several days earlier Ridgie, a young woman posted at Tilianpurth's front gate, had heard a strange sound coming from the forest—laughter. Worried, she broke the first rule of her recent training and ventured into the trees. The sound led her all the way to the glen and to laughter rising from the well's dark throat.

Stablehands murmured that beastmen had dumped Bauris down that shaft. But this was curious, for he bore no scars. The fall should have smashed his skull or drowned him. Those days in the depths should have starved him or killed him with cold. And some who paused and shook their heads in sadness at his door mused that death might have been a better end for Bauris than this delirium. But he just smiled and smiled as if enjoying some amusing secret that he could not find the words to express.

That smile annoyed Wilus, so he turned his attention to the world beyond the wall, where the ground was fraught with clover and busy with bees. The woods, ecstatic, raised those branches the snow had dragged down. They shielded chirping choirs and allowed occasional rays of sun to set the younger trees aglow. Melting snows gathered into the dry streambeds, giddy with reunion. Gorrels, the only four-legged creatures oblivious to the animals' disappearance from the Cragavar, scampered after each other, laying claim to spans of sweet grass.

Ridgie found him on the wall and reminded him that it was his day to scrape the forest for traps. The hunters among the bastion's small population were frustrated by the gorrels and game birds that they found caught and spoiled by the traps that Ryllion's men had failed to salvage. "We need this ground for hunting," they grumbled. So she helped Wilus back down to the stables, helped him climb into a vawn's sidesaddle, and strapped a quiver of two-headed arrows to his bedbag. With Pyroi's help, Ridgie rigged hooked spears for the vawn to drag behind.

As the vawn combed the ground and Wilus complained into the afternoon, he heard someone singing. "Another stranger in our woods?" he muttered. "I will not have it." He followed the sound, spurring the vawn past a flowering glitter tree and down into the glen.

He was momentarily distracted by the well. It had been ruined when last he passed this way. Someone had pieced together a new ring of sturdy stones, then painted them a soft, alluring blue.

But when the singing stopped, he halted the vawn, raised an arrow to his bow. Long, stripped branches were pinned to form an arching frame, and a stretch of canvas covered it, a span of Bel Amican weave marked with spirals depicting the wild Bel Amican tides. This makeshift tent was a soldier's work.

Wilus was about to prod the vawn forward when a man stood up from where he'd been hiding behind the crumbling stone wall. His face was skeletal, flesh grey, and blotched with scars. He squinted against the sun as if he had spent years in darkness. His hands gripped a makeshift bow. The arrow, also crude, but with a sharp stone tip, was enough to make Wilus pause.

"I'm Wilus Caroon. Bel Amican royal guard. Assigned to cleanse this patch of woods. With your general shakiness and feeble constitution, I'm inclined to drive you away, for you might be carrying plagues. I've no kind of notion what manner of man you be. You sleep beneath a Bel Amican tent, but for all I know, you might be leftovers from Abascar."

"I've lived among many from Abascar and suffered alongside them," the half-starved man declared. "One in particular has a name you will recognize, and what would I have done without her? But do you not know me, Wilus Caroon? Come and sit. I'm eager for news of my people."

"Who are you to be directing me?"

"A beastman's slave. Tunnel digger. Corpse hauler. Worse than dead I was. I was made to tend the feelers."

"Feelers?" The word made Wilus cringe, even though he had no idea what it meant.

"The Cent Regus chieftain means to strangle the Expanse. The feelers work their way like roots. They have teeth. They shatter stone. There are Abascar prisoners in the Cent Regus Core who believe the feelers had something to do with the quake that caused the collapse of their house. Soon there won't be any refuge left."

"Who, I say again, with quickly diminishing patience, are you?"

"Ask instead who brought me here. I swear upon my father's shipwreck that a beastman—yes, a beastman—smuggled me out. He brought me here as a gift, he says, for his new master."

"His new master."

"The Lady Cyndere," said the man, "my sister."

With no grace whatsoever, Wilus climbed from the sidesaddle, kicked his legs free of the bedbag, and staggered like a drunkard across the clearing.

Unfamiliar with joy, he believed himself to be feeling dismay. How could it be that Partayn, heir to Bel Amica's throne, descendant of Tammos Raak, was alive?

After many questions, and questions repeated, it became clear to Wilus that Partayn was out of his mind. For the man claimed that a beastman was scouting nearby, protecting him until he was strong enough to reach Tilian-purth's gate.

Above the edge of the glen, high in the coil tree's boughs, Jordam listened. Sunlight shone through spreads of translucent green leaves fanning in the breeze above him. The forest was steeped in colors.

A newborn gorrel cub watched him, terrified, from a nearby tree branch. *Like me,* Jordam thought, *when I first saw the Keeper.*

He had begun to find such pleasure in these thoughts. The whole world was beginning to speak. And it was not merely speech, but it was spoken especially for him. Every moment, every wonder, every ordinary thing a word, suggesting things that nothing in the crude Cent Regus tongue or even Common might reveal. Such distractions helped him endure the lasting ache of his thirst for Essence. And he was certain that the ache was slackening, that its grip on him was failing.

He looked into the trees, to where he had replanted the glen's snare-scarred apple tree. It was growing at last, branches tipped with bold white buds, roots spreading through a patch of good ground. He had tried to replant it in its grassy plot, but the tree had proved unwilling, roots ripping free of that soft earth. He found a place for it in the firmer ground above the glen, where its roots took hold and he could feed it with water he carried from the well. He had named it "Brother" for the one whose ashes he had, with trembling hands, buried beneath it.

It was a crooked tree now, injured from its ordeal. But perhaps its origins in the summery glen would enable it to bear fruit and offer shade a few years more. He counted the dark lines where the snare had seized its trunk. He thought of the lines on the wall of the old Cent Regus shack and how the ale boy had explained what they meant. "Still growing," he murmured.

Jordam rolled onto his back, folded his hands behind his head, and watched the trees waver in their ascent toward the sun. There was no white flag above Tilianpurth's tower and would not be for some time. He began to entertain thoughts of venturing back into the dark, to bring out the slaves and replant them where they belonged. Perhaps he would find O-raya's colors there. An idea began to take shape.

This is the end of the Blue Strand of The Auralia Thread.

The story will continue in the Gold Strand of The Auralia Thread—*Cal-raven's Ladder*—in which the remnant of Abascar must abandon their hideaway in the Cliffs of Barnashum and venture across the Expanse in search of a new home. Cal-raven begins to understand what Auralia's colors can reveal to him about Abascar's future. But is it too late for his people to make such a journey?

Cal-raven's progress leads unexpectedly to House Bel Amica. And when Jordam emerges from the forest at last, he brings a challenge that tests the priorities of Abascar's king. Endangered by the plotting of the Seers, Cyndere, Cal-raven, Tabor Jan, and Emeriene must make quick, excruciating decisions. And before this strand is finished, a devastating secret will be revealed in the Cent Regus Core.

And what has become of that brave and solitary boy who refuses to give his name? He's still following the Keeper's tracks, searching for souls in need of Auralia's colors.

A GUIDE TO THE CHARACTERS

House Abascar (AB-uh-skar)

ale boy—A former errand-runner in Abascar; friend of Auralia; gifted as a firewalker who can pass through fire without being burned; now a survivor responsible for leading hundreds from the rubble of Abascar south to the gathering in the Cliffs of Barnashum. Some call him "Rescue."

Auralia (o-RAY-lee-uh)—A young, artistic girl discovered, when she was an infant, by Krawg in the wilderness. Her artistry was an extraordinary revelation of color that inspired many and stirred up dissension in House Abascar. She disappeared in the calamity of House Abascar's fall, and only the ale boy witnessed what happened to her.

Brevolo (BREV-o-lo)—A swordswoman.

Cal-raven (cal-RAY-ven)—A stonemaster; king of House Abascar; son of Cal-marcus.

Copus (KO-pus)—A cave cleaner of the remnant of Abascar.

Jaralaine (JAYR-uh-layn)—Former queen of House Abascar and wife of King Cal-marcus. She ran away from the house and disappeared when Cal-raven was young.

Jes-hawk (JES-hawk)—The finest archer among Abascar's defenders.

Krawg (KROG)—Formerly a thief in House Abascar, known as "the Midnight Swindler," arrested and cast out to be a Gatherer. Now he is a harvester, famous for discovering Auralia.

Krystor (KRIS-tor)—A glass crafter of the remnant of Abascar.

Lesyl (LES-el)—A musician who was restricted to singing only songs of praise for the king during the reign of Cal-marcus.

Merya (MER-yuh)—Formerly a Gatherer; a survivor with the remnant of Abascar.

Saugus (SAW-gus)—A cave cleaner of the remnant of Abascar.

Say-ressa (say-RESS-uh)—A healer; wife of the former captain of the guard, Ark-robin, who was killed in the Abascar calamity.

Tabor Jan (TAY-bor JAN)—Formerly man-at-arms to Prince Cal-raven during the reign of Cal-marcus; now captain of the Abascar guard.

the triplets—Luci, Madi, and Margi (LOO-see, MAD-ee, MAR-gee)—Three young Abascar survivors gifted with the extraordinary power of stonemastery.

Warney (WOR-nee)—Formerly a thief known as the "One-Eyed Bandit"; then a Gatherer; now a harvester in the remnant of Abascar.

House Bel Amica (bel AM-i-kuh)

Cesylle (SES-il)—Emeriene's husband; a court representative in Bel Amica.

Cyndere (SIN-der)—The heiress of House Bel Amica; daughter of Queen Thesera and King Helpryn; wife of Deuneroi.

Deuneroi (DOON-er-oy)—A court representative; husband of Cyndere.

Emeriene (EM-er-een)—Cyndere's closest friend since childhood and highest-ranking of her attendants, the sisterlies.

Fryderoi (FRI-der-oy)—A soldier at Tilianpurth.

Garbal (GAR-bul)—A soldier and guard at Tilianpurth.

Helpryn (HEL-prin)—King of House Bel Amica; husband of Thesera; father of Cyndere and Partayn, who died in a ship-wreck while exploring the islands of the Mystery Sea.

Myrion (MEER-ee-un)—A soldier posted at Tilianpurth.

Partayn (par-TAYN)—Cyndere's older brother; heir to the throne of Bel Amica; a gifted musician; killed on the road to House Jenta.

Pretor Xa (PREH-ter kZAH)—One of the Seers, devotees of the faith of the moon-spirits who advise Queen Thesera in Bel Amica.

Pyroi (PIE-roy)—A young soldier-in-training at Tilianpurth.
Ridgie (RIJ-ee)—A young soldier-in-training at Tilianpurth.
Ryllion (RIL-ee-un)—A soldier of House Bel Amica.
Thesera (TES-er-uh)—Queen of House Bel Amica; widow of
    King Helpryn; mother of Cyndere and Partayn.
Wilus Caroon (WIL-us ka-ROON)—A guard at the Bel Amican
    outpost of Tilianpurth.

House Cent Regus (KENT REJ-us)
Goreth (GOR-eth)—One of four beastmen brothers; twin to Jordam.
Jordam (JOR-dum)—One of four beastmen brothers; twin to
    Goreth.
Jorn (JORN)—Youngest of four beastmen brothers.
Mordafey (MOR-duh-fay)—Oldest of four beastmen brothers.
The Old Dog—Father to Mordafey, Jordam, Goreth, and Jorn;
    killed when they were young.
Skell Wra (SKEL RA)—The chieftain of the Cent Regus beast-
    men; controller of the Essence.
The Sopper Crone, Kreanomos (kray-ON-o-mose)—The servant
    of Skell Wra who guards the Essence and dispenses it.

Between the houses
Cortie (KOR-tee)—The young daughter of the merchants Joss and
    Juney.
Damyn (DAME-un)—A merchant; goes by the name Fadel Tod.
Dukas (DOOK-us)—A viscorcat.
Filup (FIL-up)—A merchant and a thief.
Joss (JOSS)—An experienced merchant; husband of Juney; father
    of Wynn and Cortie.
Juney (JOON-ee)—An experienced merchant; wife of Joss; mother
    of Wynn and Cortie.
the Keeper—A massive, mysterious beast who appears in the
    dreams of all children, and some say the adults as well. It is

perceived by children as a benevolent guardian, but most determine that it is only a fancy, probably imagined out of a need for comfort. Some believe it appears in dreams because it is real and moving about in the wild with vast powers of perception and influence.

Lira (LEER-uh)—A merchant; goes by the name Anjee Tod.

Rumpa (RUMP-uh)—A vawn.

Scharr ben Fray (SHAR ben FRAY)—A renowned mage, stonemaster, and wildspeaker; former advisor to Cal-marcus of Abascar; mentor to Cal-raven.

Slagh (SLAG)—A merchant who survived the Abascar calamity; hired by the Bel Amicans to guide them into the Abascar ruins.

Tammos Raak (TAM-os RAK)—Legendary ancestor of the four houses' royal families. Stories say he led the peoples of the Expanse over the Forbidding Wall, a line of mountains in the north, to escape a curse. Accounts disagree regarding the manner and cause of his disappearance.

Wynn (Win)—The young son of the merchants Joss and Juney.